Christmas Punch

A Matthew Paine Mystery

Matthew Paine Mystery Series

Dead Spots

Prefer Death

MIA

Christmas Punch

Iced (coming 2023)

Christmas Punch

A Matthew Paine Mystery

Lee Clark

Cypress
River
Media
LLC

Burlington

This book is a work of fiction. Names, characters, and incidents are the product of the author's imagination or are used fictitiously. Any resemblance to actual events or persons, living or deceased, is coincidental.

Copyright © 2022 by Leesa K.C. Payne.

All rights reserved. In accordance with the U.S. Copyright Act of 1976, no portion of this book may be reproduced, stored in a retrieval system, or transmitted in any form by any means – electronic, mechanical, photocopy, recording, or any other – except for brief quotations in printed reviews, without the prior permission of the publisher. To use the material from the book (other than for review purposes), prior written permission must be obtained by contacting the publisher at Lee.Clark@cypressrivermedia.com.

Cypress River Media, LLC
Burlington, NC 27215
CypressRiverMedia.com

First Edition: October 2022

The publisher is not responsible for websites (or their content) that are not owned by the publisher.

Clark, Lee.
    Christmas Punch / Lee Clark. – First edition.
        Pages ; cm. – (A Matthew Paine mystery)
        ISBN 979-8-9864074-1-8 (hardcover) – ISBN 979-8-9864074-0-1 (paperback) – ISBN 979-8-9864074-2-5 (ebook) 1. Paine, Matthew (Fictitious character)

Dedication

Christmas Punch is dedicated to the brothers of the Tau chapter of Phi Sigma Pi National Honor Fraternity at East Carolina University. That all members are equally dubbed "brothers," regardless of gender, appealed to me immensely when I was in college. I find that the tripod of values on which the fraternity is built (Scholarship, Leadership and Fellowship) holds alumni together long past graduation. If you need them for anything from photography shoots to prayer for life issues, they're there!

Acknowledgments

The more books I write, the more people I need to thank and appreciate for their contributions. As always, I am incredibly thankful to my editors, Genie Clark and Dorothy Whitley, for their tireless efforts to keep me straight.

I am incredibly blessed by the loving support and encouragement of my family! And I admire and fully appreciate those who fill the gaps of my talents by providing their graphical abilities to the covers, Bill Payne and Rachael Payne.

I also want to thank Steve Spaanbroek, photographer, Tau chapter brother, and friend who took an evening to set up the scene I described for the cover and photograph it perfectly!

Contents

1 ~ Merry wallop	1
2 ~ Doctors in the house	9
3 ~ Sorting it out	17
4 ~ Crowds and throngs	27
5 ~ Breaking it gently	43
6 ~ Shadows in the night	53
7 ~ Overnight tales	63
8 ~ Plans in place	71
9 ~ Elaborations	81
10 ~ Daddy dearest	89
11 ~ Now what?	101
12 ~ Acidic answers	111
13 ~ It's not a party	123
14 ~ Hot and cold	133
15 ~ Requesting backup	143
16 ~ Chill in the air	153
17 ~ Reactions	163
18 ~ Dinner dance	175
19 ~ He's what?!	185
20 ~ True confessions	199
21 ~ Christmas secrets	211
22 ~ Dinner reservations	225
23 ~ Perfectly decorated	235
24 ~ Connections	247
25 ~ Revelations	259
26 ~ Quid pro quo	267
27 ~ New directions	281
28 ~ Dawning	291

29 ~ Nothing rational	305
30 ~ Concerning	315
31 ~ Déjà vu	321
32 ~ Miscreants for hire	335
33 ~ Nonstop	349
34 ~ Rescue who?	361
35 ~ Mourning after	371
Epilogue ~ Two and a half weeks later	379

1 ~ Merry Wallop

Matthew Paine was uncomfortably dressed to impress as he climbed the final two steps and waited on the landing while Cecelia Patterson, Cici to her friends and closest associates, pulled her access badge from her tiny purse. The top three floors of the tallest sky scraper in downtown Raleigh, North Carolina, were occupied entirely by the prestigious law firm, Markham, Denton, and Washburn, where Cici was already a junior partner. These floors were accessible from the stairwells and a dedicated elevator only by badge access.

They'd taken the back stairwell from Cici's office two floors below. Generally opting for stairs over elevators when he got the chance, Matthew figured Cici ordinarily would have balked at the idea. This evening though she was in agreement so that the one elevator which rose all the way to the top three floors could be left exclusively for the arriving guests.

The Christmas Gala they were attending was usually the event of the season and everybody in Raleigh who was anybody would be there. Though this wasn't at all Matthew's preference for spending a Saturday night three weeks before Christmas, or much of any other time, he'd consented to make at least an obligatory appearance with Cici.

Pushing the door from the stairwell open and holding it for Cici, Matthew felt a woosh of air go by his left ear. He heard the smacking impact of flesh on flesh. Startled, he realized that he'd narrowly avoided a flying fist. He paused only long enough to ensure that Cici was still firmly rooted in her spiked heels on the landing behind him. Grasping her arm firmly to prevent her from tumbling down the steps, he stepped back and half closed the door. Even in those heels, much to his amazement, she always managed to maneuver with apparent ease.

After steadying the surprised Cici, he peered around the doorway, then opened the door and stepped through. In the landing at the top of the stairwell, he saw one of the senior partners whom he recognized as Jamison Washburn sprawled on his back on the floor. Standing over him, angrily massaging his fist, was a man Matthew hadn't yet met but whom he assumed to be the newest of the senior partners. Both were similarly attired in tuxedos with perfectly shined shoes and all of the trappings of finery.

"What the?" exclaimed Cici as she too stepped around the half-opened door and into the landing between two doors, the other of which opened out onto the top floor of the building where the gala event was happening. Pushing past Matthew, Cici confronted the standing guy as only she could. "What was that about?" she demanded, looking up into his face.

"It's nothing that concerns you," he sneered down his aquiline nose. As the guy opened the door onto the top floor, Matthew could hear the sound of music, the titter of polite conversation, and fluttering laughter floating on the air. The stairwell landing grew quiet again as the door clicked closed behind him.

Leaning over, Cici asked, "Mr. Washburn, are you OK?"

Jamison Washburn, who still lay splayed on the landing, had apparently not been so fortunate as to miss the flying fist. Clad in a full-length sparkling red gown, Cici tried to kneel but couldn't, prevented by its tight fit despite the slit that revealed much of her shapely left leg.

Matthew knelt beside the injured man. He was, after all, the physician and the one who could assess the situation. At least he could assess the patient's situation, though he wasn't sure what to make of the altercation he'd just witnessed.

"I'm OK, it's all right," said Washburn, shaking off the dazed look. He pushed up into a sitting position and leaned heavily against the glossy cream-colored wall behind him.

"I'm Matthew Paine. I'm a physician in Peak," said Matthew by way of introduction. "We've met before, but it was a couple of years ago. Let me have a look before you try to get up."

Matthew could already see the angry bruise rising on Washburn's left cheekbone and he thought the man should be thankful that the connection hadn't been a bit higher. At least he wouldn't likely have a black or swollen eye from the encounter. After checking his pupils, pulse, and breathing, Matthew asked all of the usual questions, including if Mr. Washburn had hit his head when he fell.

"I don't think so. I slammed my back into the wall pretty hard, but then I think I just slid down it," replied Washburn.

After checking Washburn's head and neck to be sure that there were no further injuries, other than the rising bruise, Matthew prescribed ice. Washburn insisted that he was OK and attempted to push himself up. Matthew helped him to his feet.

"What was that all about?" asked Cici.

"It was nothing, really. Just a misunderstanding," said Washburn.

"You or Reynolds one must have misunderstood something rather severely," said Cici, looking up at her boss in concern. "Are you certain that you're OK?"

"I think so," he said. "I'm sure I'll be fine. I'm going down to my office to get some ice on this. Maybe I'll get some refreshments brought down. I'm not quite ready to join the party," he added, brushing himself off. "Would you mind making my apologies and telling the others that I'll be back up shortly?"

"Certainly, Sir," responded Cici after a momentary hesitation as Jamison Washburn pulled the heavy metal door open and Matthew held it for him. The heels of his highly polished shoes clicked slowly back down the stairwell until the door closed behind him a floor below.

Releasing the door, Matthew asked, "You have no idea what that was about?"

Cici shook her head. "Not a clue."

"Who was that other guy?"

"That was our newest partner, Kennedy Reynolds, from Massachusetts. His mother is, yes, one of THOSE Kennedys, and he's particularly keen on everyone knowing it," she added, rolling her eyes. "He's a bit pretentious, I think. He's very hung up on family history and having all the right connections. Exactly the kind of person you really don't like, but be nice. Even after whatever that was, if Jamison Washburn isn't upset about it, neither should we be."

"I'm always nice," objected Matthew.

"Matthew," she said. "Your bow tie is askew again."

Stooping to provide her access, he patiently allowed her to straighten it. Heels and all, Cici's five-foot nothing stature was nowhere near Matthew's six-foot-three broad-shouldered frame. What she lacked in actual height, she more than made up for in presence. She was a force to be reckoned with and Matthew had vowed never to want to be on the opposite side of a legal situation in a court room from her.

Escorting Cici to the annual Christmas Gala thrown by her law firm was part of an agreement that he and Cici had reached over the summer to try to bridge the gap between them. Cici was his ex-girlfriend and perhaps girlfriend-to-be again. Their current relationship, intertwined with their past history, was a seriously complicated one. All of which provided a confusing twist to his otherwise quiet and peaceful life.

"OK, I'll give you that much," she conceded. "You are one of the kindest people I know. But you aren't always engaged. It's like you check out and you're in your own world sometimes in social settings."

Probably because I am, Matthew thought, but he refrained from saying so aloud. Particularly when he was bored with conversations about who bought the biggest boat, took the best vacation, completed the most impressive business transaction, or had the nicest car or house, he knew he checked out because he really couldn't care less. In his mind, he wrote comical ditties, lyrics and tunes about the conversations, and tried not to smirk when he entertained himself that way.

Matthew, who wanted a quieter lifestyle with a wife and family in a more rural setting that didn't include regular forays into the world of the elite upper echelon of Raleigh, had purposefully chosen the family practice in Peak. He'd equivocated on his prior declaration to avoid the type of soirée that he was attending this evening at Cici's side, clad in the new tuxedo which he'd previously refused to purchase just because apparently his older one was too dated. And here he found himself.

They had both agreed to make compromises and see how it went. Until recently, he'd thought Cici too materialistic and she'd thought him too simplistic. Had that been the worst of it, he thought they might have made it past those differences and been happily married by now. The final chasm that seemed unbridgeable was the family that he wanted so badly. He adored his niece, his older sister Monica's four-year-old daughter, whom he spoiled. But he wanted children of his own, and Cici had professed never to want children. As a result, they'd split up over a year ago as amicably as was possible after having seriously dated for so long.

Reconnecting the spring before when Cici had been abducted, they'd started talking again. She'd called Matthew, who she hadn't previously spoken to in nearly a year, to come to her rescue when she was drugged and stuffed in the front trunk of her Porsche. In the aftermath, Cici had taken on an important client in London, who was trying to move partial operations into the US and needed legal hand-holding to do so. She had moved to London for a year to do just that. Recently, Cici had confessed to Matthew that maybe she hadn't meant that she never wanted children ever, but perhaps what she had really meant was just not right now.

That had been enough to keep them talking and prompt a whirlwind visit from him over the summer to London just after he'd celebrated his birthday in July. They had explored all of the sites that Cici had been saving up, awaiting his visit. In addition to all of the usual sites in London, they'd toured some in the idyllic countryside that Matthew had loved and that Cici had surprised them both by thoroughly enjoying too. Matthew wasn't entirely sure that was enough long term, but neither had he ever met anyone like Cecilia Patterson. Nor did he think that he ever would again.

They left the stairwell and entered the gala on the top floor, a large open area that had been converted from a board meeting room to a grand hall for entertaining. Mingled scents of apple and cinnamon met Matthew's nose, though he wasn't sure of their source because he saw nothing that could produce them. Alongside that, he caught a whiff of balsam, possibly Fraser Fir. Either the large tree against the far wall or the garlands of greenery strung all over, or both, must be real he figured. Or perhaps someone had mastered the happy smell of Christmas and distributed it liberally throughout the room.

Matthew loved Christmas, all the lights and decorations, food and aromas, music and traditions. They were all favorites that had captured his imagination and promised excitement through his childhood and into his young adult life. It was all the result he supposed of many happy memories of Christmases with his family over the years. Paradoxically, the truth about Christmas uplifted him with a sense of renewal and rebirth in the midst of the stark winter season and days with the least daylight of the year.

In the large room they'd entered, everything sparkled and shimmered. The lighting, crystal, Christmas glitter and gold accents, he was sure, were all placed strategically to produce that shining effect.

Down the center of the room was laid a table of every delicacy anyone could imagine. Matthew caught a glimpse of escargot and caviar, which would surely be only the finest quality, amongst other decadent choices placed along the center table. An ice sculpture of swans that appeared to be continually pouring some sort of red drink, like a fountain, adorned a high table. How many swans were swimming in the *Twelve Days of Christmas* song, Matthew pondered momentarily as he heard the melody of it gently lilting and floating through the room from a stringed ensemble in one corner, which included a harpist.

A steamship round and several other choices were available with small snowflake finger biscuits from a carving station in another corner. Alongside the adjoining wall, there was a lovely bar that seemed to be of oak, polished to a gleaming shine with brass accents and strung liberally but tastefully with greenery, lights, and glass balls that reflected the lighting. Behind the bar were three bartenders busily shaking and mixing drinks. Matthew wasn't at all surprised that no expense had been spared for the evening.

As they entered the room, Cici pushed an errant strand of her long strawberry blond hair from her face and tucked it into her otherwise perfectly coifed upswept hair. Matthew straightened to his full height and bent his right arm, offering her the crook of his elbow to escort her into the room full of the monied, both old and new, patrons of the law firm.

"Oh, there are Charles and Marshall, just on the other side of the punch fountain," said Cici of the two clients she'd been working with in London. She'd convinced them to fly back with her for a week in Raleigh to attend the annual company gala event. Matthew remembered having met them briefly.

"I offered to pick them up and bring them with us but they insisted on coming over from the hotel on their own," added Cici before turning and beginning to make her way over to them.

There was no straight path across the room Matthew soon learned. It was already strewn with groupings of people. He refrained from checking his watch for verification, lest he appear rude, but he reckoned that it wasn't yet quite seven when they had entered the room and he was surprised by the number of people already in attendance. Every male hand must be shaken and every female cheek air kissed on both sides, as if they were still back in Europe.

As they started across the room shaking hands and greeting people as they went, Cici introduced Matthew to people whose names he certainly hoped he would not be required to remember later. The women were remarking over the couture fashion of the evening. They were all impressed that Cici had shipped her designer dress, the name of which Matthew could neither remember nor pronounce very well, back from a fitting in Paris.

"It's simply stunning," Matthew overheard one of the women gush to Cici. "Who is the designer?"

Politely providing the name of the designer and murmuring her thanks, Cici moved on to the next group.

The sparkling red dress was indeed fitted perfectly to her petite hourglass figure, catching the sparkling light as she moved through the room. The effect of it wasn't lost on Matthew. Neither was it lost on most of the men in the room, Matthew noticed. Heads turned in Cici's direction, some staring discreetly and others doing double takes.

They were stopped by a newspaper reporter to be photographed when they were about half way across the room and the guy double checked the spellings of the names for each member of the group they'd been standing with before he moved on to the next one. It was important at this sort of event, Matthew supposed, to get all of the spellings correct. Circulating waiters and waitresses offered them red drinks in tall crystal punch glasses and an assortment of tiny amuse-bouche, which they politely declined.

After what seemed to Matthew an eternity later, he and Cici had finally made their way to the other side of the room to reach the London clients in the far corner when the elevator opened to their right.

They were startled by the frantic appearance of one of the wait staff. Attired in the black pants and red velvet vest with the gold insignia of the catering company on the left breast pocket, he all but ran out shouting, "Is there a doctor here? We need a doctor downstairs!"

2 ~ DOCTORS IN THE HOUSE

Without missing a beat, Cici withdrew her perfectly manicured hand from Matthew's arm and simply said, "Go. I'm fine."

Matthew and a tall, broad, older gentleman with thick silver-gray hair both rushed into the elevator. As the elevator operator punched the button to descend a floor, the guy who had summoned them said, "Thank God! I don't know what's wrong with him."

"Good evening, Eugene Miller," said the older doctor in the elevator, extending a hand calmly.

"Matthew Paine," answered Matthew, shaking it. Then turning to the server who had summoned them, he asked, "You don't know what's wrong with who?"

"I'm not sure, one of the partners I think," the guy dressed in the caterer's garb answered, looking pale, as the doors opened. Matthew and the older doctor followed the server off to the left toward the front of the building, the opposite direction, Matthew noted, from Cici's office which was on the floor below. Matthew followed quickly in the wake of the catering server who'd summoned them and down the hallway, with the older doctor trailing behind. Stopping and pointing to the last door on the left, the guy said, breathlessly, "He's in there."

Matthew entered the reception area of a large suite with an expansive seating area arranged to the left and an unlit Christmas tree looming in the far corner. Two desks stood like sentries on either side of a tall heavy wooden door with a brass handle that clearly led to the main office. Seeing the details in a sweeping glance, he walked briskly in his stiff new shoes across the cream-colored carpet that was thick and plush under his feet.

Approaching the large door that was three-quarters open with soft lighting spilling out, he resisted the urge to straighten a tray that was perched precariously on the edge of a desk to his right. The desk to the left of the door to the main office, he noticed, was neatly arranged and dark while the one to the right held a mass of clutter. A desk lamp that had been left lit and Christmas lights strung haphazardly around the edges provided a warm glow.

On the edge of the messy desk, the small tray that he'd resisted straightening held a crystal punch glass with a tiny figurine at the base. It looked like a tiny man. A crystal plate, a small gold cutlery set, and a linen napkin also adorned the tray, which was perched at a perilous angle atop a stack of papers on the edge of the desk. Some of the red punch had spilled over the tray and down onto the papers.

Taking the scene in quickly but trying to ignore it for the moment, Matthew stepped through the doorway into an expansive corner inner office. The back wall and right-side walls of the office were heavily tinted windows, floor to ceiling, that provided an impressive view overlooking the city of Raleigh. In front of the windows was a huge mahogany desk, across which was draped the prone figure of a man in a tuxedo. One arm was on the desk beside his head. From the top of his head, which was all that was initially visible, Matthew was pretty sure he was looking at the senior partner, Jamison Washburn, whom he'd just helped to his feet in the stairwell landing about an hour before.

Quickly circling the desk and seeing the man's face, Matthew also saw that his next task would be necessary but pointless. He reached in past the stiffly collared white shirt to the man's neck, which was still warm, to check for a pulse. As he had expected, he found none.

Matthew was indeed looking into the face of Jamison Washburn, but the dilated pupils staring back at him from the pale white face were unseeing. On the desk over which Washburn was draped, a puddle of what looked like drool had collected under the edge of his mouth. Matthew noticed a small bag of ice melting on the desk. There was another crystal plate of food, small gold utensils, a red cloth napkin, and a crystal punch glass, mostly devoid of punch, the base of which was adorned with a tiny charm that seemed to be shaped like a woman.

There were folders and papers protruding in every direction from under Washburn's splayed shoulders, and a phone, the receiver of which was lying on the desk just beyond Washburn's outstretched hand.

Assessing this quickly, Matthew leaned over and sniffed, looked up at Dr. Miller and shook his head, "No pulse, and I'm not betting on any hope of resuscitation, but we have to try." The older doctor nodded his agreement.

Noting that the inner office was crowded with furniture, a table and chairs, two credenzas, book cases, and more chairs, Matthew saw no floor space in the inner office where both doctors could work in tandem on their patient. "Let's move him out into the other room," he said as he slipped behind Washburn, pulled him upright in the chair. Gripping him under his arms, Matthew pulled Washburn out of the chair and around the desk.

Dragging the limp form backwards out into the reception area, Matthew placed him on his back on the floor. To the hovering server who looked to be in a near state of panic, he said, "Call 9-1-1 and ask for an ambulance to this address."

Matthew and Dr. Miller began alternating chest compressions and breathing. Matthew was administering the compressions and Miller, sealing his hands as a funnel around Washburn's mouth, provided the breathing effort.

"Don't go back into that office," warned Matthew between compressions to the ashen-faced server who was hovering in the doorway, peeking in, after having used the desk phone on the messy desk to call for emergency help. "I'm all but certain that's a crime scene," Matthew added.

After a full fifteen minutes, they had gotten no response from Washburn. Matthew checked his watch to call the time of death, noting that it was twenty minutes after eight, and both doctors leaned back from their kneeling positions to sit on their heels. Looking across at each other, they had just confirmed what Matthew already knew. Washburn was beyond help.

After a discouraged pause, Matthew got to his feet and said into the stunned silence in the room, "I know who to call to report this. You found Mr. Washburn exactly the way he was when we arrived?" he asked the guy in the caterer's garb.

The guy just nodded.

"What's your name?"

"Timothy," he spluttered.

"Thank you, Timothy, for calling 9-1-1. Would you go downstairs and bring the paramedics straight up here? They'll have to verify the condition before they'll leave, but they likely won't be providing transport. They should be arriving downstairs soon."

"OK," the guy stammered, nodding, and then disappeared as he ran through the suite door out into the main hallway. The silence that ensued felt oppressive and the air stagnant. Matthew heard the elevator ding from the other end of the hallway.

Eugene Miller stared down at the dead man in transfixed disbelief. "A crime scene, you say? Murder?" he asked, without looking up.

"I think so, yes."

"He was poisoned?"

"That's my guess," answered Matthew.

"If I were a betting man, I'd put my money on that too," said the elder doctor as Matthew pulled his phone out and poked to pull up Danbury's entry.

Warren Danbury, Raleigh Homicide Detective and a friend from the spring before though it felt much longer to Matthew, answered on the second ring, "Hey Doc, what's up?"

"I have a situation in downtown Raleigh that you're going to want to be here for. How soon can you get here?"

"What? What situation?" Danbury asked as Matthew heard shuffling noises in the background.

"I'm pretty sure I'm looking at a murder victim right now and I'm almost equally as certain that he was poisoned. We're at the big Christmas Gala that Cici's firm hosts every year. It's in their offices downtown and this is one of the senior partners."

"On my way," said Danbury. "Have you called it in?"

"Only to request an ambulance. We did a full fifteen minutes of CPR, trying to revive him, and confirmed what we thought. He's beyond being resuscitated. We got no response at all."

"I'm rolling," Danbury said, as Matthew heard his big black SUV roar to life in the background. "Is he in a public place?"

"He was in his office. There's another physician here with me and a member of the catering team who found him. He went to bring the emergency crew up."

"OK. Keep people out. And keep them in the dark. On whatever information you know," instructed Danbury in his typical staccato style.

"I can try. We moved him from his office out into his reception area for the CPR. Otherwise, we didn't touch anything in the office. Lots of people heard the call for the doctor though, and when the ambulance gets here it might be harder to contain the news. They're a floor above us. If the catering server brings them straight here, then maybe nobody upstairs will know."

"OK. Just do your best. I'll be there in fifteen. Maybe twenty."

"OK," said Matthew. Just before he disconnected the call, he heard Danbury mutter something and he put the phone back up to his ear.

"What did you say?"

"What was that about not consulting anymore?"

"Uh!" said Matthew at Danbury's ribbing, "I know, I know!"

As they disconnected the call, that realization hit Matthew harder than a physical blow. He'd relinquished his role as a medical consultant for the Raleigh Police Department the summer before because he felt that he was getting jaded. He'd reacted angrily in ways that he hadn't ever thought he would and certainly had never wanted to with some of the criminals he'd encountered. That wasn't who he wanted to be. And here he was again, being sucked back into a murder investigation.

His left eyebrow rose in disbelief as his foot tapped out the frantic rhythms in his head. He ran his fingers through his soft wavy brown hair as that realization fully settled in his mind. Here he was again. Right where he didn't want to be.

Matthew and Eugene Miller took turns washing up in the men's room down the hallway before returning to the office suite. The elder doctor slid slowly into a wingback chair in the corner of the sitting area, looking dazed. Matthew wasn't sure what sort of doctor the man was and he hadn't asked. Excusing himself, Matthew ventured back upstairs to find Jonathan Denton and Simon Markham, the other two most senior partners. They would need to know what was happening and Danbury would want to talk to them when he arrived.

Locating Mr. Markham amongst the stately revelers, Matthew offered polite apologies as he approached through the throng and whispered discreetly into his ear. Matthew watched the color drain from Markham's face before he could ask where Mr. Denton might be found.

After locating Mr. Denton, Matthew waved surreptitiously at Cici across the room and corralled the partners into the elevator. He asked if one of them would call downstairs to provide clearance from the host desk for the paramedics and Warren Danbury. He refrained from further identifying Danbury in front of the elevator operator. They readily agreed. Mr. Markham pulled his phone from his pocket to make the call. Mr. Denton instructed the elevator operator to bring the paramedics and Danbury directly to the thirty-second floor as soon as they arrived.

"Not the thirty-third floor where the party is in progress, but the thirty-second floor, here, where we're getting off now," Denton added, pointedly.

"Yes, Sir," the elevator operator nodded emphatically.

As the three exited the elevator together and the doors closed behind them, Matthew explained, "What I didn't say in the elevator in front of the operator is that I've already called Homicide Detective Warren Danbury. He's the best in this area. If anyone can figure out what happened to Mr. Washburn, it'll be Danbury."

Matthew watched the dawn of understanding on Mr. Markham's face as he was the first to realize what Matthew was telling them.

"Homicide," Markham repeated drawing a sharp breath, clearly taken aback. Regaining his composure, he added, "Thank you for your discretion in handling this horrible situation. One detective arriving on the scene will be far preferable to the building being stormed with uniformed police officers, at least from the perspective of not alarming the clientele a floor above us. If he's the best in the area, as you say, then we don't want a hoard of other officers confusing things anyway."

As they entered the office suite, Matthew hated that they both looked horrified to see Jamison Washburn's body on the floor, but he'd found nothing in the office with which to cover it, not even a spare jacket. Eugene Miller looked up and acknowledged them from the chair in the corner, but he didn't get up. The room was silent as Denton perched on one end of the overstuffed sofa in the sitting area in the outer office and Markham on the other and Matthew heard the ding from the elevator down the hallway.

The paramedics emerged with Timothy, who had brought them straight up to the corner office suite a floor below the Christmas Gala festivities. Because Timothy had found Mr. Washburn, Matthew asked him to stay there until Danbury arrived. Danbury would want to talk to the guy and he would not want him talking to anyone else in the interim. Promising to intervene with the manager of the catering company if need be, Matthew considered the murder investigation more important than the soirée upstairs.

Identifying himself and Eugene Miller to the paramedics, Matthew explained that they'd called the time of death at eight-twenty and the patient wouldn't require transport to the hospital for treatment.

3 ~ Sorting It Out

Shortly after the arrival of the emergency workers, Danbury filled the doorway to the office suite with his broad shoulders. Looking like a misplaced legendary Viking with his chiseled features, he was also taller than everyone else in the room, including Matthew. With his sandy blonde hair cut short, chiseled square jaw-line and pronounced brow, he looked exceptionally Nordic.

Matthew watched as Danbury's steel blue eyes quickly swept the scene. Approaching the emergency workers first, Danbury flashed his badge to identify himself. Matthew heard him dismiss them as he explained that the physicians present had called the time of death, the Medical Examiner was on the way, and that the ME would be providing transport. As they were about to leave, after discretely covering Mr. Washburn's prone figure with a sheet, Matthew noticed that Eugene Miller had slumped in the chair and he was shaking as he tugged at his tie and stiff collar.

"Dr. Miller?" Matthew said, "Are you all right?"

"I don't feel so well," Eugene Miller muttered as his shaking hand dropped from his collar. Matthew and the two paramedics rushed to the older doctor's side.

"We think Mr. Washburn was poisoned," said Matthew as they freed Miller from his tie, stiff- collared shirt, and coat. "Dr. Miller cupped his hands and tried to seal them as he performed the CPR breathing while I did the chest compressions. He could have inhaled something or accidentally ingested something. But it would have been minuscule," he said, half explaining to the paramedics and half talking through the problem aloud to himself. He noticed with relief that the paramedics had pulled on gloves.

"We have charcoal," said one of the paramedics. "And Ipecac," said the other. "Do we need to transport?" asked the first.

"Yes," said Matthew amidst the flurry of activity. "Flush his digestive system. Start a saline drip and be prepared to intubate. If his throat swells, he'll need a breathing tube. I don't know what that poison was but it must have been potent. Did either of you touch the deceased?"

"No," said the first paramedic, as he pulled the stretcher over and they readied it to lift Dr. Miller onto it. "You said you'd called the TOD so we were just awaiting orders from law enforcement about transport. One, two, three," and they efficiently lifted the elder doctor. Both were working over him as they piled their bags on the end of the stretcher and wheeled him out and down the hallway.

Matthew had chosen a position as a general practitioner at a family practice in Peak, a little town on the outskirts of Raleigh, precisely because it provided a calmer lifestyle than becoming an Emergency Department physician. That had been his original plan until he'd completed a rotation through an ED in medical school. He could do it, he knew, but it drained him instead of energizing him.

Danbury approached and started questioning Matthew, who felt a bit dazed by it all himself. Beginning with the encounter in the stairwell, Matthew quietly told him everything leading up to finding Mr. Washburn slumped over his desk. Then he explained the resuscitation efforts that he had been sure would be futile and had proven to be so.

"What was the time interval? What time did Mr. Washburn leave the stairwell? And what time were you summoned? By the catering employee?"

"I wish I could tell you exactly. We might need Cici to answer that one more precisely. We were making our way across the crowded room upstairs. It isn't exactly a straight shot, because we had to stop and chat a few minutes with everyone along the way, each little group as it morphed with people coming and going. I admit that I had checked out during a good bit of that and I was in my own head," said

Matthew quietly enough that he hoped he wasn't overheard. "I'd guess nearly an hour. Cici and I were almost to the other side of the room when Timothy called out from the elevator for a doctor."

"Timothy. The guy who works for the caterer? He found Mr. Washburn?"

"Yes," said Matthew. "He brought us down here and said he'd found Mr. Washburn. He's dressed in the caterer's clothing, but I didn't specifically ask him that question in all of the confusion. I just assumed."

"The guy who punched Washburn. You said his name was Reynolds. Did you see him afterward?"

"Right, his name is Kennedy Reynolds. And that's a good question too," responded Matthew, thoughtfully. "He went into the party from the stairwell, but I don't remember seeing him up there after we entered the room. There wasn't anyone else down here, at least not that I saw, when we arrived, so no, I didn't see him again."

"OK. Thanks Doc. You know the drill. Sit tight. I'll need to question everyone in the room. Find this Kennedy Reynolds. Get a guest list. Work my way through that. Do you know who's in charge? Who organized this event?"

"I don't but I'm sure Cici will know."

Simon Markham and Jonathan Denton had been sitting quietly on the sofa during all of the frenzy with Eugene Miller and under less serious circumstances, Matthew would have been making jokes, at least in his own head, about two lawyers going so long without speaking. The smaller and older but far more physically fit of the two senior partners stood. He stepped forward and to Matthew said, "I suppose I should have introduced myself properly earlier. Simon Markham." He extended a perfectly manicured hand in Matthew's direction. It was a solid handshake, thought Matthew, but the hands were soft. Yard work or anything more laborious than racquetball and golf, both of which Matthew knew from Cici that the man played, seemed to be beyond his purview.

"Matthew Paine," he answered, as he shook the proffered hand.

"You're Cecelia Patterson's, ah," he began to ask, without finishing the question.

"Date," supplied Matthew. "Yes, I'm here with Cici. Dr. Miller and I both came down when a doctor was summoned."

"Will he be all right? Dr. Miller, I mean?" asked Markham.

"I hope so, but we don't know what we're dealing with yet. Is there anyone upstairs who should know that he's been transported? His wife or anyone?"

"He came alone, unfortunately. His wife died a few years back. I'm surprised he's still here in Raleigh, to tell you the truth. He's a retired plastic surgeon and I thought he'd have moved to Florida by now. Say, haven't we met earlier?" Markham interrupted himself to ask, squinting up at Matthew. "Weren't you dating Cici when she started here at the firm?"

"I was, and yes we met a couple of years ago," confirmed Matthew.

"I knew you looked familiar."

To get the conversation back on track as Markham seemed to want to talk about anything except the current situation and the deceased partner on the floor covered by the sheet, Matthew indicated Danbury, "And this is Warren Danbury, Homicide Detective."

Turning to Danbury, Markham shook his hand and cleared his throat before he said, "You were asking about who organized our Gala event. That would be mostly Abigail Moore, Jamison Washburn's primary assistant. She's very capable and detail-oriented. I'm certain that she can provide a guest list, including those who attended and those who sent regrets. Must they be questioned, though? This is quite sensitive. Only our top clients, those of long standing and some prospects that we're trying to convince to become so, are included on the guest list for this annual event. It's the talk of the town, and it is our full intention that it should be. So, you can see why we'd rather not question the guests, if that can be avoided."

"I'll see what I can do," said Danbury noncommittally. "I'll want your input. When I get the guest list. All known relationships to the deceased."

Markham just nodded, "Yes, of course."

"For now, outline your movements. Where you were this evening.

And when. We can start there. Then find Kennedy Reynolds."

"Surely I'm not a," began Markham. "Oh, I suppose I am," he said as understanding dawned.

"Suspect," provided Danbury. "We'll know more after an autopsy. Until then, I'm gathering information. Did you see Jamison Washburn? Or Kennedy Reynolds? At any time this evening?"

"I saw both late this afternoon. We were all in the office for one reason or another on a Saturday. Our offices are in the four corners of this floor. But I don't recall seeing either of them upstairs this evening. Now that you ask," he added, furrowing his brow. "No, I don't believe that I did. A couple of Washburn's clients were asking after him. I just relayed Cici's message that he was due at any moment, but I never did see him arrive."

"You were there the whole time? Upstairs at the gala?" As Markham nodded, Danbury asked, "What time did you get there? How long were you there? Before being summoned down here?"

"It was well over an hour, probably nearly two hours," Markham amended as he pulled a gold pocket watch from his vest and flipped it open. Returning the watch to the vest pocket, he added, "I went up something after six-thirty and I was greeting our clients and guests as they arrived, mingling with them, until I was summoned down here. A whole room full of people saw that. Including Jonathan," he said, inclining his head in the direction of the shorter and younger but wider of the two remaining senior partners. "We weren't together most of the time, because we were circulating. Chatting with our guests. Making sure they were personally welcomed."

At this, Denton stood, came forward into the center of the room, and held out his fleshy hand. "Jonathan Denton," he said, as he shook both Danbury's and then Matthew's hands. His jowl shook as his hand shook and his hairline was past the point of receding, Matthew noted. It had already launched a full-scale retreat from the top of his head. The curly fringe of hair around the edges of his head hadn't bothered to turn gray yet but was still a golden reddish color. Matthew placed the man's age nearer to sixty, given the lines in the portly red face.

"Hell of a thing, here," Denton inclined his head toward the body of their former partner under the sheet. Rocking back on his heels, he stuffed his hands into the pants pockets of his tuxedo around his unbuttoned coat.

Danbury asked the same questions about having seen either Washburn or Reynolds upstairs during the evening and he got the same responses. Matthew had spoken to Denton, who had been in one of the little groups of people that he'd followed in Cici's wake to greet and chat with earlier. He had seen Markham in another nearby group, but they hadn't spoken to each other prior to Matthew being summoned downstairs. All of this, he mentioned to Danbury. Not that any of it got these two off the hook, necessarily, but there was someone at the moment of more interest than either of them, and that was Kennedy Reynolds.

"Either of you know what the disagreement was about? Between Washburn and Reynolds?"

"What disagreement?" asked Denton as he rocked back on his heels.

"The altercation in the stairwell. Earlier this evening. Between Reynolds and Washburn."

They both shook their heads as Markham answered, "There were no issues between them as far as I know. At least, nothing serious. I think Kennedy blamed Jamison for not allowing him to buy in and add his name to the firm marquee. With his experience and legal record, I think Kennedy wanted more than the remaining corner office up here and the senior partner title. I think he wanted his name added, and if he had his way, probably to precede mine," he said attempting a chuckle that fell flat. "Jamison was probably the most vocally opposed, but that was two years ago and I haven't heard them discuss it since."

Indicating Markham, Danbury asked, "Can you find Reynolds?"

"Certainly, I'll call and try to locate him," said Simon Markham, stepping out in the hallway to do so.

"And can you locate the assistant? Abigail Moore." Danbury asked Denton.

"I think I can," said Denton. "She should still be upstairs. I'll bring her down quietly."

"And Cici?" added Matthew.

"OK. If I can pull her away from our London clients, I'll bring her back too," said Denton, as he left the room and turned the corner for the elevators.

"I'm not getting an answer," said Markham, returning to the room. "It goes straight to voice mail."

"Keep trying. Do you have an address for him?" asked Danbury. "If he doesn't answer his phone. I need to talk to him somehow."

Markham nodded and Danbury said, "And can you clear the Medical Examiner and forensic team? With the host station downstairs. They'll have to be let up. Right? I'm not sure who's coming. But they'll all have ID."

"Yes, of course," said Markham, poking his smart phone and slipping back out into the hallway as Danbury made his way over to the desk on the right. He introduced himself to Timothy, the server from the catering company who'd been cowering there behind the messy desk.

"You're the one who found Mr. Washburn?" asked Danbury.

"Yeah, I did."

"OK, start at the beginning. Why were you down here?"

"Margaret sent me."

"Margaret?"

"She's the manager in charge tonight."

"Of the catering company you work for?"

"Yeah."

"What time was that?"

"I don't really know. It was pretty busy upstairs and we can't have our phones with us when we're working."

"Margaret asked you to bring the tray down?"

"Yeah, she said we'd had a request to bring down a plate of food and a glass of punch but she hadn't had a chance to get it down here. I was restocking the escargot, arranging it on the platters to replace them, so I couldn't leave right that minute. I told her I'd fix the plate and glass as soon as I was finished. And I did. I came down here to bring it to the office she'd told me to deliver it to. When I came in, I saw him. He was lying across his desk, so I put the tray down and ran to get help."

"You put the tray down. What tray? Where?"

"That one," Timothy said, pointing to the silver tray that was perched on the messy desk in front of him. "I put that tray down and ran."

"You didn't go into the inner office? Not at all?"

"No, I could see he needed help so I went to find some. I don't even know CPR so I couldn't help him."

"You were delivering this tray of food?" asked Danbury, indicating the one on the desk.

"Yes, that's what I'm telling you. I brought it in. But when I saw him, I put it down and went for help."

"There's a plate of food. On his desk. And a cup."

"Oh. Yeah, there is," he said, leaning over to peer around the corner of the door.

"You didn't bring that one down?"

"No. Just this one."

"Did you see the other food on his desk? When you first saw him. Was it there then?"

"Yeah, I guess it was. I just didn't stop to think about it, but I guess it was already there."

"And you don't know how it got there?"

"No. Maybe Margaret knows. Maybe she got it down here after all. I don't know, I only brought this one," he said pointing again to the tray on the messy desk.

"Did you hear anything? Or see anyone? While you were down here?"

Timothy paused, "No, I had a song stuck in my head. I was singing and humming it when I came down. Right up until I was coming into this office here. Everything but that inside office was pretty dark. I mean, there could have been somebody else down here. I only came in this office from the elevator. Margaret told me which one and how to get here, so I didn't look around the rest of the floor."

"How long have you worked for the catering company?"

"Lion's Share? Um, sort of off and on, really. It's not a full-time job or anything. I work some weekends and some nights. I'm a student, so it's just extra money. I've done it for over two years. Since right after I graduated from high school."

"The name of the catering company is Lion's Share?"

"Yeah, that's right," said Timothy, pointing to the gold emblem of a roaring lion's head on the pocket of his red velvet vest.

"I need your contact information. I'll print your statement. And we'll need you to read through it. Make any corrections or additions. And sign it."

"Yeah, I guess so. I have an apartment with three of my buddies near the campus downtown. If I'm not there, they can usually find me," said Timothy and gave Danbury his cell number and address.

"And fingerprints. We need yours. To confirm what you've explained. I've got a forensic team on the way. They should be here anytime now."

As Timothy was agreeing, the Medical Examiner arrived, followed shortly thereafter by the team of forensic experts that Danbury had summoned.

"OK. Thank you, Timothy. After you're fingerprinted, you're free to go," said Danbury, turning to address the new arrivals and caution them about the poison.

4 ~ Crowds and Throngs

Matthew stood, realizing that the room had gotten incredibly cramped and that Cici hadn't made an appearance yet. As he was waiting to be sure he was cleared to go back upstairs, Danbury was giving the forensic team instructions for fingerprinting Timothy to rule him out.

"Bag and tag both cups and plates. Double glove before handling those. Check for fingerprints. This one," Danbury pointed to the tray on the messy desk. "This one should have just his prints," he said thumbing to Timothy. "That one should not. Nobody else has touched it. Right?" Danbury asked Matthew as he approached the messy desk in the corner.

"Nobody touched anything in there except Mr. Washburn. After I dragged him out here, nobody went back in there so the room is preserved, at least as I found it."

"Thanks, Doc. Find me before you leave."

"OK. I was going back upstairs to find Cici. I'll check back in a few minutes. It's too much for me up there anyway, so if I can help out down here, I'm happy to," said Matthew, with a sly grin. He fastened his coat buttons and straightened his tie to be presentable before making his way to the elevator and asking the operator to go up to the next floor.

Elevator operators, he thought, were such an antiquated concept. Some of the ritzier locales in New York City he knew still employed them. Tiffany's, he remembered from a trip with Cici a few years previously, still had one. That was arguably out of necessity due to an equally ancient elevator. From previous forays into Cici's office building in past years, he also knew that this building usually did not employ them. Only the one elevator ventured all the way to the top three floors, which were usually accessed by a badge reader in the elevator. The other seven in the bank of elevators from the lobby ceased their journey two floors below the office he'd just left.

Certain that Danbury had either already questioned the elevator operator or that he certainly would, Matthew rode the quick trip up in silence. When the elevator opened, Matthew noticed a few heads turning questioningly in his direction as he stepped out into the room. He smiled and nodded without stopping to chat as he made his way in search of Cici through the room. It was crowded with throngs of people.

Finding her with her back to him in the corner closest to the carving station, he waited a beat while she laughed at something that one of the two Londoners had said. Then he slipped his hand under her elbow and she turned. "Oh, there you are," she said, stepping back from the group as she looked up into his face in apparent concern. "Is everything OK?"

"Not exactly," he said quietly. "Can you get away for a few minutes?"

"OK, let me just make my excuses here. Where are we going?" she asked, trying to be quiet but having to bridge the distance in their heights with her voice.

"Downstairs," he said and then waited while she made her apologies to the group she was chatting with, particularly the two Londoners.

"You go ahead. We'll just be faffing about," said the one Matthew thought was Marshall, the taller of the two and the more outspoken.

"OK, if you need anything, ask anyone in the red velvet vests," Cici instructed.

"Ta."

"What's going on?" asked Cici before following Matthew across the room. This time, she just nodded and smiled without stopping to talk to anyone as they made their way toward the elevator.

"Let's get downstairs and I'll fill you in," he said as they stepped aboard the elevator and asked the attendant to descend a floor. As they disembarked, Matthew pulled Cici aside before heading down the hallway and he told her what had happened.

"He's what?!" she demanded. "How can Mr. Washburn be dead? We just saw him. It wasn't from the blow from Reynolds, was it?"

"It's too early to know for sure but I don't think so. I think the autopsy will show that he was poisoned."

"Poisoned? Poisoned how?"

"It'll probably be a few days before they know that for certain. Hopefully the autopsy will be conclusive. But if he was poisoned, either he'd ingested it before we saw him in the stairwell or it was extremely fast acting and potent. I think there was only about an hour between the time we saw him and when he was found."

Considering this, Cici said, "I think that's about right. It certainly couldn't have been much longer than that." She looked up at Matthew and he could hear the alarm in her voice as she said, "Wait, you did CPR on him and he was poisoned?"

"I did, but I took the chest compressions because I thought that the breathing would be easier for Dr. Miller. Compressions take some force to do them correctly. Sometimes you break ribs." Cici grimaced and Matthew continued, "I did caution him about the probability of poisoning so Dr. Miller was doing the breathing with his hands cupped around Washburn's mouth to form a seal. It was a futile effort though. Mr. Washburn never regained any function, breathing or heartbeat, on his own. But we tried, we really did our best."

Matthew hesitated before admitting to Cici, "And then Dr. Miller was rushed off by the paramedics. He was likely having a reaction to the poison too."

"He was what? When?"

"Probably about twenty minutes ago or so."

"Are you certain that you're OK?" she asked, obviously concerned.

"I'm paying attention, believe me, but my pulse and breathing are normal. I don't feel lightheaded. Dr. Miller got immediate treatment because the paramedics were already there when he started experiencing symptoms, so I hope he'll be OK. The trouble is that we don't know what the poison was so we can only treat the symptoms. Some poisons have no known antidote anyway."

"This is so awful!" exclaimed Cici, miserably. "Has anyone contacted Annabelle?"

"Annabelle?" repeated Matthew.

"Jamison Washburn's wife. She's not here tonight because she's been undergoing chemotherapy for breast cancer. It seems to be working, but they've been through so much already. I can't believe that he's gone," said Cici in a mixture of incredulity and sadness.

"I don't know if anyone has done that yet. Your other two senior partners were given assignments by Danbury."

"Danbury is here? Oh good."

"He is. If anybody can sort all of this out, he would be the one to do it, so I called him."

"I completely agree." Pensively, she added, "Either Abigail Moore, Mr. Washburn's assistant, or I would be the best candidates to go talk to Annabelle. Or both of us together. I'm not excited by the prospect, but neither would I want some callous police officer to be the one she hears the news from. An officer would scare her just showing up at her door at night. And I'd rather we do it in person. I don't want that news delivered over the phone."

Matthew paused a moment, letting Cici's heartfelt concern sink in. In that moment he realized that he was seeing the Cici he'd fallen in love with back when he was in medical school, the one who wasn't yet callous or driven to succeed above all else.

This was but one of the obstacles that had driven them apart previously after dating for several years. The pair had met at the small private university they'd both attended south of Raleigh when Cici was finishing her undergraduate degree and preparing for law school and Matthew was in the second year of his Osteopathic Medical program. They'd dated for nearly five years and then broken up due to what seemed at the time to be irreconcilable plans for the future. Cici had enjoyed the racier lifestyle in the fast lane vowing to quickly make partner in the biggest law firm in Raleigh, where she'd been hired right out of law school.

"That's so kind of you, Cees," he said, reverting to the name he'd called her when they were seriously dating. "If you're volunteering, let's go talk to Danbury and see if that's OK and how much initial information he'd like you to provide."

"I am," she said, drawing herself up to her full five-foot-nothing stature, which was enhanced several inches by the spiked heels. "Let's go find him and talk to him about it."

Smiling down at her adoringly, Matthew formally extended his elbow and she took it as they set off down the hallway. When they entered the outer reception area of the office suite, it was still brimming with activity. Danbury was looking over the ME's shoulder at Washburn's body and both were masked, the ME gloved as he poked and prodded. Matthew caught a glimpse through the inner office door of the forensic team moving around taking pictures.

"There are no visible wounds to indicate a stabbing or shooting," said the ME. "There's no petechial hemorrhage in the eyes and no ligature marks on his neck that I can see, so I think we can rule out strangulation. I see no defensive wounds on his hands, so there must have been no struggle or physical altercation."

"Likely someone he knew. Or trusted for some other reason," interjected Danbury.

"The only mark I see is the one on his left cheek," continued the ME. "It looks to be recent. Like it had just started to bruise and swell at the TOD, and the internal temperature supports that as being something over an hour ago, an hour and a half probably."

"The bruising on his face was very recent at the time of death," announced Cici from the doorway, though she was noticeably looking at Danbury and not the ME, avoiding a direct view of the body. "We walked in just as it was happening, which was probably a couple of hours ago now. Certainly no more than that."

"Can you be more precise on the time? The last time you saw him," said Danbury. "Matthew was guessing. At maybe an hour before the 9-1-1 call. That was received at five after eight."

"That's probably close," said Cici. "We were heading up the back stairwell from my office on the floor below this one to join the event upstairs when we encountered Kennedy Reynolds and Mr. Washburn on the landing just outside the Gala. It was shortly before seven, six forty-five I think, when we left my office. It was maybe an hour later when Matthew was summoned down here. It couldn't have been much more than that, I don't think. But I'm not wearing a watch so I'm really just guessing too."

She stepped up behind Danbury where he leaned over the ME's shoulder. Standing at an angle facing him to avoid the view of her deceased senior partner, she asked, "Has anyone contacted his wife Annabelle yet?"

"Not yet," said Danbury. "Unless one of the other partners did. Is she here?"

"I'm afraid not. But maybe that's a good thing. I wouldn't want her to see him like this. Though I'm sure she'll want to see him at some point," she grimaced. "She's been through so much lately, and I hate this for her. Like her husband, she's a kind person. She is always the first to volunteer for fundraisers and civic events to support our pro-bono work when we try to help the underprivileged in the area. And he's an extremely kind and caring person. I mean he was. Who would want to hurt him?" Cici asked, choking on her words. Matthew put an arm protectively around her shoulder, pulling her back toward the doorway.

After a moment, Cici managed to regain control of her voice and said, "If the partners haven't already contacted her, I'd like to go tell her in person, if that's OK?"

"That's a hard job," said Danbury. "Are you sure?"

"I am. I wouldn't want that news to come from anyone who didn't know and adore her husband. He was a mentor to me and I want to break this news as gently as possible. I need to check with Mr. Markham to be sure that he's OK with it. He's known the Washburns far longer than I have."

As if on cue, Simon Markham returned with Abigail Moore in tow, though the woman averted her eyes when she walked in and wouldn't look to the left of her desk where the ME was still moving around the body and the two forensic experts had joined him, snapping pictures as he pointed. Their low voices of collaboration could barely be heard above Simon Markham's as he reported, "I still haven't been able to reach Kennedy but Jonathan found Abby and I brought her down with me. I've explained your request for our guest list, and she quite astutely pointed out that the gentleman at the host station in the lobby has the list marked for the evening. He and Roger the elevator operator would be in the best positions to address the arrivals and departures."

"You're Abigail Moore?" Danbury asked, turning to the woman. She was of medium height and build, blonde, and very pretty, a fact that was not well disguised behind the heavy glasses she wore on her drawn and ashen face. She wore a long green velvet dress, which looked to be from the Dickens era, with a high collar and lace ruffles at her neck and wrists.

"I'm Abby, yes," she said and she looked as if she might be sick.

"And you were Mr. Washburn's assistant?"

"Yes. The primary. That's my desk there," she said, pointing without looking at the desk to the left. "And Rhonda Cauthren occupies this one," she frowned as she indicated the messy one to the right.

"Is she here tonight?" asked Danbury.

"No, she wasn't required to be here. I mostly organized the event and she just helped out when I had specific calls she could help make or correspondence to send out. Like the invitations. She stuffed and sealed those. We still send out formally engraved invitations for the event."

"She's an assistant to the assistant?" asked Danbury.

"Something like that, I suppose. I'm Mr. Washburn's Executive Assistant," she swallowed hard. "Or, at least I was. She was his Associate Assistant."

"Did he have enemies? Anyone who might have a vendetta. Anyone with an axe to grind. Or who would benefit from his demise? Can you provide a list?"

"That would be a pretty short list," answered Abby. "But I'll give it some thought. As an attorney, he's bound to have made some enemies, though I can't think of any off the top of my head. And I can't really think of anyone who would gain from his death. He's a defense attorney, so the most likely people to hold a grudge would be a victim of someone he's defended. He screened the clients he chose to defend pretty carefully, at least he did during the fourteen years that I've been his assistant. Until he was assured that the client was innocent, he wouldn't take the case. Unless it's a child of one of our top clients who gets into trouble, or something like that, he would research it very carefully first. Those cases usually got handed to one of the junior partners to handle anyway. He doesn't take just any defense case, not these days. He could afford to be careful about whom he chose to defend, and he always was. I'm sorry, I'm babbling."

"Not at all. You're answering the questions," said Danbury, encouragingly. "You said he was careful. With the people he defended?"

"Right. If he thought they were guilty, he wouldn't take the case. 'Somebody must defend the guilty,' he'd say, 'because they are entitled to a defense. But it won't be me, if I can help it.' When he thought someone was getting a really bad deal and was innocent but couldn't afford an attorney to prove it, he took cases pro bono. He is, or was, pretty well known for that," she said, staring sadly at the floor.

"What about Kennedy Reynolds? What was their relationship like? Did they generally get along?"

At this, her head snapped up. "Kennedy Reynolds? What does he have to do with any of this?"

"It's just routine questioning," said Danbury.

"As far as I know, their relationship is, I mean was, amicable enough. I'm sure they've disagreed over something a time or two in the last couple of years that Mr. Reynolds has been here, but nothing serious that I know of. Mr. Reynolds can be," she hesitated as if choosing her words carefully. "He can be difficult to get along with. I don't know of any issues that Mr. Washburn has ever had with him. As the more senior partner, Mr. Washburn's word would have been the final one, whatever the discussion between the two of them."

"Did you see Mr. Reynolds? Upstairs at the party?" asked Danbury. "Or at all this evening?"

Taking a moment to consider, Abby finally shook her head and said,

"Only very briefly. I remember seeing him appear from the back stairwell, but I was working with the caterers so I don't know where he went after that. And then I don't recall seeing him the rest of the evening."

"Did you notice if he was carrying anything? Or if he picked up anything?"

She pondered a moment before responding, "He wasn't when I saw him. He had just come from the back stairwell into the room, but he had nothing in his hands that I saw."

"What time was that?"

"Umm, something before seven. Definitely before seven, but otherwise I'm not sure exactly."

"Were you up there the whole time? Until Mr. Markham brought you down here?"

"I was," she responded. "Orchestrating all of the details of the evening."

"Did you notice anything unusual? Anyone or anything that seemed off. Or odd. Or out of place."

After a momentary pause, she said, "No, but I was pretty busy early on. The catering company, one we've used for years, was initially short staffed this evening. Two people didn't show up who were scheduled to be here and they were scrambling to find replacements at the last minute. So that put some of the initial set up direction on me."

"Because you planned this event?" asked Danbury, finishing up the notes he was taking as she spoke.

"Right."

"And you can provide the complete guest list? Everyone invited this evening. And how they RSVPed about attending?"

Looking over her shoulder at Mr. Markham, who nodded solemnly, she said, "Yes, I can provide the entire list of invitations. The most current copy of the actual attendees is down at the reception stand in the lobby. Darren is checking the names of the invitees from a list, marking them off as they arrive. He'll have the best idea of who arrived and when this evening. Roger, the elevator operator for the evening, can also help to verify some of that if you give him specifics on who you're asking about."

"Are they working from a complete list? Of everyone invited? Or just those who said they were coming?"

"Oh. No, I suppose not. They have the list of everyone who responded that they planned to attend."

"And any guests who don't RSVP. They don't just show up? Does anyone who declined attend anyway? Maybe they changed their mind?"

"It's happened a few times. Darren has my cell number to contact me if it does, but it didn't happen this evening. He didn't call questioning the arrival of anyone who wasn't on the list this evening."

"Mr. Markham," said Cici, who'd been waiting patiently beside Matthew and listening as Abby was being questioned. "Has anyone contacted Annabelle?"

"We haven't yet," said Simon Markham, shifting uncomfortably. "Though I suppose we should. I'm just not sure how to go about it."

"May I?" asked Cici, to which Markham's face registered his surprise.

"You'd be willing to do that?"

"I want to break the news to her as gently as possible, Sir. I thought perhaps Abby and I might manage that," she said, glancing at Abby, who looked as though she would burst into tears at any moment. "If Abby's up for it, it's certainly far better than police officers banging on the door this late at night with terrible news. And I thought we could do it in person, not over the phone."

"I would be most appreciative if you would do just that," said Markham, glancing at Abby as if to gauge her intentions.

"I guess I could come too," stammered Abby, brushing a tear from her cheek. "I talked to her all the time, on one subject or another, before and after her conversations with Mr. Washburn when she called in through the office lines. Things were going smoothly upstairs when I left, but let me just slip up, check on a few things, and leave some instructions. Then I can meet you in the lobby, OK?"

"OK," said Cici. "Matthew, would you perhaps chauffer us?"

"There's plenty of room in the sedan you rented, so of course I can do that."

At Cici's request, Matthew had sold her sporty little Porsche to one of his childhood friends while she was away in London. Because of a bad experience she'd had with it the previous spring before she went to work with the clients in London for a year, she wanted to get something else to drive. She hadn't planned to buy another vehicle until she was home permanently from the year she'd committed to be in London, so she'd rented a sedate sedan to ferry around the two London clients while they were in town. Much like her previous two-seat sports car, Matthew's Corvette, which was waiting for him at her house in nearby Quarry, wouldn't hold three people.

"You got this now?" Danbury asked the ME.

"Yeah, we've got this," said the ME.

"I'll be right back. I'm going to talk to Roger. The elevator operator. And the guy at the host stand downstairs."

As Matthew, Cici, Danbury, and Abby turned to leave and headed down the hallway, Matthew glanced back over his shoulder. From the look of despair on Simon Markham's face as he stared back into Jamison Washburn's office at the scene unfolding there, Matthew was pretty certain that Markham had nothing to do with Washburn's demise. On the contrary, he looked stricken and sincerely sorrowful to lose his colleague and friend of many years.

The group stepped into the elevator and asked to be taken up a floor to deposit Abby momentarily back at the soiree. The opulent scene had gotten noisier since they left, Matthew noticed, as the elevator doors opened and Abby stepped out. As the doors closed behind her and the elevator grew quiet again, Matthew loosened his tie with his free hand that wasn't extended to Cici. Leaning back slightly against the wall of the elevator, he realized he was tired.

It had been a long week at the family practice in Peak, where he worked alongside two other Physicians, their new Physician's Assistant, and the Medical Resident that the PA had brought with her. They'd all had a week full of long days treating all sorts of seasonal ailments, from influenza and winter colds that had turned to sinus or ear infections, to strep throat and pneumonia.

Matthew was halfway listening as Danbury questioned the elevator operator, Roger, about the comings and goings of the evening. He'd seen Markham, Denton, and Reynolds, Roger reported, but not Washburn since he'd been on duty, beginning around six-thirty. Both Markham and Denton he'd ferried up a floor from the thirty-second, where their offices were, to the top floor to join the soirée.

Markham had ventured up well before seven, and Denton shortly after Markham. He said he'd taken Reynolds from the top floor to the thirty-second floor of offices just before seven, soon after Denton had ascended, and then all the way to the ground floor around seven-forty-five.

At that, Matthew's ears perked up and his eyebrow shot up as he leaned forward. That time frame put Kennedy Reynolds on the floor where the partner's offices were, and where Jamison Washburn had been murdered exactly during the time frame of the murder.

Danbury asked about the staff from the catering crew and Roger confirmed that they too would have used the elevator to reach the top floor. All but two of them had arrived before he came on shift and he wasn't sure who would have taken them up, or if they'd been issued key cards for the evening that could be scanned to provide them access.

After several more fruitless questions about overheard conversations or anything out of the ordinary, Danbury got Roger's contact information, explaining that he might have more questions later. They stepped off the elevator.

Next, they stopped at the host stand just outside the elevator while Danbury questioned Darren, who handed over his copy of the guest list. It was properly marked with the time of arrival for all guests who had checked in for the evening, and Danbury thanked him for that information, taking pictures of three pages of guests. After receiving banal answers to the quick barrage of questions about anything unusual earlier in the evening, Danbury asked for his contact information. As he was finishing up, the elevator doors opened again and Abby stepped out and joined the group.

"You all have a nice evening now," said Roger, who'd so far been left in the dark about the exact occurrences on the thirty-second floor, though he'd brought up the emergency workers, Danbury, the ME, and the forensic team. He had to know, thought Matthew, that something serious had occurred up there.

"Roger that," said Matthew. As both Cici and Abby turned to stare at him in surprise, Matthew said, formally, "My apologies. I didn't mean to say that out loud. It's just that it's been a long week and I get punchy when I'm tired. I, of all people, should never joke about anyone else's name."

"Certainly, Sir," said Roger as the elevator doors closed in front of him.

"You? Oh, you're a doctor, aren't you?" said Abby. "Doctor Paine," she added, with air finger quotes and a laugh. "I get it now. I hadn't made the connection. I'm a bit tired myself."

To her credit, Matthew thought, Cici said nothing. She looked up at him and rolled her eyes. That spoke volumes too, just not audibly, he realized.

"Yeah, I get a lot of comments about that. But I've likely heard them all by now so if you've got some new material, I'd love to hear it. Give it your best shot."

"I don't actually. I'm too tired to come up with anything original. The week leading up to this Christmas Gala is always exhausting. So many details to organize, so many things to remember to do, and all in a certain order. And all of that alongside all of my normal responsibilities. Mr. Washburn always gives me the next week off to recuperate. But this year," she started. "I don't know what's going to happen now. It's nearly Christmas and I don't even know if I'll have a job now."

"I'm sure they'll find something else for you to do, Abby," said Cici comfortingly. "Everyone knows that you're the best of the best so if anyone should be worried right now, it should be Mr. Markham or Mr. Denton's Executive Assistants."

"That's sweet, Ms. Patterson," said Abby. "Thank you for saying that. But I honestly can't imagine working for anyone other than Mr. Washburn. He was always so kind and understanding. And we had a working synergy that is rare. I'd worked in several places before I came to work for him, so believe me when I say that it's rare."

They'd made their way to the front door with Danbury trailing along behind when he spoke up. "Ms. Moore, can I get your contact information? I'll need to get you to sign your statement. I'll likely have more questions. After I review the guest lists. You worked closely with Mr. Washburn. You're the best source for office information. You can help sort out what's important."

"Certainly, Detective," said Abby, and provided her information, just as Matthew was telling Cici that he'd go get the car from the parking garage down the street and bring it right back for her so that she and Abby didn't have to get out in the cold evening air. There was a valet service for the evening but, like the elevator, Cici had insisted on not using it so that both the parking and the attendants were fully available for the invited guests. Previously, Cici had parked in the garage beneath the building and she'd recently confessed to Matthew that, despite the bad experience she'd had in that parking garage, she might have to renew her parking pass there because the nearest lot was over a block away.

Cici smiled up at Matthew appreciatively and thanked him quietly before letting go of his arm and reaching for Abby's, steering her over to the seating area of the lobby under a massive Christmas tree. The tree was cheerfully lit and decorated with balls, each of which displayed various scenes around the triangle area. Some of the Christmas balls were colored for the Universities in the area, he noticed, and each one showed some iconic emblem from the school.

Matthew didn't see the ornament for either the school his family supported or the smaller private one that he and Cici had both attended. Vowing to himself to do something about that, to find and rearrange the Christmas balls in the future, he had more important things to attend to now so he turned to leave the building.

As Matthew was about to head outside into the cold night air, Danbury stepped up beside him and pulled him gently by his sleeve, checking over his shoulder to be sure they were out of ear shot of the two women.

"Just a sec, Doc. Use your own judgment on when. But at the right time," he hesitated, "I'll need to talk to the widow. Can you prepare her for that? Give me a nice intro?" he asked as he pulled a card from his wallet and handed it over to Matthew. "Just ask her to call me. When she's ready. But let her know that needs to be sooner. Rather than later. I'll ask about her whereabouts this evening. Just to be thorough. And more importantly her insights. Anyone who might have had a grudge. Or any reason to kill him. Any past grievances with him. That sort of thing."

"OK, Danbury, will do," Matthew answered hoarsely, taking the card and slipping it into his jacket pocket before stepping outside. A misting of something cold had begun to fall from the sky while they had been inside and he flipped up the collar of his tuxedo. The street lamps, as well as the lit Christmas wreaths that hung from them, shone with what Matthew feared was either ice or what could become so. He recalled that the forecast had predicted low temperatures hovering just above freezing and he hoped that was correct.

Despite the lovely sparkle and shimmer of Christmas lights in the cold December misting rain, he felt the deep sadness of lost life and the pain that he knew it would cause a family this Christmas and likely every one hereafter. As he glanced back over his shoulder, he could see that the building he'd just left was lit at the top in alternating colors of green and red. He knew that there was an ice-skating rink and a tower of Christmas ornaments forming the shape of a Christmas tree over a walkway nearby on Fayetteville Street, and he usually loved seeing those.

Normally, these Christmas scenes would be cheerful ones and he'd love to pause and drink it all in, exulting in his childlike joy of the season. Instead, this night he shivered as he walked up the street toward the parking garage to retrieve the rental car and go deliver news that he dreaded having to relay.

5 ~ BREAKING IT GENTLY

Finding the car easily enough on a weekend night, Matthew climbed in and started it up. After he'd paid to park, he pulled out onto the wet streets and then down alongside the curb in front of the tall building. Setting the parking brake, he climbed out to open the doors for Cici and then Abby Moore.

After they were settled, Cici pulled up the street address that Abby gave her on the navigation app on her phone and placed it in a slot on the front dash.

"They're in one of the older ITB neighborhoods just down Glenwood," Abby explained. Raleigh, Matthew knew from having grown up there, was very much divided in the minds of some people as being either inside the beltline, ITB, or outside of the beltline, OTB. The beltline, so called by natives who had lived there for forty years or more, was I-440 to newer arrivals and actually just a highway that made an oddly-shaped oval around the city of Raleigh.

Having grown up in north Raleigh very much outside of the beltline, Matthew had been oblivious to this delineation. His childhood home in which his parents still resided was in a very nice older neighborhood but not one with which descendants of "old" Raleigh money would be very impressed, purely due to the location. Where they were headed, he soon learned, was one of the more impressive "older monied" neighborhoods around Carolina Country Club. To meet Mr. Washburn though, you'd never have known that. He was as down-to-earth as it got from what Matthew had known of the man.

Of the three senior partners, Matthew thought that Denton was far more aware of the "older" versus "newer" money delineation in Raleigh, probably because he came from the latter group. The only one of the three who had not grown up in Raleigh, much less the old monied areas of Raleigh from which the other two originated, Denton seemed to need people around him to know about his accomplishments.

Markham and Washburn were both old names that were well known in the Raleigh area. From what Matthew could determine, Denton hadn't come from money at all. He seemed to think that he had more to prove in that area. His aspirations at achieving the kind of old southern charm and style that Markham and Washburn both naturally emanated seemed to fall short, which only made him try harder and the differences in the three of them, therefore, were brought into sharper contrast. As far as a legal mind though, Matthew had it on good authority that Denton was brilliant.

Matthew's musings were interrupted by Cici speaking up, "We need a plan for when we get there, Abby. I don't want to scare her by showing up unannounced this late at night. Maybe you could text or call and tell her you need to stop by for something urgent or important when we get close?"

"Good idea. There's no need to panic her before," Abby stopped up short. "Well, before we have to. This is going to be so hard," she said on a shuddering breath. "They've been married for thirty-four years! Did you know that? Jamison was only fifty-eight, and I think Annabelle is just a couple of years younger. Their youngest daughter Elizabeth lives close by, thankfully. She's just finished her undergraduate degree and will be starting on a Master's or PHD or something at Duke in January."

"They have two daughters," she continued. "The older one, Sophia, doesn't live in this area anymore. She's out in Seattle, Washington. Their son, Jamison the fourth, is the middle child and he lives just over the Georgia line. Not too far away, but not as close as Elizabeth. Maybe she'll just come and stay with Annabelle for a while."

Abby blew out a breath and she seemed to be fighting for control. Maybe she wasn't the best person to have come along and talk to Annabelle, Matthew thought. But then again, maybe she was the perfect person to mourn alongside the new widow. Maybe her sorrow would be comforting. He certainly hoped so as he turned off Glenwood Avenue into the neighborhood surrounding the golf course of the Carolina Country Club and Abby made the call to Annabelle.

He had to give the woman credit for keeping her cool as Abby told Annabelle that she needed to stop by for something for Jamison. She cut the conversation short, saying that she would be turning in momentarily, while he assumed that Mrs. Washburn was wondering what that "something" might be. He did indeed turn quickly between two tall square brick pillars. Each were each adorned with a large lit wreath of greenery and what looked to Matthew to be gold and burgundy ornamental balls and a large bow.

The driveway was lined on both sides by tall trees with overhanging branches and balls of light hung at exact intervals along them. Matthew realized that the driveway was actually U-shaped, and the other side of it was nearly a mirror image, as he pulled to the front of a large brick house which was set well back off the road.

There was a central center section of the house, two stories with a pillared porch. The pillars dropped from the roof of the second story down to ground level. A little balcony hung from the second story above the front entrance. Roping of lit greenery was draped in swags along the front edge of the porch ceiling, pulled up in front of each pillar and along the balcony railing above the door. It was draped around the ornate carvings above the double front doors and down the outside edge of the side lights on either side. Large lit wreathes of greenery with gold ornaments and burgundy ribbon graced the tops of the pillars and both front doors. Candles glowed warmly and invitingly in all of the windows of this main section of the house. It all glistened invitingly in the cold misting rain that was still falling.

Lower brick sections protruded on both sides of the center structure, each a story and a half with dormer windows. No lights were on in the windows of these side sections. Bushes and landscaping shrubs, meeting the perfectly manicured grass in grand sweeps on either side of the circular drive, prohibited Matthew from determining how far the two side sections extended off into the darkness of the night. To the left Matthew could see that the driveway continued from the front circle around the corner of the house.

This was some house, thought Matthew, wondering about its age. A self-confessed history buff, Matthew would indeed be interested in the narrative of the house, its tale of antiquity. On any other occasion, he likely would have asked. Usually, in his experience, the owners of family homes of long standing knew the full history of them and they were happy to enlighten interested guests. This though was not one of those visits.

Matthew parked carefully along the drive to ensure that there was extra pavement available along the passenger side of the car. When he opened the doors for the women, he wanted them to be able to step out onto solid ground. Other than the quietly spoken thanks as Matthew handed each woman out of the car, the group was silent as they stepped up the two broad curving steps onto the expansive front porch and Abby rang the bell.

The greenery was all real, Matthew realized as the heavy scent of it hung in the air around the porch. It looked to be a mixture of pine and fir with ivy and holly intertwined. Hearing the doorbell chime echo within the house, Matthew was half expecting a tuxedoed butler named Jeeves to answer the door. Instead a diminutive woman, who was probably much younger than she looked at that moment, appeared wearing a Christmas head wrap. A matching shawl adorned her small shoulders and she was otherwise clad in a silky cream pant suit that hung on her as if it were two sizes too large.

She seemed initially taken aback by his and Cici's presence but she recovered quickly from her surprise and invited them all in. "I'm Annabelle Washburn," she said, offering her hand to Matthew.

"Matthew Paine," he answered. "You have a lovely home."

"Thank you," she answered quietly, "And I do remember you, don't I? But please refresh my memory on your name," she said, offering her hand to Cici.

"Cecelia Patterson, Junior Partner at your husband's law firm."

"Oh yes, of course. Nice to see you. And you too, Abigail. How can I help you all this evening? Was there something that Jamison sent you to retrieve?"

"No Ma'am, not exactly," said Abby, stepping forward. "We need to talk to you. Is there some place we can sit for just a moment?"

"Certainly. Please, this way," she said motioning them into a large high-ceilinged foyer into which ran a hallway with a grand staircase swirling down to the right. The handrail, Matthew noticed, was draped with greenery that was only slightly narrower than that which adorned the outside of the door. Like the outdoor greenery, it too was obviously live and adorned with Christmas balls in gold and burgundy and a large bow of the same colors at the base of the handrail. It smelled wonderful, he noted as Annabelle Washburn led them through a set of French doors to the right.

Flipping a switch to illuminate a beautiful sitting room, comfortably furnished in creams, mauve, and gold accents, she invited them in. In the corner to their right, a large Christmas tree lit with the flip of a second switch. It was decorated with ornaments, balls, a garland, and a tree skirt that perfectly matched the décor of the room. Beneath the tree were stacks of wrapped presents in varying sizes that also matched that décor, cream and mauve packages with gold bows and gold foil packages with cream and mauve bows.

If she was concerned about the purpose for their visit Mrs. Washburn hid it well, Matthew thought, as she said, "Have a seat, wherever you'd like. I'd offer you something to drink but I've given the staff the night off and it would take me a bit to prepare anything."

"Please don't bother with any of that," said Cici. "We've been quite well refreshed at the Christmas Gala this evening." She hesitated, not certain how to continue.

"I must admit that I'm surprised to see you here this evening. Isn't the Gala still in progress?" asked Mrs. Washburn.

"Probably so, Ma'am," said Abby. "And I'm so sorry to disturb you this late in the evening. We wouldn't have if we didn't have something very important and timely that we need to discuss with you."

"Yes, of course," she answered as she perched on the end of an overstuffed suede sofa and swept her arm for them all to be seated around her.

Cici sat down beside her and Abby took the small chair opposite while Matthew perched on a large overstuffed suede wing-back chair on the other end of the sofa.

"I don't know how to begin to tell you this," started Abby.

Annabelle's look of curiosity changed quickly to one of abject terror as she asked, "What's wrong? Is Jamison all right?"

"No Ma'am, I'm afraid he's not," was all that Abby had managed to get out when what little color there was in Annabelle Washburn's face drained completely out of it and, had Cici not been sitting beside her to catch her, she'd have pitched forward onto the floor.

Matthew quickly strode forward and took charge, laying Mrs. Washburn out on her back on the sofa and propping her calves up with nearby pillows from the back of the sofa. "Abby, can you get a damp cool cloth, please? And maybe a little bucket or small trashcan, just in case?"

Abby nodded and ran from the room. Cici had moved out of the way onto the edge of the nearby chair that Abby had occupied, sliding it forward, as Matthew checked Mrs. Washburn's vitals, her pulse, breathing, and pupils.

"I pulled these from the hall bath," said Abby, dashing in and handing Matthew a small wet finger towel and a brass wastebasket that, Matthew was thankful to notice, contained a plastic liner.

"Thank you, Abby. She'll come around in a minute," he said, dabbing her face with the wet towel and then lifting her head gently and swiping the towel behind her neck. "Is she diabetic or does she have any other health issues?" he asked, knowing that she was receiving chemotherapy for something and the head wrap was covering her head for a reason.

"She's been battling breast cancer," said Abby. "But Jamison said she was doing better and the outlook was pretty good. She's not diabetic or anything else that I know of. Why?"

"If you can find a little juice, natural sugar, that would be good for when she comes around. You said she had a daughter close by. Do you know how to reach her?"

"Um …" began Abby, just as Annabelle Washburn's eyes fluttered open and she looked up into Matthew's concerned face.

"It's OK, Mrs. Washburn," he reassured her. "I'm a physician. You just fainted." He looked up at Abby and nodded. She slipped from the room and back out into the main hall, Matthew hoped in search of juice. "Is there anyone we can call for you? Abby says you have a daughter nearby. Elizabeth, correct?"

"Yyyyes," she stammered, as if not at all sure what was going on around her yet. "Her number is in the little address book in the top desk drawer in the library. It's diagonally across the hallway. I'm afraid I left my phone upstairs. What happened?" she asked, and then the memory must have returned as she looked up at Matthew in horror and said, "Jamison!"

"I'm so sorry, Mrs. Washburn," said Cici, leaning as far forward as she could in the little chair and touching the woman's hand compassionately. "I'm so very sorry."

"He's," started Annabelle Washburn but then couldn't finish the sentence right away. "He's gone, isn't he?"

"I'm afraid so," said Cici soothingly, as a tear started down her cheek and she brushed it away quickly.

"What? How? What happened?" asked Annabelle Washburn, as she tried to push herself up into a sitting position. Cici quickly gathered more pillows and put those and the ones Matthew handed over from under her calves behind her to prop her up.

"We're not completely sure yet, Mrs. Washburn. Cici and Abby wanted you to hear the news from them in person and not have police officers knocking on your door this late at night," said Matthew.

"Police officers? That would have been a fright. That means that something ... happened."

"Yes, Ma'am," said Abby, handing Matthew a small glass of liquid.

"When was the last time you've eaten anything?" he asked, sitting the glass on a marble coaster on the little table at her head.

"I had a little chicken and some steamed vegetables for dinner around five-thirty," she said. "But I couldn't eat much. The chemotherapy has all but obliterated my appetite. Where is Jamison? Please tell me what you do know. I'm not the weak old lady that I appear to be. It's just the cancer. I was strong, active, and vibrant before that. And the doctors seem to think that I will be again. So please, tell me everything."

Matthew nodded to Cici and switched places with her. As she

perched on the edge of the sofa, Cici took Annabelle Washburn's hands in hers and told her about the events of the evening. Handing over a nearby tissue box that was cosseted in a heavy marble and gold holder, Matthew slipped quietly from the room and Abby followed.

"Can you get her daughter Elizabeth on the phone, please?" asked Matthew and then explained about the little address book in the desk drawer in the library.

"What do I tell her?"

"Don't deliver the news over the phone. Just ask if she can come and sit with her mother who isn't feeling very well this evening. Mr. Washburn can't get here and Mrs. Washburn has dismissed the staff. Something like that, which is the truth, just not all of it yet. Ask if she's able to come for the night. She'll know that her father is out at the gala event. We can tell her the rest of it when she gets here, so that she doesn't have to drive over knowing."

"Sure, Dr. Paine. I'll go find her number."

Matthew hovered in the doorway when he returned to the room. Tears streaked both of the women's faces as the elder woman listened intently, asking an occasional question, primarily about the whereabouts of Kennedy Reynolds and if they really thought that he'd killed her husband.

"Mrs. Washburn," began Matthew, returning to the room. "We don't know enough yet to know precisely how it happened, but there is a homicide detective who will want to talk to you. He's a friend of ours," he said, including Cici in the description. "I called him after we'd tried unsuccessfully to resuscitate your husband. If anyone can determine what happened and who orchestrated it, that would be Detective Danbury." Reaching into his pocket, he pulled out the card Danbury had given him and handed it to her.

She studied it a moment and then looked back up at Matthew. "Thank you, Doctor. May I have that juice now?"

"Of course," said Cici, reaching across and handing it to her.

"Detective Danbury said he'd wait for you to call him, but he will need to talk to you as quickly as he can. He'll ask you lots of background questions, mainly about any enemies that your husband could have had or made over the course of his legal career. That sort of thing," explained Matthew. "I'm sure he'll be thorough but as kind and considerate as he can be in the process."

"I'll call him as soon as Elizabeth arrives," promised Mrs. Washburn, handing Cici the business card, asking her to slip it into the front of the table drawer above her head, and sipping her juice. "Is she on her way? Were you able to reach her?"

"Abby is calling her. She's not telling her the whole story over the phone, just that you need her this evening."

"That's so thoughtful. Thank you," said Mrs. Washburn with a sniffle.

"We'll wait with you until she gets here, if you'd like?" asked Cici.

"Yes, please. I'd be so appreciative if you would."

Matthew loosened his tie and released the top button on his starched white shirt, thinking it would be a long night yet and it was hardly early now.

6 ~ SHADOWS IN THE NIGHT

As uncomfortable as Matthew was in his stiff new shiny shoes and the heavily starched white shirt, from which he'd removed the tie and then the vest hours earlier, he couldn't imagine how Cici was holding up in the spiked heels and restrictive dress. She was a trooper. He was entirely impressed with her sincere care of the older woman both before and after her daughter, Elizabeth, arrived.

Elizabeth, a lanky blonde with a thick ponytail that hung to her shoulders and bright green eyes, hadn't fainted at the news of her father's demise. She'd put the brass trashcan to good use instead, immediately apologizing profusely afterward. Matthew was unfazed by it all. He was a physician, so he'd signed up to deal with blood and bodily fluids when he'd chosen to attend medical school.

Annabelle Washburn was as good as her word about being tougher than she appeared. She'd shed tears off and on and she was clearly distraught. She had also risen to the occasion and called Danbury immediately after Elizabeth settled tearfully on the other end of the sofa from her mother.

After explaining how the mechanism in the fireplace worked, Annabelle said she was chilly in the sitting room and sweetly asked Matthew to build a fire. Inside, the fireplace was old brick with the addition of an elaborate gas lighting system that had been much more recently installed. It still burned wood, which Matthew collected from outside the kitchen entrance at the back of the house, but bars burning gas had been installed beneath the grating so that kindling and paper weren't needed. Matthew simply stacked the logs, flipped a switch to turn on and ignite the gas, and then waited for the logs to catch and burn on their own.

It was an antique but modernized ornate fireplace surrounded by marble trim and a highly polished mantle intricately carved of a light wood that seemed to float above it. Along the mantle were collections of small nativity scenes that seemed to be from all over the world. Some were glass, others carved wood, some ceramic, and one clay that featured what were obviously African figurines. When Matthew admired them aloud to Annabelle, Elizabeth rolled her eyes at him.

"Please don't encourage her," said Elizabeth in mock disdain. "Mother has collected those from all over the world. From the Holy Land to Europe, Asia, and Africa. There are sets of varying sizes and styles, created in varying medium, all over the house."

"They're lovely," agreed Cici, joining Matthew by the fireplace to examine the figurines. Then, she turned her back to it as the wood began to catch and a blaze lifted from the logs. "Oh, that is nice," she murmured.

"Thank you for getting that going. You can turn off the gas feeding the fire in probably another five or ten minutes," instructed Elizabeth. She was reclined against the back of the other end of the sofa from her mother with her feet propped on a stool in front of her. She'd mostly recovered from the shock, Matthew realized, to be joking about the figurines. Or she'd shifted into denial. Still, they'd asked him to wait for Danbury to arrive and to do the introductions. He'd readily enough agreed. How could he refuse to help when asked under the horrific circumstances?

When Danbury finally did arrive, it was nearly two in the morning. Matthew and Cici had curled up together in an overstuffed chair with their feet propped on the ottoman in front of it. When Annabelle Washburn had asked them to stay, she'd also told them to please make themselves comfortable and they'd taken her at her word. Abby was likewise curled up in an overstuffed suede wingback chair staring into space as if not seeing anything or anyone else in the room.

The chimes they'd heard when they arrived rang through the house and Matthew rose, slipping out and around Cici who'd had her head under his arm on his chest. "I'll get it," he said. "It can't be anyone but Danbury at this hour."

"Do you have any chamomile tea?" Matthew heard Abby suddenly ask as he and Danbury stood in the foyer just outside the sitting room behind her. "I could make you some to help with the chill." It was obvious that the rest of the unspoken reason was the underlying nerves that were about to get frazzled by the questioning process.

"That's an excellent idea," said Cici. "I'd be happy to help."

"There's a selection of teas and coffees in the butler's pantry off of the kitchen," replied Annabelle. "Elizabeth, would you show them where to find everything, Sweetheart?"

"Certainly," she said as she rose and the three women left the room. Elizabeth eyed Danbury suspiciously as she passed him in the large foyer but she didn't linger for introductions.

"Please come in," said Annabelle. "And please forgive my daughter's manners this evening. She's undergone quite a shock, as you can imagine. She was very close to her father. If ever there were a 'Daddy's girl,' Elizabeth is the poster child."

"Mrs. Washburn, this is Raleigh Homicide Detective, Warren Danbury," said Matthew.

"Please, come in and have a seat," she said. "I've heard that you are Raleigh's best at determining what happened in this sort of situation."

"I don't know about that," said Danbury, perching on the edge of the wingback chair that Abby had just vacated and looking uncomfortable as if he felt like the proverbial bull in an expensive China shop. "But I'll do my best."

"Thank you," she said, tearing up as she spoke. "I'm sure this process won't be an easy one, but I'll try to answer all of your questions as honestly and completely as I can. I do want to know what happened to my sweet Jamison. If he was indeed murdered, then his murderer must be apprehended before he or she can cause any other family this degree of suffering and anguish."

Matthew reached for the tissue box and placed it on the rectangular gold and marble coffee table in front of her. She took a tissue and blotted her pale drawn face with it, then said to Danbury, "Now, you may begin anywhere you would like."

"May I record this conversation?" asked Danbury, formally. "I need your permission to do so."

"Certainly. If that will help find my husband's killer, you may record anything you'd like." She choked on the statement only slightly but otherwise her voice was strong and clear.

The first questions were the most awkward ones. Her whereabouts for the evening and those of her husband leading up to his appearance at the Christmas Gala had to be established. Technically, she had no alibi for the time of what Matthew was all but certain would soon be classified as a murder. She was home alone. She had dismissed the staff for the evening, claiming that she wanted to enjoy a peaceful evening reading a new and intriguing biography of some long-dead relative which had just been published the month before.

Having dozed off while reading in bed, Annabelle wasn't sure exactly what time anything had transpired after Jamison left the house shortly before six. "He was dressed in his tuxedo and said he wanted to quickly attend to something in his office before the big gala event."

"He was going to his office first," summarized Danbury. "Was he meeting anyone there?"

"Not that he mentioned. He just said he had one last thing that he hadn't finished this afternoon before he left to come home and have an early dinner with me. He insisted on spending time with me this evening before attending the annual event of the season without me. Or yesterday evening, I suppose it was now," she said, acknowledging that it was the middle of the night. "I usually attend with him, but I wasn't feeling up to it this year," she added, sinking back into the pillows she was propped up on.

"Completely understandable," said Danbury, having been briefed when Matthew called him that she was dealing with cancer and chemotherapy treatments. "Mrs. Washburn, we can do this tomorrow. Or later today. If you need to rest."

"No, no, it's quite all right," she waved off his objection with her hand. "Despite having a veritable pharmacy of sleep medications upstairs, I do precious little of that these days anyway. I catch naps when I can but it's harder to sleep for long stretches of time. I think I did sleep for quite a while earlier this evening. I'm as up for this as I'll ever be, so please proceed."

"OK. Can you think of any enemies? Anyone your husband didn't get along with? Anyone he disagreed with? Or who had a disagreement with him?"

"I've been trying," she responded. "If there was anyone from a client perspective, I believe that it would have been from years ago. He was so very careful about who he defended, at least these past twenty years or so. Once he was able to choose his clients and still maintain a client base, he certainly exercised that option liberally. If he thought someone truly guilty, he refused to represent them. The only exception would be perhaps children of clients who had some brush with the law. He'd helped to defend them on occasion. But otherwise, he chose much more judiciously, particularly if there were another party alleged to have been injured in some way."

"I see," said Danbury. "Over the course of that time. Twenty years or prior. Do you know of anyone with a long-standing grudge?"

"That I don't know," she said, frustrated, rubbing her forehead with her thumb and forefinger. "I feel as if I'm no help at all. His colleagues should be able to help you with that. I'm sure Simon and Jonathan can answer that question far better than I can."

"How about in Mr. Washburn's personal life?" asked Danbury. "Has he made any enemies? Made anyone mad? Or jealous?"

At this last question, she seemed to draw into herself, but after a moment she looked Danbury squarely in the eye and said, "My husband was a kind and generous man. With me, our family, his friends, and strangers in need. He hasn't made enemies of anyone, or if he has it wasn't due to anything he did or didn't do."

That, thought Matthew, was an interesting answer to a seemingly simple question. In his experience, working alongside Danbury, in his medical career, and just in his life in general, he thought that everyone had something to hide. Everybody concealed some secret, whether a past sin or just knowledge of something awful that they didn't want known. He wasn't sure what she could be hiding, but he was certain that Annabelle Washburn was withholding something just then when she answered the question in a rather roundabout way.

As he pondered what that secret could possibly be, Abby and Cici returned with a tray and set a beautifully decorated mug of steaming liquid in front of Annabelle. It was delicate and looked to be hand painted with sprigs of holly leaves and berries, ivy, and tiny silver bells. "Elizabeth said that you like honey in your tea, so she put a dollop in for you," said Abby.

"Thank you, Dear," said Annabelle absently as she watched the steam rise from the mug and seemed to lose herself in it momentarily.

Finally, she sighed deeply and said, "The only person I can think of from Jamison's distant past who might still hold any serious grudge would be Aubrey Bartles."

"Aubrey Bartles," repeated Danbury, adding the information to his notes, "Tell me about him. And why he might still hold the grudge."

"It seems like another lifetime ago now," she began, as Abby and Cici both took seats to listen. Transfixed by the beginning of what seemed to be an interesting story, none of them had seen Elizabeth move into the doorway behind Danbury. "We were all students at University and Jamison and I had just met and begun dating. I had spent a little bit of time with Aubrey Bartles, but he apparently thought our relationship was a serious one already."

"Oh Mother, not the story of that hideous man again!" exclaimed Elizabeth from the doorway. "Please stop and do not tell this story again!"

"Again?" asked Annabelle, in surprise, as if only then realizing that Elizabeth was there. "When have you ever heard this story before to know about it?"

"I just have," Elizabeth replied. "And I don't wish to hear it again. I beg of you, please do not share this story."

"Elizabeth, Dear, perhaps it's relevant. The detective was asking about long-held grudges against your father. This is certainly the longest of which I'm aware."

"How could it be? That was like a million years ago," she protested. "I for one have no desire to dredge it all up again – the secret society, the pact and broken promises," she said. Turning, she fled from the room. Instead of the quiet footfalls they'd heard so far about the house, Elizabeth's feet could be heard running, as if stomping, up the curving stairwell that graced the spacious center entrance of the house.

"Elizabeth! There was no secret society or pact and you weren't even there!" Annabelle protested, then, turning back to the room, she said, "I apologize."

"No need," said Danbury. "As you mentioned, Ma'am. I'm sure she's very upset." Then he paused, waiting her out to begin again on the story about Aubrey Bartles, someone from the long ago past and about whom Elizabeth did not want to hear. Matthew stood and paced to the window, looking out and noticing that all of the outdoor Christmas lighting had either gone out on its own from timers or been turned off at some point. The night was dark except for the light cast on the lawn from the windows in the room where he was standing and others from above and to the right of the house. That must either be the room that Annabelle Washburn had vacated, he thought, or the one to which Elizabeth Washburn had fled.

As he turned to face the room, he noticed that the fire was getting low and Annabelle still had not spoken.

"Mrs. Washburn, would you like to have the fire refreshed?" He asked. "Or did you intend for it to burn out now?"

She looked confused by the simple question initially but then seemed to come back to life as she said, "Would you mind refreshing it? This room is comforting somehow, and I'm not yet ready to go back upstairs alone to the bedroom that Jamison and I share. I might never be ready," she said, and choked.

"Certainly, I'd be happy to," said Matthew, handing her a tissue from the box on the coffee table before excusing himself to bring in fresh logs.

As he passed the bottom of the stairwell, he could hear what he first thought was singing from above, but then he realized that it was crying. Not wailing exactly but a higher pitch could be discerned periodically, keening. Poor thing, he thought, as he moved through the house to get the wood. He knew that he wasn't in a position to do anything to ease the current suffering in the house except to keep the home fires burning, quite literally.

He knew he'd have to have his tuxedo cleaned anyway, but particularly so after he stacked the second load of wood up one arm. As he was turning to reenter the house, he saw something out of the corner of his eye and turned back to the expansive back yard that was lit only by a dim light mounted above a detached carriage house. There was definite movement and it was too large to be a wandering dog. Besides which, dogs didn't walk upright like he saw the shadowy figure do as it moved along the edge of the tree line.

"Hello?" he called, "Who's there?" His inquiry was met by silence as the figure slipped into the tree line and disappeared from sight. The misting rain that was falling earlier had ceased and the night was silent except for the sounds of distant traffic, presumably from Glenwood Avenue or perhaps even as far away as the Beltline, but he heard nothing more.

As he turned to return indoors, he was certain that he could hear the careful retreat of footsteps heading off into the trees that surrounded the back and sides of the property, a stealthy footfall, the snap of a twig. "Odd," he murmured to himself, raising an eyebrow. He closed the door and carefully locked it, sliding a large dead bolt home with his free hand. Then he flipped the row of light switches by the back door until he found one that lit the brick patio area behind the house.

When he returned to the sitting room, Annabelle Washburn was in tears and Cici was trying to comfort her. The story of the vendetta or grudge or whatever it was had yet to be resumed. Matthew placed the wood and stoked the fire, then turned to Danbury.

"Danbury, can you come with me for a minute?"

"Sure, Doc," said Danbury, looking confused. He dutifully followed Matthew from the room.

"Do you think they're in any danger here?" Matthew whispered in the hallway beyond the foyer.

"Why would you say that?" asked Danbury.

"We don't know definitively yet that Mr. Washburn was murdered. We're all but certain. Assuming that he was, we don't have any idea why yet. And I'm pretty sure I just caught someone leaving the property out back. I called out to them but they slipped into the tree line and disappeared."

"There's a golf course. On the other side. Right? Beyond that tree line."

"I think so," said Matthew. "I think this property backs up to the country club, so if it's not the golf course, it would be tennis courts or the clubhouse or some part of that."

"That could have been anybody," said Danbury. "Having come from anywhere. For any number of reasons."

"True," said Matthew. "But when I called out, the shadow moving along the tree line very quickly disappeared into the trees. And there was something about it that seemed," he hesitated. "It seemed menacing, furtive at the very least."

"You got all of that. From a shadow?" asked Danbury dubiously.

"Yes," said Matthew with certainty. "There was something about the person skulking in the yard that concerns me."

"OK," said Danbury. "I'll see what I can do. We can bring in patrols. Have them rotate through. Down this street. Every couple of hours."

"Will that be enough if someone is meaning to harm this family?" asked Matthew. "They certainly could afford to add security if you have any suggestions for who to hire. I don't want to scare Mrs. Washburn by suggesting that she's in danger. But I'd far rather do that than have her be in danger and leave her here isolated if she is."

"Yeah, I agree," said Danbury, rubbing the stubble on his chin with his thumb. "You're right. We don't know what we're dealing with. Not yet. Let's go hear the rest of the story. If she's willing to share it now. And we'll bring that up afterward. At some point."

Matthew nodded, adding, "I did lock the back door securely and I turned lights on back there to discourage the visitor from coming back tonight." Both men returned to the sitting room, where the fire had caught nicely and was burning brightly in the grate, casting a warm glow that should have been a happy one out into the room.

"My apologies, Mrs. Washburn," said Danbury, reclaiming his seat. "Where were we? You were about to enlighten us. About who might be holding a grudge. A long one by the sound of it. Against you. Or your husband."

7 ~ Overnight Tales

"Ah yes," said Annabelle Washburn with a faraway look in her eye as she picked up her mug of now cold chamomile tea. She sipped it absently, as if by doing so, she could be transported back in time. "I was a freshman in college at Vanderbilt in Nashville, Tennessee. Jamison was a junior. He had thought that he wanted to pursue a career in medical research but he was changing his mind about that and trying to figure out what might be a better fit for him when I met him."

"We were both from Raleigh but with the two-year age gap, we hadn't known each other growing up. I knew his younger brother, but I'd never encountered Jamison." She took a sip of tea but her gaze was into the middle of the room as if only her body were there and her mind had been transported back in time to another place.

"Anyway, I met Aubrey Bartles first. He was a friend of Jamison's, though I use that term very loosely. I had gone out with Aubrey a couple of times when I met Jamison, but there was no comparison in the way I felt about them. Jamison and I started dating seriously pretty quickly and we dated until he graduated. Aubrey had faded into the background, or so I thought."

"By that time, Jamison had decided to pursue a degree in law, corporate law, specifically. He was accepted at both Harvard and Yale, but he chose Yale. We split up when he left and it broke my heart. I already knew that I loved him deeply and I'd go anywhere to be with him. Even to New Haven, Connecticut, as cold as it is up there. But that was just me. He needed to want the same thing, so I backed off and quietly let him go."

"Those next six months were the worst for me. I returned to Vanderbilt but I was beyond lonely. I didn't want to date anyone else there and I felt completely lost without him. Despite my mother's promptings, I was determined to make my own way and not rely on a man for my future or my happiness. So I got it together and put all of my time and energy into my coursework. I thought I'd graduate, find a good job, and start over somewhere else."

"What I didn't know at the time was that Jamison was lonely and struggling just as much without me. It didn't take him long to realize that he loved me and missed me as intensely as I was missing him. We went through the next year apart, he through his first year of law school, and me through the junior year of my undergraduate program."

"Meanwhile, Aubrey, who was between Jamison and me in age, befriended me again. He was in his senior year during my junior year. We started spending a good deal of time together. I later learned that he was seeking me out when we "just happened to run into each other." He was serious about me but I just wanted the friendship. He was gregarious and charming, lots of fun to be around, and I did enjoy his company."

"Aubrey Bartles," she said as if she'd just bitten into a lemon. "I should have seen it then, but I was young and naïvely trusting. I suppose now you'd call it stalking. At first, I thought he was a good friend to Jamison and me both but then I realized that he wanted more than friendship from me. Initially, I was flattered with his attention. Then I realized how serious he was becoming and I tried to pull away. The more I tried to put distance between us, he just came on all that much stronger. I finally told him that I thought we should go our separate ways because I believed he wanted more than I did from our friendship."

"How did he react to that?" asked Cici, who was clearly as enthralled with this unfolding story as Matthew had become.

"I could tell that he was angry, particularly with Jamison, though he tried to hide it. There was a vein that would pop out in the center of his forehead when he was upset. I had seen it before but never directed at me. He spoke calmly when he told me that he 'cared deeply' for me, or some such verbiage. Thankfully, we were near the end of the year at that point and I just tried to avoid him, although he made it quite difficult, until I could come home for the summer. He wasn't from this area. He was from Ohio, I believe, and he was graduating so I thought that would be an end to it."

"But it wasn't?" asked Cici.

"Hardly," said Annabelle. "That summer Jamison and I both came home. We reconnected and he told me how he felt about me. I reciprocated and we were happy, at least for that summer. Jamison was interning at a local law firm and I was working with a friend who had her own business but we spent all our spare time together."

"Did you tell Jamison about Bartles?" asked Cici.

"Not at first. I honestly didn't think there was anything to tell. Aubrey had graduated and, as far as I knew, he'd gone back to Ohio."

"He hadn't?" asked Cici, while Danbury just looked on, his amusement showing clearly on his face that she'd taken the lead in asking the right questions to get the story out of Annabelle. She was a professional at asking the right questions too, thought Matthew.

"No. I didn't know until later that he'd followed me to Raleigh and he was watching us, or having us watched, all summer."

"Oh! That's creepy!" said Cici.

"I agree. I thought I'd caught a glimpse of him a couple of times, but I told myself that wasn't possible. I was so involved with Jamison that I didn't think much about it at the time. But then the summer was over and Jamison was going back to Yale and Connecticut. I had the one year left at Vanderbilt so we sadly parted company again. Jamison and I wrote letters and called, back and forth, all through that next semester. We were both so head-over-heels for each other that we didn't think anything could come between us. You know how that is," she said, indicating Matthew and Cici.

That caught Cici off guard momentarily as she looked up at Matthew and their eyes met over Annabelle's head.

Danbury took up the line of questioning, pushing Annabelle Washburn to get to the point. "When did he resurface? Bartles. How did he interfere? And why the grudge?"

"I was just about to go home for Christmas and Aubrey came strutting up to me across campus, knelt, and presented me with a diamond ring, asking me to marry him. He said he'd never loved anyone like he loved me and that he never would. He said he was desperate without me, or something akin to that. Of course, I refused. I told him bluntly that I was in love with someone else. And that's when he tipped his hand."

"How so?" asked Danbury.

"He said if I was talking about that sniveling Yale guy I'd spent so much time with over the summer, he was a mendacious traitor. Aubrey informed me that he, himself, was far superior and that only he could make me happy. He was my future, not that turncoat Yale guy."

"So, he pretty much admitted that he'd either followed you or had you followed?" asked Cici.

"Pretty much," she said. "I told him that who I loved was none of his business and that I wanted him to leave me alone and never contact me again."

She paused and Cici said, "How did he respond?"

"He stood, looking sadly down into my eyes, and said something like, 'I'm sorry but I can't do that. I have to make you see that I'm the one you're meant to be with. I'm your destiny,' or some such nonsense. When I tried to turn away, he grabbed my wrist and wouldn't let go. When I yelled for help, he wrenched it slightly and told me that I'd be sorry I'd done that because if he couldn't have me, Judas wouldn't either and he'd make sure of that. The look in his eyes was one of insanity and I'm sure the one in mine was one of abject terror."

"Oh!" exclaimed Cici. "Judas? Meaning Mr. Washburn?"

"I assumed so, yes."

"What did you do?"

"What I should have done long before. I went to the campus police and reported the incident. Then I finished my exams and went home for Christmas, hoping to put the whole debacle behind me. But I did tell Jamison at that point. He took me to the law firm he'd been working for. It was over near North Hills. And he helped me to take out a restraining order on Aubrey that was effective in both North Carolina and Tennessee."

"But that didn't work?" asked Cici.

"I didn't see or hear anything else from him for a while. Or if he was lurking around anywhere, I was too preoccupied to notice him because Jamison proposed on Christmas morning and I was completely giddy about marrying him. I love Christmas," she said. "Or, at least I used to love Christmas." Her voice broke on that statement and she sobbed openly.

It took more tissues and tea to regain her ability to speak again. Even then, her voice was hoarse and raspy as she tried to finish the story.

"Then what?" asked Danbury. "Why still hold a grudge now?"

"Then he went after Jamison."

"Went after?" repeated Danbury.

"Oh, we could never prove it, but that's just the thing. He never got caught. There were a few little unexplained accidents that Jamison survived, which he clearly wasn't meant to. After the first one, we thought it was just an accident but by the third, we were pretty sure that we were dealing with a psychopath. I thought I caught a glimpse of him a few times again, but I was never certain that I'd actually seen him. We had a security team following us for three months before our wedding, which was Christmas a year later. That whole ordeal definitely cast a long shadow over what should have been the happiest time of our lives. And now this," she choked up, apologizing profusely and took a deep breath to steady herself and continued with the story.

"Aubrey showed up at the wedding but we had security there too and he was handcuffed and removed from the premises for causing a disturbance and violating the restraining order. Thankfully, that was outside of the cathedral. Nobody inside was aware of the scene he'd created. Or the one he'd likely intended to create inside had he made it that far. Apparently, he was removed from the premises still yelling about objecting and not holding his peace."

"When was the last time you saw him? Or heard from him?" asked Danbury.

"It was about ten years ago," she said quietly. "He contacted me by phone and told me that he'd just gotten out of a facility where he'd faced his demons and he was trying to make amends. He had contacted me to apologize for trying to ruin my engagement and marriage to 'that guy.' His apology wasn't very convincing."

"Why were you not convinced?"

"There were many reasons, starting with his inability or unwillingness to say Jamison's name. He said he'd married and had a daughter. I'll give you a single guess as to what he named her."

"He didn't!" exclaimed Cici as the men looked at each other in confusion.

"He did."

"He did what exactly?" asked Danbury, still confused.

"He named her Annabelle," said Cici.

"He did," confirmed Annabelle. "But he'd gotten divorced and his ex-wife took the girl and disappeared. He didn't know where they were and he couldn't find them, though he said he'd tried."

"He came back for you," asserted Cici.

"Something like that. He let me know that he still had feelings for me. When I told him that he needed to move on with his life because I was happy with mine, he let me know that he knew about my children. I don't remember how he stated it exactly. It wasn't blatantly a threat. It was in more couched terms but it sounded menacing, particularly coming from him."

"By that point, Jamison had the law firm here. I informed Aubrey that, as soon as we hung up, there would be restraining orders issued against him coming anywhere near Jamison or me or any of our children. I told him that if he contacted any of us again or if there were any further incidents, I'd swear out a warrant for his immediate arrest and I'd be sure that he wouldn't be coming out of the next facility he visited."

"Wow!" said Cici. "How did he respond?"

"He was silent and then the line went dead. I do believe I saw him skulking outside of my children's school several times when I'd pick them up or after sporting events and extracurricular activities. But I couldn't prove it and by the time anyone got there to investigate, he'd have gone."

"You didn't report it then?"

"No, I didn't."

"That was ten years ago. You haven't seen or heard from him since?"

"No."

"Do you think he's still around?"

"I don't honestly know. I hope he hasn't been skulking around again. That's chilling to contemplate. If he has been nearby and watching since then, he got better at doing it surreptitiously. But if Jamison is really truly," she choked, unable to finish the sentence, and began to weep bitterly again.

8 ~ Plans in Place

When Mrs. Washburn was finally calm again with Cici's consoling help, Danbury simply said, "What about the pacts? And secret societies? The ones your daughter mentioned. What did she mean?"

"I have no idea. I don't know how she knows about Aubrey Bartles. I've certainly never told her."

"I need to talk to Bartles," said Danbury. "Do you know how to find him? Last known address? Anything like that?"

"I truly don't. I purposefully avoided him, I tried to extricate myself from him, and I made no effort to keep up with him. As long as he was away from us, I was most content. I'm not sure how or where the restraining orders were served to him ten years ago. Jamison handled all of that and tried to shield me from it, I'm sure. Someone at Jamison's firm might know."

"I'll see what I can dig up," said Cici. "Just as soon as I get a chance to get back to the office."

"I can help with that," Abby piped up from the corner by the front window where she'd been quietly curled in a chair. "I had been working for Mr. Washburn a couple of years when those papers were served. I helped to create them. I'm sure there's a record somewhere of where they were served. I seem to remember that a private investigator was hired. I can try to find those records."

"Thank you, Abby," said Annabelle. "I can see why my husband was so fond of you."

"What does Bartles do, occupationally?" asked Danbury.

"Do? That's an excellent question. I've never known. He was living on a trust fund when we were in college. His major was in the science research fields. That's how he met Jamison, I believe, before Jamison changed course. Neuroscience maybe? He's really very brilliant, but I don't know if he ever channeled that intelligence into any worthwhile endeavors."

"Mrs. Washburn," said Danbury, changing direction. "Are you familiar with the name Kennedy Reynolds? Have you met him? Has your husband mentioned him?"

"He's one of the new partners in the firm, I believe. He came from somewhere else a couple of years ago. The Midwest maybe? I think I met him once or twice before the cancer. Why do you ask?"

"Did your husband ever say anything specific? About Reynolds? Anything negative? Did he mention them disagreeing? Over something important maybe? He and Reynolds?"

"Those are all very odd questions," she said. "No, I don't recall having heard Jamison mention anything negative about Kennedy Reynolds. Nor did I hear of any altercations between the two from anyone else. As far as I know, their relationship was a sound professional one. If they had issues, Jamison never mentioned them to me. I'm sure Simon Markham or Jonathan Denton can provide more insight into their working relationship than I can."

"The other thing," began Danbury, but hesitated. "I'll need to talk to your daughter. Not tonight, necessarily. But soon."

"Of course. Perhaps tomorrow, or I suppose I mean later today, she'll be up to it. Shall I contact you when she is awake and coherent?"

"Yes. Thank you, Mrs. Washburn," said Danbury, as he rose from the chair. "Would you also contact me if you think of anything else? Any small detail might be important. You have my card?"

"I do," she said, pointing to the drawer in the end table beside her. "And I will."

"Just one more thing," said Danbury. "You mentioned having a security detail. Early in your marriage. Have you had one since?"

"No, I'm very thankful that we've had no need of one. Why do you ask?"

"Because it might be a good idea. To hire a security company now. I can have patrol cars cruise the area. Every couple of hours. But I don't have probable cause. Not to assign anyone here. Not to be here twenty-four-seven. Not yet, at least. Adding security might be a good idea. Until we know more."

"You think we're in danger?" asked Annabelle, as if trying to assimilate the information and decide whether it was worth the effort to be alarmed.

"Possibly. Until we know what happened to your husband. Whether he was, ah, murdered. And, if so, how. If it was poison. That's not usually an accident."

"I see," she said, staring down at her hands as she twisted and shredded the tissue she'd been holding. Then she looked up at Danbury, her chin out, and the determination in her face evident. "Do you have any recommendations on who I should hire? Someone you'd trust? Jamison's father provided the security detail all those years ago and I have no idea how to contact them, or if they're even still in business."

"I can make some calls. But it will take a day. Or two. At least. Maybe longer. The best companies staff closely. They ramp up as needed. Temporarily, in this case. If this is short term. And I hope it will be. We find the murderer, and the threat disappears. If there is one. I would advise taking the precaution. In the meantime."

"OK, thank you. What do I do in the interim? Should I be concerned?"

"What sort of staff do you employ?"

"All petite women indoors, I'm afraid. A cook, a maid, and a personal assistant that Jamison insisted on hiring for me when I began the chemo treatments. I've been doing so much better. I gave Louise, my personal assistant, the rest of the month off. She flew out to be with her family in Montana Friday. Jamison was planning to take some time off over the holidays and we were going to spend some time together, just the two of us," she choked and couldn't finish what she was trying to tell them. Matthew handed her a tissue.

After blowing her nose profusely and apologizing, she continued, "There's a cleaning service that comes twice a week and a gardener who's here twice a week during all but the coldest winter months. Everyone except our gardener is female and Mr. Marchuto is rather aged. His grandson comes with him on occasion to help with heavier tasks, but that's it for staff. It's minimal, I suppose, for the house and grounds. We don't have any live-in staff like many of our friends, but it's all we need."

Danbury looked over at Matthew and Cici tilted her head to summon him out into the foyer.

"Pardon me," Matthew said, as he stood and slipped from the room, following Cici out.

"Matthew, we need to stay here with her until she can hire a proper security team," said Cici urgently.

Matthew stared at her in amazement. "You're volunteering to give up your established routine in your well-ordered house to come and care for Mrs. Washburn?"

"Yes," she hissed at him, clearly annoyed with his question. "If she'll have us. Her husband gave me my first job, coached me along the way, and pushed for my promotion to junior partner last year. I owe him a lot more than this, but I definitely want to be sure his beloved wife is cared for. And it doesn't sound like her daughter will be of much help to her. At least not this one," whispered Cici, as she motioned up the staircase. "Can't you pack up and come for a few nights, until she can get a full security detail in place? Or until we know that she doesn't need one? You can bring those guns you adore, just in case."

At this, Matthew knew his jaw had just dropped. Cici had always hated that he had guns in his condominium and a concealed carry permit. She had also always wanted him to come and be a part of her well-ordered life, not the other way around. She was showing a much stronger concern for someone she didn't know well than Matthew remembered her having done for several years. Not since before she was finishing law school had he seen much of this side of her. It was as if the education had frozen her somehow. He was surprised but thrilled to see the thaw happening before his eyes, even in the December chill.

"OK, Cees. We can spend a few nights here. If she'll have us. We'll still have to commute to work, or at least I will. And I'll need to go by my house each morning and evening to care for Max and spend some time with him. He got moved around enough last spring. I don't want to do that to him again."

Max, Matthew's large gray tabby cat, had been foisted on him as a tiny kitten by his older sister Monica when they learned that her husband, Stephano, was highly allergic. The spring before, Matthew's house had been firebombed by a disgruntled guy who blamed Matthew for his life falling apart when, in truth, it had been held together by the paperclips and duct tape of his own lies before Matthew ever met him. Matthew had gotten the fire out quickly and Max out safely, then they both went to stay at Cici's empty house while she was in London and his condo was being repaired.

Before the repairs on Matthew's condominium were completed, Max had stayed with friends in Peak while Matthew went to Miami for a week to help find the missing daughter of his friend and colleague, Dr. Rob. That, Matthew figured, was more than enough upheaval for the sweet big cat and he didn't want to uproot him again.

"I can get my things packed pretty quickly but I'd love a bit of sleep," said Cici, yawning. "I was up earlier this morning than I'd intended to take Marshall and Charles for breakfast to that biscuit place I'd told them about. They're only here for the extended weekend, not even a full week, so we were packing a lot into it."

"I need to go home and feed Max breakfast and I'd love a couple of hours of sleep too. But that leaves Mrs. Washburn alone," he grimaced. "Why don't you ask her if she'd like the extra help and if she agrees, I'll stay and take the first shift."

Danbury appeared behind Matthew and said, "I think I'm done for now. I'll track down Aubrey Bartles. And we're working to find Kennedy Reynolds. He wasn't at home. I sent two officers to his house. Before I got here. They found no recent sign of him. Nobody seems to know where he is. Where he'd have gone. Nobody we've asked so far."

"Can I help locate security for Mrs. Washburn?" asked Matthew. "Cici is advocating staying here until we do to be sure that she's not alone." Then, lowering his voice so that it wouldn't carry up the stairs behind him, he added, "I'll admit that Elizabeth doesn't seem capable of being much help at the moment. Do you think it's necessary for one of us to stay with her?"

"It couldn't hurt. I don't know what we're dealing with yet. It's hard to advise you. Maybe it has nothing to do with the family."

"I'll ask her about us staying," said Cici, slipping back into the sitting room.

"Or maybe," said Matthew, "if this Aubrey Bartles person is involved, it has everything to do with the family."

"We're working on it. With the catering company. Somebody had access to the food and serving pieces. But nobody saw Reynolds go near the serving table. Just in the door and then down the elevator. Timothy only went down once. His whereabouts are accounted for. Someone brought that food and drink. It was from upstairs. The catering manager identified both sets of plates and cups. The ones inside the office. And the ones Timothy brought up. In the outside reception office. Both are theirs. The same as was at the party upstairs."

"They're certain? Somebody couldn't have replicated what was upstairs?"

"Possible, but not probable. It would be hard to replicate. Without a connection to the catering company. The plates and glasses are Waterford. Very specific Waterford. It's called the Eileen cut. The twelve days of Christmas collection. Each punch glass had a little charm. Attached at the stem. To help keep the glasses straight. When people put them down. The charms are of the twelve days of Christmas. From the song. A lady dancing was on the glass inside the office. The outside office glass had a lord leaping charm."

"Ah. I noticed those, but I didn't stop to examine them or try to figure out what they were. Were there prints on either glass?"

"Hey Doc, are you consulting again?" asked Danbury pointedly.

Matthew raised an eyebrow, sighed, and hesitated. "I suppose I am. I'm neck deep in this one already, aren't I?"

"You are. Probably the last to have seen him alive. You and Cici. Other than the killer."

"If I can sign up for this one case, yes, I'm in. I want to help if I can."

Danbury looked as if he were about to say something profound and then changed his mind, "OK, Doc. Prints are hard to get. Off of footed crystal punch glasses. Preliminary testing shows prints. The victim's partial on the glass on his desk. And Timothy's on the glass outside the office. None others yet. We'll do more testing at the lab. But that's all the initial results showed."

Danbury changed the subject. "I can take Abby back. If you're staying here."

"That would be helpful," said Matthew, considering how to arrange the logistical puzzle pieces so that they made the most sense.

"Matthew," said Cici, reappearing in the hallway. "Mrs. Washburn is very relieved to have you stay with her. She said she'll have her staff freshen rooms upstairs for her other two children, and one for us in the mother-in-law wing off to the right of the kitchen. It'll be tomorrow though before her staff arrives so we're on our own tonight. She gives them Sundays off."

Matthew's eyebrow shot up at Cici's mention of a single room for the two of them. Until they knew what sort of footing they'd be on when she came home permanently from the remaining few months in London, Matthew had been holding her at a distance. He'd flatly told her that losing her when they broke up over a year and a half prior was the hardest thing he'd ever had to do and he didn't want to do it ever again.

They'd made progress on compromise and Cici was considering the issue of children, but Matthew wasn't ready to commit to her again just yet. Neither was he, at the moment, wanting to argue the point so he just said, "Danbury has offered to take Abby back to the office to retrieve her car so that you can go home and get some rest. Unless she's staying too?"

"She didn't make that offer when I discussed our plan, so I'm assuming she's not. Thank you, Danbury, for taking her back."

"No problem. I need to go back to the precinct. It's downtown too. Not far from your office. Lots of reports to file. And more forensic testing to authorize."

Matthew had seen, over the past year, that Danbury needed very little sleep. Even so, he was amazed that the man was still standing. Matthew felt as if he wouldn't be standing much longer himself. It was four in the morning, he saw as he checked his watch, and he was well past just being punchy from exhaustion.

"Can you get her settled wherever she wants to be before you leave with the rental car, Cees? She mentioned not wanting to go back upstairs to the room she shared with her husband."

"She doesn't. She said she wants to try to rest there on the sofa in the sitting room, at least for what's left of this first night. I'm going upstairs to retrieve her cell phone and medications from her nightstand and I'll be right back."

Cici slipped up the stairs and Danbury stepped back into the sitting room, leaving Matthew in the hall, eyebrow raised and foot tapping in concentration, wondering what had just happened.

"Ms. Moore," he heard Danbury call from the sitting room doorway. "I'm going back downtown. Can I drop you at your car?"

"That would be wonderful," she said wearily. "Thank you." She stood and followed Danbury out into the foyer hall.

Cici returned with the requested items and got Mrs. Washburn settled in with pillows and a blanket on the sofa for the remainder of the night. Danbury, Abby, and Cici vacated the Washburn home and Matthew retrieved more wood and added it to the fire, stoking it to a warm blaze. He could hear that Annabelle Washburn was breathing deeply and rhythmically so he placed his jacket and other entrapments of the tuxedo on the back of the nearby wingback chair and perched on the edge of it.

Typing and sending a text message to his family group, which included both of his parents and his sister Monica, he explained that he wouldn't be at church with his family later as he usually was. Nor would he be decorating his Christmas tree with his little niece as he'd planned that afternoon. He'd been up all night to that point, he texted, and he'd explain later.

He sincerely hoped that they all had their phones on mute as he saw that it was something after four in the morning. Settling back into the reclining wingback chair to at least rest while on guard, he thought maybe he'd be able to watch the inside of his eyelids for a few precious minutes. His thoughts turned hazy as he drifted off for what seemed like minutes but was actually hours until he was startled awake by a shrieking sound.

9 ~ ELABORATIONS

Matthew jumped from the wingback chair to see Elizabeth standing in the doorway of the sitting room. She held what appeared to be a stuffed animal, the exact type of which was difficult to determine because it was so well worn as to look more like a lump with limp arms and legs hanging from it.

"Mother!" shrieked Elizabeth. "How can you sleep? Daddy's gone! And why is he in here with you?" she demanded, pointing at Matthew.

Annabelle groggily propped herself up higher on one elbow, sliding up on the pillows and said, "Come sit with me, Elizabeth, and let's talk for a minute. I know you're overwrought but getting hysterical won't help the situation at all."

"I'm not," Elizabeth began to screech. Then taking a deep breath, more calmly she said, "I'm not hysterical." Slowly, she walked to the sofa and perched on the edge beside her mother. "He's really gone. How can he be gone?"

Returning to his seat and pulling the wingback chair into an upright position, Matthew leaned over and pushed the tissue box across the coffee table to the young woman as tears streaked down her face. "I'm sorry that my presence here upsets you," he said. "I'm sure your mother can explain. Or I can try."

Holding up a hand, Annabelle said, "This is my mess. I'll explain it."

"Elizabeth," she said calmly. "Last night you didn't want to hear about a man I was talking about, one who I didn't know you knew about at all. Eventually, we're going to need to hear your story and you're going to have to tell us what you know. For now, suffice it to say that there's a strong possibility that someone poisoned your father last night and there's a chance that Aubrey Bartles might be behind it. If he is, I know that he's a danger to us. To me, to you, to your brother and sister. We're going to hire security temporarily to guard and protect us but until we can get them in here, Matthew Paine has graciously agreed to spend the nights here with us. He sat with me last night so that I could sleep without worrying about you and me being vulnerable here alone."

"Security? You mean like body guards?" Elizabeth asked, looking stricken.

"Something like that," said Matthew. "Danbury, the detective who was here last night, is compiling a short list of companies that he's had enough experience with to know that they're capable and dependable. Mrs. Washburn will choose one and then it sounds like they might have to ramp up to carefully vet and create a team for round-the-clock protection here. That process could take a couple of days but meanwhile, Cecelia Patterson and I will stay with you."

"Please, call me Annabelle, and thank you for offering to do that. I'll call my son this morning and maybe he can get here today. I don't know how much protection he'll be. That's not exactly his forte."

"That's stating it mildly," said Elizabeth, rolling her eyes.

Matthew wondered what they were alluding to but he was too polite to ask, so he just said, "It is daylight now and Cici should be back shortly. Checking his watch, he noted that it was just after ten on Sunday, December the eighth.

Checking his phone, he saw that both parents and his sister had responded to his text. Monica said that he was just mean to make her have to tell his little niece Angelina, who adored him, that he wouldn't be picking her up from children's church or decorating his tree with her. Both parents expressed concern, and his bet was that they were all blaming Cici, though it was only inadvertently her fault.

Glancing at the fireplace, he noticed that he'd let it burn almost completely out.

"Would you like the fire rebuilt?" he asked.

Considering a moment, Annabelle replied, "I'd like to go clean up and change and then I do believe this room is the best one for visitors and family today. I think it got colder than it was supposed to overnight, so if you wouldn't mind too terribly, that would be lovely."

"No Ma'am, I don't mind," he replied as she raised her tiny frame slowly from the sofa and asked Elizabeth to accompany her upstairs.

"To your bedroom? Mother, I'm not sure that I can," and the tears started flowing again.

"It's all right Elizabeth, I'll just be a moment," she said to both of them as she left the room alone.

Matthew followed her out of the room and then he went down the hallway and out the back kitchen door to the large woodpile that was arranged in some sort of decorative round iron container which was open on both sides with sturdy legs. Pausing momentarily, Matthew looked around the yard. The carriage house to the left blocked most of the view in that direction and a wooded area surrounded the rest of the expansive well-manicured back lawn. Like the front of the house, the perimeter of the yard had raised flower beds that ebbed and flowed neatly and decisively between the grass in the yard and the wooded area beyond.

Curious, Matthew stepped off the brick patio and down a walkway to the edge of the wooded area where he'd seen the stealthy shadow the night before. The ground didn't feel frozen. Overnight temperatures apparently had dipped just below freezing but hadn't frozen the ground which squished audibly under his feet from the rain. Maybe, he thought, he could find something out here. Before he'd finished his thought, he saw them. There were footprints sunken into the edge of the flower beds that ran along that side of the yard. The prints ran down the edge of the flower bed and disappeared into the tree line.

What he couldn't tell was which way they had come from. The thick winter rye grass wasn't showing them if the person had come through the yard and the underbrush in the tree line offered the same protection for the interloper from that direction. The prints were larger, likely male, but otherwise nondescript in the mulch and mud at the edge of the flower bed. Pulling his phone from his pocket, he snapped pictures, getting as close as he dared without interfering with any of them, and sent the pictures to Danbury.

"*Someone was out here last night,*" he texted. "*I found footprints in the flower bed on the edge of the tree line where I saw the dark figure.*"

Turning, he went back to the wood pile, stacked the wood along the sleeve of his now potentially ruined tuxedo shirt, and glanced back one last time before he entered the house, making sure that he'd locked the door carefully again as he closed it behind himself. Thinking he smelled coffee brewing, Matthew chalked it up to his wishful imagination. Elizabeth had disappeared and Matthew was alone as he returned to the sitting room to rebuild the fire that was all but embers.

While working on the fire, he felt his phone vibrate repeatedly in his pocket. When he was happy with the burgeoning fire, he pulled his phone from his pocket. Cici had texted that she was heading his way but needed to meet Abby at the office a bit later to help locate the restraining order from ten years prior. Another text from Danbury was thanking him for the pictures and promising to send someone out to do a quick evaluation, though it sounded like he didn't think it would help much.

As he was putting his phone down, relieved that Cici was on the way and he could finally get back home to a shower, some hot coffee, a nap, and some fresh and casual clothes, Elizabeth appeared in the doorway holding a tray that she set on the coffee table. On the tray were two up-side-down mugs, cheerfully painted with the same Christmas motif as the one he'd seen the night before, and the best sight he'd seen since sometime the day before. A carafe of coffee with sugar and cream containers that matched the mugs adorned one end of the tray and there his eyes stopped.

"Would you like some coffee? Dr. Paine, was it?" she said with a smirk.

"Just call me Matthew. Yes, it is 'Dr. Paine.' And yes, I've heard about that for years, but give it your best shot if you think you have some new material."

"It's just too easy," she shrugged, leaning over the tray and flipping the mugs upright.

"I'd love some coffee, but with lots of sugar and some cream. I can fix it myself if you'd like. Thank you," he added as she liberally scooped sugar into both mugs and added the steaming coffee before stirring in the cream. They had that in common, he realized. She'd put as much sugar in her own mug as she had in his.

After the first few sips, he noticed the pastries on the other end of the tray. Because they were on the other side of the coffee, they'd initially escaped his notice. Seeing him eyeing them, Elizabeth slid a breakfast plate over to him on the coffee table and handed over the plate of pastries. For the first few minutes, they sipped and ate in silence, Matthew savoring what he had determined was really good coffee.

"Tell me about this Danbury guy," said Elizabeth, breaking the silence. "He seems very abrupt."

Matthew chuckled. "He can be. He's ex-military and he's very much no-nonsense when he's working on a case. But he has a heart of gold and he really cares about the people he's trying to help. It's not just a job to him. I haven't quite known him a year yet but in that time he's taken vacation from his job twice to help solve cases for people he cares about. He's a good guy. You can trust him to do everything in his power to figure out what happened to your father. And he's thorough, so if anybody can get to the bottom of it he can."

After a few more moments of silence, she looked pensive and added, "I suppose you're wondering about my outburst last night over that horrid man mother was talking about."

Matthew nodded, his mouth full of a pastry that he was chasing down with the wonderful coffee.

"He really is horrible," she said.

"How do you know about him?" asked Matthew. "Your mother said she'd never told you about him."

"I met him," she said softly.

At Matthew's surprised but concerned expression, she decided to elaborate. "I was with a group of friends back when I was in middle school and we were hanging out at the food court at the mall, just down Glenwood from here. Mother didn't know I was there and she'd have had a fit had she known, because she never thought it was a safe place for us to gather. Retrospectively, I suppose she was right."

Matthew nodded in encouraging acknowledgment but said nothing, so she continued, "Three of my friends had gone down to a clothing store that was very much in vogue back then and just Ella and I were sitting there eating ice cream when this guy walked up. He was older, but handsome and he started talking to us. Ella could talk to a stump and have a full conversation, but he started asking questions that made me feel uncomfortable."

"What sort of questions?"

"Where we lived, what school we went to, were our parents still married. Things that I knew, even at thirteen, were too personal to be telling a complete stranger. But Ella lacked a proper filter and she was happily telling him her life story and starting in on mine when I kicked her under the table. She was clueless as to why I'd do that and she reacted."

"What do you mean?"

"Well, I didn't want her to TELL the guy that I'd just kicked her under the table. I wanted her to shut up about our lives. But she said something like, 'Ow! Why'd you do that?' I saw the guy's face darken and cloud over like he was angry about it. He leaned over the table and was just about to say something when Jillian's mom came in to pick us up. He slunk away quickly and we left with her to go down the mall to find Jillian and the other two girls, but I think he followed us. He gave me the creeps."

"Did you tell Jillian's Mom about that?"

"No, but I told my dad when he got home."

"What did he say?"

"He said he'd handle it but to let him know if I ever saw the guy again."

"And did you?"

"Just once more."

"Really? He showed back up again?"

"Yeah, it was after a soccer practice one day."

"What happened?"

"I was sitting on the brick wall out behind the school near the soccer fields waiting. My parents were both busy, so a driver who worked for my dad was coming to pick me up. He was running late, stuck in traffic somewhere. My friends were already gone and I was just sitting there, all sweaty after practice. This Bartles guy came out of nowhere and sat down beside me."

Matthew was quiet so that she'd continue the story, which to his relief, she did.

"He struck up a conversation like we were old friends and had just talked last week. This time, though, it was entirely personal and I was looking around for other people. Across the field, I spotted the coaches so I got up and started walking that way. Of course, he followed me across the field."

"What did he say that was personal?"

"He went on and on about how I should be his daughter because he had been in love with my mother first and that he and Daddy had belonged to this secret society in college, I forget what he called it. Anyway, they all had a pact not to interfere with a girl if another member of the society was dating her first. My Dad, he said, broke the pact and violated the trust of the brotherhood, or some such nonsense, and that he'd never paid the penalty for that breach."

"What penalty?"

"I have no idea. By the time he got to that part of his tirade, I was nearly to the coaches across the soccer field and he veered off into the edge of the woods and disappeared."

That last bit sounded familiar to Matthew, entirely reminiscent of the dark figure disappearing into tree line in the back yard the night before. He swallowed a bit of pastry before he said, "And you told your father about that encounter?"

"I did," she replied.

"How did he respond?"

"He looked shaken and upset by it, which is something I didn't see in my dad very often. He was an eternal optimist and not much bothered him. I still can't stand talking of him in the past tense like this. He should just be walking through that door any moment now. I just can't," she said, setting the mug down and reaching for the tissues again.

"I'm so sorry you've lost someone so important to you," soothed Matthew. "Your encounters with Bartles might be important though. Danbury needs to know about them. Would you be willing to tell him what you've just told me? On the record, I mean."

She nodded her consent and blew her nose loudly before adding, apologetically. "I'm sorry. I'm not myself today."

"Who would be under these circumstances?" asked Matthew, as he heard the front doorbell sound. "That should be Cici. Do you mind if I answer it?"

"Please," she said, blotting tears. "I'm not up for it anyway."

"Maybe she can help with answering calls and doorbells today, if you'd like her to," said Matthew as he rose to go let Cici in. After she was situated and he could excuse himself, he slipped out to take the rental car that Cici had just arrived in. On the way out, he called Danbury to tell him what he'd learned from Elizabeth. Danbury, of course, wanted to hear her account for himself but thanked Matthew for the information in the interim.

Realizing that his plans for Sunday afternoon were a wash and the few hours of sleep he'd gotten in the chair would likely suffice for the day, Matthew began to plan the things that he knew he needed to do to return and spend the night at the Washburn's home. He'd have to figure out how to navigate the beginning of the week until the real security team could be brought in and he wasn't sure what that would entail since nothing that had happened so far was at all predictable.

10 ~ DADDY DEAREST

After spending the rest of the afternoon enjoying the peace of his condominium just east and slightly south of Peak, Matthew packed a small bag with his toiletries, sleep pants, soft t-shirts, boxer briefs, and a pair of shoes for work with socks stuffed inside. Remembering Cici's words, he unlocked the safe in the top of his closet, pulled out both his Glock 19 and the little 1911 with two loaded magazines and a holster for each one and added those to his bag. Sure, he had two handguns but he'd always hoped never to have to use them except on a range or in shooting contests, neither of which he'd had the time to do lately he realized.

He placed clothing for a couple of days at work, long-sleeved dress shirts and gray and beige khaki pants with belts, into a travel hang-up bag and folded it up. Bringing those out of the bedroom, he picked up from his sofa his leather satchel that contained his computer. He still needed to check his patient schedule for the next morning some time before he went to bed that night, he thought, as he piled it and the other bags by the door.

The partially sunny Sunday had clouded over and what light there had been from the cloudy afternoon was quickly waning as he fed Max and rinsed and refilled his water bowl. Matthew had topped off the watering dispenser on his Fraser Fir Christmas tree that he had gotten the lights on and was supposed to have decorated with Angel, his niece, that afternoon. That was just one more way he was sure he had disappointed his niece lately, he thought sadly. He was spending some time scratching Max behind the ears as he prepared to leave for the night when his cell phone dinged.

Pulling it out of his pocket, he saw what looked like a frazzled text from Cici, "*Are you on your way yet? Things have deteriorated here. I could use your help.*"

"*Just leaving my house now,*" he texted back, with an eyebrow raised. Like tapping his foot and bouncing his knee, the raised eyebrow was a subconscious habit that emerged when he was pondering something. Unlike the tapping and bouncing, the eyebrow also raised in amusement or confusion. He wondered what situation had deteriorated at the Washburn house. Certainly nothing would ever be normal there again.

Matthew locked up, leaving a few strategic lights on, and carefully set his security system on the way out. His condominium was the last one at the end of his community on the right side of the complex with woods along the far side and the back corner of a golf course behind him. It was isolated and it had been broken into the previous spring. He'd always been cautious, but that experience had made him all the more so.

He'd left his Corvette at Cici's the night before and he didn't have a garage door opener in her rental car, so he'd parked it in his short driveway. Exiting through the outside garage door to get to Cici's rental car, Matthew carefully locked that behind himself too. The Honda Element he'd driven through high school, college, and medical school and the Corvette that Cici had encouraged him to purchase when he'd paid his student loans from medical school off early usually occupied his garage. He wished they had taken the time to go get his car today so that they could stop swapping off the one car.

All was quiet as he was pulling out of his condominium complex and admiring his neighbors' Christmas lights and displays. Matthew saw none of his neighbors out and about. Most of them were retired and his neighborhood was usually peaceful, which suited him nicely. He was surprised not to see Cordelia Drewer out walking her little Pomeranian Oscar at this time of evening. Even she, the neighbor he'd once thought was the nosiest on the planet before he'd befriended her, was apparently tucked warmly inside like the rest of the residents on this chilly December evening.

Matthew drove the mile or so down Chester Road quietly, not bothering to pull up his Christmas playlist on his phone. Because he so loved Christmas, he had a large and rather eclectic playlist of all of his favorite music for the season. Turning left onto Highway 20, Matthew passed King's Country Club, with the golf course that his condominium complex backed up to, on his left.

Considering the plight of the Washburn family as he drove, Matthew knew that the family would go through stages of grieving. That included sorrow, anger, guilt, and denial. If he'd learned one thing about the grieving process over the course of the past few years in dealing with his patients and, more recently the families left behind after murders, it was that the mourning process was never predictably linear. It was recursively very messy, and any two people were hardly ever at the same place in the process at the same time. This did cause issues for families who were trying to grieve together, however close they had been and continued to attempt to be.

Traffic was light on this Sunday evening as Matthew made his way up Highway 64, up the edge of 440, and around to Glenwood Avenue. He wondered what Mr. Washburn's autopsy was revealing and he wondered what Danbury was doing. It was a Sunday but he knew that Danbury would work through most of every day until he determined the truth behind what happened to Mr. Washburn.

A light rain was falling as Matthew was pondering the mechanics of getting the cars swapped around so that Cici had exclusive use of the rental and he had one of his cars at his disposal without leaving the Washburns unattended. As he parked in front of the house, he thought surely they could both slip out momentarily in the morning when the staff was present and Cici could drop him at her house to retrieve his car. She could return for the day if she was needed, he reasoned.

As he pulled his small bags from the rental car, his thoughts shifted back to their current situation and the dilemma that had prompted Cici to text him. It didn't take him long to figure out what that was. As he stepped up onto the porch, he could hear yelling from inside. As soon as he rang the bell, Cici quickly pulled the door open and motioned him inside.

She said nothing as she looked up at him with huge eyes and they both stood in the large foyer, transfixed by the loud bickering voices they heard from somewhere further down the hallway.

Then, she whispered conspiratorially, "Jay, that's Jamison's son, drove in from Georgia. He arrived just ahead of Sophia, the older daughter, who got on the first plane headed this way from Washington state. They're with Elizabeth in Jamison's study. Annabelle asked them to have a go at Jamison's obituary to honor their father's memory and that broke out into a bickering match which has escalated rather severely. I can't believe they're still at it! I feel like I'm intruding and I don't know what to do."

Not knowing what to do was a first for Cici, Matthew thought, as he heard a female voice that wasn't Elizabeth's ring out accusingly, "Well, of course you'd want it that way! You are the baby and you were always his favorite!"

"If I was his favorite, it was just because I listened to him and tried to follow his sound advice, unlike the two of you!" a voice that Matthew thought was Elizabeth's hotly replied.

"But you weren't the huge disappointment to him that either of us were!" a male voice chimed in angrily. "I could never do anything right in his eyes. But you could do no wrong!"

"That's not true!" retorted Elizabeth angrily. "When you came out, he was entirely reasonable and he tried his best to understand and be supportive of you and your lifestyle. He really did! He was very supportive. Because he loved you!"

"And how would you know much of anything about his understanding, Lizzie? Or his reasoning?" demanded the male voice. "He said he was trying to be supportive of my lifestyle choice, as if anyone would ever CHOOSE to make their lives more difficult! He never understood that it isn't a choice I consciously made. His great disappointment was that, clearly, I'd never marry a woman and I would not be providing him with his legacy grandson, Jamison Harrison Washburn the fifth! At least not in any traditional way would I ever provide that heir to the Washburn legacy."

"He loved you, Jay Jay! He really truly loved you and he didn't care about that. Why would you think that was more important to him than you? It wasn't. It never was!"

"Neither of you had the pressure of being the first-born Washburn and having to be perfect!" yelled the other female voice. "I was sick of crinolines and cotillions and all the right friends and interests that were carefully cultivated for me! I might have liked to have played soccer too, but I'd never have been allowed!"

"You, Sophie Washburn, play soccer? That's hilarious!" yelled Elizabeth's voice. "You would never have played a team sport if your life depended on it. You were far too busy rebelling against the establishment to want to participate in anything organized by it, with rules and team cooperation required! Unless it was a march or demonstration. And Daddy tried to understand how you felt about all of your causes. Like when you became a vegan. You and your hippy dippy lifestyle. He tried!"

Matthew and Cici had stood, dumbfounded, at the base of the stairs until they heard a stirring upstairs and both of them turned in unison and slipped into the sitting room they'd been in the night before. It was like watching the proverbial train wreck, thought Matthew. You didn't really want to see it, but neither could you tear yourself away. The voices were still heated, though they could understand less of the words as they moved over to the fireplace, which was starting to burn low again. Somebody had obviously added wood while he was away and Matthew assumed that his first chore would be to restore it to the blaze that Mrs. Washburn had been enjoying earlier.

Matthew and Cici faced the fireplace, keeping their backs discreetly to the doorway as they heard Mrs. Washburn's heels click onto the hardwood foyer floor at the base of the staircase and all but march down the hallway. Her voice rang out clearly and far more assertively than Matthew would have thought possible from her diminutive frame, "Stop it! Stop it this instant! All of you! I cannot imagine what your father would think of this incessant bickering! I'll write the obituary. Out! All of you, out! Go to your rooms and unpack your things. Dinner will be served promptly at seven and I expect you all to be in the dining room, dressed, and properly conciliatory!"

Matthew could hear murmured responses but he couldn't make them out and then he heard feet shuffling down the hallway behind him and tromping up the stairs. He turned only when, to her credit, Annabelle Washburn chose to address the issue instead of pretending that it hadn't happened. She said, clearly and strongly, behind them, "I'm so sorry you had to hear that. They haven't done that since they were children."

Going to her, Matthew held out an arm and escorted her to the sofa, where she seemed to be headed. "It's all right. Everybody handles grief in different ways at different times and it's bound to cause some conflict here and there."

"He's right. Think nothing of it," added Cici. Then to Matthew, she said, "I've already put my things in the suite down the hall off the kitchen. We can take yours down and then, Mrs. Washburn, would you like your fire rebuilt?"

"That would be lovely and I'd be very appreciative. Particularly with this damp weather, the chill goes right to the bone. As I'm sure you heard, dinner will be at seven in the dining room. My staff has been in this afternoon and cooked a pot roast with the trimmings. I hope you like that."

"That sounds wonderful," said Cici as Matthew nodded his agreement. "If you're certain that we're not intruding."

"Hardly," she answered. "To the contrary, I'm very thankful for your willingness to stay with me, particularly during the nighttime hours, until a security team can be brought in. Your friend Danbury, true to his word, has already sent me the names of two firms and one individual who he highly recommends. I'll contact them in the morning."

"That's great, Mrs. Washburn," said Matthew. "I'm glad he could help. Speaking of Danbury, do you think Elizabeth will be up to talking to him after dinner? He'll want to gather all of the information available as quickly as possible."

"Certainly, she can. Jay and Sophie too if it would be helpful. Neither of them has lived here in quite some time, so I don't know how much help either of them would be. Perhaps he should speak to them individually as to avoid a repeat of that heated conversation you unfortunately had to endure just now. We should be finished with our meal by seven-thirty or so if he'd like to come by then," she added.

"I doubt my daughter Sophia will touch dinner anyway. We're heating up some frozen soup, but the vegetable soup has beef in it. I haven't had time to prepare for her dietary preferences. This was all so sudden. Thankfully, she's not a vegan any longer, but she's still a vegetarian. She left here at eighteen for Stanford and never really looked back, I'm afraid. And Jay did the same. He set off for the crimson tide of the University of Alabama and then a graduate program at the University of Georgia. Like Sophia, he never moved back to North Carolina."

To Matthew's mind, she seemed to be talking to avoid her own sorrowful thoughts, so he and Cici just waited until she'd finished before excusing themselves to take his bags to the guest suite. He promised to return quickly to rebuild the fire and scooped up his bags as Cici led him out through the central hallway and kitchen, past the butler's pantry off to the right, and down a short hallway to a beautifully furnished suite with a bedroom, a sitting room, and fully furnished bathroom.

The immaculate bedroom held a cherry furniture set with a queen-sized poster bed, a long dresser with a mirror, a highboy chest of drawers, and matching bedside tables. The teal, navy, and cream drapes, bedspread, and an area rug all coordinated beautifully. Matthew couldn't help but notice the perfection of the room. The small sitting room had what appeared to be a daybed, an antique cherry writing desk and chair, and two overstuffed chairs that were pulled in front of a fireplace.

The bathroom featured a small corner shower, a dressing table that was built into the bathroom counter between two sinks with an upholstered stool, and a large sunken tub. It was replete with a linen closet full of toiletries. On a quick inspection, Matthew noted sheets, extra blankets and pillows, towels, soaps of varying sorts, individually packaged toothbrushes, toothpaste, and pretty much anything else that he thought they could possibly require. Their hostess had apparently planned for all of her guests' needs and he was duly impressed.

"How far did that argument set you back, Cees? Five years? More?" he asked, returning to the bedroom.

"Set me back? On what?"

"Ever wanting children."

"Oh, that," she grimaced. "It's not as if Mr. Washburn was the monster they made him out to be. I'd take Elizabeth's side on that argument. I never saw him in a parental role when they were young, but I knew the man and I've heard him talk about them. He was proud of them and their achievements. All of them. I suppose I hadn't gotten around to thinking what a thankless job parenting is, until you pointed it out."

"Great," said Matthew. "I'm sorry that I did."

"Eyes wide open is always best, Matthew," she said, standing on tip toe to kiss him. "I wouldn't ever want to become a parent without realizing and agreeing to what I was getting into."

He pulled her in close and kissed her, feeling her return much of the pent-up emotion that reflected his own. To his surprise, she pulled away first. Taking him by the hand, wordlessly, she led him back out to the main part of the Washburn house.

Returning to the sitting room, Matthew and Cici were introduced first to Jamison Harrison Washburn the fourth, a small-framed man who Matthew was guessing to be in his mid-twenties. He had a serious expression with lines already forming between his eyebrows that Matthew guessed was present even when the circumstances weren't so dire. His sister Sophia entered the room shortly thereafter and introductions were made. Sophia was taller than both Elizabeth and Jay, even in her flat shoes that peeked out from under a colorful long flowing skirt that accompanied a beige gypsy blouse.

All three siblings had large luminous green eyes, the feature that was most noticeable in Jay's more drawn narrow face and least so in Sophia's fuller one. They gathered, amicably enough now. They all made their way toward the dining room, from which Matthew could smell wafting down the hallway what promised to be a delicious dinner.

*****

Danbury arrived precisely at seven-thirty as they were just finishing the meal. Matthew escorted a dubious Elizabeth into the library with Danbury where Annabelle Washburn insisted that they'd be most comfortable to talk. Elizabeth perched nervously on the edge of a leather upholstered chair while Danbury and Matthew took up residence on opposite ends of a matching leather sofa and Danbury wasted no time in beginning to question the young woman.

After a couple of attempts to get her to tell her story and getting only murmured responses, Matthew said, "Elizabeth, just tell him exactly what you told me earlier, about the two times you were approached by Aubrey Bartles and exactly what he said to you each time. Tell him about your impressions of the man and then about how your father responded when you talked to him."

"OK," she began uncertainly. With a few promptings from Matthew, she told the story about both encounters and Danbury took over the questioning.

"Did your father ever explain? The pact? The society? What Bartles meant? About being in love with your mother first? Why any of that was important years later?"

"Somewhat. At Vanderbilt, there was some sort of society, not Greek or I'd have known what it was. Latin maybe? I don't remember the name of it, though I'm pretty sure my father told me. He said that it was a college society and that it was just for fun. It was never meant to be carried throughout life like some sacred alliance. Or something like that."

She took a breath, settling back into the chair, and said, "Daddy said that Bartles had met my mother and fallen for her but the feeling wasn't mutual. Then he came along, they realized they were both from here. They started talking about their families and growing up in Raleigh. The first time they went out, they talked almost all night. He said he knew then that she was someone special and she obviously felt the same way about him. She told him that she'd been out with Bartles, so my father knew that. He brushed it aside because she told him that she didn't have feelings for Bartles. What Daddy didn't know at the time was how strong Bartles' feelings were for my mom."

"Bartles confronted my father and told him to back off because he was dating her first and, as members of their society, it was part of their pact not to pursue a woman that another of them was dating. My Dad refused and Bartles took a swing at him. Daddy held him off and then managed to walk away, but Bartles wouldn't let it go and he kept badgering my dad to stop seeing my mom. I don't know exactly what else happened, but apparently it got ugly."

"And how did he respond? Your father. When you told him. About Bartles approaching you?"

"As an attorney, my dad usually had a pretty good poker face. But I could see first anger and then fear in his eyes. He told me that he'd take care of it and that he'd be sure I wasn't alone after school anymore, ever again. I don't think he told my mom, but he had this big guy following me everywhere I went for the next two years or so. He was my driver, but he stuck around when he'd take me and my friends places and I wasn't allowed to go out without him. My father made that perfectly clear. His name was Brutus or Bruno, or something like that and he looked like one of the infamous Raleigh oak trees. He was huge. At first, I remember being more scared of him than I was of Bartles. And then I was annoyed because he scared other people too, like boys that I wanted to go out with."

"What about your brother and sister? Did Bartles ever approach either of them?"

"Not that I know about, but you'd have to ask them. I mean, neither ever mentioned it, so I'm assuming not. I'm the youngest, though, so maybe I was an easier target. I'm not sure what he even wanted, but the guy gave me the creeps," said Elizabeth, hugging herself at the memory.

"You went out on your own? Two years later?"

"It was probably a little more than that. When I started driving, Daddy bought me a powder blue convertible Mustang. My dream car. And I was allowed to drive that around, to school and school activities, as long as I reported in regularly and didn't go anywhere my dad hadn't approved ahead of time. I think I saw Brutus or Bruno, or whatever his name was, hovering a few times after I started driving but I guess Daddy figured I was safe enough after several years had passed. At first, Daddy asked me regularly if I'd seen Bartles again, even at a distance. But I hadn't, so I guess he figured whatever he'd done to get rid of the guy had worked. I don't know," she added with a shrug.

"You never discussed this with your mom?" asked Matthew.

"My Dad said not to. He didn't want to upset her or worry her. But he told me, very sternly, that if I ever saw that Bartles guy again, I was to contact him immediately. I had a cell phone by then, of course, and I agreed. So, I guess it was just our little secret."

Danbury asked a few more clarifying questions and then if

Elizabeth knew of anyone else who might want to harm her father. She had no other ideas, so she left and first her older sister and then her older brother were brought in and questioned. Neither of them admitted to having seen or been approached by a guy matching Bartles' description and neither could think of anyone who would want to harm their father.

After they'd left, Danbury took a moment to update Matthew on his progress, "Abby found the records. When the restraining order was served. Bartles hasn't been at that address in over six years. But we're tracking him down. Kennedy Reynolds will be easier. He has a cabin. Up in the Virginia mountains. It's on a big swath of land. Owned by his father's family. He goes up there to relax. Mostly in the summer months. Best guess, that's where he is. We'll find them both. Eventually."

"Reynold's father's family-owned land in Virginia?" asked Matthew. "I thought the guy was from Massachusetts or somewhere?"

"He grew up there. His mother's family is from there. But his father is from North Carolina. The piedmont region. Just west of here."

"Huh," was all Matthew could think to say to that.

After Danbury left and the Washburns had retired to bedrooms elsewhere in the house, Matthew banked the fire, checked all of the locks on the downstairs doors and windows one final time, and followed Cici down the back hallway to the guest suite.

"Cees," he began and she spun abruptly, holding up a hand and staring up at him, shooting daggers with her big brown eyes.

"Don't," she said. "I know you don't want to sleep in the bed with me tonight. I know it, Matthew! You don't have to say it, so don't!"

"It's not that I don't want to," began Matthew. "It's just that...."

"It's just that you can't commit to getting fully back into a relationship with me and risk losing me again. I know, you've already told me. You're scared to try. You're scared of me. Matthew, every relationship, ever, every single one, involves some degree of risk. Ours is no different and you weren't the only one who was badly hurt when we broke up."

"I know I'm kind of risk averse. I admit that. But you've still got, what, four or nearly five more months in London before you come home for good? You know none of this has ever been casual to me. It's all or nothing and it's the only way I can do this."

"I know, I know. And just so you know, it's never been casual for me either. At least never with you. I was devastated when we split up too, but I'm willing to try it again." She paused a moment and Matthew could hear a clock chime somewhere in the house. Then Cici said, "OK, Matthew, you win. We'll do it your way, but I don't have to like it. I'm merely concurring with your wishes, though I do not agree with the reasoning behind them."

He laughed at her legalese and kissed her again before pulling away and offering her use of the bathroom first.

"Always the gentleman, Matthew Paine, even when it hurts."

Matthew refrained from admitting to her just how much it hurt and how much he did not, in that moment, want to be a gentleman.

11 ~ Now What?

Monday morning at the Washburn home was a blur of activity. Sophia, Jay, and Elizabeth all emerged at breakfast alongside their mother and none of them looked particularly refreshed, though Sophia looked more disheveled than the others. She had changed time zones quicky and drastically, thought Matthew over his morning oatmeal, omelet, fresh fruit, and the requisite steaming cup of coffee.

Cici seemed refreshed and perky, though Matthew thought she should since he had insisted that she take the queen-sized bed in the bedroom and he'd opted for the little day bed in the sitting room. He'd checked his schedule for the week, researched a couple of issues for patient visits the next morning, and then tossed and turned through a good bit of the previous night. Following the sleepless night prior, he'd thought sleep would be instantaneous and deep. He was sorely disappointed to have been wrong on both counts.

They'd arranged to drop Matthew at Cici's early to pick up his car and still have time to go by his condo to feed Max. Annabelle Washburn was preparing to meet with the funeral director, who was coming to her instead of the other way around. Cici said she planned to "pop into the office" and then return to the Washburn house to help run interference, which had proven to be a necessity.

Well-meaning neighbors and friends had begun calling that morning, as the word got out, offering condolences and promising meals and food trays. As Matthew and Cici were just about to leave the house, two floral arrangements and an elaborate potted plant arrangement arrived with sympathy notes and promises of visits later that day. Cici seemed up for the challenge of organizing it all and

Matthew was glad of that because it all seemed more than a little bit overwhelming to him. The Washburns were well known in the community and the outpouring of condolences and well wishes would be over the top, he was sure.

When they arrived at her house where his Corvette waited in her driveway, Cici stood on tip-toe and kissed him longingly. Then she climbed into the driver's seat of the rental car that he'd driven over and slid the seat drastically forward. She waved sweetly as he climbed into his Corvette and fired it up, then pulled off and headed back to the Washburns in Raleigh as Matthew headed for Peak. Thankful for an uneventful drive back to his condominium, he was also happy to see that all was undisturbed there when he arrived.

Max immediately came to greet him as soon as he opened the door and then wound between his legs as Matthew tried to walk into the kitchen to feed him breakfast and rinse and refresh his water bowl. "You missed me, huh, Big Guy," he said, finally scooping up the big cat in order to take more than a halting step forward at a time. Scratching Max under his chin, Matthew heard a rare purr and paused for a few moments to fully appreciate that, scratching behind his ears and around the side of his face.

After caring for Max, locking up, and setting the alarm, Matthew got in the Corvette and headed back out. His Christmas playlist was a welcome respite from the distressing events of the past thirty-seven hours so he cranked that up too, loudly. As he was backing out onto the dead-end street, he spotted Cordelia Drewer bundled up like pictures he'd seen of Eskimos in fur parkas. He knew that it was her because she was walking Oscar, her persnickety Pomeranian, who was likewise clad in a coat.

As he turned down his music and pulled alongside her, she scooped up Oscar and Matthew lowered his window to greet them both. "Good morning, Mrs. Drewer."

"Hi Matthew," she said. "I hope all is well with you." Oscar leaned over for a quick head scratch. The little dog was initially very protective of his owner and had growled at Matthew every time he got the chance. After Mrs. Drewer and Matthew had become friends, Oscar had apparently decided that he could be friendly too.

"Mostly. It'll no doubt be all over the papers this morning, if it wasn't already yesterday, and I know you read those," he began.

"Let me guess," she said, looking at him with a slight smirk. "You are somehow involved in investigating the death of that very prominent lawyer who died in Raleigh Saturday night."

"Yes Ma'am, I am."

"How on earth did you get involved in that?"

"I was there when Mr. Washburn was found. He was one of the senior partners at the law firm where Cici works and we were at the annual Christmas Gala. A doctor was summoned urgently and I went to try to resuscitate him. It was too late though, and I wasn't able to do anything at all to help him," admitted Matthew sorrowfully.

"He leaves a family behind, doesn't he?"

"Yes, Ma'am. A wife who adores him and three grown children. The youngest just graduated from an undergraduate program and is headed for a masters at Duke, I think they said."

"That's so sad," she said, and Matthew knew that she could relate, having lost her newly-wed husband to the Vietnam War shortly before it ended.

"I'm not sure which is worse, losing the man you loved before having the chance at a life together or losing one you've had a long and happy life with," she said, pensively. "Either way, I hope you find who killed him."

"That was in the news? That he was killed?"

"It was today. His death was mentioned in the papers yesterday but this morning the report was that it was being investigated as a homicide. There weren't many details, so I won't ask you for any."

Matthew grinned at her, surprised in the change since they had become friends. Previously, he knew she'd have drilled him for those details and lectured him on some topic or other if he failed to provide them to her satisfaction.

"Thanks, Mrs. Drewer. I'll tell you what I can when I can. I'll be in and out here for a few days this week. I'm staying nights with the Washburn family. Nobody is sure yet if it was personal and the family is in danger or if it was professional and Mr. Washburn was the only target. Until they know that the family isn't in danger or until a security team is hired, I'll be there."

"Oh my," she said. "You really are in the thick of it again."

"Yes Ma'am, I really am. Again."

"I'll be happy to keep an eye on things here," she said. "I have your number and a key to your house, so let me know if you need me to take care of Max or anything else."

"Thank you, Mrs. Drewer. I appreciate that. Enjoy the rest of your morning walk."

"It'll be a short one," she said, shivering noticeably and drawing her hooded coat more tightly around her neck. "I don't like the cold. I should really consider moving to Florida."

"Just don't go to Miami," he said with a knowing wink as they said their goodbyes and he put the window up and set off again. It was warmer this morning than it had been over the weekend, Matthew thought, and he wondered how she got Oscar out during the really cold mornings. The afternoon promised to be nicely warm for December in North Carolina with predicted high temperatures around sixty.

The short four-mile trip into Peak was relatively unobstructed this morning, Matthew noticed, and he arrived in well under ten minutes. As he was parking the Corvette in his usual spot in the parking lot adjacent to his office building, he saw a text pop in from Danbury asking about his afternoon plans. He wanted to know if they could meet at the catering company at four-thirty to talk to the manager and some of the serving staff. Matthew checked his watch. It was already eight-thirty on a Monday morning, a half hour after he normally arrived at work. Particularly in the winter months, the staff scheduled fewer regular appointments on Mondays because they knew that there would be a heavier influx of call-in and walk-in patients who had waited over the weekend to be seen for myriad seasonal ailments.

Before retrieving his satchel and going in through the back door of his office building, he quickly texted back, *"I'll let you know at lunch. Mondays are hectic this time of year."* His office was a two-story brick structure that he thought was meant to mimic the style of the Cultural Arts Center which was on the block in front. It seemed to be a mixture of French provincial meets Romanesque, or maybe neoclassical was what the architect was going for. Their senior partner, Dr. Garner, had called it Palladian but Matthew had never been sure.

He pulled off his coat and switched it for his lab coat from the coat rack just inside his office door, pulled his computer from his satchel, and stashed the satchel bag under his large wooden desk. Having checked the morning roster the night before, he had some idea of what to expect and he set off down the hallway to Exam Room Six to see a teen-aged boy with chronic tonsillitis who might need a tonsillectomy.

Gladys, Matthew's most trusted nurse and self-appointed protector who was short and rather stout, waddled down the hall from the other direction to meet him at the exam room door. She looked a bit like a mother hen strutting toward him with her short legs, and that description matched well with her tendency to mother him. She was not a fan of Cici's and thought that the woman was bossy and not good for Matthew. She had at least refrained from pointing that out regularly in the past six months since Cici had been marginally back in Matthew's life.

"Good morning, Matthew," she said cheerfully. "I hope you had a restful weekend."

"Not exactly," said Matthew, with one eyebrow raised.

"Oh? Are you OK?"

"I'm fine. Just tired. I'll tell you about it later," he said, as he opened the door and stepped into the room. Matthew's ears were immediately assaulted by a string of profanities in some form of rap that was emanating from the teenager who was perched with his back to the door on the edge of the exam table. With ear buds in and cell phone in hand, he was attempting to keep up with whatever rapper he was listening to and profane lyrics were flowing freely.

Gladys marched around Matthew to stand in front of the boy, hand on hip, looked into his face and said, "Boy! Do you kiss 'yo Mama with that mouth?"

Startled, the guy sat up straight, pulling out the ear buds and then clicked the phone to turn off whatever he'd been listening to. "Excuse me, Ma'am," he said politely, looking as if he thought her next move might be to slap him silly. "I was just listening to some beats." Gladys, non-pulsed as usual, was also not impressed as she pursed her full lips and circled to the other side of the exam table without commenting further.

Matthew stifled a laugh at the encounter and stepped forward professionally, "Good morning, Carlos, I'm Doctor Matthew Paine." He waited for the reaction he usually got to his name but, getting none, he proceeded. "I know you usually see Dr. Rob but he's booked solid all week so you're stuck with me this morning. This is, what, the third severe sore throat that you've had in the past two months?" he asked, checking the chart.

"Yes, Sir, it is."

"And you've been on two full runs of antibiotic?"

"Yes, Sir," he said, politely, seeming to want to make amends for his earlier performance.

"And you've taken them all? You didn't stop taking them when you felt better?"

"No Sir, I mean, yes Sir," he glanced nervously at Gladys before clarifying. "I finished them all. My mama kept a schedule on the fridge so I got one every morning and every night until they were gone."

"OK, let's have a look," said Matthew, putting down the tablet he was carrying, washing his hands thoroughly in the sink, patting them dry, and then retrieving the overhead light and a tongue depressor. "I'm sure you know what to do by now," he said. "Stick out your tongue and say, 'ah'."

The boy did as he was told and Matthew was amazed that the kid was talking or singing at all, as red as his throat was, with the telltale white patches. Matthew stepped back from the boy's foul breath and asked, "Do you ever get tonsil stones?"

"You mean those nasty white lumps that come up out of my throat and taste awful?"

"That's a perfect description, yes."

"Yeah, all the time."

Laying the instruments aside, he said, "I'm just going to feel your neck." When he did, the boy flinched. "That's sore right there?"

The kid just nodded.

Then to Gladys, Matthew noted, "The lymph nodes are both swollen and sore."

"Have you run a fever or had any body aches?"

"Not this time. My mama called Friday afternoon right after my throat got sore again."

"OK, let's get a quick sample for a rapid test, though I'm pretty sure we're dealing with both strep and tonsillitis."

Gladys was ready with the swab and Matthew repeated the routine with the tongue depressor and got his sample, handing the swab back to Gladys to process.

Matthew asked all the usual questions about allergies, just to confirm what he'd seen in the notes on the boy's chart, then he said, "We'll do a quick test so it'll just take a few minutes to get those results back. There's a different antibiotic that we can try to see if it works better. If it doesn't knock this out, or if it comes right back again, we'll refer you to an Ear Nose and Throat Specialist for a tonsillectomy."

"A tonsillectomy?" the boy repeated, alarmed. "That's when they cut your throat open, right?"

"Not exactly," said Matthew, realizing that the boy was likely mentally younger than his biological age and wishing that "his mama" could be there with him. A perusal through the patient file the night before had told Matthew both why she wasn't there and that he'd try this one final antibiotic before recommending the tonsillectomy.

"It is a surgical procedure and you are anesthetized, or put to sleep, for it. So you don't feel anything. But nobody cuts your throat open. The surgeon goes down your throat through your mouth to remove your tonsils. They don't cut the outside of your throat at all." Noting the boy's continued alarm, he added, "The ENT surgeons have done so many of these procedures that they could do them blindfolded with one hand tied behind their backs. What I'm telling you is that if you do need the surgery, there's very little risk involved. You just have a very sore throat for a few days and you get to eat lots of ice cream."

At this, the boy's face lit up. Matthew envied his colleague Dr. Rob's way with children, putting them at immediate ease. Apparently he'd gotten this one thing right in allaying the boy's fears. If he were to place bets on the outcome, his bet would be that the surgery would be needed eventually.

After getting Carlos squared away and treating several other similar ailments that morning, Matthew slipped up to the second-floor break room where he found Gladys already stirring cream into her coffee to somehow match the exact color of her flawless skin. She glanced over at him and asked how many cups of coffee he'd had so far that morning.

"This is just the third," he responded, picking up a cup. "I had two this morning with breakfast but I haven't managed another one until now."

"You need a thermos with a big 'ole straw is what you need. It won't have to keep the coffee warm long because you drink it so fast. But you sure drink lots of it. And all that sugar," she shook her head at him as he dumped it into the bottom of the cup before adding the coffee.

"You gonna give yo'self diabetes before you're forty," she warned, lapsing into her southern drawl as she did when she was either comfortable with whoever she was talking to or admonishing them. Having raised three children of her own and then helping her overwhelmed children when the grandchildren started appearing in doublet, she probably did a lot of admonishing, he thought. Her youngest daughter had barely been married a year when she produced the first set of twins, which Gladys swore did not run in her family. A daughter in the middle produced a second set, and then the youngest daughter accidentally produced yet another set of twins. Her oldest child, a son, had therefore fearfully sworn off starting a family for a while. His wife, who Gladys said initially wanted to start a family immediately, was in full agreement.

"Thank you for caring about my health, Gladys," he said to her with a wink. "I'll take it into consideration."

"I'm not criticizing you. You are the doctor, but why did you give that boy with the strep and tonsillitis another antibiotic this morning? He's already had two."

"Because there is a chance that this one will work and it's a chance that we needed to take, given his circumstances."

"What circumstances would those be?"

"He's from a single parent low-income family. His mother works multiple jobs, which is why she wasn't here with him this morning, and she has three other children. She can't afford the surgery or the time away from work to care for him after he has it. They have no insurance and she has a very limited support system in place."

"You got all of that from his file?"

"There were notes to that effect in his file that Dr. Rob had recorded, yes."

"Well, when you put it like that, it makes perfect sense. I knew you had to have a reason. I just didn't know what it was."

"He said he took all of the medications he'd been given previously, so that shouldn't be an issue."

"I just hope this one works then."

"Me too, Gladys, me too," said Matthew as he pulled his phone from his pocket and saw that while it was on silent when he was with his patients, he had three missed messages. One was from Danbury and two had come in from Cici. All were telling him that Kennedy Reynolds had been located up at his family cabin in the mountains and he was being escorted back to Raleigh for questioning. Cici added that she was going to be there for that process and wondered if Matthew would want to be too.

He quickly texted that it all depended on the timing because he had a full day of patients and asked them both to update him when they knew what that timing was likely to be.

"What are you into now, Matthew Paine?" asked Gladys suspiciously. "Now what?"

"What makes you think I'm into anything?"

"Because I can read you like a book. Your eyebrow went up and your foot went to tapping, and you're thinking hard about something. And it's not about your patients. It's something you read in a text message."

Chuckling at her acuity, Matthew told her the basic version of what had transpired over the weekend, what was still happening with the Washburn family, and his role in all of it.

"Mmm mmm mmm. Honey, you can't keep yo'self out of this stuff for trying, can you?"

"Not for lack of trying," said Matthew. "But no, I don't seem to be able to stay out of it."

"And that little Cici is back from across the ocean and all up in this mess too, huh?"

"She is. It was her idea to stay with the Washburns and try to help them."

"Really?" asked Gladys. "That don't sound like her."

"She admired Mr. Washburn. She said that he was her mentor. He gave her the job and then fought for her early promotion. She says she owes him a few things. I've seen a softer side of Cici since she's been back. More like when I first met her, before she went through law school."

"Huh," said Gladys as she slipped a lid on her coffee cup, holding it carefully. "I'll see you in Exam Room Three." Waddling out and down the hallway, she was muttering to herself.

Matthew leaned back against the counter for a moment, sipping his coffee and staring out the French doors that opened from the break room onto the little covered balcony with café seating. Following in Gladys' manner, he muttered to himself, "Great question. Now what?"

12 ~ ACIDIC ANSWERS

After a full day at the office, Matthew drove out of Peak toward his house with the waning light behind him. Knowing that Max was far more interested in his food than attention, Matthew stayed only long enough to rinse and refill the big cat's water and food bowls for the night before grabbing a protein bar from the pantry and setting out again. He was heading for the downtown Raleigh police station, where Danbury had left his name to be admitted. Unsure of his role, if he had one, when he arrived, he was going to hear whatever was still underway with questioning Kennedy Reynolds.

Matthew was lost in his own thoughts as he made the drive up to Raleigh, munching his protein bar to tide him over until dinner. Had Reynolds poisoned Jamison Washburn? Reynolds clearly had some grievance with Washburn to punch him in the face. The fact that he'd slugged Washburn was indisputable. Matthew had very nearly gotten in the way of it himself. But why? Rational people didn't just go around punching each other for no reason. What, he wondered, could be the reason?

Either because he was completely immersed in his thoughts or because the traffic was exceptionally light on that Monday evening, he seemed to arrive at the downtown police station and up into the parking deck behind it in record time. He hadn't driven at warp speed, he knew, but the trip seemed short. Shrugging that notion aside as he slid from the Corvette, he grabbed his jacket, picked up the wrapper of his protein bar, and found a nearby trash receptacle to deposit it in.

As he approached the low, two-story brick building and rounded the corner, Matthew glanced over his shoulder. With the leaves off the trees that were planted along the sidewalk across the street, he could catch glimpses of the shimmering oak tree on the side of the Raleigh Convention Center wall. An iconic part of the downtown scene, at least in Matthew's mind, the shimmer wall depicted a swaying oak, celebrating the "City of Oaks," that was Raleigh, North Carolina.

He wasn't sure exactly how it functioned but he knew there was some creative brilliance behind the design as the tree appeared to sway and shimmer in the wind. There were, he knew, small squares that made up the wall and they were hinged somehow so that they swiveled to reveal either light or dark and create the movement of the tree. At night, as he was seeing it, the tree was back lit with programmable LED lighting so that it continued to shimmer.

The evening was warmer than usual in December, which enabled him to pause and admire the oak tree for a moment longer before climbing the steps and entering the building that housed the downtown police precinct. His name was on file with the front desk attendant so, after providing his identification and receiving a temporary guest badge, Matthew was directed through the double doors and down the hallway to the fifth door on the right.

He'd been in the tiny observation booths behind the interrogation rooms before so he knew the drill. Knocking lightly once, Matthew stepped through as the door was pulled open from within. He was surprised to see Danbury in the observation booth watching Cici talking to Kennedy Reynolds in the interrogation room beyond.

"What'd I miss?" he asked.

"Most of it," said Danbury. "She's just finishing up with him. She thought she could get more out of him. You know, attorney to attorney. He's been tight-lipped."

"What's his story about Saturday night?"

"He won't say why he slugged Washburn. Or directly admit that he did. He is denying that he poisoned him."

"He's revealed nothing useful at all then?"

"Maybe he has. He says he went downstairs. To the thirty-second floor. Right after the encounter in the stairwell. That maps to what Roger said. He says he wanted to apologize to Washburn. He regretted the altercation immediately. His words."

"He regretted hitting the man or he regretted getting caught in the act by Cici and me?"

"Good point. Either way, he didn't get to apologize. Or so he says."

"Why not?"

"His story? He went to the men's room. Then he went to Washburn's office. He heard voices within. So, he didn't interrupt. He figured he'd apologize later. He went by his office. Picked up some things. Checked a few things. Printed files to review. And then left for the rest of the weekend. He said he wasn't up for the party. Not after all of that."

"He heard voices in Washburn's office when he went downstairs?"

"That's what he said."

"Which would have been right after Washburn went downstairs."

"Right. Pretty soon after."

"The caterer said he called up and asked for refreshments to be delivered, right?"

"Yeah."

"So maybe Reynolds just heard Washburn's voice on the phone."

"Can't be. If he can be believed. He said the other voice was female."

"He says he heard a woman in the office talking to Washburn?"

"That's his story."

"Did he recognize the voice he heard?"

"He says not. Says the conversation was muted. He couldn't hear what they were saying. And he didn't see anyone. He just assumed it was Washburn. But didn't go in the outer office. He paused in the hallway. When he heard the voices, he moved on. Back to his office. And then left the building. He drove by his place. Packed some clothes. Then up to the mountains. Says he was coming back today anyway. But who knows? Maybe none of that is true."

"But he won't say what the altercation in the stairwell was about?"

"Nope. He won't even discuss it. Flatly refused to talk about it.

Says it was personal. Wouldn't admit to hitting Washburn. Not directly."

"He was up at the mountain cabin ever since then alone?"

"That's what he claims. Says he drove up that night. And hadn't been back in town. There's no radio or TV up there. He didn't know about Washburn. That he was killed."

"Who told him?"

"A couple of officers. The guys who located him."

"What was their impression? Did they think he seemed genuinely surprised?"

"One did. The other didn't."

"Oh," said Matthew.

"But the one who didn't. He's been on the force a long time. He's more jaded. He'd say his own mother was lying," added Danbury with a smirk.

"You're saying that Reynolds could have been genuinely surprised to learn that Washburn was dead?"

"Possibly. The younger officer thought he was."

Danbury perched on the edge of one of the stools in front of the two-way mirror and Matthew slid onto one beside him. Danbury flipped a switch and Matthew could hear Cici's voice clearly.

"Why are you refusing to answer the question about why you assaulted Mr. Washburn?" asked Cici.

"The Kennedy and the Reynolds families are the epitome of civility," responded Reynolds. "An altercation as you describe, had it occurred, would have been merely a momentary lapse in good judgment, for which I would have sincerely apologized."

"I'm asking for a motive, as you well know Mr. Reynolds. Are you pleading the fifth?" prodded Cici.

"Certainly not. I'm pleading that it's none of your business or that of anyone else," he replied acidly. Matthew thought that his tone alone could burn through the two-way mirror in front of them.

"I'm not pleading the fifth," Reynolds continued. "Because I cannot incriminate myself. There can be no evidence produced where none exists," he said sharply. Looking down his aquiline nose that was perfectly set in his patrician face, he stared at her as if she were some lesser species from another realm.

"And we all know that where no evidence exists, I can neither be arrested nor held against my will," he continued, lecturing Cici as if he were instructing a class of novices on basic legal concepts. "I acquiesced to the request to come in and answer questions, which I've now done to the best of my ability. And now, I'll take my leave."

He rose from the chair and walked to the door, staring at it expectantly as if his penetrating stare could burn straight through it and it would open for him immediately simply because he willed it to do so.

Cici had been completely correct in her assessment that Kennedy Reynolds was the kind of person that Matthew did not like. Matthew saw that now and he understood exactly what she had meant. Reynolds was haughty and exhibited disdain for everyone around him. He clearly thought he was a superior breed of human being. Cici had been right. Matthew had absolutely no use for people who behaved that way.

"One last thing, before you go," said Cici, rising from her seat but not moving toward the door yet. "Did anyone tell you how Mr. Washburn died?"

"Not directly, but I can ascertain from the earlier line of questioning that he was poisoned. Hemlock, was it? That grows all over North America, not just on my property in Virginia. It hides in plain sight. Many people confuse it for Queen Anne's Lace. I've worked tirelessly to rid my property of it, but I haven't been entirely successful. Check with the state of Virginia and they'll confirm my tireless efforts. I've contacted them multiple times when I've encountered new growth of the intrepid weed. Any connection is, of course, purely circumstantial and we both know that it won't hold up in court."

"No, Mr. Reynolds, it will not. I have no further questions," said Cici, over her shoulder in the general direction of the two-way mirror.

"Hemlock?" repeated Matthew in surprise.

"Initial lab work indicates it. They're isolating it now. They found traces of chemicals. Some I won't try to pronounce," said Danbury, pulling his phone from his pocket, poking it, and then holding it out to Matthew to review. "Derived from poison hemlock."

Studying Danbury's phone, Matthew read aloud, "Coniine, g-coniceine, and piperidine alkaloids. Poison Hemlock. That grows everywhere. There's no antidote for it and it's all extremely poisonous, the whole plant. It sometimes gets confused with carrots, parsley, and Queen Anne's Lace, as he said. Is it possible that Mr. Washburn accidentally ingested it?"

"Possible. Not probable," said Danbury. "Where would he get it there? At a formal event?"

"His symptoms do align with that sort of poisoning. If he ingested it, his stomach could have been pumped if we'd found him in time and he could have survived it. It's highly toxic and often fatal, but not always."

"If it's found, yes. But death can happen quickly. Symptoms in thirty minutes, easily. If it's potent. Toxicity of the plant varies. It's readily available. All over the country. It has a sweet taste. Or so I'm told. Which points to the punch as the delivery mechanism. I'd like to have a look around the Washburn property. In the daylight. Just to rule it out. To be sure it isn't growing there. Harder to tell in winter. But it's still seeding now. So if it's there, we can still see it."

"You think that somebody doctored his punch with hemlock," repeated Matthew slowly, taking that in.

"Best working theory so far. Explains why he had two punch glasses. One delivered by the caterer. One delivered earlier. We just need to figure out who delivered it. How they got to the refreshments from upstairs. And how they got it to him unnoticed. He must have trusted the person who brought it to him. If it was in the punch. Otherwise, why drink it willingly? There were no signs of struggle in his office. Or on his body."

Danbury rose and left the observation booth and Matthew heard a buzzer, after which the door to the interrogation room opened and Kennedy Reynolds, looking annoyed at the delay, stepped through a free man. At least he was free for the time being, Matthew thought. He remembered Danbury's words earlier, that not all horrible people who you didn't like were guilty. While it was technically true that meanness didn't necessarily equate to guilt, it did heighten the possibility in Matthew's mind. And Kennedy Reynolds was definitely not a nice person.

Matthew checked his watch and saw that it was nearly seven. Dinner time at the Washburn household. He'd watched the family pick at their meal the evening before and he knew that they were mostly going through the motions, but he didn't want to disrupt their daily routine any more than necessary during this difficult time.

Stepping out into the hallway from the observation booth, Matthew nearly collided with Cici who was on her way in. "Hey there," she said, smiling up at him. "How long have you been here?"

"Not long. Just long enough to hear Reynolds deny pleading the fifth, tap dancing around admitting that he'd hit Mr. Washburn, and denying any involvement in his death. Danbury said he went down to apologize to Washburn but didn't get the chance because he heard a female voice in conversation with him in his office and he didn't go in."

"That's what he claims. He also claims not to have known that Mr. Washburn had been killed because he was up at the mountain house alone. He has no alibi for any of it. Nobody saw him up there or even knew that he was there apparently. He says he rarely went to the cabin in the winter months because it isn't centrally heated, but he needed to get away and clear his head so he kept the wood stove burning and ate food he'd transported up."

"Do you think he's guilty?"

Cici screwed her face up in thought before answering, "I wish I knew definitively. If he is, it'll be impossible to prove from the little we know so far."

"Don't lawyers usually have a sense of guilt? When you're working with clients and potential clients?"

"Sometimes. But I only try cases involving corporate law, not murder, and it doesn't usually work that way anyway. You learn to believe about half of what they tell you," she said, slipping into the interrogation booth and retrieving the leather messenger bag she'd left there. Matthew was sure that it was some expensive designer brand, but he couldn't keep all of them straight to know what it was. Neither did he care overly much. He said nothing and she continued, "You have to build the case based on facts and evidence. In this case, there are precious few of either of those to support his guilt. We have to assume innocence at this point as the authorities continue to search for the evidence."

Taking her arm, Matthew steered her back down the hallway. "It's nearly dinner time at the Washburns. Any progress there on getting a security detail in place?"

"Some. Mrs. Washburn will be interviewing candidates tomorrow. Her children have insisted on being part of that process, which is disturbing because they've agreed on very little else so far. But she has claimed her right to veto as their surviving parent, the only full-time occupant of the house, and the widow, so maybe it'll be OK."

As they pushed through the double doors out into the entrance lobby, Matthew saw Danbury in conversation with a young police officer in full uniform, but from another place, not the garb that Matthew had come to recognize as that of Raleigh police officers. "Are you certain?" he heard Danbury ask. "You'd testify to that in court?"

"As sure as I can be. And yes, I'd testify to my impression in court. It's just an impression though and not based on anything concrete except my useless degree in psychology and a few years of experience in reading people." As Matthew stepped up alongside the officer, he could see that the guy had a lopsided grin and a freckled face. He didn't look young exactly, just earnest.

"OK, thanks," said Danbury, as he turned to acknowledge Matthew and Cici. He didn't introduce them and the uniformed officer slipped out through the front doors and into the chilly night air, a blast of which Matthew felt as the doors swished closed behind him.

"Hey Doc," Danbury said. "What did you think?"

"Of Kennedy Reynolds? I think he's not a nice person but as you said earlier that's not necessarily indicative of guilt."

At that, Danbury laughed and said, "Good to know. You heard what I said. And remembered it." Then, to Cici, he said, "Nice try. You didn't break this one, did you?"

"I had no expectation of breaking him or even tripping him up. That man is like hardened steel and he has many years of successful litigation experience beyond mine. I was hoping to get some impression from him though."

"You didn't?"

"No, none. He gives absolutely nothing away. He refuses to explain the reason that he hit Washburn in the stairwell, or even directly admit that he did, while simultaneously insisting that he was going to apologize and that he didn't kill him. He's maddening. What we need at this point is evidence, either inculpatory or exculpatory, something to indicate if he's telling the truth about any of it."

"We're working on that," said Danbury. "And I agree. For whatever that's worth. He has no 'tells.' None of the usual mannerisms. I've interviewed people who were lying. Many times. And I can usually get a sense of when they are. They give something away. They look down. Or won't make eye contact. They have some facial expression. Or do something with their hands. They fidget. Something. He's either telling the truth, or...."

"Or he's a very practiced and capable liar," Cici finished the sentence for him.

"Right. And I'm not sure which it is. Are you headed back to the Washburns?"

"We are," answered Matthew. "At least for the night. Cici says they're interviewing the security teams you recommended tomorrow, so hopefully it won't be for much longer. Have you found anything on Aubrey Bartles yet?"

"We're tracking his movements. But we haven't located him. Not yet."

As they were about to say their goodbyes, the guy behind the desk where Matthew had checked in was frantically waving his hands as he blurted out, "Detective Danbury! I'm glad you're still here. Dispatch has just called in another death and you might want to be there for this one."

The trio stepped over to the desk where Matthew and Cici turned in their temporary badges and Danbury took the phone that the guy behind the desk was waving in his face.

"Danbury here." After a pause, he said, "Uh huh. Yeah. OK, what's the address? Yeah, I know it. I'm on my way."

"What's up?" asked Matthew as they all walked out of the building together.

"A young woman was found this evening. Hanging in her apartment. She worked for Lion's Share."

"The catering company for the Christmas Gala," said Cici, her eyes widening in alarm.

"Right," said Danbury. "Looks like a suicide. But they're not convinced. I've gotta run. I'll keep you posted."

"OK," said Matthew to Danbury's retreating back.

Like Matthew, Cici had parked in the deck that was off to the right behind the police station, so they walked that way, hand in hand. They were crossing the street to reach the sidewalk on the other side of the parking deck and Matthew had glanced back over his shoulder at the shimmering oak tree when suddenly the roar of an engine made him look back in time, as a Bentley shot out of the parking garage, nearly running them over. Matthew managed to pull Cici up onto the sidewalk and as he looked over at the driver, he was all but certain that he'd seen Kennedy Reynolds sneering at him from behind the wheel.

"That man is horrible!" said Cici vehemently, confirming Matthew's impression. He certainly didn't argue with her on that score.

After they'd recovered from the shock and determined that they were both unharmed, Matthew walked Cici to her rental car and tucked her in it safely. "See you there," he said and he waited for her to lock the doors and start the engine before he moved away.

She blew him a kiss and waved, then backed out and headed out of the deck as he went to retrieve his Corvette on the next level up from where she'd parked. Was there another murder, he wondered? Or had the catering staff member had good reason to commit suicide? Danbury had clearly said, "young woman" and Matthew wondered if it had been her voice that Reynolds had overheard in Washburn's office

Saturday night. If he'd actually heard voices and hadn't made up that story to cover his murder of Washburn. There were far too many unknowns to jump to either of those conclusions yet, Matthew chided himself.

He fired up the Corvette and then cranked up his eclectic Christmas playlist that he enjoyed, tapping his fingers on the steering wheel and singing along on the way to the Washburn house. Normally, that would put him in the Christmas spirit. This year though there were a few confounding factors and he felt the need to work a little harder to kindle that spirit.

Knowing that he was arriving late for dinner, Matthew was surprised to see not just the Christmas lights lit but the entire house ablaze with lights as he pulled into the circular driveway in front of the Washburn home. There were multiple cars in the driveway, none of which Matthew recognized from earlier. Thinking that perhaps the Washburn offspring had procured rental vehicles for their time in Raleigh and maybe a few well-meaning friends had dropped by, he tucked his Corvette in behind Cici's rental car off on the edge of the main driveway to allow room for anyone else to get by. He wondered what he'd find inside, but he was in no way prepared for it.

13 ~ It's not a party

Pulling his satchel and jacket from the car as he slid out of the Corvette, Matthew could hear what he assumed to be upbeat Christmas music as he approached the Washburn house. The door opened for him as he was trying to decide if he should ring the bell or just walk in without disrupting the dinner that he assumed was already in progress. Cici pulled him inside and whispered, "Welcome to the house of insanity."

"What?" asked Matthew.

"There are about twenty extra people here and they're talking and laughing as if Mr. Washburn didn't just die," she hissed, obviously angry with that development.

"Where is Mrs. Washburn?"

"I haven't found her yet. I just got here a few minutes ahead of you."

"OK," said Matthew, processing this information. "Let's start there. Are Sophia, Jay or Elizabeth here?"

"Yes, yes, and I don't know," she replied. "Sophia is in the other room in the middle of it all, pouring drinks and laughing with a group of people. Jay is over in the corner obviously flirting with some guy, and I haven't seen Elizabeth. The table is set for dinner in the dining room, but nobody is in there."

"Let's divide and conquer. Why don't you ask Sophia where her mother is and I'll ask Jay. Maybe one of them will know."

"Or care. This is unbelievable," Cici added as she marched off leading Matthew toward the kitchen then down a side hall to the left. This hallway, it seemed, ran opposite the one they took to the right to reach the suite where they were staying. Like the hallway on their side of the house, Matthew noticed a door to the left and two to the right that were closed. If it was a mirror image, then one of the doors on the right was a bathroom and the other a stairway going up to the half floor above.

Straight ahead of them, the hallway opened out into a large room, undivided into separate spaces as the wing they were staying in was. This room was furnished with a seating area of plump sofas and chairs on one end. The other end was set up with entertainment in mind. There were a few seats interspersed with a billiard table, foosball table, dart boards, and a huge screen TV that was blaring Christmas music videos.

On the wall opposite the TV was a wet bar where Sophia was busily shaking some sort of drink concoction and laughing at a guy leaning over the bar talking to her as if what he'd just said was the cleverest joke she'd ever heard.

"Excuse me, pardon me," said Matthew, pushing his way through to get to the corner where he saw Jay in animated conversation with a tall slender man who looked to be twenty-something as well. Jay would reach up and touch the guy's shoulder every now and again to emphasize some point. Cici was right. He was clearly flirting.

"Hey Jay," said Matthew above the din. "Do you know where Mrs. Washburn is?"

"Oh Mom? She said she had a headache and I think she went upstairs a while ago. I told her that she should eat some dinner but she rushed out and was gone."

"OK, thanks!" Matthew called out, turning back the way he'd come. He met up with Cici in the hallway and learned that she'd heard a similar story from Sophia.

"Maybe we should see if the kitchen staff is still here and have a tray sent up to her," offered Cici. That plan sounded more reasonable than anything he'd witnessed so far, and Matthew followed her into the kitchen where a frustrated cook was slamming pans around.

Catching a glimpse of them, the woman tried quickly to compose herself, "Good evening. What can I help you with?"

"We understand that Mrs. Washburn hasn't had dinner and went upstairs with a headache," said Cici.

"Can you blame her?" asked the cook, motioning toward the hallway from which the racket was still extremely loud. "I had her favorite dinner all cooked and I was ready to serve it when all of these people started showing up! It's an invasion of the rabble rousers."

"I don't blame her at all," said Cici. "I was just wondering if we could perhaps send a tray up to her. I haven't seen her eat much today and you did say you'd cooked her favorite meal."

"I did," answered the cook proudly. "She loves my lasagna and I made a big batch 'specially for her with a nice salad and some homemade rolls that she likes."

"Is that what that wonderful smell is?" asked Matthew.

Beaming, the cook said, "Sending a tray up is a good idea. Would you two like to eat in the dining room this evening? The door closes, you know. Slides right out from inside the wall there."

"Ah, good, pocket doors," muttered Matthew, thinking that was a wonderful thing indeed given the current noise level.

"That would be lovely," answered Cici. "What about Elizabeth? Have you seen her? Has she eaten?"

"Nobody has eaten anything," replied the cook, throwing her hands in the air. "And I haven't seen Elizabeth since earlier this afternoon. I was just trying to decide what to do with all of this food with nobody here to eat it. I can package it up and freeze it once it cools. I was going to put some in the freezer for them for later anyway. But it's hot and ready now. I'll fix Mrs. Washburn a nice tray. Would you like to take it up to her?"

Cici looked only momentarily startled and then answered, "Certainly. Where is she?"

"She's in the upstairs west wing," said the cook, gesturing generally in the direction of the suite that Matthew and Cici were occupying. "Thankfully, on the other end from all of that racket, poor woman. Can't anybody get any rest in this house with all of that going on. Give me just a minute and I'll fix it up nice for her."

"OK," said Cici. "I'll be right back for it." She gestured to Matthew and they went down the hallway toward the suite they were occupying so that they could talk.

"Should we stay here tonight?" she asked him. "It's not like this house isn't obviously occupied with too many people to count. And I feel a bit intrusive now."

"It is well occupied. So was the gala Saturday night when Mr. Washburn was off by himself just like Mrs. Washburn is now. The trouble with large gatherings is that it's easy to hide in plain sight and disappear then reappear without anyone noticing. I wonder if Sophia and Jay actually know all of these people."

"Or any of them," Cici echoed his thoughts.

"I don't think we can leave Mrs. Washburn here with all of this tonight, as much as I'd love to be in my own bed," he said, trying and failing to stifle a yawn.

"I agree. OK, then we take a tray up and then eat in the dining room?"

"I guess we do," he answered and they returned to the kitchen. As she had promised, the cook was creating a tray for Mrs. Washburn with steaming hot lasagna on a beautiful Christmas plate accompanied by a bread plate with a roll and pat of butter shaped like a flower. She added a small bowl of salad, gently pouring over some sort of vinaigrette concoction from a cruet, a glass of iced water, a napkin, and cutlery as they watched.

"That should do it. Mrs. Washburn loved a glass of wine with my lasagna before her illness but she isn't drinking anything alcoholic again yet. I have a chocolate chess pie down here too if she'd like a piece when she's finished with her tray. Come on back when she's settled and I'll set you two up in the dining room," she said, looking pleased that there were appreciative diners to serve after all.

"OK, thank you," said Cici, looking at the tray uncertainly.

"I'll take it up. At least to her door," said Matthew. "You can check on her and see if she's appropriately dressed for visitors."

"Thank you," she said as Matthew lifted the tray, carefully balancing it. Cici went ahead and opened the door to the back side stairway of what Matthew realized was apparently called the west wing. Five steps ascended and then were interrupted with a small landing before the stairs turned back and continued up to the second floor. On the landing there was a little table with a dimly lit lamp on it.

Cici looked back when Matthew had reached the landing, checking to see if he was OK with the tray. "I've got it, Cees. Go ahead," he told her. They walked around a railing at the top of the landing and over to a closed door on which Cici gently tapped.

"Mrs. Washburn?"

Hearing a faint response from within, Cici cracked the door and said, "Mrs. Washburn, it's Cici. Matthew and I brought some dinner up for you. Your cook prepared a lovely tray for you. May we come in?"

Matthew couldn't hear the reply, but Cici slipped into the edge of the room and said, "Yes, Ma'am." She motioned for Matthew to enter behind her and pulled the door wider for him and the tray to fit through it.

The room was dimly lit, as the stairwell and hallway outside of it had been, and Mrs. Washburn was draped across a chaise lounge looking like she belonged in a black and white film from the 1940s. A long light blue silk and lace robe mostly covered a matching negligée and her feet were clad in matching slippers trimmed in something that looked like feathers. The only thing missing, Matthew thought, to complete the movie scene would be an opera length cigarette holder. He was glad to see that in her hand, she instead held a damp folded washcloth which he assumed had been over her eyes.

"Thank you for bringing that up for me. That's so thoughtful of you. Cici dear, could you pull that little table over? You can place it just there," she pointed as Cici slid a small table over and Matthew set the tray down on it.

"Your cook said that her lasagna is your favorite and it smells wonderful," said Cici.

"It is and it does. Claudette is a wonderful cook and her lasagna is always delicious," Mrs. Washburn responded.

"She also said there's a chocolate chess pie down there. We can bring you a slice of if after dinner if you would like. Do you need anything else right now?"

"No, thank you so much. I just needed to be somewhere quiet and dark. I had a headache come on rather suddenly."

Cici seemed to be choosing her words very carefully. "I can certainly understand that, with the entertaining downstairs. I'm sure the party is a bit loud if you have a headache."

"It's not a party exactly," said Mrs. Washburn. "It's just Sophia's way of working through her grief."

As Matthew and Cici exchanged a confused glance between them, Mrs. Washburn explained. "It's Sophia's way of coping. Whenever something sad, disappointing, or upsetting happens to her, she calls her friends, hosts a party, and then begins to deal with it the next day. She'll be completely hung over in the morning and then she'll start to process what's happened to her father."

"I suppose everyone deals with grief in their own way," said Cici.

"Indeed they do. Please enjoy your dinner and don't worry about me. I don't' have much appetite but I'll try to eat at least a little bit of this."

"Mrs. Washburn, does Sophia usually invite people she knows well?" asked Matthew.

"I don't honestly know. She hasn't lived here in quite some time, you know. I'm not sure who's in my house right now but it'll all settle down again in a couple of hours. It always has. Please don't be concerned about it. Just enjoy your dinner."

"We'll check on you after we eat," said Cici.

"Thank you, dear. You've been a godsend," said Mrs. Washburn as Matthew and Cici slipped quietly out and closed the door behind them.

"Now what?" whispered Matthew.

"Now I guess we get dinner," said Cici.

"OK, but let's not close the pocket doors. I want to keep an eye on the people coming and going. Somebody needs to."

Cici just rolled her eyes before admitting, "I know that you're right, even with all of that racket." She turned and descended the stairs quietly and they closed the door at the bottom behind themselves.

After washing their hands, they slipped into the dining room and Matthew chose a seat where he had a view through the open archway without closing the pocket doors. Claudette served them salads and rolls and then the best lasagna Matthew could remember eating. Cici laughed at him when he moaned audibly over it.

"Hey Cees, did you mention to Mrs. Washburn that Kennedy Reynolds had been found and was being questioned today?" Matthew asked, breaking the silence as they were finishing up their meal.

"I did not, no."

"Does she know that her husband was poisoned with what they think is hemlock?"

"I have told her nothing about any of that. She's talked to someone at the police department a couple of times today, mainly about when Mr. Washburn will be released from autopsy so that she can finalize arrangements for him. I don't know what they've told her. I didn't ask and she didn't offer any information about that. Why?"

"She just didn't seem very concerned about the party that isn't, at least according to her, really a party down here."

"You're right. She didn't seem concerned. Though I think she's really just going through the motions right now. I'm not sure she has any emotional energy left to expend on it."

"That's understandable," said Matthew, who was lost in contemplation. Among other things, he was debating the best way to remove all of the revelers from a house that wasn't his and then to ensure that it was properly locked up behind them for the night. As he and Cici took their dishes into the kitchen, he noticed that some of the partiers had spilled out onto the brick-tiered patio area out back. Strategically placed area lighting that he hadn't known was there had been turned on and he had a decent view of it all from one of the kitchen windows.

"Oh, I'll get those," said Claudette, reappearing from the butler's pantry and taking their dishes. "I didn't realize you'd finished. Are you ready for some chocolate chess pie?"

"Twist my arm," said Cici with a grin. "That was fabulous. But maybe I should take some up to Mrs. Washburn first," she amended.

"I have three slices already plated right here," said Claudette. "Do you want coffee with that? It's decaffeinated."

It was an unusual unseasonably warm night for December in North Carolina with temperatures still up around sixty degrees, so they certainly wouldn't freeze out there, Matthew thought, still staring out the kitchen windows at the partiers. He noticed a couple returning to the group, seemingly unnoticed, from somewhere farther out in the back yard as he was pondering the dynamics of large groups of people.

"Matthew, do you want decaf coffee with your pie?" Cici asked him with a nudge.

"Oh, no thanks," he said without turning around.

"I'm going to take dessert up to Mrs. Washburn before we have ours," said Cici.

"That sounds good. I want to check in with Danbury. Can you take hers up? I'll bring the tray down later if you can't manage it now."

"I'll try," said Cici, as she picked up one of the three dessert plates with the chocolate chess pie and a tiny dessert fork and slipped out of the kitchen.

"Danbury here," Matthew heard after he'd made the call.

"It's Matthew. I was just checking in."

"Hey Doc. How're things there?"

"A little crazy right now. One of the daughters invited friends over and there's a loud party going on."

"What? How did that happen?"

"I'm not sure, but Mrs. Washburn says that's how her older daughter copes with upsetting things. She hosts blowout parties. The party dynamics made me think about the gala Saturday night and the general confusion of large gatherings, from which people can come and go, seemingly unnoticed because there's so much going on. Then I was thinking about the woman whose death you just went to investigate who worked for the catering company. I think it was Abby who said earlier that a couple of the catering workers didn't show up Saturday night, right?"

"That's right. They called in back-up workers."

"This woman, the one who just died, she was one who didn't show up, wasn't she?"

"How could you possibly know that?"

"Just a hunch. I'm also betting that she was there Saturday night. And that her death today wasn't a suicide."

"I don't think it was a suicide. I agree with that assessment. Why do you think she was there? Saturday night?"

"I think she was the voice that Reynolds heard talking to Washburn. I think she was there to do exactly what she did in poisoning him but Reynolds, by clocking him, did her a favor and provided easy access to Washburn when he went down to his office instead of into the party. Unless Reynolds was in on it and the encounter in the stairwell was planned to keep Washburn out of the party. Had she worked for the catering company long?"

"No, she was newly hired. But carefully vetted. At least according to the manager. That's a very interesting theory. And it provides a motive. For murdering her."

"She wouldn't be listed on the guest list, would she? Didn't the elevator operator say that the catering company arrived before he did? And likely also before the host arrived who was checking in the guests. But didn't he also say that two members of the catering crew arrived late?"

"He did. I'll get a picture of this woman. And the other worker. The guy who also called in sick. Then I'll contact Roger. He might be able to identify them. If they're the ones who arrived later. You might be onto something."

"How could they know that Washburn was downstairs if he never entered the party unless it was all planned in advance? If they were the ones who arrived later, wouldn't the other caterers notice when they did arrive if they went upstairs into the gala event? Or would that be part of the crowd dynamic in which people come and go, seemingly unnoticed, because there are so many of them and there's so much going on? They'd have had to have been dressed in the caterers' uniforms for Roger the elevator operator to know that they were with the caterers, if they were the ones who arrived late. And they'd have needed access to the food and those specific serving pieces, right?"

"Good questions. But maybe it's why she was murdered. She wasn't working alone. If your conjecture is right. She had an accomplice. Maybe the other absentee worker. Who might have just cleaned up loose ends. And she was one of them. I'm on it. I'll let you know what I find out. Thanks for the call."

Matthew started to answer, but Danbury was already gone.

14 ~ HOT AND COLD

Sitting at his desk for just a moment after arriving at his office on Tuesday morning, Matthew was contemplating their odd stay at the Washburn house and wondering how much longer he'd have to be there. He had managed to clear the house of visitors the night before, most of whom were too drunk to object by the time Matthew and Cici were preparing for bed. He'd gotten rides for several of them who had no designated drivers and then carefully locked up the house. Leaving several key outdoor lights on for the night, he hoped to discourage the wrong sort of visitor.

The night had been uninterrupted by any unwanted visitors, but he'd still slept fitfully in the little daybed dreaming of shadows lurking in stairwells and rooms so full of people that he couldn't breathe. He awoke to a warm morning, showered, quickly downed a breakfast of eggs and toast with lots of coffee that Claudette had prepared, and then dashed out to go back to his own house to care for Max.

He and Cici had been the only ones up when he'd left the house and he wished that he'd asked Mrs. Washburn the night before how the interviews had gone with the security companies. He had been a full half hour later than usual arriving at work again so he had no time to linger in his office or to hang the Christmas lights he'd bought but still hadn't put up on the little tree on his desk. Instead, he donned his lab coat, retrieved his laptop from the satchel on his desk, and stashed the satchel under the desk.

Calling Trina, the young and energetic office manager who had instigated ordering daily lunches as a perk for anyone who wanted to participate, he placed an order. It was taco Tuesday and that sounded good to him. He felt lighter somehow, being back in his own world and he was whistling a Christmas carol as he stepped out into the hallway with his computer under one arm.

Dr. Rob was headed in his direction from the front lobby. They briefly exchanged pleasantries and Matthew filled him in on Carlos, the teenage boy he'd seen the day before who was usually Dr. Rob's patient.

"Good call," said Dr. Rob. "That would have been my next step too, given the circumstances. I'm afraid he'll eventually need the surgery, but I sure hope this antibiotic works. It's worth the try. How are things with you and your family? I hope you're enjoying the Christmas season together."

"We're all well, though I haven't seen my family much lately. How's Ariel?" Matthew had helped to rescue Katherine Ariel Roberts, Dr. Rob's only child, when she was abducted in Miami in the early summer and he had become her long lost uncle in her eyes and in his as well.

"It's a busy time of year, isn't it? Ariel just got home for a month between semesters so we're doing all of our traditional Christmas things. We have the tree up and decorated. We each make one new ornament together every year and I think Ariel is gathering supplies today so that we can do that this evening. Why don't you come for dinner and join us? She'd love to see you."

"I wish I could," said Matthew, and he told Dr. Rob a little of what was going on with Cici and the Washburn family situation.

"Oh, that's right. I forgot that Cici was already back for the holidays. That's awful what happened to her senior partner. I hope you can help. If you need me to cover any for you, just say the word."

"Thanks, Dr. Rob, but I saw your schedule this week and yours is worse than mine as it is. It's why Carlos got assigned to me yesterday morning. But I do appreciate the offer."

They parted in the hallway, Dr. Rob heading to check on a small child in Exam Room Six, who was running an unexplained fever, and Matthew for an older patient with a chronic cough in Exam Room One.

*****

After a brisk morning of back-to-back patients, Matthew picked up his tacos from the front desk. He admired the festive tree and decorations that Trina had put up in the front reception area before joining a group that was already convened on the upstairs balcony off of the break room. The day was partly cloudy, but temperatures were hovering above seventy degrees, exceptionally warm for December but perfect for eating on the café furniture outdoors. Maybe children being able to be outside to play would stave off a few shared colds and other ailments, he thought hopefully.

Gladys, Megan Sims, the Physician Assistant that their senior partner Dr. Steven Gardner had brought in over the summer, and Sadie Peterson, the resident Megan had brought with her, were already seated. They slid around and made room for Matthew.

After saying a blessing over his tacos, he was just about to dive in when his cell phone began to vibrate in his pocket. The taco in his hand made it entirely tempting to ignore the call but he put it down and pulled out his phone.

"Hey Doc!" said Danbury's voice. "Just wanted to give you an update. You were right. The murdered woman arrived late. Saturday night. Roger identified her from a picture. And the caterer confirmed it. She called in sick at the last minute."

"But then showed up anyway? Interesting," said Matthew, rising from the table and stepping back inside the break room to have the conversation without disrupting lunch for the gathering around the café table.

"What about the guy?"

"Roger was less sure about him. The other late worker arrived with early guests. A guy in a catering uniform. But Roger wasn't sure of his face."

"Then it could have been either the other missing worker or someone who'd gotten his hands on a uniform."

"Exactly. But there's more," added Danbury. "Remember the little charm? The one on the base of the glass in the office? It was a lady dancing. From the twelve days of Christmas. There were multiple sets of those. Twenty sets, the caterer said. There should have been two hundred and forty glasses with charms. But they ran out of charms. Before they ran out of glasses. That was the only lady dancing. The one on Washburn's desk. There were twenty sets of all of the other charms. But not that one."

"You're saying it was purposeful, that there was only one with that charm because it marked the glass to be given to Mr. Washburn?"

"It's pure speculation. I can't prove it yet. But that's what I'm saying."

"That makes sense. It's the obvious conclusion and not something that would be noticeable until you started digging into it. The killer probably thought that it would go completely unnoticed. Or at the very least nobody would tie it back to the murder. Nice work."

"When you're hot, you're hot," said Danbury with a smile in his voice. "But trails can turn cold. Very quickly. We still haven't located Bartles. Are you back at the Washburns tonight?"

Matthew sighed heavily, "I will be if I have to be. I really hope that Mrs. Washburn can hire a security company today, one that's already staffed and they can step in and take over. I'd really love a good night's sleep in my own bed and soon."

"The companies I recommended are top notch. They do it all. Surveillance, security equipment installation, protection detail, all of it."

"Then, let's hope I'm only going back there tonight long enough to pack. I'm sure Cici will keep me posted. She's mostly been there during the daytime hours helping Mrs. Washburn."

They said good-bye and Matthew went back to the balcony to quickly down his tacos because he had a mere ten minutes before his next patient was due to be seen. The three women were already picking up their lunch wrappers and stuffing the trash in paper bags when Matthew returned.

"Sorry, Dr. Paine," said Sadie Peterson, the young resident. "Megan and I have a patient to see now so I can't keep you company."

"That's OK, Sadie. I have a patient in about ten minutes myself," he said between bites.

"You just slow down and don't choke on your lunch," said Gladys. "I'll go get vitals and ask all of the usual questions and have that ready for you when you get down there."

"Thanks, Gladys," said Matthew, swallowing too quickly and then reaching for the water bottle that accompanied his lunch order. "I'll be there in just a minute."

Most of the time, he thought, he was very thankful for Gladys' mother hen tendencies and her protectiveness over him. Finishing his last taco and washing it down with the last of his water, Matthew scooped up his wrappings and stuffed them in the bag, tossing the whole thing in the trash on the way out of the break room. He had a full roster of patients to see that afternoon and he knew he needed to get to them.

His next patient was a middle-aged woman that he'd seen only once several months before when she had been recovering from an episode of diverticulitis. Currently, she was experiencing more abdominal pain, but cyclically and not constantly, with a recurring sepsis that Dr. Garner had been treating with antibiotics. After pouring over her records, Matthew feared that her symptoms were indicative of a colovesical fistula, a rare but painful condition when a connection forms between the colon and bladder.

She'd had no previous surgeries, he'd noted as he had studied her chart, so there wasn't an obvious reason for the condition he suspected. If he was correct about his diagnosis, the condition was serious and would require surgery to repair. That was beyond his purview, so he referred her to a team of colorectal surgeons. They conduct the right tests to diagnose and then repair the damaged organs, if he was right, he explained to his patient. Much to Matthew's relief, Gladys eagerly contacted the practice and managed to get the woman seen immediately. It wasn't something he wanted to let linger.

He was headed down the hallway to see his next patient when he felt his phone vibrate. Pulling it from his pocket, he saw a text from Cici, "*I have good news and bad news, which do you want first?*" It was a little game of sorts, a method that he and Cici would tell each other things.

Slipping into the alcove between exam rooms, he quickly called her. "Hey Cees, I'm between patients. Let's have the good news first."

"The good news is that Mrs. Washburn has hired a security agency and I agree with her that it was the best choice."

"And the bad news?"

"We have one more night at the Washburns. They're starting tomorrow, installing a state-of-the-art security system with cameras, multi-layered locks, and alarms. They walked the entire property today with Jay and Mrs. Washburn and made some very specific recommendations. They'll bring in a team and provide round-the-clock security and surveillance tomorrow. But that's tomorrow. I'll switch beds with you, if you're still insisting on not sharing one with me. Really, Matthew, you don't fit on the day bed. Surely you can't be getting any sleep."

"That's mostly all good news, Cees. And I can manage one more night on the day bed. Did she get an answer about when they'll be finished with the autopsy testing yet?"

"Not that she's mentioned. It sounds like all of the arrangements are in place, except of course for the date. She isn't rushing anyone for that though. She's being pretty smart about it. He'll be cremated before interment," she said, choking on her words and pausing a moment. "So, she wants to ensure that any information which will ever need to be known from the autopsy is gathered now to provide the evidence if the killer can be caught. They have space in a mausoleum at the cemetery on the other side of 440 from here. The one with the statue of Jesus with his arms out. She says she loves that statue and finds it comforting."

"I know the one she's talking about and I agree with her. I've got to get to my next patient and I'm not finished today until five-fifteen so I'll be there by six-thirty or so, after I get the patient records straight and go feed Max. I need another set of clothes too. But I'll do my best to be there in time for dinner at seven. Let me know if anything changes."

"Will do. See you by seven." She blew him an air kiss and was gone.

*****

After a full and exhausting afternoon treating patients at a pace that Matthew didn't enjoy because he felt like he got no time with any one individual patient, he was on his way to his condo to spend a few minutes with Max and pack clothing for the next day when a text came in from Danbury. He had the text message read to him over his car speaker system and Danbury was asking him to call when he got the chance. Figuring he had the chance because he didn't have far to go and he could talk over the car system and still have his hands free to drive, he told the car system to call Danbury.

"Hey Doc!" said Danbury. "We've had some further developments. Thought you might want to know. And share with the Washburns when you get there."

"OK, what's up?"

"We got an address on Aubrey Bartles."

"Yeah? Where is he?"

"Up in Ridge Woods."

"Oh! Then he is local. That's what, maybe twenty miles north and slightly west of the Washburn's house. How'd you find him if he's been off the grid?"

"He's sub-leasing a place up there. So no records online. But he got a speeding ticket. Turns out it was the night of the gala. Up in Morton."

"Morton? Everybody knows you don't speed through there. The speed limit on I-40 drops to fifty-five and the police station is right off of the interstate."

"Apparently not everybody."

"Which way was he headed?"

"He was headed west."

"What time was it?"

"Just before seven."

"And he was issued a ticket? Is that how you found him? By the record of the speeding ticket?"

"Not quite. He has a better alibi than that for the night of the murder."

"Which is what?"

"He was doing over a hundred miles an hour. They didn't just give him a ticket. They took him in. He spent the night in lockup. Until he could make bail. The next morning."

"You're telling me that he was in jail in Morton all night the evening of the gala?"

"Right."

"Wow! Well, back to Kennedy Reynolds as the primary suspect then, huh?"

"Nobody ever said he wasn't always the primary suspect. But we have to run down all leads."

"Oh," said Matthew. "Well, he definitely had the opportunity and some sort of motive. It's odd that he won't answer any questions about it since he claims to be innocent. Why wouldn't he clear himself if he can? Maybe he really is 'pleading the fifth,' though he clearly told Cici that he wasn't."

"Anything he could say would be incriminating," said Danbury. "Without an alibi. It's no wonder he's not giving any details. About the argument in the stairwell. The guy's too smart for that."

"Yeah, wily like a fox," said Matthew. "By the way, the Washburns picked a security company. I didn't ask which one, but Cici said she thought it was the best choice. They'll be there tomorrow morning to install what sounds like a pretty sophisticated security system and begin round-the-clock surveillance."

"You're there tonight then?"

"Yeah, I'm headed to my house now to take care of Max, water my tree, and pack clothes for tomorrow. But then I hope I can come home tomorrow night. I need a full night of sleep in my own bed."

"I bet so."

"Thanks for the update. I can share it with Cici, right?"

"Carefully. And only Cici. The less details shared, the better. At least at this point."

"OK, will do."

"Have a good one, Doc."

"You too," replied Matthew, but Danbury was already gone.

Matthew decided to turn on the radio to see what was going on in the world around him and he searched for a weather forecast to know what to take for the next day at work. He heard that the high temperature for the day had been up around seventy-five. That was unbelievable in December, he thought, but temperatures were dropping. According to the weather forecast, the lows would be below freezing and in the high twenties overnight on Wednesday. He'd always heard the old adage that if you don't like the weather in North Carolina just give it a minute and it will change. It wasn't far wrong, he thought.

As he turned from Highway 20 onto Chester Road, at the end of which was his condominium complex, he noticed with relief that the car which had been following him since he'd left the little town of Peak kept going past his road. He chided himself lightly for being paranoid. What he didn't see were the brake lights a quarter of a mile later when the car turned around to circle back.

15 ~ Requesting Backup

After a leisurely but sad dinner with the Washburn family reminiscing, Matthew and Cici were alone in the sitting room of their suite discussing their day and enjoying each other's' company. Realizing that he hadn't told her about Danbury's call, he said, "Hey Cees, there's good news and bad news on the Washburn case. Which do you want first?"

"Umm…" she said, as if it were a difficult decision. "I guess the good news."

"Actually, good choice. That's really the only way this works," he said, grinning at her. "I talked to Danbury and he said they found an address for Aubrey Bartles up in Ridge Woods."

"Oh!" said Cici. "That isn't really great news. He's way too close! What's the bad news?"

"He was taken into custody for speeding nearly fifty miles over the speed limit in Morton Saturday evening about the time that the gala event began and he spent the night in jail there."

"So, he wasn't here Saturday night," said Cici slowly. "Which way was he headed?"

"West," said Matthew. "I asked that question too."

"Like he'd just left here? How far away is Morton?" she asked and then pulled up a map on the notebook computer that was resting in her lap to answer her own question. "Wow, that's well over two hours away, nearly three. He was long gone from this area before the Christmas Gala even started. But why would you speed that fast in

Morton? Everybody knows you'll get ticketed faster there than nearly any place else along the I-40 corridor in North Carolina."

"That's what I said too. But he isn't from North Carolina, is he?"

"No, I guess not."

"I'm about ready to wash up and turn in," said Matthew. "Do you want the bathroom first?"

"No, you go ahead. I was going to do one more thing on my computer before I shut it down for the night."

"OK," he said, leaning over to kiss her softly before he got up.

After they'd said their good-nights and gone to their respective beds, Matthew was lying wide-awake in the little daybed. Happy that he'd be in his own bed the next night, he hoped he could actually get some sleep. He was thinking about how Max loved to curl around his head while he was sleeping, and he smiled to himself in the dark. He called it "hair by Max" when he awoke the next morning to his short brown hair standing out in all directions as a result.

Matthew didn't realize he'd gone to sleep, but he knew that he must have drifted off when a dream sequence that he couldn't quite remember afterward was interrupted by a crash. Jumping upright on the tiny daybed, he retrieved his Glock 19 from the table above his head and ran out of the room in the direction of the crash.

As he raced into the kitchen from the side hallway, Jay was coming into the kitchen from the center hall. "What was that?" said Jay in a stage whisper that he might as well have spoken aloud.

"I don't know. It wasn't me. I just heard it and came running," answered Matthew.

"Oh!" said Jay, seeing the gun in Matthew's hand. "Put that away, please!"

Ignoring this request, Matthew responded instead, "It's too dark in here. I left lights on outside of that back door and they should be shining through the windows." He also felt a slight chill, as if a breeze were flowing through the kitchen somehow.

"Oh yeah," said Jay. "Those outdoor lights were on when I went up to bed."

"What's going on?" asked Elizabeth, as she trundled into the kitchen from the center hallway in a robe and slippered feet.

"We don't know yet," said Matthew, undecided as to what to do next. He was vacillating between turning on a light to see better and not lighting the inside to make themselves targets if there was someone skulking around outside who would then be able to see them without being seen.

Elizabeth removed the need to make a decision when she reached over and flipped a light switch. Jay shielded his eyes and Matthew flinched in the sudden glare. It was then that Matthew saw it, the source of the crash they'd heard. There was broken glass on the kitchen floor.

"Stay back," Matthew said as Elizabeth was walking into the room. "There's glass all over the floor over there by the back door," he added, pointing. Clad in his favorite flannel sleep pants and a soft T-shirt but with bare feet, Matthew wasn't thrilled with the idea of investigating too closely either. Surveying the back door from where he stood, he saw the source of the broken glass.

"Call 9-1-1," he said. "And report an attempted break in at this address. Let's get out of the light of the kitchen and I'll get my phone and call Danbury."

"OK, I have my phone," said Elizabeth, stepping back into the unlit hallway. Matthew saw the light from the phone as she retrieved it from a pocket of her robe, then heard her placing the call and providing the address.

"I'll be right back," said Matthew. "Stay in the shadows and away from the windows in case somebody is still out there." He dashed down the hallway and into the suite, nearly colliding with Cici who was approaching the doorway. She wore a negligée that would have made him drool had he not been so intent on retrieving his phone and donning his leather boat shoes.

"What on earth?" she asked.

"Somebody was trying to get in here," said Matthew. "Elizabeth is calling 9-1-1, but I'm going to call Danbury. Somebody took out the back lights and then cut a perfect circle in the panes of glass on the back door right by the door handle and dead bolt lock. But then the glass on the inside layer fell inside and broke all over the floor. I'm guessing that wasn't part of their plan."

He'd been poking his phone as he spoke and he heard Danbury's voice, sounding sleepy, say, "Danbury." And then, more alertly, "Oh, hey Doc. What's going on?"

"Somebody just tried to break in here at the Washburns," he explained. "Elizabeth called 9-1-1 to report the attempt, but I thought you'd want to know too since it might all be related to the murder investigation."

"I'm rolling," said Danbury, sounding fully alert, then Matthew heard a lot of background noise. Danbury sounded very far away, obviously having switched to speaker phone, when he said, "Talk to me. What happened?"

Matthew explained the sequence of events and Danbury said, "OK. It'll take me about twenty to get up there. I'm on my way."

Hating to have to wake the guy up and drag him out late at night yet again, Matthew took his phone and the Glock back down the hallway. He heard the murmur of voices as Sophia and Annabelle had joined the huddled group. Cici had pulled on a robe and she followed behind him.

"Let's move to the front sitting room," said Matthew, as he went down the hallway and peered out the front entrance to see that the lights on the front of the house were still burning brightly. "The drapes are drawn and there's no visibility into the house from outside there. I'm going to go check the rest of the downstairs windows and doors. To make sure that was all there is before the police arrive."

Glock and cell phone with the flashlight enabled in hand, Matthew made his way slowly through all of the rooms downstairs that had outside windows and doors. He checked each one to ensure that it was locked and nothing was broken. After making his way through the central part of the house, he checked the east and west wings. Finding nothing amiss, he returned to the gathering in the front sitting room.

"Everything else looks secure," he reported. "The windows are all still locked, as are the doors and all the glass is intact. I guess we just wait here for the police to arrive."

As he said it, he realized that it was a moot point because he heard sirens in the distance before they silenced and then they could all see the lights flashing through the stained-glass side lights on either side of the front door. Noticing that none of the family members had moved, he motioned to the door and asked, "May I?"

Jay just nodded and Annabelle Washburn answered softly, "Yes, please do."

Matthew stepped forward, meeting the officers at the door, opening it for them and introducing himself. He quickly summarized the reason they'd been called but said, quietly, as he led them down the hallway to the kitchen, "But there are some other circumstances."

"What's that?" asked the older heavy-set officer and Matthew quietly explained about Mr. Washburn's murder Saturday night.

"Think it's related?" the officer asked no one in particular as he shone a flashlight around the hole and the door handle, then donned gloves to open the door and step outside as a rush of cold air blew into the kitchen. He held a powerful flashlight away from his body but shone the long beam all around the back yard before returning his attention to the door.

"I'll go check behind the garage out there," offered the younger officer and set out with a similar flashlight illuminating the darkness in its path to nearly daylight, or so it appeared in the dark of night. The grass and shrubbery shimmered in the light and Matthew realized it had rained after he'd gone to bed, though it didn't appear to be raining at the moment.

"You say there were lights on out here?" asked the older officer.

"Yes, both here beside the door and floodlights on the corner there that shine out into the yard," Matthew added, pointing to the darkened corner. "There is area lighting for entertaining that wasn't on. Let me find the switches for that." Those switches weren't by the back door.

"Sophia? Jay?" he called back down the hallway. "Where are the switches for the area lighting out back?"

"I've got it," said Sophia and came in to turn them on. The younger officer returned from his more extensive search of the yard and started asking questions, most of which Matthew could answer. He escorted the officer down the hallway to the sitting room to have the family fill in those questions that he couldn't answer while the older officer was processing the scene at the back door and snapping pictures.

Plopping unceremoniously into a nearby chair in the front sitting room, Matthew ran his fingers through his hair, chagrined that it would be another long night. He listened impatiently as each member of the household was asked the same string of questions about where they were, what they heard, and at what times. They each provided the same basic story of being awakened by the crash or being awakened but they weren't sure after the fact by what. The 9-1-1 call had been placed at two-thirteen so that put the time of the crash shortly after two.

Both Jay and Elizabeth reported turning on lights upstairs when they heard the crash. The officers were speculating that had "sealed the deal," as the younger officer said, on the intruder deciding to leave the premises.

After the details had been sorted, the officers asked about finger printing everyone. Matthew and Cici both explained that theirs were already in the police database, Matthew's because of his concealed carry permit and a break in at his own house the spring before, and Cici's because of her profession. "Mine are likely the last ones on the doorknob, other than the intruders if he wasn't wearing gloves," said Matthew. "Because I locked up and double checked all of the doors before I went to bed."

Matthew heard Danbury's big black SUV arrive out front and he met him at the door. "Hey Doc. Show me," was all he said. Matthew led him back down the hallway to the kitchen.

After surveying the scene, Danbury stood back, staring pensively at the glass on the ceramic tile floor, around which they'd all been stepping as best they could. Then, he went outside onto the brick back patio and shone his flashlight up to where the floodlights had been and then down on the ground underneath. He did the same thing on the light fixtures on either side of the door and then shone the light carefully around the tiered patio before reentering the kitchen looking concerned.

"What?" asked Matthew.

"Somebody planned well. And executed well, up to a point. The floodlights were knocked out. Shot out, maybe. But not with anything high powered. Nothing that made a noise."

"You mean with something like a BB gun? It would just be a pop," said Matthew.

"That's possible. It would make a slight noise. But breaking glass makes more. The bulbs on either side of the door were removed. Those weren't broken out. They're missing. There's no glass outside. And they're not lying around anywhere."

"The intruder took them with him?"

"That's my operating assumption. So far," said Danbury. "And then the glass here on the door. It's double-paned. Both were cut with a heavy precision cutting tool. Probably a cutting tool with a suction cup in the center. Looks like they took the outer one. And the inner one went the wrong way. It fell into the house. Instead of being pulled out. Doesn't look like enough glass here. Not for both panes."

The older officer who had arrived earlier came into the room and introduced himself. Apparently, thought Matthew, not everyone on the Raleigh police force knew everyone else, but the guy knew Danbury without introduction. They discussed how to carefully clean up the glass and bag and tag it, though neither thought they would find prints on it, even if it could be reconstructed. But it might yield something useful. Sometimes, they agreed, they found unexpected things in the oddest of places.

The younger officer, he'd said, was in the car reporting in. After comparing notes on what they'd found so far, Danbury and the officer left the house together to make a complete sweep around the perimeter of it. Daylight was still several hours away but Danbury seemed unwilling to wait for it.

Matthew returned to the quiet tired-looking group in the sitting room and stifled a yawn as he realized that they weren't likely to get more sleep that night. He slid beside Cici into the huge chair with the ottoman and they snuggled together quietly with her head on his chest until Danbury returned.

"We found footprints," said Danbury. "It rained earlier. They're fresh in the mud. Made by a nondescript flat sole. Like those," said Danbury, pointing to Matthew's boat shoes. "What size do you wear?"

"They're twelve and a half," said Matthew.

"Can I borrow that?"

"You want my shoe?" asked Matthew.

"Just to compare. I'll bring it right back."

"Sure," said Matthew, reaching down to remove one and hand it over. He'd done odder things during investigations so why not, he reasoned.

"I'll be right back," said Danbury.

The room grew quiet and then the younger officer came back in through the front door with a bag and unpacked a digital fingerprint kit. He made his way around the room to each member of the Washburn family. As he was repacking the bag, Danbury returned with Matthew's shoe. "It's likely a man's shoe," he said to the Raleigh officers. "Smaller than a size twelve and a half. Maybe a ten or eleven. But a similar shoe sole. I got pictures. I'll share them."

"OK, we'll get them in the report," said the older officer.

"What time is your security company arriving?" Matthew asked Mrs. Washburn, thinking that it couldn't be soon enough for him. He wanted the professionals to take over.

"First thing this morning, at eight." she replied, looking truly exhausted. Her face was drained of all color, and she looked bedraggled.

"OK if Mrs. Washburn goes back up to bed for a few hours?" Matthew asked Danbury.

"Yeah, good idea."

"I don't know if I can sleep," she said, "But I can try. I know I need the rest, if nothing else."

Elizabeth rose to escort her mother out as Danbury stepped to the doorway. "Tell you what," he said. "Why don't you all go back to bed? I'll stay the rest of the night. I doubt anything else will happen tonight. But just in case." Turning to the two officers, he asked, "You're finished with all of them?"

"Yeah, we've got what information we can gather for now," said the older officer. "If you find anything else in the daylight, let us know."

"I'll do it," said Danbury, walking them to the door as Sophia and Jay both rose from their chairs and wordlessly followed them out into the foyer, heading for the staircase in the other direction.

"Are you sure you want to stay the night?" asked Matthew when Danbury returned.

"That chair looks good," he said, pointing to the one Cici and Matthew were in. "I can sleep on a rock. Trust me, I've done it."

Having heard a few of Danbury's stories about his days as a Marine in the middle east, Matthew was sure it was true. "Yeah, your credo is sleep when you can and eat when you can because you don't know when you'll have the chance do either again, right?"

"That's it," said Danbury.

Matthew checked his watch and decided that the two and a half hours he could still sleep might get him through his busy Wednesday schedule of back-to-back patients. It was the cold and flu season, after all, and even with the addition of Megan Sims and Sadie Peterson, the three doctors were still very busy. It was smart of their senior partner, Steven Garner, to have hired the PA in the spring, thought Matthew as he slid out of the chair and held his hand out to Cici pulling her out behind him.

"Thanks," said Matthew over his shoulder to Danbury as he and Cici followed the path of the others out into the foyer.

"I'll stay until the security team arrives," said Danbury. "I want to talk some specifics with them anyway."

"Thank you," Cici added, as they turned and headed toward the back hallway for what Matthew hoped would be the last time before turning his watch over to the professionals. "I really appreciate all you're doing for this family."

Matthew sincerely hoped his tired brain would stop turning all of the events of the night over and allow him to get those last two and a half hours of sleep.

16 ~ CHILL IN THE AIR

After showering, dressing, and packing his things Wednesday morning, Matthew joined two of the Washburn siblings, Cici, and Danbury at the dining room table at seven for breakfast. Mrs. Washburn sent her apologies and her thanks, Elizabeth explained, but she wouldn't be joining them and Sophia had claimed not to be on eastern time yet and wouldn't be making an appearance either.

Danbury had already piled his plate with eggs, sausage, and biscuits when Matthew arrived and he was quickly and systematically working his way through the contents of his plate. Matthew had thought that he could eat a lot – until he met Danbury. Nobody he had ever known ate as much or as fast as the tall, broad-shouldered homicide detective, he thought.

There was plenty of food on the table, so Matthew piled his plate, though not nearly as high, and thanked God for it before digging in.

Jay had been looking down at his plate since Matthew arrived and Elizabeth, he noticed, wasn't looking in Jay's direction. Wondering what he'd missed that had caused the definite chill between the siblings, Matthew smiled over at Cici and ate his breakfast quietly.

Checking his watch when his plate was empty, Danbury said, "I'm going to sweep the grounds. One more time. Now that the sun is up. Then, could I get a shower?"

When neither Elizabeth nor Jay looked up from their plates or responded, Cici piped up, "I'm sure you could use the one in the downstairs west wing where we have been staying."

Matthew glanced curiously at the two siblings, who still hadn't responded or looked up to acknowledge the discussion. He looked across at Cici who merely shrugged. Danbury nodded, took his plate into the kitchen, said he'd be back in a few minutes as he went down the hallway, and went out the front door to more thoroughly survey the property.

A gust of cold air blew through the house as the front door opened and closed reminding Matthew that somebody would have to oversee the glass in the back door being replaced. Mrs. Washburn, who had looked frail to begin with, had looked specter-like the night before. He was concerned about her well-being, wishing that in his medical capacity, he had asked her more questions. She didn't need to deal with anything else, he thought.

"Are you sticking around a while today?" Matthew asked Cici.

"I thought I would, just to try to be helpful if Mrs. Washburn needs anything. She mentioned something yesterday about picking up medications from the pharmacy if they couldn't deliver them today. I offered, so I suppose I'll at least wait until she gets up to determine how long I'll stay. I need to get back by the office at some point. Charles and Marshall flew back out for London this morning and I haven't even seen them since Saturday night at the gala."

Matthew was impressed that Cici had put the needs of Mrs. Washburn so high above those of her clients, and he determined to tell her so when they were alone. With the others at the table, he just said, "I should have asked Danbury if the security company will want any input on the back door glass being replaced. That will need to get done today, too, but maybe we could at least tape some plastic or something over the hole until then. Temperatures won't be nearly as warm as yesterday, and they're forecast to dip below freezing tonight."

"I can handle that so that you can get to work," said Cici, much to Matthew's amazement. Cici had historically been eager to get to her job and she wouldn't have let much get in the way of that.

"Elizabeth," Cici said, "Do you know where there might be some packaging tape? And maybe some paper bags or plastic ones?"

Being asked a direct question seemed to shake the young woman out of whatever trance she'd been in and she looked up and said,

"Packaging tape? There's probably some in the study. Or maybe out in the rec room."

"After breakfast, could you find it for me please?" prodded Cici.

Elizabeth produced an obligatory, "Sure," before she returned to staring at her plate. She'd been mostly moving her food around, Matthew noticed, and had eaten very little of it.

Matthew went back to his own plate and he and Cici munched and sipped their coffee in silence until Danbury returned. "We found all there was to be found last night," he said. "The guy came from the country club property. Into the back corner of the yard. Where you saw somebody before, Doc. Maybe they were staking things out then. I see no signs of hemlock. Nothing that resembles it."

"Do you think the intruder knows that the security company is coming in today? Is that why he chose last night? And what could he possibly have wanted?" asked Cici.

"Those are the right questions," said Danbury, scratching the stubble on his chin with his thumb. "If we can answer those, we'll get somewhere."

After determining from Danbury that the security company might have a recommendation on a company to replace the glass because they wouldn't likely do it themselves, Matthew went to retrieve his bags from the west wing.

Cici followed him down the hallway. "Matthew, do you want to have dinner tonight?"

"Honestly, Cees, if I can just get through the day, what I most want is to get something quick for dinner and then get in my own bed early. I'm pretty wiped out."

"OK, tomorrow night then? You could come over after work and we'll have a nice quiet evening together, just the two of us, without all of the hullabaloo that drives you nuts."

Matthew grinned down at her. "That sounds great. It's a date." He leaned down and kissed her, instantly feeling the tingle up his spine. "We'll talk later. Keep me posted on any new developments with the Washburn investigation from here and if I hear anything from Danbury, I'll do the same."

"OK, have a good day," she said, standing on tiptoe to kiss him one last time.

"You too, Cees. I'll talk to you later," he said before heading down the hallways and out the front door. The chill in the air was a brisk reminder that, despite the warmth of the day before, it was still December in North Carolina and Christmas was right around the corner.

Going through his mental Christmas checklist, Matthew warmed up his car and then made his way out through the Raleigh morning traffic. He had managed to get his tree up at home with the lights on a timer and he'd installed the automatic watering feature. He needed to check the reservoir on the device again when he got home. He still had a few presents to purchase, though he brought or shipped most of them home from his visit with Cici in England the previous summer. Some were very special, he thought, and he was anticipating the reaction of the recipients.

Not that she'd appreciate it as much now as in years to come, but from a gift shop across from the Canterbury Cathedral in Kent, he'd bought two beautiful little angel figurines to add to Angelina's collection of angels. Trite as it might be that he'd been contributing to the collection, he thought it was appropriate for his little niece whose nickname was Angel. He'd get her something she could play with as well, once he got her annual Christmas wish list from his sister.

His sister Monica was getting a pair of Hunter wellies that he'd shipped back for her. That was an easy one because she'd dropped every hint imaginable that there was "a cute pair of tall rain boots" that she'd love to have, specifically from London, in a size eight. He'd added a couple of pairs of tall Hunter socks to the purchase to add some splash to the basic boots. His mother Jackie was getting a lovely cashmere sweater. Though the cashmere itself was shipped into England from the Himalayan plateaus of China and Mongolia, Burberry was a well-known purveyor of beautiful cashmere clothing.

He had yet to purchase a present for Cici, though he knew exactly what he was going to give her. Planning to ask his father for some help in that department, Matthew knew that Joe Paine had a good friend from college who owned a long-standing family jewelry store in Ridge Woods. Over the years his dad had given his mom some beautiful jewelry from that store. Checking his watch, Matthew confirmed that it was Wednesday and his dad usually called to check on him mid-week. He made a mental note to contact Joc, his dad, if he didn't hear from him this week.

Nothing was wrapped and under the tree yet, he thought. He loved to see the packages sparkling under the tree and normally they were there early in December after he got his tree up and decorated. He still had a couple of weeks, he reasoned. It was only the eleventh of December, but if this year was like every other, the next fourteen days would fly by.

*****

Matthew had made it through that Wednesday morning running on caffeine and he'd lost count of the cups of coffee he'd consumed. He had just gotten off of the weekly call with his dad, who had sounded somewhat reluctant to agree to set up an appointment with his friend at the jewelry store for them Saturday morning, but he did agree. As Matthew was picking up the lunch he'd ordered from Trina, the office manager at the front lobby of his office, his phone vibrated in his pocket.

"Hey Doc," he heard Danbury say as he pulled out his phone and clicked to accept the call. He juggled the phone and bag of food as he made his way through the double doors and back down the main hall to his office. "I have some photos I need you to look at. And Cici too. What are your plans after work?"

Realizing that his evening plans had just been shattered, Matthew sighed, "Honestly, I was planning on a quiet evening at home and an early bed time," he replied. "What do you need?"

"I have photos of the wait staff. From the catering company Saturday night. Can you look through them? See if you recognize and remember any of them?"

"I can try. But to what end?"

"You know the woman who was killed? The one who called in sick. And then showed up anyway."

"Yeah. You're saying that she was killed, meaning that you're sure now that it was murder and not suicide?" said Matthew, setting his lunch bag on the floor outside his office to pull his office key from his pocket and unlock the door.

"Nearly positive. Ligature marks don't match. Looks like she was strangled first. And then hung. To make it look like a suicide. There was a note. Hastily scrawled and short. Handwriting analysis is due back soon. Nobody we've interviewed who knew her thought it was hers. We're looking into her background. But it doesn't look like suicide. Looks more like a clumsy attempt to cover up a murder of passion. Not a planned murder. Not carefully staged to look like a suicide."

"Huh," was all Matthew said as he retrieved the bag from the floor, closing the door with his foot, and plopped his lunch on his desk.

After a moment he said, "Why did you want us to look at pictures then?"

"Remember the second staff member? The guy who called in sick? Like the woman, it was at the last minute."

"Right, the guy who Roger the elevator operator couldn't positively identify. What about that?"

"We wanted to question the guy. In connection with both murders. He's missing. Nobody seems to know where he is. The woman showed up at the event. After calling in sick. I think he did too. I want to know if you saw him. It won't take long. There are only ten pictures. You just look through them. And point out who you remember seeing. The catering company manager hasn't been much help. I gather she was too busy to notice much. Abby is looking through them. As are the partners from the firm."

"I can try," was all that Matthew could promise. "I tend to check out in crowds, so I'm not sure how much help I'll be. Cici will likely be more help than I will. And probably Abby. She worked closest with the catering company anyway."

"Could Cici meet us? Maybe for dinner at Peak Eats?" Peak Eats was the little diner and soda shop that had evolved from a historic apothecary with a soda fountain in downtown Peak. It was just down Winston Avenue from Matthew's office and very accessible to him, though not as much so to Danbury and Cici.

"I can ask, unless you'd rather."

Danbury just laughed. "I've seen her look at you. If she'd agree for anybody, it would be you. And I've seen you look at her too, Doc."

Matthew cut him off before he could say anything further, "I'll call her and see if she can meet us at Peak Eats. How about six? Does that work?"

"Yeah, see you there at six."

Before Danbury could disconnect, Matthew asked, "Hey, how did the security team work out this morning?"

"They're pros. I didn't have to say a word. I left them to it."

"Great to hear that!" said Matthew. "I'll feel a lot better with a professional team in charge there until all of this is sorted out."

"Yeah, me too, Doc. See you at six." As Matthew was well accustomed to, Danbury was gone without any formal goodbye. Putting his phone down and opening the bag, Matthew was determined to at least eat his lunch before he called Cici to ask about meeting up for dinner. He was sure she'd agree, though he wasn't sure what she'd think of him agreeing to meet with Danbury after he'd put her off for dinner. But then, one was a quick working dinner and the other was not at all that.

He'd just downed the last of his sub sandwich when his phone went off and he saw that it was Cici, saving him the effort of contacting her. "Hey Cees," he said as he clicked to answer it.

"Hey, I just left the Washburns and came by the office. We're being called in this evening to look at pictures of the catering staff to see if we can identify them. Do you know what that's about?"

"Ah, you're doing that there? Danbury just called and asked me the same thing. He did explain though."

"Enlighten me?"

Matthew explained what Danbury had told him just moments before and that Cici could choose to have dinner with them instead.

"I can't," she said. "Mr. Markham has called an official meeting with all of us who were there. All we were told was that we'd meet in the big conference room where the gala was held at five-thirty and be pulled out, one at a time, into one of the smaller rooms to look at pictures of the staff. The meeting invitation was mandatory, not optional. Maybe you can join us here?"

With one knee bouncing in concentration under his desk, Matthew took a deep breath and then blew it out, "Sure, Cees, if you'd rather I do that, I can meet you at your office. Say five-fifteen?" he asked, realizing that was cutting it really close behind his last patient on his schedule for the day.

"Sounds good."

"I'll text Danbury and tell him. Maybe he can just meet us there too. If he wants to be directly involved in seeing all of the reactions, that's his best bet anyway."

"True. OK, good."

Just as he was about to say good-bye, she said, "Oh, and Matthew, remember the glum breakfast this morning?"

"You mean when Mrs. Washburn and Sophia weren't at the table and Elizabeth and Jay weren't talking to or looking at each other? Oh yeah, I noticed a definite chill."

"They were apparently up after we went back to bed this morning discussing some of the arrangements for the funeral and the security team. They had a big disagreement. Mr. Washburn might not be cremated after all, but it sounds like he'll be released to the family on Monday. Services will be next week sometime. I'll keep you posted when I get the details."

"OK, Cici, I'll be there for you whenever that happens."

"I know you will. You are my rock, Matthew. I love you."

"I love you too," he answered before they disconnected. Her rock, she'd called him. His eyebrow raised involuntarily as he turned that over in his mind. Cici had been fiercely independent every moment of every day since he'd met her. He did love her fiercely but was it enough?

Putting those thoughts aside, Matthew saw a text come in from Danbury, *"Change of plans, Doc. Law firm agreed to request to talk to all staff. To view pictures. And be questioned. Five-thirty. Tonight. Can you meet there?"*

"*Sure,*" Matthew texted back.

"*Good. All reactions at once.*"

"*I'll be there.*"

As Matthew put his phone back in his pocket, threw his trash away, and picked up his notebook computer to begin his afternoon round of patients, he was thinking how quickly plans changed and how flexible he was having to be these days. Feeling his phone vibrate in his pocket, he pulled it out just before locking his office door to see that Danbury had sent back a single word.

"*OK,*" the text said.

17 ~ REACTIONS

Matthew rushed through switching his lab coat for his blazer, stashing his computer in his satchel, snatching up the satchel, and locking his office to slip out for the evening without updating his patient charts or checking his roster of patients for the next morning. Resolving to do that as soon as he could get away from the gathering downtown and get home, he stepped out the back door that was nearest his office. He slid into his Honda Element, which he'd retrieved from his house that morning when he'd gone by to feed Max.

The drive into Raleigh took him over a half hour and he was rushing into Cici's office building through the front lobby entrance when he noticed the huge Christmas tree to his right with the ornaments from around Raleigh and the state of North Carolina. Glancing around, Matthew saw that the lobby was deserted, so he circled the tree twice until he found one of the ornaments he was searching for. It was around the back of the tree, hanging high, just barely within his arm's reach. If he'd been any shorter, he'd have been unable to reach it without risking toppling the tree.

Carefully removing it, he happily switched it with the ornament from the school that was the rival to the one his family cheered for. That ornament he moved to the back of the tree as high as he could reach up it. Red, the color of the big university that his family supported, was a better color to be front and center on a Christmas tree anyway, he reasoned. He couldn't find the ornament, which he assumed would be orange, for the school that he and Cici had attended, but he resolved to address that issue later when he had more time. He knew that he needed to get upstairs. Feeling slightly lighter after the ornament switch, Matthew made his way across the lobby.

After waiting at the desk for a concierge to return and give him a temporary badge for the elevator to access the top floors, he scanned the badge and punched the elevator button. He felt himself shooting quickly upward without interruption. The doors opened on the thirtieth floor, the third from the top floor, and he stepped out and headed for Cici's office.

She was just locking up her office door when he met her in the hallway. "Oh, there you are," she said. "I was afraid you wouldn't make it after all." She stood on tiptoe to give him a quick kiss before they circled back to the elevators and rose, stopping to take on two partners from the floor above, to the top floor.

As they stepped off the elevator, Matthew looked around assessing the transformation. Gone was the glitz and glamour of Saturday night. In its stead, the long board room table in the center of the room was uncovered, unadorned, and surrounded by professional rolling office chairs. The large room had smaller desks and chairs, partially obscured by potted plants and partitions, now arranged around the periphery. The only remnant of the party that gave any indication that there had been a huge Christmas gala event was the large tree which still stood proudly glittering in one corner.

Already getting seated around the table were some of the partners, senior and junior, including the arrogant Kennedy Reynolds, Matthew noticed. Many of them he had met at one time or another, but it was a large gathering so there were still some that Matthew didn't know. The firm employed an array of attorneys with a variety of specialties so he was quite sure that he hadn't met all of them. Several of the people at the table Matthew remembered as being spouses or significant others he'd met at the gala event. Two police officers sat at one end of the table with Simon Markham and Jonathan Denton on either side of them and they were talking quietly.

As Matthew and Cici were getting settled, the elevator opened again and Danbury and three others stepped off and found places at the table. Matthew recognized only one of them, the one he'd hoped to avoid. Danbury sat beside Matthew and, much to Matthew's annoyance, Mitch Moorestrom slid into the chair on the other side of Cici and greeted her a little too warmly and familiarly in Matthew's opinion.

Over the year that Matthew and Cici had been apart before she'd left for London, she had casually dated Moorestrom. Their relationship was more in the way of having a second to social functions than anything serious, at least as she had explained it. But still, thought Matthew, there were plenty of other chairs at the extremely long table that were not occupied.

After exchanging pleasantries, they all turned expectantly to the other end of the table. Simon Markham, the senior most partner, rose to address the group.

"It looks like nearly everyone is here, so let's get started. First of all, I want to thank you for your time this evening. I have assured the police department of our full cooperation with their investigation into the murder of our senior partner, colleague, and dear friend, Jamison Washburn." Markham paused reverently before continuing, "We'll talk more about arrangements for his memorial service and our own personal remembrances later, but I want to use the officers' time judiciously this evening."

"This is Officer Atkins," said Markham, motioning to the officer on his left. "And this is Officer Garrison," he motioned to the officer to the right of Jonathan Denton. "They will be pulling you each, in turn, aside to ask you some very specific questions about your experience at the gala event Saturday evening, including people you might or might not have seen there. It goes without saying that I expect your full cooperation with the officers in answering their questions and volunteering any other information that you might deem helpful to the ongoing investigation. Jonathan and I have already answered everything they've asked and tried to recall the details of the evening to the best of our ability."

"Also, we will have some refreshments brought in shortly. Nothing fancy, just some trays of sub sandwiches, chips, and soft drinks as a thank you, particularly at dinner time, for being here and answering questions this evening. Officer Atkins?"

As Officer Atkins was getting to his feet, Matthew wished he'd had something other than a sub sandwich for lunch. He figured he'd partake of the refreshments anyway to save him time when he got home. That way, he could take care of Max, update and check his patient charting, and maybe still manage to get to bed early. He stifled a yawn as the police officer addressed the group.

"Thank you, sir. I see Homicide Detective Warren Danbury is also here," he nodded in their direction. "He might have more questions when Garrison and I have finished with ours. Thank you for your time and patience with this process. We'll get through it as quickly as possible. We'll be calling you over to talk to one or the other of us in those workspaces in the corner." Without further preamble, he began with the list of names he'd been supplied, calling the first two people over to two of the corner desks. Each desk had chairs positioned behind sectioned dividers and plants along the outer edge to at least partially screen the occupants from the eyes in the rest of the room.

Danbury rose and joined the two uniformed officers, hovering between the two desk areas of adjoining workspaces. The murmur of voices, Matthew first thought, precluded his hearing what was happening in the corner but then he realized that white noise was being piped in on a speaker system and he yawned, not bothering to stifle it this time. Some of his favorite naps as a child had been with a fan running in the summer and he thought he could easily put his head on the table and take one now.

Cici reached for his hand under the table and he smiled at her, trying to enjoy the moment. They sat quietly, hand in hand, until a disturbance from the middle section of the table caught Matthew's attention. Not surprisingly, it was from the group of people seated around Kennedy Reynolds. Above the din of voices, Matthew heard Reynolds loudly exclaim, looking pointedly down the table at them, "The alleged altercation in the stairwell!"

"But we heard that you hit him," said someone Matthew didn't recognize on the other side of Reynolds.

"Did you now? And from whom might you have heard that?" he asked. "If there were an altercation in the stairwell, it must have been properly witnessed to be anything other than defamation of character, both libelous and slanderous. Has anyone reported witnessing such an act, first hand?" His patrician face was twisted cruelly as he stared, pointedly, down his nose at Cici.

"Asked and answered," said the guy who had apparently made the accusation, as if he were in a court room.

"Defamation of character is an actionable offense," continued Reynolds, still staring at Cici, daring her to speak up in front of the table of her peers and superiors. "One would have to be absolutely certain of precisely what one saw in order to avoid a slanderous statement or libelous allegation. I dare say that no one at this table saw such a thing nor would they want to risk reputation or disbarment to assert otherwise."

They hadn't actually seen Reynolds deck Washburn, Matthew realized. They saw the result and he'd ducked the blow as he was opening the door, but they had missed seeing the owner of the fist as it was flying and the actual connection to the face. Still, it was more than arrogantly brazen to challenge them on that technicality, he thought, and he knew that Cici was fuming.

Matthew supportively squeezed Cici's hand under the table. A pall fell over the room and nobody spoke, even in murmurs or whispers, as they all stared between Cici and Reynolds. The gauntlet had been thrown and Matthew could see the angry color rise in Cici's face as she stared coldly back at Reynolds. She had initially wisely chosen, probably against every fiber of her being to do otherwise, to remain silent.

More powerful, in Matthew's opinion, than the forceful bluster of Reynolds' words farther down the table were Cici's when she chose her moment to interject softly into the silence so that most of the occupants of the table leaned in to hear her, "If you're addressing me, Mr. Reynolds, the relevant discussion about what I might have seen, heard, or suspected, I have already had with the police. Nothing more need be discussed in this forum."

The standoff of intense stares between the two of them was interrupted as the elevator doors opened and carts containing platters of sandwiches, condiments, and chips were wheeled in. This was not, Matthew noticed, the catering company that had served them the night of the gala event. The three servers loading platters onto the table had logos on their matching golf shirts, but they were a swirl of overlapping letters and not the lion's head.

"Please, help yourselves. The catering staff can explain what sort of subs are available and they will restock any that run low," said Markham from the other end of the table, choosing to ignore the standoff. "As you know, there are more drinks, cups, and ice in the break room if these bottled soft drinks don't appeal to you," he added, waving toward to the wall to his right, which was directly in front of Matthew and Cici.

The wall had a long pass-through window in it with a narrow counter running the length of the outside of it. The shutters above the counter had been closed and the counter draped with greenery Saturday night, Matthew remembered. He hadn't realized that there was a break room back there but neither had he paused to consider what would be passed through the shutters, had they been open then. He raised an eyebrow speculatively about that. Had the catering company used that room Saturday night? He tried to remember if they'd been coming and going from any particular direction but he couldn't recall.

Cici and Matthew had each eaten one small section of a sub sandwich when her name was called and she stood and walked over to look at the pictures and answer their questions. Mainly, Matthew knew, it was about the pictures because she had answered endless questions already, as had he.

When she returned to the table, his name was called and he made his way over to the corner. Danbury explained, as Matthew had expected, that all they needed from him was to look at the pictures. He'd been on the scene that night and already thoroughly questioned. "His responses were part of the initial report. The one you already have," he added to the officer behind the desk on the other side of which Matthew was motioned to sit.

Danbury, who was still hovering between the officers, handed Matthew a notebook and asked him to take his time looking through the pictures in it. All were in clear plastic sleeves, easily flipped through. Some were headshots that were clear while others were grainier more distant shots.

One face he knew well, and that was Timothy, the guy who had summoned him and Dr. Miller after finding Jamison Washburn draped across his desk. He pointed out three others that looked somewhat familiar. One of them was Margaret, the manager of the catering service, and another was one of the women who was circulating with cocktail trays of hors d'oeuvres. Both of them were quickly dismissed like Timothy. When Matthew pointed out the next picture, that one immediately caught their attention.

"You saw this guy?" asked Danbury, leaning over the desk and tapping his finger on the picture that Matthew had indicated.

"I can't be positive, but I thought I saw a guy who looked like that."

"When and where?"

"It was right after we'd come through the stairwell door. I was paying more attention at that point due to the 'alleged altercation,'" he said with finger quotes. "The one we had just witnessed in the stairwell."

Danbury looked at him strangely but didn't ask about the air quotes. Instead, he said, "You saw him up here? On this floor?"

Matthew nodded, "If it's the same guy, yes, over by the elevator as we came through the stairwell door."

"Anything else can you tell us about him?"

Matthew thought back to Saturday night and tried to remember why he'd even noticed the guy to begin with. A photographic memory wasn't one of his gifts, but he finally recalled the reason that the guy stood out. "He looked disheveled and ill at ease."

"How do you mean?" asked Officer Atkins, leaning in from across the table.

"The other servers seemed calm and perfectly put together, the women's hair pinned back neatly, shirts tucked in and pressed, vests nicely fitted and buttoned up tightly. His shirt sleeves were wrinkled and one side of his white shirt was visible between the vest and the top of his pants as if it weren't tucked all the way in. His hair wasn't perfectly combed into place either and he seemed jittery, like maybe the elevator wasn't getting there fast enough for him or something. But he couldn't have gotten back on the elevator or Roger would have recognized his picture. So maybe that wasn't it."

Matthew's foot was tapping in rapid rhythm and his knee was bouncing behind the desk as he was concentrating intently on the image that was slightly hazy now. An eyebrow raised of its own volition as he considered what he'd seen and tried to recall more details.

"I didn't see him full in the face," began Matthew as he tried to recall what he had seen. "I only saw about three quarters of it. But he doesn't really resemble any of the others, does he?" he asked, flipping back through the pictures, looking again at each one. "He was gaunter looking, somehow. Lanky, wiry, more angular. He had a long face like in his picture and a long torso, which isn't visible. Or maybe that was just the untucked shirt. I'm not positive it was the same guy, but the impression fits. Cici didn't see him?"

"She didn't point him out."

"She was probably too busy searching the crowd for the two clients she's been working with in London to notice him. She was scanning the room for them as soon as we walked in. What about Kennedy Reynolds? He says he went straight from the stairwell to the elevator, right? That would have been just moments before we entered from the stairwell and passed the elevator, so Reynolds could have walked right by the guy."

"We'll call him next," said Officer Atkins to Garrison who had joined them at the table. "Let's move him up our list."

"Thank you for your time. You're free to go now," said Officer Atkins. "Just let us know if you think of anything else," he added, handing Matthew a card.

"No problem. Danbury knows where to find me," said Matthew, jovially as he stood. Rounding the partition, he noticed Mitch Moorestrom leaning a little too far over into Cici's personal space to suit him, with his arm around the back of her chair and talking animatedly about something. Taking a deep breath and blowing it out slowly, he reminded himself that though he and Cici certainly acted like were in a committed relationship again, technically they were not yet.

"Are you ready to go?" he asked Cici, approaching the table. "They said we could leave after they talked to us."

"They told me that too," said Cici. "I was just waiting on you to get back. Did you want another section of the sub sandwich?"

"Maybe one more for the road," agreed Matthew, sliding back into his seat and pulling another section of the turkey and provolone on whole wheat out of the pile and onto a paper plate. "Did you get another one?"

"One was enough for me, but I knew you'd need more. Want to place any bets on Danbury cleaning up whatever is left over?" she asked, conspiratorially.

"I'm not betting against that one," he swallowed and answered with a chuckle.

As he walked Cici out and down to her rental car, she was ranting and venting about Kennedy Reynolds. "He's the most vain and arrogant man I've ever encountered and he was so cool and calm, challenging me as if scolding a child in front of the whole office, daring me to talk about what we witnessed in the stairwell, something that he himself perpetrated. He's an assailant at the very least, and most likely a murderer! A murderer, Matthew, and he was challenging me to make me back down from my statement that he'd assaulted Jamison Washburn! How dare he sit there so smugly! Literally thinking that he's getting away with murder!"

Matthew certainly didn't disagree with her. He just walked along beside her as she held onto his arm and ranted while he nodded in unspoken agreement. The man was, as Cici said, some piece of work. And, like her, Matthew couldn't imagine why the senior partners had brought him in except that, as she explained, he did get the results they wanted on the cases he handled. That, Matthew supposed, made up for all of the arrogant bluster at least in the minds of the senior partners. But why they allowed him to stay, now that he was under serious scrutiny for the murder of one of their own, that he couldn't begin to explain.

"I detest that man with great loathing, redundant as that is. He's incredibly rude, obnoxious, and grandiose!" she summarized, beginning to wind down a bit. "I wish he were merely pretentious, like some of the new monied clients we deal with, but he isn't. He truly has old family money, so why does he feel the need to flaunt it?"

When she took a momentary breath, Matthew interjected, "I was proud of you, Cees. The way you handled him, that whole situation, was perfect. You didn't raise your voice and you didn't challenge him. You diffused the situation while still holding your ground. That was impressive."

She just looked up at him and smiled brightly. "Thanks, Matthew. That means a lot."

Cici had parked in the parking garage beneath the building. After tucking her safely into the rental car, ensuring that it started and that she was on her way, he walked out to the street and down to the parking lot where he'd parked his Element. Matthew pulled the collar of his blazer up closer around his neck and stuffed his hands into his pockets. He hadn't taken an overcoat into the building and the temperature had dropped considerably while he'd been inside. A stiff breeze just added to the chilly evening.

The Christmas lights were nice, he thought, as he walked along the sidewalk. He was whistling to himself until he realized what he'd been whistling was *The Twelve Days of Christmas*. He wasn't sure that song would ever be the same for him after the weekend events. Like the reliable champ he'd always bragged about it being, when he reached the Element, climbed in and turned the key in the ignition, it started up immediately.

An uneventful drive back to Peak was a most welcome respite from the usual traffic on the cold Wednesday night, though it wasn't officially winter yet. Matthew had seen none of his neighbors out and about and assumed that they were all hunkered down inside where it was warm for the evening. After pulling his Element into the garage and clicking the button to close the door behind him against the chill, he slipped into his house, locked the door, and set the security alarm.

Max met him at the door, rubbing up against his legs, so Matthew plopped his satchel on the end of his leather sofa and scooped up the big cat, scratching him behind his ears for a few minutes before returning to the kitchen to refresh his food and water bowls.

Deciding to get comfortable before attacking the work he'd left unfinished earlier, Matthew trundled down the hallway to his bedroom. The bags he'd brought from the Washburn house were still on the floor in his bedroom where he'd dumped them that morning and he nudged them into the closet to deal with later. Donning his favorite flannel sleep pants and a soft T-shirt, he fought the urge to climb into his comfy bed but went instead back out to the desk in his living room and fired up his computer to get his work done.

A glass of wine and an hour with his computer later, Matthew was beyond yawning and had moved on to bleary-eyed. He shuffled down the hallway and barely managed to brush his teeth and wash his face before collapsing into his bed and dropping into a deep sleep. Even as concerned as he'd been about the recent murders and his patient load this time of year, if he dreamed of anything at all, he was unaware of it.

18 ~ Dinner dance

After a long day in the office on Thursday, Matthew arrived at Cici's house in Quarry five minutes early and was surprised to smell both something sumptuous in the way of dinner emanating from the kitchen and a strong evergreen fragrance, the source of which he couldn't pinpoint.

"Oh, good, you're here!" said Cici, meeting Matthew at the door and stating the obvious as he walked in. She raised to her tiptoes to give him a quick kiss and he leaned over to her. "The chicken cacciatore is nearly ready. We're having it over risotto with a salad. Would you pour us some wine?" she said, as she turned and went back into the kitchen.

"Sure," said Matthew as he entered the kitchen behind her and froze in his tracks at the domestic scene. He wasn't sure which surprised him more, that Cici had apparently cooked for him or that she'd worn an apron while doing so. Their usual dinners were either take-out from their favorite Italian restaurant or sushi or wraps and salads. Cici had gone to a lot more trouble and expended effort cooking his dinner. He was impressed.

Pulling a bottle of pinot noir from the wine rack hanging above the wine cooler that was built in under her counter and extracting two glasses from the cabinet above, he poured them each a glass. "That smells delicious, Cees. I can't believe you went to so much trouble to cook dinner."

Cici rose to her tiptoes to kiss Matthew and he leaned over to get within reach, pulled her in close, and kissed her with pent-up passion.

Afterward he was struggling to remember what he had been thinking about. "Where's the nice fresh evergreen smell coming from?" he finally managed to ask.

"I know you love the smell of Christmas trees, so I got candles that I thought smelled as real as they come," she motioned back to her sitting area through which he'd just come. "I lit two of them on the mantle in there."

"It does smell nice. Almost like Christmas should smell," he teased.

Cici just rolled her eyes, smiling up at him as he handed her a glass of wine and she took a sip. He felt his stomach rumble in response when she set the wine glass aside and lifted the lid on the fancy frying oven, stirring the chicken gently before replacing the lid. "I'm declaring it done," she said.

Matthew set the table in her little eating nook while she scooped out parmesan risotto onto their plates and then added the chicken cacciatore atop it. She'd made a nice vinaigrette dressing for the salad, he noticed, as she handed him the cruet and he added that to the table along with the salt and pepper grinders. They sat down opposite each other, Cici beaming across at him, proud of her culinary accomplishments.

"I know you'd have loved bread and whipped butter with this. But I'm trying not to gain five pounds while I'm home over the holidays," she said. "Unlike you, I cannot eat everything in sight and not gain weight."

"It doesn't need bread," Matthew said honestly.

"Will you bless it?" she asked.

Pleasantly surprised, Matthew just said, "Sure." They bowed their heads and he made certain to bless the hands that prepared the meal, as he'd heard his grandfather do so many times over the years at family gatherings. They chatted amicably, munching through their salads as the main course cooled to a palatable temperature on their plates on the counter.

"I've got it," Matthew said as he rose and cleared the salad bowls and dressing from the table, bringing back the plates still steaming slightly with the chicken cacciatore. All conversation ceased as they dived in, though Cici laughed at Matthew who was moaning softly as he ate.

"That's amazing, Cees," he finally managed to say.

"I'm glad you like it, but I'd rather hear you moan over other things," she said meaningfully.

The topic that he'd been avoiding, the one they'd been dancing around since she'd been home, was out in the open. It had reared its head again. It wasn't at all that he didn't want her. He was fighting a constant battle not to sweep her off her feet and carry her up the stairs to her bedroom and he told her as much.

"Then why don't you just stop fighting and do it?" she asked pointedly.

He took a deep breath and tried to calm his nerves before he responded. He knew he couldn't fight for them both and he was struggling to control himself. "Because that's never been anything casual for me, Cees. I can't just sweep you off your feet before you fly out again in a few weeks, not knowing if we can work through all of our issues when you get back."

"I long for you when I'm gone. And it's just as bad or worse when I'm here!" she said, standing and flinging her cloth napkin into her vacated chair. "And it's like we've been tap dancing around this issue of intimacy and we need to get it out in the open and address it. I know you have high moral standards and usually it's one of the things I love about you. But right now, Matthew Landon Paine, it's driving me nuts!"

If she weren't so angry, he'd have laughed at how cute she was when she stood there, one hand on her hip, calling him by his full name. Instead, in an attempt to diffuse the situation, he stood, threw his napkin in his chair, and said, "I know, Cecelia Lindley Patterson, but I'd like a little help here because I can't fight us both off and I don't want to get completely involved with you until I know that we're fully back in this for good, for the long haul. I can't go through a break up with you again, Cici, I just can't."

"Don't mock me! And why would you think you'd need to go through a breakup again? I have no intention of breaking things off with you if we can get it back together!"

"We didn't intend to the last time," he retorted.

"Why can't we just agree to that and work through our issues? I've been trying so hard!"

Realization dawned. He had been afraid of the changes he'd seen in her, the compassion for the Washburns, the willingness to help. Was it, he wondered, because she was trying too hard to change for him? He hadn't had the time to slow down and ponder what was bothering him about their situation, but there it was. It was plain to him now.

"I feel like we're in this intricate dance where we take one step forward and two back, Matthew, and I don't want to do that anymore. I want to be all in," she said as his thoughts continued to whirl.

"Cees," he said, as he was quickly thinking through how to broach the underlying issue that had been bothering him, but that he was just figuring out himself. "I have seen changes in you. You've been more like when we first met, the woman I fell in love with in the first place those nearly seven years ago, caring for the Washburns and wanting to help them. Somewhere in law school it was like you hardened, became competitive and distant. Maybe because you thought you had to be with all of the stiff competition for bar exam results and placement afterward. I don't know why, but I thought that was it. That was for good. That was who you'd become. And if it is, it is. I don't want you changing for me or trying to be something that you're not just to please me."

"What? Who do you think you're talking to?" Her voice rose indignantly. "You know me better than that, Matthew! You do! I am exactly who I am and I'm not trying to change that to suit you or any other man! I thought caring for the Washburns was the right thing to do and I knew you'd be all in because you genuinely care about people, but how dare you accuse me of pandering to you! How dare you!"

"Cici," he said, stepping toward her. "That's not what I meant."

"No?" she asked, stepping back, "Because that's exactly what you just said!"

"I just mean that I don't want you to marry me with the expectation that we're going to have children if that's not really what you want. I don't want you to resent me or them if you have them and wonder what your life could have been like if you hadn't settled. Settled for me. Settled for a quieter life than you've wanted for the past few years. I don't want to be part of your 'settled for' life if you want more, no matter how much we love each other."

"Oh," she said, more calmly in the wake of his raw admission.

"When you get back from London for good, if you still feel the way you do right now, and if we resolve the issues between us, the big ones, then we'll work on it. I mean, there are the small issues like the fact that I love live Christmas trees and you think they're too messy. We can compromise on those."

Cici nodded her agreement as Matthew continued, "But there are still some pretty big life issues that we don't agree on. I want a family. I want a quieter lifestyle. You have said you never wanted children and you love being in the middle of the glitz and glamour, at least in Raleigh, and sometimes you make forays into the New York scene. You've talked about wanting to move there. I don't want to move to New York. Ever. Visiting is fine, but I'd be miserable trying to live there."

"We don't have to move to New York, Matthew. I'm happy in North Carolina. Really, I am. And maybe I can commit to children. Eventually." After a moment, she added pensively, "But I'm scared to have children."

"What?" he asked, not understanding what she was saying at all.

"I like my body the way it is. And it'll never be this way again if I have children. Especially yours! I'm more than a foot shorter than you are. You're six-foot-three and, well, not so tiny. Your Mom is about nine inches taller than I am, so she managed just fine. Didn't you say that you weighed nearly ten pounds when you were born?"

"Something like that. But at least I don't have huge bones like Danbury, Cees, so that should be some consolation," he said, teasingly, pulling her to him and holding her there.

"Maybe we could adopt?" she asked playfully, calming considerably and sounding reasonable again.

"These are the things that we need to figure out," he finally said, seriously, with his head over hers, which was tucked under his chin into his chest. "I don't want to get intimately involved with you only to lose you again. If we get back together, it's going to be for keeps. Expect rings and proposals and wedding bells, consolidating households and yes, eventually, children. That's what I want most, Cecelia Patterson, and I want all of that with you. But you have to want it too or it'll never work. You'll resent me and the demands I've made on you. And I don't want that. I don't want you to feel forced into doing anything you don't really want to do, no matter how much you love me."

"I do, you know," she said, pulling back and staring up at him. "I do truly love you."

"I truly love you too," he said, as he bent and she stood on tiptop and reached up to kiss him. He felt the heat go down his spine and he didn't know how much longer he could maintain control. Pulling back, she did it for him. She tucked her head back under his chin, wrapped her arms around him, and clung tightly.

He wrapped his arms around her and they held each other, locked in an embrace that both seemed reluctant to release lest they never have it again. At least, that's how Matthew felt and he was attributing the same motivation to Cici as she clung to him too.

Finally, she broke the spell, pulling back to look up into his face as she asked, "Rings and proposals and wedding bells when I get back, huh? So that's not what I'm getting for Christmas?"

He laughed at her upturned earnest face that he saw the amusement in, "That's not what you're getting for Christmas."

"Have you bought it yet?" she asked, still playfully. "My Christmas present?"

"No, but I've picked it out. I just need to go pick it out more specifically."

"Well, that's cryptic," she said, still smiling up at him.

"And that's all you're going to get. No shaking packages, no guessing what it is, no twenty questions about it."

"Harsh!" she quipped. "Would I do that?"

"If you thought you could get away with it."

"You're right," she smiled broadly up at him. "I absolutely would. So not even a tiny hint? I'll give you a hint about yours. I've already bought it. I just need to wrap it and get it under the tree." Cici's tree was a fake one in her living room with white tips on the branches as if it had snowed on it. It was pretty, Matthew thought, as far as fake Christmas trees went. And it definitely suited Cici.

He pulled her left hand up to his face, absently, as he was thinking about the future and kissed her ring finger. "No hints," he said. "Not for either of us. That spoils the surprise, the magic of Christmas."

"You're such a kid when it comes to Christmas, Matthew," she said and he couldn't begin to disagree with her. He knew it was the truth.

Then, she grew serious as she said, "There is something else that you should know, Matthew."

Bracing himself, he asked, "What's that?"

"You're right that I hardened when I was in law school. And it's not as if I'm unaware of it. I'm very aware and I want to try to explain it to you. Let's sit," she said, pulling him into her living room. "I'll clean that up later," she said, motioning to the kitchen that they were leaving uncleaned.

That was new, thought Matthew. She usually was set on cleaning up any and every mess immediately. "I'll help you clean up after we talk then. It's only fair. You did all of the cooking."

"Deal," she said as she sunk into her plush sofa and patted a spot for him next to her.

He sunk in, putting his arm around her, and she leaned into his chest. "Just gathering my thoughts," she said after a moment and then leaned back to look up at him.

"I know this might be hard to explain because you're both male and so very comfortable in your own skin with nothing to prove to anyone." While he didn't think that last bit was entirely true, neither did he interrupt her train of thought as she continued. "The legal world has made great progress over the past twenty years or so but it's still a man's world. And it's hard for a woman, at least it was hard for me, to find my voice in it. But I'm finally getting to that point, finding my voice, finding my style, breaking stride in it."

Taking a deep breath, she continued, "I really appreciated what you said about the way I handled Kennedy Reynolds last night, because I was proud of me too. Many of my male counterparts bluster and raise their voices and are entirely intimidating in that process. That works for them. Women get called nasty names when they do that and it's not nearly as effective anyway. You know me, Matthew. I'm not averse to having people call me nasty names. But my effectiveness, that I can't forgo. I'm learning that I don't have to be hard and harsh to be effective. I can be softer and quieter and sometimes, like last night, that packs a bigger punch. Does that make sense?" she asked, looking up and searching his face earnestly with her big brown eyes.

"It does. I understand what you're saying, but I'm surprised to hear you say it."

"Why?"

"Because you've always packed a wallop," he said, smiling down at her. "You're intelligent and well-spoken and rarely do you mince words. You've always been a force to be reckoned with, in or out of the courtroom."

"Thank you. I appreciate your vote of confidence. I know I became demanding, expecting everything to be done my way and I'm sorry for that. I am happy that you stood up to me, even tempered as you are, and as much as you loved me when we broke up. You put your foot down and I'm glad that you did. As painful as that was, it was all part of the journey to get here."

Matthew nodded, surprised at this admission but not wanting to disrupt her thought process by interjecting.

"It's just that I was trying too hard to be that force. I had to find my own voice, my own style, to be fully confident in being effective. I started to find it before I left for London. Remember when I questioned that thug who locked me in the frunk of my Porsche?"

"I do. Very well. That was a gutsy move," he said. He was amused that she'd adopted the slang for the front trunk of her Porsche that she had previously said was a ridiculous word, but he refrained from pointing that out.

"I felt it then, the beginning of the transformation. I was softer and quieter but I twisted him around my little finger into the palm of my hand and then smacked him down onto the table, figuratively of course, without ever raising my voice or shouting at him. It was my lack of intimidation tactics that got the result I wanted, not my employment of them. I don't have to be hard and cold and brash to be effective. I'm not any of those things and I can't imitate a man's tactics and be effective."

"Being in London, I've been the expert in the room on international corporate law. I haven't had to convince anyone of that fact. It just is. That's helped the process along quite a bit. I'm frequently the only woman in a room full of men and I can hold my own, but I'm doing it in my own way now."

"Wow, Cees," was all he could say as she leaned into him with her head on his chest and he stroked her hair. "That's some pretty incredible insight." He felt the warmth between them grow and crescendo, though they were just snuggling and talking on her couch.

"It's also what makes me think that I'm closer to being ready to be a mom," she added softly. "I don't feel the need to go out and conquer the whole world anymore. Just my tiny corner of it. The whole pregnancy and birth process still terrifies me."

"You are one very amazing woman," he said, in wonderment that anything ever terrified Cecelia Patterson. "I've always known it but you do continue to surprise me."

"In good ways, I hope."

"In all the best ways," he said, still holding her close and stroking her silky strawberry blond hair lovingly and longingly.

19 ~ HE'S WHAT?!

After helping Cici clean up her kitchen, restoring it to the pristine spotless order that he knew she preferred it to be in, he reluctantly took his leave and drove home. He didn't mind her neatnik tendencies, he thought, as he drove home pondering their evening together. In fact, they complimented his messier ones nicely. He wasn't a total slob but he could surely stand some neater habits in his life.

Reluctant was a significant understatement to describe how he felt to be leaving her and going home alone. Their evening had been evolutionary. Cici had been angry but then vulnerable, their fight having led to a much deeper understanding as he realized what was bothering him and she'd shared with him how she felt, how she had struggled, and how she was growing both personally and professionally. It was a fight well worth having, he thought, and they hadn't discussed the murder investigation all evening.

He arrived home, locked up and set the alarm, refreshed both the food and water bowls for Max, and checked the water level on his Christmas tree. Standing in his closet, he checked the weather forecast for the next day before looking for clothes to lay out for the next morning. Tomorrow would be Friday the thirteenth, he noted, thankful that he wasn't the least bit superstitious, and the weather would be rainy again with a high near fifty. Well, at least that precluded ice and snow, he thought as he noticed the bag in the edge of his closet that he still hadn't unpacked from the Washburns. Starting with that, he determined to make a concerted effort to be neater.

After unpacking the bag and putting it away, he laid out his clothes for the next day, washed his face, brushed his teeth, and slipped into his soft flannel sleep pants and T-shirt. He plugged in his smart phone on the bedside table to recharge after checking it one last time to be sure there were no new messages. Retrieving his notebook computer from the end of the sofa where he'd plopped his satchel, he climbed in bed with it to check his patient roster for the next morning. He was having trouble concentrating on his patient records with Cici filling the forefront of his mind.

Max was head-butting his hand to get his attention so Matthew put the computer aside and scooped up the big gray tabby cat. He had largely neglected Max this week he thought regretfully, as he'd tried to help the Washburns through a difficult time. He scratched Max behind his ears and under his chin as the big cat purred and Matthew thought about how amazing Cici had been throughout the week. His feelings for her were stronger than ever, he realized, much to his chagrin. He'd been trying to keep her at arm's length and not feel so deeply for her but he realized that holding her off physically had only allowed her to get closer emotionally. That was the exact opposite of what he'd intended, he thought as he turned off the light and snuggled down under the covers. But here he was again.

As he drifted off to sleep, his heart felt full. Even in the midst of a murder investigation, he felt a lightness that he hadn't in quite some time. He didn't know what their future together would hold, but he met the dream world with the warmth and certainty that he was head over heels in love with Cici Patterson and that she was the only woman in the world that he wanted to spend that future with.

That, he supposed later, was the reason why he was so startled to wake up several hours later in disbelief from the dream he'd just had. It wasn't about Cici at all. She had appeared nowhere in it. Instead he was searching for something or someone that was totally elusive. He realized that he was chasing someone in the dream realm as that world solidified in his mind. It was very important that he catch him. He didn't understand why it was so imperative that he find the person. He knew only that it was of the utmost importance.

The more he searched, the farther he felt he was getting from his quarry. The shadowy dream world morphed and shifted. There were corners to turn, obstacles to climb over, and pitfalls to avoid as he realized that he was chasing a man. He was chasing an arrogant and distasteful man that he realized he'd rather not find, but felt compelled to chase anyway. Why was it so important that he find Kennedy Reynolds when he wanted so badly to avoid the man, he wondered in the dream. Even in the dream, it wasn't making sense. As Matthew struggled to make sense of the chase without ceasing in it, he heard a booming voice like thunder say to him, "Stop. Look deeper, see beyond."

"Deeper? Beyond what?" he'd asked in the dream, searching then for the source of the voice. It wasn't a scary voice, just a commanding one that he knew he must heed.

"He's not what he seems," the voice said. "He's innocent."

"He's what?" asked Matthew as he was surfacing from the realm of the deep dream world and back into the physical reality of his bedroom. He'd had realistic dreams before, some in which things he couldn't possibly know had been revealed to him. This one left him feeling shaken and confused. Matthew was all but certain that he'd been chasing Kennedy Reynolds in the dream and that he'd intended to harm him if he'd found him. That was enough to shake him up, but then to be told that he should look deeper and see beyond something, though he didn't know what, because the man was innocent? That was just too much to comprehend in the middle of the night.

Matthew tossed and turned, trying to shake the after effects of the dream before giving up and trundling to the kitchen for a glass of water and an Advil. He rarely experienced headaches but he had one now. Kennedy Reynolds was nothing but a headache, he thought. Matthew hadn't witnessed the man being kind to anyone that he could recall, just less obnoxiously arrogant to some than others.

Max met him in the doorway as he returned to the bedroom and climbed back in bed. Turning on the bedside lamp, he patted the bed beside him for Max to jump back up. As he scratched the big cat behind the ears with one hand, he picked up from the night stand with the other a book he'd been reading. He was trying to distract his mind from the dream. After a few minutes, Max curled up into a ball of fur beside Matthew's leg and seemed to go happily back to sleep. Matthew wished that it were just that easy but he was still haunted by the dream and wide awake. What could it mean to look deeper and see beyond? Beyond what? An arrogant veneer? Reynolds' exterior seemed real and impenetrable enough to Matthew.

Eventually giving up on the book, Matthew slid under the covers and turned the light off, deciding to try again to sleep, this time hoping for dreamless and less disturbing sleep. What would Cici think of his dream, he wondered. There wasn't much room for interpretation, he thought with a yawn as he finally felt sleepy again and drifted off into a restful dreamless sleep for the rest of the night.

Awakening to the alarm from his phone, Matthew removed Max from where he was curled around his head and checked the weather forecast again. He had just managed to prop up in bed when the phone vibrated and dinged in his hand.

"Good morning, Sleepyhead," he heard Cici's soft voice say as he clicked to answer it.

"Good morning. My alarm just went off."

"I know. That's why I called you now. Before you got up and busy with your morning."

"Did you sleep well?" he asked.

"It could have been better," she said and he could hear the alluring smile in her husky morning voice as she said it.

"It could have, I can't disagree with that sentiment," he said, though he wasn't planning to elaborate on his disturbed sleep over the phone this morning.

"How does your day look? Are you up for dinner this evening? Nothing fancy. I'm thinking I'll grab a pizza from Franco's and bring it to your place, if you'd like."

Franco's was their favorite Italian restaurant that was between her house in Quarry and his in Peak. It was one that they had frequented before they'd broken up because it was conveniently located between them, easy to access with their full schedules, and it had delicious traditional Italian fare that they both loved.

"Sure, Cees, but I'll come to you and bring the pizza if you'd rather. You cooked last night."

"I know, but Matthew I really want to be part of your world. Integrated. Fully integrated. I've been thinking a lot about that. I wasn't before and I truly want to be now. I want to see Max. He needs to trust me and like me. We can talk about it tonight, but as I've watched the Washburns this week, I've had an epiphany or two."

Officially intrigued by all of the things that Cici had never cared about before, Matthew just said, "OK, I'll look forward to tonight then. What time?"

"Um, sixish maybe? Is that too early? I don't have a key anymore so I'll need you to be home when I get there."

"Six is great, Cees. I don't have patients scheduled after two, but there will be walk-ins galore this afternoon. There always are this time of year on a Friday. All the parents who don't want to wait until Monday to address sniffles that could worsen over the weekend. Parenting isn't for wimps, you know."

"I'm beginning to see that," she said, seriously. Then she said, "I don't want to hold you up. I know how busy you are during this time of year. I'll pop into the office this morning but probably be out by four. That leaves me plenty of time to get by my place to change into some jeans, pick up the pizza, and be at your place by six."

"I'm looking forward to it," he said.

"Me too. And Matthew," she hesitated. "Thank you for last night. It was really very,"

"Cleansing," they both said in unison and then laughed. "And healing," she added. "See you tonight. I love you Matthew Landon Paine."

"I love you too, Cecelia Lindley Patterson."

She blew him an air kiss and was gone.

Never in his wildest imagination could Matthew have planned for things to go so well with Cici, he mused as he climbed out of bed, feeling refreshed and rejuvenated even with the interrupted sleep. He'd have to figure out what to do about that situation with the dream too, but the first thing on his agenda this morning was to go get a cup of the coffee that he'd set up the night before to brew. Having perfected the timing, it was ready just as he was clambering out of bed. He could smell it and the aroma drew him to the kitchen like one of those summoning fingers in cartoons.

After his usual routine with a long hot shower and shave, cooking and cleaning up eggs and toast, and rinsing and refilling the food and water bowls for Max, Matthew retrieved his notebook computer and shoved it in his satchel. He'd pulled an all-weather coat from the closet in his hallway, knowing that the day was going to be rainy and chilly but not, thankfully, freezing. Choosing to drive the Element in the nasty weather, he'd just pulled the key fob from the hanger by his side door that led to his garage and locked the door behind him when his cell phone went off in his pocket.

Juggling the satchel and travel mug of coffee he carried, he opened the car door, put those inside, and pulled the phone from his pocket.

"Hey, Doc," said Danbury. "Two things," he began, without preamble. "Can you meet for lunch today? Peak Eats. Maybe around one?"

"I think I can ask Maddie to juggle my schedule to free up an hour around one. I have patients scheduled until two, but I can shuffle them a little, I think." Maddie, the cute young receptionist in his office, had settled in nicely. Initially, she had been a bit in awe of Matthew for some reason that he couldn't fathom and she was shy to the point of embarrassment around him.

"Good."

"But that's just one thing. What's the second?"

"Penn wanted me to ask you and Cici over for dinner. I keep forgetting. She's getting annoyed. Say you're free tomorrow night, Doc. Keep me out of the doghouse."

Matthew just chuckled at the relational bliss that the stoic Danbury was finding himself in now that he and Penn, a woman he'd had a serious crush on in high school, were an item. Penn and her brother Leo lived in their ancestral home, the historic Lingle Plantation house that most people in the town of Peak thought was haunted, though only the youngest residents would openly admit it. Both Lingles had moved back to Peak after their brother was murdered. Danbury and Matthew had been instrumental in finding his killer.

"I think we're free tomorrow night," Matthew finally said. "I'll check with Cici to be sure and let you know at lunch."

"Thanks, Doc. See you at one. Text if that doesn't work."

"OK, see you then," said Matthew to thin air because Danbury was already gone.

Climbing into the Element, he clicked to open the garage door and turned the ignition. He backed slowly out, clicking to close the door behind him, and out through the deserted streets of his condominium complex. The elder residents who were his neighbors must be staying warm and dry inside this morning, he thought, as he pulled up his eclectic Christmas playlist and blasted the happy music through his car.

After an uneventful drive to his office on that rainy Friday morning, he parked in his usual spot and slipped in through the side door that was closest to his office. He unlocked his office door, placed his satchel on his desk, pulled his computer from the satchel, and stuffed the satchel beneath his desk. Whistling Christmas music as he swapped his heavy coat for the lab coat, he picked up his travel mug and the computer. He went first to the front lobby to ask Maddie about blocking an hour for him from one to two and to let Trina know that he wouldn't be needing the "lunch train" as she called their daily office lunch order program.

His next stop was the second-floor break room where he refilled his travel mug, now mostly empty after his short drive in. Sadie Peterson, the resident, and Megan Sims, the PA who'd been at the practice in Peak since the previous June, were already there discussing their day ahead.

"At least things will calm down in another week or so in time for Christmas," observed Sadie. "After the schools go on Christmas break and the little Petri dishes are separated so that they can't wander around swapping specimens."

Matthew chuckled at the analogy as he greeted the two women and wished them a happy Friday. Children were very much like little Petri dishes, he mused, having overheard their conversation. The two women returned his greeting before they slipped out and he could hear their conversation growing quieter as they went down the hallway. After refilling his travel coffee mug, he followed and headed back downstairs behind them. Diane, one of the nurses who rotated between physicians, met him at the bottom of the stairwell and cheerfully said, "Good morning, Doctor. You're with me this morning, or I'm with you, however you define that." He returned her cheerful greeting and they headed down the hallway together to the first patient who was waiting for them in Exam Room Five.

*****

After a morning that was more rushed than Matthew would have preferred, because he felt like he wasn't spending quality time with each patient, he swapped his lab coat for the all-weather coat and went to meet Danbury at Peak Eats. He didn't mind walking in the rain. With that particular coat at least, he was well protected.

As he rounded the corner onto Winston Avenue, he remembered that he hadn't yet asked Cici about Saturday night, so he quickly called her on the way.

"Cecelia Patterson's office," said a bright young male voice that he didn't recognize.

"Is Ms. Patterson in?" he asked.

"Whom shall I say is calling?"

Hesitating, momentarily, Matthew realized that he was about to say, "her boyfriend" before he corrected himself and simply said, "Matthew Paine."

"Just a moment, Mr. Paine."

He heard Cici's voice promptly asking, "Hi Matthew, why on earth did you call the office number?"

"If you were in meetings or something, I didn't want to disturb you by ringing your cell."

"Oh," she said. "I'm mostly meetingless today. I'm just catching up on paperwork. What's up?"

"I'm walking down to meet Danbury for lunch at Peak Eats and I was supposed to have called you already and asked if we're free for dinner tomorrow night. Penn wants to have us over."

"That would be lovely. I'd enjoy getting to know her and Leo both. If they're friends of yours, they're friends of mine," she said cheerfully. "Do ask what we can bring," she added, as if she were the one who'd been raised in the south and he'd grown up in Boston, instead of the reverse.

His eyebrow raised in amusement, but he simply said, "Yes, Ma'am. Will do."

"Great. See you at six," she said and blew him an air kiss. He blew her a kiss back and tucked his phone back into his pocket, happily whistling *O Tannenbaum* as he walked the rest of the way down the sidewalk.

Shaking the rain off under the awning outside as best he could, Matthew heard the bell jingle overhead as he entered Peak Eats. Danbury motioned to him from a booth in the back corner as he walked in. Matthew felt like he was shedding an equal amount of water on the floor as he'd shaken off outside when he walked across and removed the coat. Hanging it on a peg for that purpose on a post between the booths, he slid in across from Danbury. As usual, Danbury had his back to the wall like a cowboy in an old western movie.

"Hey Doc," said Danbury. "I ordered you a glass of water. The special today is meatloaf."

"Thanks," said Matthew. "That sounds good. I think I'll have a cup of soup too," he added with a shiver.

"What did Cici say?"

"That she'd love to come to dinner and get to know Penn and Leo."

"Great," said Danbury, clearly relieved. Danbury hadn't, Matthew realized, been around when he and Cici had split up so he wasn't jaded in any way toward her like some of the other people in his life were. His parents and Gladys, his motherly protective nurse, most notably. He wasn't sure what his sister thought but neither had he ventured to ask her.

Mallory, the flirtatious waitress arrived with their drinks and she didn't bother to hide the fact that she was checking their ring fingers as she handed the drinks over. When Matthew and Danbury had first met to discuss a case at Peak Eats the spring prior, neither of them was attached. Neither wore a wedding band yet, but both were seriously involved. Flashing her dimples and her toothy grin at first Matthew and then Danbury, she asked sweetly, "Have you decided what you'd like?"

Matthew hadn't opened the menu that was on the table in front of him, but knowing that the special was meatloaf, neither did he need to. "I'll have the meatloaf special with mashed potatoes and string beans," he said. "And what's the soup of the day?"

"Vegetable beef," she said, flashing the dimples. "We also have a nice French onion and a broccoli cheddar."

Mathew opted for a cup of the broccoli cheddar. Danbury just doubled Matthew's order, but chose a bowl of the vegetable beef instead. "OK, now what did you want to talk about?" asked Matthew after Mallory had left the table.

"Just a few things," said Danbury. "About a couple of twenty-somethings. With diverse resumes."

"That was cryptic. What does that mean?" asked Matthew.

"First things first," said Danbury, pulling a sheaf of paper from a folder on the bench seat beside him and handing it and a pen over to Matthew. "Sign here. Initial here and here," he said, pointing to the relevant lines. As Matthew hesitated, Danbury added, "It's the same as before. The form hasn't changed."

It was the form that Matthew had signed when he agreed to be a medical consultant with the police department the previous spring.

"You sign, we'll talk. It needs to be official. Nondisclosure and all," said Danbury, leaning back against the tall booth seat.

"OK," Matthew sighed as he signed and then initialed the form. He remembered it from before. It paid nothing, but put his medical knowledge at the disposal of the police department, and the non-disclosure section swore him to complete secrecy about the cases he helped with. His medical knowledge, he knew, was just the beginning of what would be expected of him, at least by Danbury.

"Now, what did you want to talk about?" asked Matthew, sliding the form and pen back across the table.

Returning the form to the folder, Danbury pulled another set of papers from the folder and slid them across the table to Matthew. "Alicia Laws and Joseph Hayden," he said.

"The servers from the catering company? These were the two who called in sick at the last minute but then showed up anyway?"

"The same," said Danbury. "And then disappeared again. Around the time of the murder. Joseph is the guy you ID-ed."

"Huh," said Matthew, flipping through the pages. There were unflattering headshots of each of them which he recognized as arrest photos along with the accompanying RAP sheets. "These two have a record already," he said, stating the obvious.

"They do. Hers is much longer. His is recent. Both have diverse resumes," said Danbury.

"Meaning, what? That they can't hold down jobs for long?"

"Can't or won't. Not sure which yet," said Danbury between sips of his tea. "And an array of petty crimes. Nothing serious. Drug possession. B and E. Stolen car."

"Breaking and entering to drug possession," Matthew repeated. "But nothing violent? Not even bar brawls or anything?"

"Not that they've been arrested for. At least not yet."

"Alicia was found murdered so she's not likely to commit any," Matthew said sarcastically. "Though Joseph here could be facing charges if he's the one who killed her, huh?"

"Yeah, we like him for that murder. He had full access. Means, opportunity. All of it."

"And motive?"

"Possibly. We're working on that. Both had money wired to their accounts. Both wires the day after Washburn was killed. Twenty thousand each. On Sunday the eighth. Hers disappeared the next day. Monday. The same day she was found dead."

"Disappeared? Where'd it go?"

"We're chasing that down now. Both where and how. Looks like another wire transfer. We haven't located where it went. Yet. Both accounts were otherwise pretty flat. Small amounts came in. It all went right back out."

"Do you think it's all related to Jamison Washburn's murder?"

"Do you believe in coincidence?"

"Not really, no."

"Neither do I," said Danbury. "Betting pool likes Reynolds. For all of it."

"He's innocent," Matthew blurted out before thinking that he'd have to explain that statement and he wasn't prepared to do so yet.

"Come again?" said Danbury.

Thinking quickly, Matthew said, "Hey, it's your supposition that just because someone isn't a nice person and we don't like him does not make him guilty. I have to assume he's innocent until provably guilty, right?"

"Now you quote me?" asked Danbury, with a chuckle. "He doesn't have an alibi. He was in the building at the time. On the same floor. And he's admitted that."

"That's Washburn's murder, but how could he be responsible for hers?" asked Matthew, thumping the picture of Alicia Laws. "Isn't Joseph Hayden a more viable suspect? Were they involved? I mean with each other. I guess I just assumed so, but you haven't really said."

"They're known associates. We're digging into the duration. And the relationship. But they moved around a lot. So that's not an easy task."

Just then the food arrived and Mallory asked if they needed anything else as she handed Danbury a ketchup bottle and extra napkins from her apron pocket, anticipating that he'd ask for both. They assured her that they had everything they needed.

Matthew remembered to ask what they could bring Saturday night before digging into his meal. "We can bring dessert or wine at least or both. What's on the menu? Red or white wine?"

"Couldn't tell you," said Danbury between bites.

"Just tell Penn we're bringing wine and dessert," said Matthew.

Danbury's mouth was full so he just nodded his consent. The man was a marvel, thought Matthew, to be able to polish off the quantities of food that he did in such a short span of time.

*****

Matthew finished with patients at the office shortly after five and packed up to drive home. He just needed to be there before six to let

Cici in and he had plenty of time to drive the ten minutes or so home. Getting comfortable and having a glass of wine to begin updating his patient charts before she arrived sounded like a great idea.

On the way into his neighborhood, he was admiring the Christmas lights glistening in the misty evening when he saw Mrs. Drewer out walking Oscar. The rain had let up, at least momentarily, so he stopped to greet her. Lowering his window as he pulled alongside her and she scooped up the little dog, he said, "Hi Mrs. Drewer. How are things on your end?" She occupied the other end of his condo unit with one neighbor in between them.

"All is well on my end," she smiled in response. "I was just getting Oscar out quickly before the rain starts back up again. It's been raining all afternoon. I hope you're well and enjoying the holiday season."

"I am, thanks. The Washburns hired a security company round-the-clock so I'm happy to be back home and sleeping in my own bed again."

"There's nothing like your own bed and home for rest," she said. "Are you making any progress on that investigation that you can talk about?"

"I wish I could tell you that there's been lots of progress, but from what little I know, not much headway has been made yet. I'm not directly involved now that I'm not staying at the Washburn home, though I just signed back on as a medical consultant this afternoon so who knows what I'll get dragged into next."

"Oh Matthew," she commiserated. "You just can't get any peace this Christmas season, can you?"

He laughed at that and just said, "Not so far. I'll let you finish your walk before the rain starts back up. Enjoy your evening." They waved as he drove off and he clicked to open the garage door. Instead of putting the Element in the garage, he pulled it up behind the side of the garage where the Corvette was parked inside, leaving the space and the door open for Cici.

20 ~ TRUE CONFESSIONS

Matthew had gotten a little bit of work done on his patient charts when Cici arrived with a Greek salad and two medium pizzas that the two of them would never finish in a single evening.

"Are you feeding the neighborhood?" asked Matthew as he leaned over and kissed Cici softly, taking the pizza boxes from her.

"No, I just know how you love leftover pizza."

"And I know how you used to tease me about eating it cold for breakfast."

She crinkled her nose at him and said, "That was just back in college, right? You heat it up and eat it later in the day now, I hope."

"I make no promises when it comes to leftover pizza consumption," he said jovially as he lifted a corner of the lid on one of the pizza boxes, appreciating the aroma that wafted up to meet his nose. They stacked the pizzas in the oven and turned it on warm before splitting the salad into bowls to share and pouring glasses of wine.

They settled happily at the little table in front of the bay window in Matthew's eating nook that overlooked the back corner of the golf course, none of which they could see now in the dark.

"Everything looks nice," said Cici, as she glanced around his open living area. "I'm glad you were able to get it all restored after that awful fire."

"And thank you for the new furniture," he said. "That was really too much for a birthday present, you know."

"For you? Never! Besides, I picked out the original set and I didn't want you selecting anything hideous to replace it," she said, laughing.

"That was a great set. This is nearly a replica of it, so it's perfect." And it was. Matthew had loved his soft buttercream leather sofa, chair, and ottoman, all of which had been damaged by smoke or water or both in the fire. The set Cici had selected and sent for his birthday back in July was not exactly like the first set, but it was very close. He had yet to replace his area rug but he'd nearly convinced himself that he didn't really need one anyway.

"I'm glad you like it," she responded and then bowed her head expectantly.

After blessing their meal, they both dived in. The meatloaf lunch, Matthew realized, was long gone and he was hungry. After they'd finished their salads, he rose and put the bowls in the sink, pulling down plates and then loading them with pizza that had gotten hot again in the oven while they'd languished over their salads and wine glasses. They weren't in any hurry, he noticed, neither wanting to rush through their evening together.

Cici laughed at Matthew moaning quietly over his favorite pizza, a meat lovers, and she asked, "Does that make it taste better somehow? Maybe I should try it," she added, popping a piece into her mouth and moaning exaggeratedly over the bite.

Matthew marveled over Cici being silly again like she had been when they'd met. Before they'd broken up, she was still fun to be with. She joked and they laughed together, but she had gotten much more serious and far less prone to silliness just for its own sake. This was the Cici he'd fallen in love with and he was thrilled to see her reemerging.

After finishing their meal, they rinsed their dishes and stuck them in the dishwasher. Matthew piled the leftover pizza in glass containers with lids and left them on the counter to cool before going in to the refrigerator. After tearing down the pizza boxes and throwing them away, Matthew poured them each a little bit more wine and said, "Let's go enjoy the Christmas tree lights. Obviously, there aren't any decorations on it yet. Normally, you know those would have been up long ago. I waited this year because I had a date with Angel to decorate it last Sunday. Obviously, I had to postpone that because we were at the Washburns. I'm hoping I can make it up to her this Sunday and we'll try that again."

As they settled into the new soft buttercream leather sofa, Matthew blue toothed his Christmas playlist to his speaker system and turned it down to be background music. Max appeared from somewhere and jumped up onto the end of the sofa expectantly.

"Hi Max," said Cici, invitingly. "It's nice to see you again," she crooned. The big cat looked her over and then, apparently deciding that she was OK, walked across Matthew's lap to bask in her appreciation of him. It was a cat's life, thought Matthew as Cici scratched Max under the chin and behind his ears as she'd seen Matthew do so many times while talking sweetly to him. Max eventually snuggled into the tiny crevice on the sofa between them where he didn't really fit and Cici just laughed at him.

"OK, Cees, the suspense is killing me."

"Suspense?"

"You said, this morning, that after spending time with the Washburns you'd had an epiphany or two."

"Oh. Yeah, I have. I don't know where to start, so I guess I'll just dive in. You know that my parents are divorced and my family disjointed. There's no pressure there at all, nothing to live up to, nobody to disappoint. Your family, though," she said and paused. "I've seen your parents work together as a team, you're all so close that it was overwhelming. You wanted to bring me in as a part of it when we first started dating and it terrified me. Becoming a part of that was scary and it felt smothering to me when we were younger."

"Really? I didn't know that."

"Of course not. It's not like I ever told you. I'd never have dared to criticize your family," she said.

"Cees, it's not like my family is above reproach. They're not perfect," he began, but she held up a hand.

"Just let me finish this thought," she said. "That was then. But now I understand the importance of family, close family. The Washburns, Jamison and Annabelle, they weren't happy because of Jamison's success. They were happy before it and they continued to be happy together during that success. His success wasn't a prerequisite to their happiness. I still want to make senior partner but there's no rush. My happiness, our happiness, isn't dependent on that external success. I don't have to be at a certain place in my life to be ready for you, ready for your family, ready for us."

The floodgates had apparently opened on Cici's introspection and Matthew was excited to be hearing the result of that, so he kept quiet as she continued.

"I know they aren't thrilled with me and I understand that. I'd been quite aloof for several years and dug my heels in against being a part of your close-knit family. On top of that, I'm betting that they blame me for our breakup and your heartbreak."

"Only marginally," said Matthew, trying to level with her as she was being so openly honest with him. "I don't think they blame you for the breakup, but they saw how devastated I was afterward and they don't want to see me go through that again. I think they are wary of you. I had been so certain that you were the one, that we had a future, that we were going to go through life together. After all of that blew up, I was still trying to redefine my future without you when we were pulled back together last spring. It took me awhile to get it back together. I was just going through the motions. Most people probably didn't know that, but my family did. They saw it very clearly."

"I get it. It's why you've held me at a distance all this time too."

"I have," he admitted. "But last night backfired on me."

"How do you mean?" she asked.

"I was so busy trying to hold you off physically that I had my guard totally down emotionally. You've been very open and honest and I appreciate that. But the cleansing conversation we had last night was more than that. I let you back in again, Cees. Some of that is OK because I finally understood what it was that I was afraid of, your eventual resentment if we got back together and you were forced to make changes you didn't really want to make. To give up dreams of bigger and better things to settle for being with me."

"That's just it, Matthew. I've never felt like I'm settling when I'm with you. Quite the opposite really. I feel pretty empty without you. I know what you mean about going through the motions. I tried to convince myself that I was better off without you, that you'd hold me back and keep me from being everything I wanted. But that's insane. You've never done anything but encourage and support me. Ever. I'm so much better in every way with you than without you."

He tried to pull her close, but she resisted. "Just a minute, I'm not quite finished yet."

He just shook his head and grinned at her.

"I want to be part of your family too, Matthew, if they'll have me. If we're going to make a go of it, I need to be an integral part of what's most important to you. I enjoyed the time I spent with them right before I left for London last spring."

"They did too. Mom commented that she was pleasantly surprised that you chose to spend Mother's Day with them, the last day you were here before flying out for the year in London."

"Well, that's encouraging. I thought maybe I'd start with the easiest to win over. You said you were going to bring Angelina over Sunday after church to decorate your tree. Can I invite myself to be a part of that?"

"You think Angel will be the easiest to win over?" asked Matthew, laughing. "She's the most blatantly honest person I know and at four-years-old she parrots everything the adults say without a filter. If you want to know what they're thinking, she's your best bet."

"Is that a yes?"

"Of course, it's a yes, Cici," he said, thrilled beyond words that she wanted to be part of his family, but he figured he'd try. "You're right that my family is very important to me. And any woman I'd seriously consider marrying would need to be a part of that family. So yes, I'd love to decorate the tree with you and Angel. Are you planning to come to church and then out to lunch with my suffocating family afterward?"

"Of course," said Cici, laughing at his summary of her previous feelings for them. "I thought that was a given."

Miracles really never did cease, thought Matthew as Cici asked, checking her watch, "Can we call her? Tonight? What time does Angel go to bed?"

"In about a half hour," said Matthew, also checking his watch to see that it was already eight. "As upset as Monica was with me for having to cancel last Sunday, it serves her right if we call now and get Angel all excited right before bedtime. Let's do it."

Cici laughed. "Be careful there, little brother. I don't want the payback when we get around to having kids."

Matthew felt a warm glow emanating from his toenails to his scalp. Cici had just said they'd have children, he and she, together. Picking up his phone from the coffee table, he clicked to call the Valenti household which still had a land line. Stephano, Monica's lanky Italian husband answered.

"Hey, Stephano, it's Matthew. Is Angel still up?"

"Hey Matthew. Who are you talking about? You know she's still up. The only way to get her to bed on time during this season of year is with that crazy elf that's anywhere except ever on a shelf. Did you want Monica? Or did you want to talk to Angel?"

"Both," said Matthew. "But I think I'll ask forgiveness instead of permission and start with Angel."

Stephano just laughed as he said, "Hey man, she's your sister. You understand the wrath you're risking." He called his daughter to the phone and Matthew put his on speaker, laying it back on the coffee table between Cici and himself.

"Hiya Uncle Matt!" she said, delightedly. "Are you calling to reschedule? Because you'd better be! I don't like bein' standed up."

"Stood up? Who told you that?" he tried not to laugh because he knew the precocious child hated being laughed at when she was being serious. Likewise, Cici stifled a laugh in her sleeve but Matthew could see the amusement dancing in her eyes.

"My momma told Granddad you were standin' me up when you didn't come to church Sunday. And I didn't get to come decorate."

"How would you like to come decorate after church this Sunday with Cici and me?"

"With Cici too?"

"Yeah, she's here now. Do you want to say hello?"

The normally chatty child grew quiet. Then Angel said softly, "Do YOU want her to help decorate, Uncle Matt?"

"I do. Very much. But only if you do," he said looking up at Cici, who just nodded.

"OK, Momma says more is merriest and it's Christmas!"

"Like the more the merrier?" asked Matthew, trying not to chuckle.

"That's it! That's what she said. Can we go Christmas caroling too, Uncle Matt? I really wanna go Christmas caroling."

"That's a wonderful idea!" Cici chimed in. "Let's! Matthew, most of your neighbors are older and retired. They'd love to have Angel come sing to them."

"Can my Momma and Daddy come too? And Grand and Granddad?"

"The more the merrier," chimed in Cici from beside Matthew.

"But, Uncle Matt," began Angel, sounding concerned. "Can they just come later? I want to decorate the tree, just us. But don't tell them. It might hurt their feelings."

"You can come home with us after lunch and they can come later if they want. How's that?" asked Matthew.

"That's the merriest!" chortled Angel.

"I should probably talk to your mom about all of this now, Sweetie. Is she there?"

"Oh Mooooommmmmmma!" Angel called and Matthew could tell that she was skipping through the house with the phone by the way her voice bounced along over the long, drawn-out word. "Uncle Matt wants to talk to you! We're going to decorate on Sunday! And then we're gonna go Christmas caroling to all of Uncle Matt's tired neighbors!"

Cici couldn't hold it together any longer after that and she had to get up and walk down the hall to laugh aloud. Matthew nearly had to pinch himself to keep from laughing out loud himself, but he managed as Monica was getting on the line and then he lost it too, laughing in her ear.

"What is it?" asked Monica. "What's so hilarious?"

"Your daughter," said Matthew. "Didn't you hear her? She sounds like a miniature adult most of the time but every now and then she gets something close to right, but her twists are funny. I tried not to laugh because she was so serious, and I managed until she handed the phone to you. She said that we were going to sing Christmas carols to my tired neighbors. They probably are, but what Cici had said was that my neighbors were mostly older and RE-tired."

"Oh," said Monica quietly. "Cici is there?"

"She is, and you're on speaker," warned Matthew lightly and then continued quickly. "We want to bring Angel back with us after lunch on Sunday to decorate. But then Angel asked if we could also go caroling and she wanted to know if you and Stephano and Mom and Dad could come too."

"Well," said Monica slowly, sounding to Matthew as if she were thinking aloud as she spoke. "I suppose we could do that. What time are you thinking? Not too late for Angel's bedtime. We'll need to get her home and calmed down before eight-thirty. It gets dark pretty early now. Did you check the weather forecast?"

"It's supposed to be sunny and warm on Sunday. You're right, though, sunset is officially around five now. It'll get cooler fast after that."

"OK, let's do five. Will your neighbors be OK with that?"

"Yeah, it's probably almost dinner time for them, but that should be OK."

"And dinner. We could do that right after and still have time to get Angel home and to bed on time."

"Let me take care of that," said Cici, stepping back up to the phone. "We can eat here afterward. Any special Christmas requests?"

"None that I can think of," said Monica. "Our family, including Angel, eats most things. If you really want to make a hit with her, spaghetti with meatballs is her favorite."

"OK, Christmas spaghetti it is then," said Cici. "And maybe some apple cider or hot cocoa to take caroling."

"She'll love either one," said Monica. "Just not too much before dinner or she'll bounce off the walls and then crash from the sugar. Trust me, you don't want to see the crash. She gets cranky fast."

"We'll listen to Christmas music while we decorate to brush up on all of the Christmas classics," said Matthew getting easily into the spirit of planning for the season he loved. "Do you think the adults will need printed versions of the songs?"

"That surely couldn't hurt where I'm concerned," said Monica. "Mom walks around the house singing Christmas carols before Thanksgiving so she's probably OK, but the rest of us might need the help."

"OK, I'll work on printing those out for us," said Matthew.

"Are you going to call Mom and Daddy and see if they're free? Mom has her women's Bible study group on Sunday nights, usually, but I think they break for the month of December and attend Christmas cantatas and programs together instead."

"Sure, I'll check in with them next," said Matthew.

Cici suddenly piped up, "What size does she wear?"

"What?" asked Matthew, looking up at her.

"Angel. What size is she?"

"She's tall for her age but slender," said Monica. "She's four, but she wears a seven or eight, depending on what it is. She needs an eight slim in pants but can sometimes wear a seven in tops if they're cut long enough and not too wide. Why?"

"I was just thinking I'd surprise her with something Christmassy to go sing in. What's her shoe size?"

"She's mostly in a size one youth, but lots of those are too wide for her, so adjustable is good."

"Great!" said Cici, her face alight with excitement. Matthew wasn't sure what she was up to but he was happy to see her excitement about planning the event with his family.

"OK, I'll call Mom and Dad next. I need to talk to Dad anyway about some plans for tomorrow."

"What plans?" asked Monica.

"Sis, you know better than to ask questions like that this close to Christmas," he said mysteriously.

"OK, I won't ask. See you both Sunday?" Monica asked instead.

"Looking forward to it!" said Cici enthusiastically.

As they said their good-byes and Matthew clicked to end the call, he looked up at Cici who still hovered beside him. "What?" she asked.

"Who are you and what did you do with Cecelia Patterson?" he asked, laughing.

"I am the original, and the new and improved version," she said. "I want this to work, Matthew. I am committed to making this work. And I am excited about spending the day with Angel. I need to learn how to be around kids. I have no experience with that whatsoever."

He smiled up at her, taking her hand and pulling her down to the sofa beside him. Christmas miracles apparently did happen, he thought as he kissed her passionately. Reluctantly, he pulled away with a shiver.

"Me too. I want this to work," he said simply. "Just a sec," he added, getting up and going into the kitchen. He returned with a key hidden in his hand. He'd replaced the locks on his house after the fire, and he'd had five keys cut. He put one on each car key ring and had three extras made. One, he'd given to his parents, one to Mrs. Drewer who had helped keep an eye on the renovations while he was away in Miami, and one that he'd put in the desk drawer in his kitchen, just in case.

"I have something for you," he said, sitting back down and handing her the key.

"They key to your heart?" she joked.

"Apparently, you already have that. But this one will get you in any of the doors here. They're all keyed alike."

"Thanks, Matthew. That means a lot."

"Well, I can already get in your house any time I want with your security codes that I memorized, so I suppose it's only fair."

"I might need to come and go a bit tomorrow, if that's OK. While you're off with your dad on the mysterious Christmas errand, I'll get set up for Sunday. Hey, what time are we eating with Danbury and Penn tomorrow night?"

"That's a good question. I'll check with Danbury and let you know what he says. But now, I need to call my parents and ask them about Sunday," he responded as he picked up his phone and started poking at it. "I'm not putting this one on speaker."

"OK, well then, I guess I'll go wash the wine glasses. Unless you want more?" she asked, rising from the sofa and carefully picking up the two glasses by the long stems.

"No thanks, Cees." And then into the phone, he said, "Hey Dad. Are we still on for tomorrow?"

"Hi, son. We are. I set it up with Lawrence for one. He'll be closing up to the rest of the world then. Can you be here by noon? It won't take us that long to get up there but your mom will want to see you too."

"Sure, that's great. Thanks, Dad."

"Is there anything in particular that you're looking for?" he casually asked. Matthew saw right through that ploy, knowing that what his father was really asking was if he was going ring shopping for Cici.

"Oh, it's a Christmas secret," he said, instead. "Are you taking Lawrence a bottle of that special bourbon for staying open just for us?"

"I always do," his father replied.

"Thanks, Dad," said Matthew, sincerely. "For setting this up. Oh, just one more thing. Are you and Mom free Sunday evening to come join us for Christmas caroling and dinner?"

"Christmas caroling?" repeated Joc Paine dubiously.

"I'm bringing Angel home from lunch to decorate and she wants to go caroling afterward. She specifically asked if you and Mom could come too. Cici apparently thinks this is a great adventure and she's planning to have hot drinks to take caroling and spaghetti with meatballs for us afterward. Well, mostly for Angel, but I guess we can have some," Matthew added with a chuckle.

"I'll check with your mom. Can we just tell you tomorrow? She's out at a Christmas play with her Bible study women this evening and she'll be in later."

"Sure, that works. I'll see you tomorrow."

"OK, Matthew. Have a good night."

"Thanks, Dad. You too," said Matthew, clicking to end the call.

"What was that mysterious call all about?" asked Cici from the sink as she rinsed the glasses she had just washed and flipped them up-side-down on his bamboo drying rack as Matthew came in behind her. He put the leftover pizza container in the refrigerator.

"I'll never tell," he said. "It'll have to remain a Christmas secret. For now at least."

21 ~ Christmas Secrets

After finishing his patient charting and some household chores that morning, Matthew drove to his parents' house in north Raleigh, the home he'd grown up in. Pulling into the driveway at exactly noon, Matthew looked around the cul-de-sac where he'd played as a boy and noticed that not much had changed over the years except the color of the trim on some of the houses and the seasonal addition of Christmas decorations. The houses on this end of the street were mostly varying shades of brick, so that hadn't changed.

There had been no rain or messy weather in the forecast so he'd driven the Corvette. He offered to drive so that he and his dad could have a little fun on the way up to Ridge Woods to visit the jewelry store. Lawrence, the store owner, was one of a few friends that Joc Paine had kept up with since college and Matthew knew that he was also a car enthusiast.

Joc almost always shopped for his wife's gifts at family-owned Hudson's Jewelers and Lawrence Hudson habitually remained open after hours so that Joc was the sole customer in the store. As a result of many years of gifts, Matthew knew that Jackie Paine had complete sets of ruby, emerald, and diamond jewelry including rings, earrings, necklaces and bracelets. She'd shown him and his sister Monica how to access the wall safe in her dressing room, lest they should need to do so without her presence. Both siblings balked at the notion but noted the instructions anyway.

Joc had started on a sapphire set and Matthew knew that he was going to look at some tear-drop earrings to match the necklace he'd given Jackie for her birthday. His father, aided by Lawrence Hudson, had great taste in jewelry and he was hoping they'd help him pick out something equally as wonderful for Cici this year, but he'd kept what he was planning to buy for her to himself.

Matthew shut the engine off and climbed out of the Corvette. The front door opened as he stepped up onto the porch. Jackie welcomed him warmly and hugged him tightly as he entered.

"Come on in, Sweetheart, and visit for a minute before you head off into your mysterious adventures with your father," Jackie said, smiling. Matthew figured that his mother probably knew exactly where they were going and generally what Joc would be doing there.

"Would you like some coffee? Maybe a chocolate chip cookie or two?"

She knew how to offer the right things to get him to sit down and stay for a bit. He'd give her that much. He readily accepted both, following her through the house and into the kitchen.

"I'll let you add your sugar and cream," she said, reaching for a mug and handing it to him. "I know I'll never get as much in your coffee as you'll want," she added, sliding a little tray with a cream pitcher and sugar bowl over and handing him a spoon from the drawer.

While they chatted, she pulled out a plate and napkin for him and handed him the cookie jar. He sat at a stool behind the island in the kitchen and munched happily. She joined him in a cup of coffee but said she'd already eaten too many of the cookies while she was baking them that morning.

When Matthew's plate of cookies was gone and the coffee mug empty, he asked about the Christmas caroling and dinner for Sunday night. "I guess Dad told you about that?"

"He did, and it sounds wonderful," she said. "What a great idea. Do you need me to bring anything other than the rest of the chocolate chip cookies? I made a double batch to share with Angel. That child could eat her weight in them," she added with a fond smile.

"I don't think so, but Cici volunteered to do dinner so I'd have to ask her what she's planning. I know it'll include spaghetti and meatballs because Monica told her that's Angel's favorite, but I didn't ask any questions."

"That was sweet of her to offer to provide dinner," said Jackie as Matthew stared into her face trying to read her thoughts. Convinced that his mother's words were sincere, he turned as his father entered the kitchen from the back staircase.

"Hey Matthew, all ready to go?" he asked, carrying a brown bag by the top of what was obviously a bottle of liquor. If his mom hadn't already known where they were going, Matthew thought, that was a complete giveaway because she knew the history of the special bourbon that Joe and his college fraternity brothers favored better than Matthew did.

"Ready when you are," said Matthew, getting up and taking his coffee cup and plate to the sink and rinsing them.

"Just leave them there," said Jackie. "The dishwasher has just finished running so I'll need to empty it before those can go in."

"OK," said Matthew, turning and raising an eyebrow. He had been well trained by Jackie to always rinse his dishes and put them in the dishwasher. It was one thing about which she had been particular when he was growing up. He and Monica were expected to clean up behind themselves and not leave messes behind.

After hugging his mother, Matthew said, "I'm glad you can come tomorrow night. That should be fun. I love you."

"I wouldn't miss it," she answered. "And I love you too."

Matthew and Joe slid into the Corvette and Matthew fired it up and backed out of the driveway. As quietly as he could, he made his way down the street. He made the turns, as if on autopilot, to leave the Mill Pond Estates subdivision where he'd grown up and head north to the jewelry store in Ridge Woods.

"What are you planning to buy for Cici, son?" asked his father. "I could tell that your mother was dying to ask but she was pretending not to know where we were going."

Noting the concerned look on his father's face, Matthew decided that he'd worried his parents long enough with his mysterious gift idea and he answered directly, "No, I'm not going to look at engagement rings."

Matthew felt a prick of annoyance at the look of relief on his father's face that he caught out of his peripheral vision.

"I am, however, going to look at a diamond ring of another sort," he teased mischievously thinking himself justified in prolonging the mystery just a few more seconds. "I want to get her a diamond tennis bracelet. She saw one she particularly liked in London but she wouldn't buy it for herself. It is a ring of diamonds. But it has a clasp so the ring can be broken," he added meaningfully.

"Ah, that's a nice gift. You know your mom has one that I got from Lawrence a few years ago. She loves it."

"I remember. It completed her diamond collection. And yes, she does love it. I'm hoping to pick out something equally as wonderful for Cici and I figured Lawrence can help me with that. Cici usually goes over the top with gifts, like ordering the replacement furniture for my living room and having it shipped for my birthday, so I wanted to get her something nice."

Matthew's cell phone chirped and he saw on his car display that he had an incoming call from Danbury. "It's Danbury," said Matthew, stating the obvious to his father. "OK if I take this?"

"Sure, go ahead."

Matthew clicked to answer the call over the car speaker and immediately heard Danbury get right to the point as usual, "Hey Doc. Two things. Dinner tonight is at six. I was supposed to confirm that with you." He sounded like he might have gotten an earful from Penn for not having done so already. Matthew chuckled to himself but refrained from teasing the big detective about it with his father in the car.

"Hey Danbury. I'm in the car with my dad right now and you're on speaker. We're doing some Christmas shopping up in Ridge Woods. I'm sure dinner at six is fine," said Matthew. "I'll double check with Cici and let you know if it isn't but consider it confirmed. What's the other thing?"

"Can you meet me at the law firm? Monday after work. I need to talk to Kennedy Reynolds. I have some questions for him. Can you get there?"

"Cici's office on Monday," Matthew parroted, trying to remember his schedule without being able to look. "I think so. What time?"

"How about five-thirty? That enough time for you? He's agreed to talk to me again. But at his office this time. He's finished with meetings by five."

"OK, I'll block it on my calendar. We schedule fewer appointments on Mondays because we know we'll get a lot of walk-ins, particularly this time of year. Lots of people get sick over the weekend, and many of them children whose parents are frantic by Monday morning."

"Thanks Doc. I'll give you the update tonight. There are some new developments."

"OK, that works," said Matthew, as the phone line went dead.

"He doesn't waste words or time, does he?" asked Joc with a chuckle.

"Not at all. Nobody could ever accuse Danbury of wasting either."

"I hadn't asked you about that. How is the investigation going? Do they have suspects yet? Anybody who stands out?"

"Two people, so far. One has a pretty iron-clad alibi, but the other is much more suspicious. I'm pretty sure he's innocent though. He just acts like such an arrogant jerk that it's hard to get past that."

"Why is that? Or can you tell me?"

"I will, but you can't say anything about it."

"I'm not mentioning any of this to your mother, if that's what you're worried about. I don't want to worry her."

"Dad, not to anyone."

"I understand. Who else but your mom would I tell?" Matthew nodded, both understanding what his father had initially meant and knowing very well that his father was one of the most trustworthy people he knew.

"The guy I thought was guilty, it was because Cici and I saw him punch Jamison Washburn in the stairwell about an hour before Mr. Washburn's body was found. He doesn't have an alibi at all. And he won't tell anybody why he hit Washburn. He went out of state immediately afterward and he was in an isolated spot. He says he didn't know that Mr. Washburn was dead. Some people believe that to be true, but most think that he's the murderer."

"But you don't?"

"I wish I could say otherwise, but no, not anymore."

"What changed?"

Matthew was considering how to answer his father when the phone rang again and he saw that it was Cici.

"Dad, OK if I take this?"

"Fine with me," his father responded.

"Hey Cees."

"Hi. I started to say good morning, but it isn't anymore, is it?"

"Not quite, no."

"I've been so busy, I guess I lost track of time. OK if I run by your place and drop off some things for tomorrow? You're not there, right? You're already off on some mysterious Christmas mission with your dad?"

"I am. We're in the car so you're on speaker with both of us," said Matthew, glancing over at his father. "Oh, and Danbury just called and said that dinner is at six with him and Penn this evening. Does that work OK for you?"

"Sure. I'm busy but flexible. Having a deadline is probably good to keep me from going too far overboard."

Matthew raised an eyebrow at this admission and wondered what she was up to. "Have you talked to the Washburns in the past couple of days? I keep forgetting to ask you that."

"I spoke to Annabelle yesterday morning," said Cici. "Abby and I were combing through files trying to see if anyone else jumped out at us as having a potential problem with Mr. Washburn. We had a couple of questions for her. Nothing really stands out though. I think we're back to Aubrey Bartles with his iron-clad alibi and the horrid Kennedy Reynolds, who has none. At least as far as motive. We're hitting dead ends on finding any others with a strong motive. Nothing recent at least. Abby pulled case files from the past fourteen years since she's been there. We haven't looked back farther than that yet."

"Is Annabelle holding up OK?" asked Matthew, thinking that it was probably a really ridiculous question, but wishing for an affirmative answer.

"Under the circumstances, I think she's doing well. She told us that she was tougher than she looks and I'm inclined to believe her. Jay went back to Georgia until the service, which will likely be the end of next week, probably on Friday. Annabelle told the Medical Examiner to take his time and be certain that he gets all the evidence that he needs. He's telling her that'll be the beginning of next week when they finish with the testing. Sophia is still in town but I get the impression that there's tension in the house with her there."

"I wonder what they're testing still?"

"I have no idea. She wants them to be thorough and preserve any and all evidence, so I suppose that's what they're doing."

"I guess that's good then. Are we meeting up at my place to go to dinner together? I can pick you up if you'd rather."

"No, that's fine. I'll plan to be there and ready by five-thirty. Did you get any update on what we can bring?"

"None whatsoever. I offered to bring wine and dessert. But you know Danbury. The less he has to say, the happier he is."

"Yeah, that's true. I guess he talks to Penn, at least sometimes. Or maybe she's really talkative and he just nods and grunts a lot," Cici speculated, laughing.

"Turn here," said his dad.

"Oh, yeah, I almost missed that."

"I'll let you go do your Christmas secret stuff then. I still have lots to do before five-thirty too. See you in a bit."

"OK, I should be back long before five-thirty."

They said their quick good-byes, sans anything personal because the presence of Matthew's dad put a bit of a damper on that. Matthew made the final two turns and parked in the lot that was, but for one other vehicle, deserted.

"Want to get a reaction?" asked Joc Paine, grinning.

"As long as it's a good one," said Matthew.

"Rev it up one good time when you park it."

"OK," said Matthew and did as his father requested before turning the car off and climbing out. Before they'd taken two steps toward the glass door of the store, Lawrence Hudson appeared in it and stepped through.

"What have you got there?" he asked, one car enthusiast to another.

After he and Matthew talked cars for another five minutes, the three men went inside the store to talk jewelry. With the expert help, Matthew easily chose a beautiful tennis bracelet and his father chose a pair of lovely tear-drop earrings, pear-shaped sapphires surrounded by tiny sparkling diamonds. Lawrence Hudson wrapped up both boxes, tying them neatly with sparkling gold bows. The man was practiced, thought Matthew, and he was thankful for the professional job because he realized that he had never quite mastered the art of neatly wrapping presents. They were never perfectly square with carefully folded ends when he finished with them.

Both Matthew and Joc thanked Lawrence profusely for staying open just for them, and they said their good-byes.

"Thanks, Dad, for that introduction. That's one I might need again," he said, cryptically, enjoying the way his father's eyebrows knit in the center. It looked like Joc was trying to hide his look of concern, but Matthew had always been able to read his father's expressions.

After dropping his father at home with the promise of seeing his parents in the morning at church, Matthew slid back in his car and called Cici to tell her that he was on his way home. Tempted though he was to drive through one of his favorite coffee shops and get a latte to go, he opted for brewing his own when he got home instead. Then he cranked up his eclectic Christmas playlist for the ride home.

He was looking forward to knowing what it was that Danbury had discovered on the case, but for once his curiosity about the investigation was taking a back seat to his excitement about the Christmas season. His plan for the afternoon was to go home, wrap presents, and retrieve the bin of Christmas tree decorations from the spare bedroom where he'd stashed it when he pulled it, dusty though it was, down from his attic. He'd have it all laid out and ready for Angel tomorrow. He had "standed her up," as she had accused, he realized. He hadn't at all meant to but that was all pretty hard to explain to a four-year-old. His only recourse, he thought, was to just make it up to her. With Cici's help on the caroling and dinner, Matthew thought that Angel would be well made up to.

As he drove down Chester Road and into his condominium complex at the end, he noticed a gray sedan driving very slowly past him in the other direction. He recognized neither the car nor the driver, though the driver was mostly obscured behind dark sunglasses and a baseball hat. That was odd Matthew thought because the day was only partially sunny and the sun was completely obscured by clouds at the moment. It was in the fifties and too warm to snow but it surely looked like it could rain at any time, Matthew thought. Maybe the guy was just visiting one of the residents who lived down here, a son or more likely grandson. He saw Cici's rental car already in his driveway, so he forgot all about the strange car and driver, returning to his thoughts about the evening and all of the plans for the next day.

As he pulled into the driveway, Cici was coming out his front door. He parked the Corvette and doubled back without closing the garage door to see if she needed his help with whatever she seemed to be unloading from the car.

"Hiya handsome," she said, stepping up on tiptoe to kiss him. He leaned over and brushed her lips gently with his there in the middle of the driveway.

"Hello gorgeous," he responded grinning at her and easily picking up the old habits from their dating in previous years. "Need any help with anything?" he asked.

"I'm just bringing things in, but you're welcome to grab a few if you'd like," she said as she popped the trunk. "Just don't go in the backseat."

"OK," he said slowly.

"You're not the only one who can have Christmas secrets, mister," she said by way of explanation.

He helped her carry bags of groceries and packages marked with the name of a store that he didn't recognize into the house and then doubled back to close the garage door. As he came back in, he was dancing and singing, "Why's that partridge up that pear tree? I've no clue so just go ask him."

"Ask who?"

"The partridge."

"I don't think that's how the song goes," said Cici, rolling her eyes but laughing at him. Matthew was well known by the people closest to him for his habit of rewriting song lyrics or making them up entirely on his own.

"It is in my version."

"I swear, I've never known anyone else to get as excited about Christmas as you do. Christmas brings out the goofy in you."

"Yeah, I guess it does. Christmas was always special at the Paine house."

"It wasn't such a big deal for me growing up," she said, solemnly.

"That's just sad and we need to fix it," he said, grabbing her as if he were going to waltz with her, but swinging her around the kitchen and singing his version of the Christmas song. When they were both flushed with laughter, he pulled her to him and kissed her. Releasing her, he realized that the look on her face was sheer bliss and he cherished the moment. It was after all exactly what he wanted most to give her.

"I've got cooking to do," she announced.

"I've got wrapping to do. What are you cooking?"

"Oh no, you first. What are you wrapping?"

"I'll never tell."

"Well, me neither then!" she answered, laughing, as he detoured down the hallway.

Stopping up short, he asked, "Do you need any help with any of it?"

"No. It's all under control. Oh, by the way, is it OK to invite Mrs. Drewer for dinner tomorrow evening?"

That caught him off guard. "Sure, Angel befriended her last spring and she's met my family."

"Good, because I kind of already did."

"You talked to Mrs. Drewer?"

"I did. I saw her out walking her dog and I stopped to chat. I told her what we were planning and that I was trying to figure out how to seat us all with your kitchen situation. I figured the leaf on your little table in the eating nook flips out and you have four chairs, right? Two at the table, one at the desk in the living room, and one at the desk in your spare bedroom that we can pull in."

Matthew had returned to the kitchen and he just nodded.

"You have the little café table outside on your back porch, but it's pretty small. It only seats two and there are only two chairs. She offered us her card table and another chair. I told her to make it two chairs and join us and we'd have a deal."

"Wow," said Matthew, because that's all he could think to say. When they were dating previously and Matthew had moved into the condominium complex, Cici had been particularly annoyed with Mrs. Drewer's nosiness. "I'm impressed."

"Don't be. She's bringing fresh baked bread too," said Cici, grinning widely so that the merest hint of dimples showed. "With garlic butter."

"Sounds great. And really, I just need to wrap the presents that I bought for my family in London last summer, so there aren't any secrets down here," he thumbed down the hallway over his shoulder.

"Oh," said Cici, sounding mildly disappointed. "Well, I'm just going to start the spaghetti sauce and cook the meatballs so there really aren't any in here either."

"You're making it yourself?"

"From all but fresh tomatoes," she answered from the kitchen. "I didn't go quite that crazy. I'm using tomato sauce as the base. I found a recipe to make the meatballs out of ground beef and sausage. And I got wine to take to Penn's this evening, red and white, so that we're prepared for whatever she serves."

"Thanks Cees. Sounds like you've thought of everything," said Matthew, over his shoulder as he disappeared back down the hallway.

"Hopefully so," said Cici. "Would you mind getting the card table and chairs from Mrs. Drewer? Either this evening or tomorrow?"

"No problem," he called, as he slipped into the spare bedroom that was outfitted partially as a bedroom, where his life-long friend Justin slept whenever he was in town, and partially as an office that he never really used as such. He preferred to work at the desk in his living room instead. Pulling the boxes of presents over to the daybed and retrieving wrapping paper from the closet and tape and scissors from the desk drawer he went to work.

Humming to the Christmas music he'd set up to play on his speaker system while he wrapped, Matthew enjoyed looking at each gift one more time, thinking about how the recipients would like them, and wished again that he could wrap neatly. As he worked, he began to smell garlic and onion and other mingled spices emanating enticingly from the kitchen.

When the presents were all wrapped, Matthew stacked them neatly on the daybed, thinking he'd put them under the tree after it was decorated, and meandered into the kitchen. Cici had pulled her long strawberry blonde hair up into a messy bun and she was slightly flushed from working over the stove.

"Anything I can do to help?" he asked, hugging her from behind.

"Just the card table and chairs, if you don't mind," she said, smiling up over her shoulder at him, without stopping the work she was doing. "I'm nearly finished here for the night. I'll cook the pasta and put the finishing touches on tomorrow, but I wanted to get the sauce and meatballs done ahead so that the spices mingle together and settle in overnight."

"It smells wonderful," said Matthew, grabbing a jacket and heading for the front door. "Hey, what is in all of these other bags?"

"Get out of those!" she said, rounding the corner and smacking his hand out of the closest of the bags that she'd left stacked on the end of his sofa. "Those are surprises."

"For me?" he grinned at her.

"Well, for Angel," she admitted, grinning back.

"Why can't I see them then?"

"Because then you wouldn't be surprised too."

"I'll be right back with the table and chairs," he said, sighing as he slipped out the front door.

When he returned, he found the sofa cleared of gifts and Cici comfortably ensconced on it with Max in her lap. The big cat was happily purring as she scratched his face and behind his ears with her perfectly manicured fingernails and crooned softly to him. Matthew put the folded table and chairs in the kitchen, pulled his jacket off, and sat down with Cici and Max.

"There you are, Big Guy. Where have you been hiding this afternoon?" he asked, scratching Max behind the ears. "Are you ready for your dinner?"

Max turned his face to stare at Matthew with huge luminous eyes at the mention of food. It was the fastest way to the big cat's heart.

"Show me?" asked Cici.

"About feeding Max?"

"Sure. He gets food and fresh water mornings and evenings, right?"

"He does. There's a measuring scoop in his food bin."

"And it's always dry food?"

"Yeah, I tried giving him some of the fancy canned food when he was a kitten and he turned his nose up at it. You'll like this way better anyway. The canned food is messier and smellier."

"I'll like whatever Max likes just fine," she said, rising from the sofa as Max jumped to the floor and ran to the kitchen yowling expectantly for his dinner. Matthew followed them in to show Cici the routine.

"This is the easy part," Matthew said, with a chuckle as he pulled the bin of cat food from his pantry. "The litter box is another story."

"You have one that automatically cleans the box, right? You just add litter once in a while and change the little collection bag thing in the front?"

"That's right," said Matthew as he rinsed and refilled the bowls, wondering how she knew that and surprised that she suddenly cared. He figured he'd just chalk it up to Christmas miracles, pondering how many more of those he might get this year.

22 ~ Dinner Reservations

"Are we driving together to dinner at the Lingles?" asked Cici as she put the last of the food she was preparing into the refrigerator and pulled out two bottles of white wine. Adding those to the two bottles of red in the carrying bag that was specifically designed for wine bottles, she turned expectantly.

"We can if you'd like," he said. "I don't know how late we'll be there."

"I'd like," she said. "Let me grab the strudel I got for dessert from the car and I'm ready to go whenever you are."

"I are," he said, grinning at her and replicating her response. "Let's take your rental car. It's already out of the garage and available."

"Sure. If you're OK with driving it again."

They both found their coats and Matthew turned on outdoor lights, picked up the wine carrier, locked up, and turned on the security system on the way out. They left his house through the side door and out through the side garage door. Matthew stashed the wine carrier on the back floorboard and they climbed in.

"I can't as easily play my Christmas playlist in this car," he said, and Cici just rolled her eyes as he backed out and headed down the street.

"Hey, did you happen to see a gray sedan parked or driving around my neighborhood earlier today? Like when you came home?"

When she didn't answer immediately, he looked over to see her grinning at him. "Home, huh?" she asked. "That has a nice ring to it."

"Does it? Would you really want to live here?"

"I might. I guess I just figured we'd sell both places and buy something that was ours when we got around to that. But of the two houses, I do like the quietness of your neighborhood better. Even though my house is detached, it's still close to the street and the lots are tiny so it might as well not be. And there are lots of noisy neighbors hosting parties and such at all hours. I'd rather be here than there on New Year's Eve. I guess that's telling."

"I guess it is," said Matthew, taking her hand and holding it on the console. Then, more solemnly, he asked, "When do you have to go back to London?"

"I'm planning to be here until January second, though I haven't booked my flight back yet. They celebrate Boxing Day the day after Christmas there and the banks are all closed. The twenty-sixth of December is a Thursday this year, but Charles and Marshall are taking off that whole next week, so I'm not in a rush to get back."

As they drove the short distance into Peak, Cici asked, "Matthew, what would you think if I decided not to finish out the next four months in London?"

After carefully considering her question for a moment, Matthew asked, "How would you do that and not feel like you're letting your clients down? And maybe even yourself?"

"I was talking to Mitch Moorestrom," she began. Matthew gave an involuntary twitch and his eyebrow rose at her mention of the name and she asked, "You really don't like him, do you?"

"I don't really, no," Matthew answered honestly.

"Because I dated him?"

"That's not it."

"He's perfectly nice to me. He's been very helpful actually, like when I got promoted to Junior Partner so quickly. Doing so that fast is unheard of, but he showed me the ropes and helped me through that process as he did it himself."

"He seems possessive of you, I guess, and that annoys me," Matthew admitted. "I can't completely describe it but there's just something about him that comes off as insincere. He's too highly polished. It's like everything he says is rehearsed and not genuine. I guess maybe that's the legal training, but I don't trust him."

"We weren't ever seriously dating, you know."

"Yeah, I don't think he got that memo."

In his peripheral vision, he saw Cici roll her eyes at him as she said, "He is the only other junior partner who could handle an international client like this. The banking industry is complicated when you start working internationally, with world currencies and trade restrictions. There are so many rules and regulations and they're all different in different countries. Mitch has worked more with pharmaceuticals but he's dabbled into banking law. He's very interested in it, and he's good at international law with the big pharma companies. He's agreed to come back to London with me for a month to make the transition and then I could come home without finishing out those last three months. If the senior partners are willing and if," she left that sentence hanging, and Matthew could feel her eyes imploringly on him.

"If I want you to? Cees, I'm not going to make a decision like that for you. I never want to hold you back from your career advancement, from doing what you want with your career."

"I'm not asking you to make it. I'm just asking you to weigh in on it."

"You know I'd love to have you back here after a month instead of four," he said, squeezing her hand that he still held on the console between them. "But only if that's what you really want."

"I do. I miss you and this past week has done nothing but show me how much. I want to move forward with you and I feel like we're stalled out and in a holding pattern if I'm back in London for four more months."

"If that's what you really want then I'm all for it. I'm not too excited about you spending a month in London with Moorestrom, but otherwise I fully support the plan if that's what you want."

They pulled into the long gravel driveway of the Lingle Plantation, the name that the residents of Peak had traditionally called the old historic homestead of Penn and Leo Lingle, and Matthew parked the car in front. As they were climbing out Matthew retrieved the wine carrier with the four bottles from the back floorboard and Cici pulled the strudel from the back seat. The front of the house was well lit with Christmas lights. In addition to the porch lights, candles burned welcomingly in all of the windows.

Penn and Danbury appeared at the front door to greet them. The big detective looked more domestic than Matthew could ever have imagined with one arm around Penn's shoulders and the other holding the door open for their guests. What a homey scene, thought Matthew, as he took in the lights and greenery that was artfully draped across the front porch rails, with red bows at each post, and along the railings in the main hallway inside.

After the initial greetings and introductions, Penn led them down the main hallway toward the kitchen. Matthew noticed that the top of all of the portraits which hung along the hallway wall, mostly of long dead Lingle relatives, were adorned with greenery and red berries. Only one of the frames had a gold strip of a light fixture above it that had been added since the last time Matthew had been in the house. The illuminated portrait was that of three children, who Matthew had earlier correctly assumed to be the Lingle siblings Penn, Allan, and Leo.

In the warm cozy kitchen, there was a delightful smell emanating from somewhere and Leo stood by the stove stirring something in a sauce pan.

"Hi Doctor," he began. "I mean, Matthew," Leo corrected himself.

"Good to see you, Leo," said Matthew, as they entered the kitchen and he handed the wine selections and the strudel over to Penn.

"Oh, good!" she said. "You brought a nice selection of wines and that strudel looks delicious. Oh, a Bordeaux and a cab. We're having roast beef with carrots, onions, and potatoes. These will go nicely," she said, selecting the cabernet sauvignon. "Warren, would you pour our wine, please? And some water glasses too," she added, handing him a cork screw and placing the other bottle of white wine in the refrigerator.

Penelope Lingle, Matthew noted, was one of very few people he'd ever heard call the big detective by his first name. Most everyone else called him either Detective Danbury or just plain Danbury.

"We'll have salads first and the rest should be ready in about five minutes," said Penn over her shoulder as she rearranged the refrigerator and pulled out a large salad bowl. "Leo is stirring the gravy, the finishing touch, now. Have a seat wherever you'd like," Penn added, motioning to the table in the kitchen that was already set with plates, bowls, and cutlery.

"There's nothing we can do to help?" asked Cici.

"Not a thing," replied Penn as she joined them at the table and Danbury followed. Leo slid the pot over to another burner on the stove and covered it before also taking a seat at the table.

"Matthew, would you bless our dinner?" asked Penn. "I've seen you do that, just quietly. Growing up, we said blessings regularly but I'm out of practice. Do you mind?"

"Not at all," said Matthew and Cici reached for his hand as he blessed the food and the friendships at the table.

As they began eating, Matthew asked how Malcolm was doing. Malcolm had been Allan's caregiver and he'd been getting his nursing degree meanwhile. At Penn and Leo's invitation, he'd stayed on at the Lingle Plantation to complete the degree.

"Malcolm finished his degree a couple of weeks ago and took a job at a small hospital just over the Virginia state line to be closer to his sister up there. He was so meticulous and caring with Allan, I know he'll do a great job up there. I'm sure he'll be busy but hopefully he'll stay in touch."

*****

After a wonderful dinner with much laughter and conversation, the dishes had been cleared and Leo, Penn, and Cici were working on those while Danbury pulled Matthew aside.

"Penn, we'll be back. OK if Matthew and I talk in the study?"

"Sure, going off to smoke cigars and drink brandy?" she asked with a wink.

"Right," said Danbury jokingly.

"Talking work, huh?" asked Penn seriously.

"He's signed back on. Literally. I want to get him up to speed."

"Be right back," said Matthew to Cici, as he kissed her on top of the head.

"OK," said Cici. Matthew neither saw nor heard any concern in her voice or demeanor so he followed Danbury down the hallway to the study.

Danbury closed the door behind them and they took seats in leather chairs opposite each other as he said, "There are cigars in here. They're old. But they're supposed to be really good. If you want one."

"I hear that's an acquired taste," said Matthew. "It's one that I've never acquired."

"Me either. But I had to ask. I'm trying to be less abrupt. And more hospitable."

"Ah, by Penn's request? You're the epitome of civility," said Matthew, grinning as he teased Danbury. "Seriously, though. I know you had a crush on her all those years ago and you look happy together. That's great."

He couldn't be certain, but as Danbury looked down, Matthew could have sworn that he saw the big detective blush. That was very much out of character for the guy, Matthew thought, so maybe he just imagined it.

"You have updates on the Washburn murder?" Matthew prompted, changing the subject.

"Yeah. A couple. Important ones."

"Anything I can help with?"

"Maybe. When we talk to Reynolds on Monday."

"OK, catch me up."

"Money was wired. Into the catering servers' accounts. Both who didn't show up. But then did. The woman who was murdered. And the guy who's still missing."

"That is important information."

"But then it was moved. Out of the woman's account. The night she was murdered. Looks like it went into his. The missing server's account. And then all of it back out again."

"That's pretty incriminating," said Matthew, leaning forward in the chair he was seated in. "What do you know about this guy?"

"Not much yet. We're working on it. But he's a ghost. Didn't exist before two years ago. His RAP sheet started nearly two years ago. And there's not much on him prior."

"Wow!"

"It gets better. Tracing the funds forward was easy. The guy didn't know what he was doing. He didn't cover his tracks. We're watching the funds. So that we can locate him. When he tries to access it. We also traced the fund transfers backward. Our tech forensic experts did. To a bank that most of Cici's law firm uses. That was much harder. We just have the routing information of the bank. But we need a warrant. To see a specific account. The one it came out of originally. And we need more concrete evidence. To get the warrant."

"So you have no idea who the funds came from?"

"Not yet. We're still searching. Finding what we do know was hard. Should have been impossible. Whoever moved the money originally. To the two caterers' accounts. They knew what they were doing. They ran it through multiple other locations. Before it landed in those accounts. But our tech guys are better," added Danbury with a grin.

"That's impressive work on somebody's part," agreed Matthew.

"That looks incriminating. For Kennedy Reynolds. That's why we need to tread carefully. On Monday. I can't arrest him. But we don't want to spook him."

"I see."

"Do you? You tread more carefully. More so than I do."

"Ah, that's why you want me there. Not because there's anything medically forensic happening."

"Right."

"But I have serious reservations."

"You had dinner. You don't need reservations," said Danbury, cracking a smile.

Matthew had to chuckle at Danbury making a joke. "I have serious reservations about Kennedy Reynolds' guilt."

"Really?"

"I know, I don't like the guy. It sounds like not too many people do, not any that I've met so far in fact. But I think he's innocent, at least of the murder."

"Huh," said Danbury, rubbing the stubble on his chin. To Matthew's relief, he didn't ask any further questions, particularly about why.

"A payout could also have come from Aubrey Bartles, right? Because he could have paid off the catering company workers and staged the night in jail many miles and a couple of hours away. Why else would you speed that fast through that particular town, where everybody knows the speed limit drops and the police station is right off the interstate? Unless you had another motive, getting caught and providing yourself what appeared to be an airtight alibi. A night in jail so far away appears to provide him with the perfect alibi."

"We know where Reynolds banks. We don't have banking information on Bartles. Not yet. But we're working on that too."

"And there are no other likely suspects at this point?" asked Matthew. "I mean, is unrequited love really a strong enough motive for murder?"

"The word 'likely' is key. We haven't found any other suspects yet. And you'd be surprised. Motives for murder aren't often complicated ones. And love is a strong one. Unrequited or unfaithful. Either way."

"Cici said that she and Abby had gone through files and hadn't found any other likely candidates. At least, no obvious motives jumped out at them."

"Yeah, I know. Most people loved Washburn. We are low on motives. Even from Kennedy Reynolds. Bartles is the only one with a motive. So far at least."

"How can I help in talking to Reynolds on Monday? Were you looking for a good cop to play against your bad one?"

"Something like that. Most people are cagey about financial information. Reynolds seems to have no problem with letting people know that he has it. Substantial financial resources. He's not all that likely to divulge specifics. But I have to try. I'm running out of angles to come at this one from."

"You want me to ask him for access to his banking records?" asked Matthew skeptically.

"Just if he banks at the First Trust Bank of Raleigh. I know it sounds inane. I thought I'd ask him. And then you can listen. To see if he's sincere in his response. And complete. If he chooses to answer the question."

"He's a highly trained lawyer with a reputation of complete control in the courtroom. I don't know what I can glean from him that you won't, but I'll come along if you think it'll help."

"You are less abrupt. Your mannerisms are more polished. More like his. If nothing else."

Eyebrow raised, Matthew just chuckled as he said, "Penn really has been working you over about this abrupt thing, hasn't she?"

"She might have mentioned it. Once or twice," said Danbury ruefully.

23 ~ Perfectly Decorated

After a restless night of tossing and turning, Matthew crawled out of bed Sunday morning and poured a large cup of coffee with the usual surplus of cream and sugar. He knew that he'd upset Cici when she wanted to stay for the night and he had, once again refused. She was closer than he'd wanted her until she got back from her remaining time in London, however long that might now be, he thought.

Maybe she was right that they were both too far gone emotionally for it to matter. But it did matter, to him at least. Morally it mattered. Pulling away from her the night before though had been the second hardest thing he'd remembered doing in his personal life in a while. It was right behind having broken up with her nearly two years prior. Like it or not, he didn't think he could become any more emotionally attached to her no matter what they did or didn't do.

He had mulled those thoughts over through his morning routine all the way to church and through a good bit of the church service that he realized later to his chagrin he remembered precious little of. Cici seemed distant this morning too, he thought, adding insult to injury. But why wouldn't she be after he'd pushed her away yet again? It wasn't that he had commitment issues, or was it? He'd been committed to her before. Completely so.

But maybe that was the problem. Maybe he was truly afraid of being that deeply hurt again. And the only way to be that deeply hurt again was to love her that deeply again. Could that be it, he wondered? If Cici had remained the person she'd been when he met her and she'd never gotten jaded by her legal career aspirations, would they be married by now? Would they have children of their own? Was she right that he couldn't be more connected to her than he currently was? But she had gotten jaded and she had thought his life choices too simplistic. They had broken up and it had broken his heart when they did.

He was still pondering those thoughts over lunch when his sister Monica spoke up, "Matthew, did you hear what Angel just asked you? You're a million miles away again, aren't you?"

"I'm sorry, sweetie, what did you say?" he asked Angel as they were finishing their lunch at the restaurant they'd chosen after church. It was a weekly ritual to discuss the restaurant, bringing up new choices regularly, and then settle on one of three of their favorites most weeks. This week, it was a French café because they were having spaghetti for dinner so their favorite Italian place was quickly ruled out.

"I said you're not standing me up again, right?" She looked genuinely concerned, probably due to his preoccupation with his own thoughts when she asked, "We're decorating today, OK?"

"You bet we are! The tree will be perfectly decorated when we're finished with it!" he responded, hoping that the enthusiasm that he put into his response sounded genuinely excited and didn't fall flat. Kids were perceptive, he knew, and this one exceptionally so.

"OK. Just checkin' 'cause you can't stand me up again."

Casting a glance across the table at Monica, who Matthew had been told had made the initial comment about standing his little niece up, his eyebrow went up involuntarily. Angel was apparently not letting it go. Monica met Matthew's eyes briefly and then unsuccessfully tried to hide a smirk before looking away.

"I'm ready when you are," said Matthew. "I drove the Element so that your car seat easily fits. Let's go decorate a tree!"

"OK!" said Angel.

"Matthew, she could finish her meal first," protested Monica.

"I am finished, Momma," said Angel, jumping up and pulling her coat from the back of her chair.

"I'm sorry. Cici, are you finished? Or are you still working on your quiche?" Matthew thought to ask.

"I was mostly finished," said Cici, looking up at Matthew calmly.

"OK, I'll go find our server and settle our bill. That'll give you both a few more minutes," said Matthew, including Angel in the comment.

With a heavy sigh, Angel climbed back into her booster seat and plopped down, "OK, OK," she muttered as she stuffed her ham and cheese croissant into her mouth and chewed loudly in apparent annoyance at the delay.

*****

After the bill was settled and the car seat had been transferred, Matthew, Cici, and Angel set out for Matthew's house. He'd picked Cici up that morning so they all went together. They arrived after multiple games of "I spy with my eye." Angel was relentless at the game. Matthew had to go drag Max out of the back of his closet where he'd apparently hidden when he heard the noise of a child so that Angel could pet him before she was ready to start the decorating.

Cici put a big pot on the stove and poured in a large jug of apple cider from the refrigerator, turning it on to simmer and adding cinnamon sticks. Meanwhile, Matthew had pulled up his *Christmas Favorites* playlist and connected it by Bluetooth it to his home stereo speaker system. After getting Angel seated on the floor putting gold metal hangers on the non-breakable ornaments, Matthew wandered into the kitchen.

"Are we OK?" he asked Cici as he wrapped his arms around her and kissed her gently on top of her head.

"You tell me," she said, turning to face him. "Are we?"

Not knowing what to say to that he spluttered, "I hope so."

"Me too," she admitted. "But last night I wasn't so sure."

"We'll be OK, Cees. We've got the rough spots after that horrible break up to work through, but we can be OK." He leaned over to kiss her. She wrapped her arms around his neck and he lifted her off the floor, pinning her up against the cabinet as he kissed her with all of his pent-up emotion.

"Ewww!" he heard from behind him. As he gently set Cici back on her feet, they both turned to see that Angel had wandered into the kitchen behind them and she'd scrunched up her face in dismay with the exclamation. That fully broke the ice and Matthew and Cici both laughed.

"Are you gonna get married and live in a tree?"

"What?" asked Cici.

"You know, Cici and Matthew living in a tree K S S K I K G," Angel answered earnestly, misquoting the rhyme.

"You mean, sitting in a tree K I S S I N G?" asked Matthew, eyebrows raised as he tried not to laugh at the serious child.

"Yeah, you live happily ever after when you kiss and live in a tree," explained Angel. "Uncle Matt, I'm ready to get lifted up to hang the glassable ones," she said, dismissing the conversation before turning and skipping back into the other room.

"Well, I guess it's a tree for us then. You want to hang some glassable ornaments?" asked Matthew, quickly kissing Cici and then following Angel back into the other room.

"Just a sec. I want to get the sauce back on the stove on simmer first."

"OK," he said.

As he turned the corner into his living room, Angel was holding up one of the glass balls that Matthew had put aside and told her that he'd handle. He figured there wasn't much that was breakable which held any sentimental value, so he shrugged aside even a light reprimand and lifted the expectant child so that she could carefully place the ornament.

They repeated the process until the tree was decorated and Angel stood back, arms crossed, to examine their work.

"OK now?" asked Matthew.

Angel inspected the front of the tree where it stood in the corner with close scrutiny. "OK now!" she exclaimed as he flipped a switch to turn on the tree lights.

"Ooooo!" said Angel, hands clasped and eyes wide. "It's perfectly decorated!"

After they all admired it, Matthew retrieved the presents and Angel helped him to carefully stack them around the skirt under the tree. "Whose is this one?" she asked with each new package. After they'd all been placed, the child who missed nothing looked up at Matthew in concern and whispered, "Where's Cici's? Doesn't she get one? She'll be sad if you forgot her."

Matthew leaned over conspiratorially and whispered back, "Hers is the best of all. But if I put it under the tree, she might guess what it is."

"Ohhh!" said Angel. "And it has to be a 'sprise."

"Exactly," said Matthew.

"What are you two whispering about?" asked Cici, returning from stirring the sauce.

"Christmas secrets!" exclaimed Angel.

"I'm not sure that I can stand any more of those," said Cici with a laugh. "The tree is lovely, Angel. You did a great job."

"Thank you," she said somewhat shyly under Cici's praise. The two hadn't interacted much over the years when he and Cici were previously seriously dating, Matthew supposed, and Angel had been too young then to be completely relational back then anyway.

"OK, now on to printing out Christmas caroling music and setting up for the spaghetti dinner after caroling," said Matthew. "What are your favorite Christmas songs?" Matthew asked Angel, expecting responses like Frosty and Rudolph.

"Oh Christmas Tree, what are you doing!" she exclaimed.

"Oh Christmas Tree?" repeated Matthew, realizing that the rewriting of song lyrics seemed to have been handed down another generation. "Like this?" he asked, playing the song.

"That's it!" said Angel, singing her version of the song along with the music.

"OK, what else?"

After they'd compiled the list of songs and Matthew had printed them out and put them in binders, he and Angel set up the tables, placing the chairs around them. Just as he was thinking it looked very slipshod, Cici returned from his guest bedroom with one of the bags she'd brought in the day before. She pulled a lovely long Christmas tablecloth with golden bells embroidered around the edge from the bag and Matthew helped her to spread it across their collection of tables.

"It could stand to be ironed," she said. "You have an iron and ironing board somewhere, right?"

After pulling the requested supplies from the laundry room, Matthew watched in awe as Cici, who had insisted on doing the ironing, carefully removed the fold creases from the table cloth. Matthew put the iron and ironing board back in his laundry room and then he and Angel set the table with all but the plates. Meanwhile, Cici was busy in the kitchen preparing dinner and humming Christmas carols as she worked. In that moment, Matthew realized that if someone had told him two years ago that Cici would be doing any of those things, much less happily humming meanwhile, he'd have laughed in disbelief.

"You're not putting the plates on the table?" asked Matthew.

"Nope. I'm fixing the plates myself when we're ready to eat," she announced. "It's nearly five, so let's go get you all ready, Angel."

"I'm not ready?" asked the child.

"Not quite," said Cici, taking her by the hand and leading her down the hallway to the guest bedroom. "We have some packages to open first." When they reappeared, Angel and Cici both carried boxes that looked to have been professionally wrapped, Matthew noticed.

"OK, let's start with this one," said Cici, handing Angel a rectangular box that was, Matthew thought, only slightly smaller than the breadbox that all mysterious things got compared to.

"This is for me?" asked Angel.

"It is," said Cici. "It's an early Christmas present. So are these," she added, indicating the stack of boxes they'd just carried out. Cici patted for Angel to sit down beside her on the sofa and Matthew perched on the ottoman of the chair opposite them.

"Oh boy!" said Angel, ripping the beautiful wrapping off and tossing it aside. The lid was off of the box even more quickly than the wrapping paper came off and Angel held up a brown lace-up leather boot with a low heel and admired it. "Boots!" she exclaimed. "They look like yours."

Angel, Matthew admitted to himself, was more observant than he was because Cici was indeed sporting a heeled version of the same brown boots that laced up over her ankle.

"Can I wear them?"

"That's the idea," said Cici, laughing at the child's delight.

"Do you want to put them on now? Or open the rest of your presents?"

"Now!" exclaimed Angel, kicking off her velcroed shoes and tugging on the laces of the boots.

"Can I loosen those for you?" asked Cici.

"OK," said Angel, handing them over.

After the boots were on, Matthew watched as Cici checked to be sure they fit. How she knew to do that, he had no idea, but then Angel pranced proudly around the room in them. "I'm Cici, and I'm beautiful," said Angel, flipping imaginary hair off of her shoulder. Her own dark hair was held back from her face by a ponytail. Matthew and Cici both laughed at her antics.

"OK, next box?" asked Matthew, joining in the female adventure and curious himself because Cici hadn't enlightened him as to the contents of the boxes.

"OK! Which one next?" Angel asked Cici.

"Why don't you try this one?" said Cici, handing her a large robe box.

As the wrapping came of the box and the lid followed that to the floor, Angel pulled out a green velvet dress trimmed in mottled cream and brown faux fur with a matching cape. "I love it!" said Angel excitedly and suddenly flung her arms around Cici.

Cici just smiled as she hugged the child back. "I'm so glad. I thought you could wear it caroling tonight. And then maybe to any other Christmas parties or plays or musicals that you go to."

"Yea!" exclaimed Angel. "I want to!"

"You have a couple more boxes over there yet," said Matthew, who figured that he might be enjoying this even more than Angel was, but for totally different reasons.

"This one is not very exciting," said Cici, handing over the smallest one.

Without another word, Angel laid the green dress carefully across the box on the sofa beside her, and tore into the next box that Cici handed her. "It's tights and a bow," said Angel. "Does it go with the dress?"

"That's right," said Cici. "The tights go with the boots and the dress. The bow is for your hair."

"OK, thanks," said Angel matter-of-factly as Cici handed her another box. This one contained a little faux fur hand muff with a cord that snapped around the neck and a matching hat, both of which matched the trim on the dress.

"It goes with the dress!" exclaimed Angel, plopping the hat on her head at a jaunty angle. "But what's this?"

"That's a hand muff. You snap the cord behind your neck so that it hangs down in front of you. When your hands get cold, you stick them in to warm them up."

"Ohhhh!" said Angel, grinning broadly at Cici. "It's so soft!"

Matthew was beginning to get the picture, quite literally, in his mind. Angel would be dressed for the evening looking like a child out of a Dickens Christmas display. He just shook his head, grinning at Cici, "Where did you find this?" he asked.

"I saw it in the window of a darling little children's shop over in Woodburn Village when I took Marshall and Charles to that biscuit restaurant down there last Saturday. Then I remembered having seen it when Angel started talking about Christmas caroling and I thought she would look adorable in it."

"She will. You're amazing, Cees," he said, rising and picking up the final box from the floor. Kissing Cici on top of the head as he leaned over to hand Angel the box, he enjoyed the fragrance of her hair. It was alluring, he thought, or maybe that was mostly the woman herself.

The last box, the biggest of the stack, contained a long cream-colored coat that was trimmed in cream faux fur. It was all lighter than the trim on the dress, cape, hat, and hand muff but it all coordinated nicely, Matthew noticed. Trust Cici to have put all of that together in a single afternoon. The woman had an intrinsic sense of style and an effortless class about her. He'd have to remember to tell her that, he thought, as his parents knocked and then came through his front door.

"Hi Mom, Dad," he said, rising and taking their coats, kissing his mom on the cheek and motioning them in.

"Look at my Christmas presents!" exclaimed Angel, sliding the boxes apart and pulling the clothes out, spreading them out across the sofa. "I get to wear my new outfit to go Christmas caroling! And to parties!"

"I see. That's lovely," said Jackie appreciatively as Angel picked up each item for her inspection.

"And the tree! We decorated it perfect!" said Angel as Jackie murmured appreciative comments over the tree as well.

After hanging his parents' coats in the hall closet, Matthew said, "Let me get this mess out of the way so you can find a seat." He scooped up and scrunched the wrapping paper while Cici picked up the boxes, stacked them on the coffee table, and made a neat pile of the clothing on the arm of the sofa.

"We have hot apple cider on the stove with mugs on the counter, if anyone would like some," said Cici, easily assuming the role of hostess. "And there's hummus and vegetables and also cheese and crackers on the island in the kitchen. The little dessert plates are out, so help yourselves."

"I think I might," said Joc. "It's hard to carol on an empty stomach," he winked at Angel.

"Do you want to go put your new clothes on before your parents get here?" Cici asked Angel.

"Yes! Momma will love it!"

"OK, let's go back to your Uncle Matt's room and get you all dressed up." She scooped up all but the coat from the sofa in one arm and took a beaming Angel by the hand. Matthew could hear their excited chatter down the hallway before he heard his bedroom door close behind them.

"Did you do that?" Jackie asked.

"You do know better than that, right?" asked Matthew with a grin.

"Cici did that?" she asked, the surprise showing in her face.

"She did. She kept it a secret from me too. I just now saw it all as Angel was opening the boxes."

*****

The group had taken lots of pictures of Angel in her outfit and set out for the caroling adventure shortly after five. They'd almost made their way through Matthew's small condominium neighborhood singing when Cici excused herself to return to his house to put the finishing touches on dinner.

"Can I help with anything?" Mrs. Drewer asked her.

"Sure, I'd love your help," said Cici.

"Good. I'm not much at singing anyway. They'll sound better without me," declared Cordelia Drewer, following her back to Matthew's house.

"Six more?" asked Angel, who did seem to be wearing down from all the excitement, but who looked adorable, as Cici had promised, in her Christmas outfit.

"Yep, are you up for it?" asked Matthew.

"Yeah, we can't disappoint your tired neighbors," replied Angel, taking a deep breath and stepping up the walkway to the next house as the adults all muffled chuckles and followed.

After those last six houses, a tired Angel returned to Matthew's house an hour and a half after they'd begun with an assortment of treats including candy canes, chocolates, a gold dollar coin, and homemade cookies. Christmas caroling, thought Matthew, was better than Halloween trick-or-treating. The adults emptied the goodies from their coat pockets onto the coffee table before reconvening in the kitchen to await orders from Cici and Mrs. Drewer.

"Sit anywhere you'd like," said Cici. "The salads are waiting for you, dressings are on the island, and I'll have plates ready for everyone in a moment."

"It's a special Christmas 'spasghetti!'" exclaimed Angel. The child seemed to have two speeds, Matthew thought, full on and full off. She had been running down after the caroling but she seemed to have gotten a second wind.

"What can I do?" asked Matthew, slipping up behind Cici and kissing her on top of the head.

"Pour wine for anyone who wants some," said Cici, who was pulling green angel hair pasta from the pot with tongs, twisting it around itself, and arranging the twisted strands in an open ring on each plate. She hadn't shared her "Christmas 'spasghetti'" plan with him at all. He had just thought they were having spaghetti and meatballs, so he watched in fascination before she looked enquiringly up at him and he moved on to pull down wine glasses, take wine orders, fill glasses, and hand them out.

After the salad that was accompanied by Mrs. Drewer's homemade bread which was a resounding success, Cici asked Matthew to help hand out the plates. She'd put them in the oven warmer while they ate their salads. What she pulled from the warmer, Matthew thought, was a remarkable work of art. Each plate had a twisted ring of spinach pasta that was drizzled with sauce like ribbon. Two large meatballs that roughly formed bows adorned the bottom. Cici was adding grated parmesan cheese that looked like it had snowed, and sprigs of fresh basil around the meatballs on each plate before Matthew picked them up to distribute them.

As he brought the plates to the table, first for his mother and Mrs. Drewer before the others, Angel was unable to contain her excitement any longer and exclaimed, "Christmas reefs of 'spasghetti and meatballs! Cici made the noodles green!"

"It's just spinach angel hair pasta," clarified Cici to Matthew's relief because Angel's description sounded less than appetizing.

"It's lovely!" said Jackie as Matthew, with his hand clad in an oven mitt, placed her plate carefully in front of her. "Where did you get this idea?"

Cici pondered for a moment and then said, "I think it just came to me in the pasta section of the grocery store when I saw the spinach angel hair pasta. It had to be angel hair pasta, of course," she added, winking at Angel. "And the rest sort of just took shape from there. I hope you enjoy it."

After asking a blessing on the meal and those gathered around the table, Matthew realized that he hadn't thought about the Washburn murder case all day. He wondered how the Washburns were doing as he glanced appreciatively around the makeshift table at the family, woman, and neighbor he loved. He decided to pause and drink in the moment before digging into his Christmas spaghetti wreath.

24 ~ Connections

It had been a busy Monday but Matthew had managed to slip out of the office in time to meet Danbury at Cici's office by five-thirty. Still a few minutes early when he arrived, he parked in the parking deck below the building and took the elevator up to the lobby.

Not seeing Danbury or anyone else in the lobby after hours, Matthew slowly circled the huge Christmas tree looking for the other ornament that he hadn't located earlier. It was elusive, but he finally found the orange and black ornament low on the left side and quickly switched it with the other blue ornament hanging front and center on the tree. A private and academically challenging university, this darker blue ornament at least had a right to be somewhat arrogant. He noted that his red ornament was still exactly where he'd put it just above where the orange one now hung. Satisfied with his effort, Matthew stepped over to the main desk in the lobby to request the required badge that enabled access to the top floors.

After a few minutes when nobody appeared, he pushed the button marked for that purpose. It was a necessity sometimes, he realized, but he'd always rather give the desk concierge a moment to appear from wherever they were when not at the desk before ringing a bell. It was silent in the lobby, but a young woman quickly appeared from a tall wooden door behind the desk.

"May I help you?" she asked.

Matthew provided his identification and explained the purpose of his visit. The woman looked a bit ashen at the reference to the Washburn case. She quickly handed over a temporary access badge and provided the instructions, which Matthew already knew, for which elevator to use and how to access the top three floors.

Matthew stopped briefly by Cici's office on the thirtieth floor. She already knew he'd be there so she didn't appear surprised when she looked up from her desk and saw him standing in her doorway. "Dinner later?" Matthew asked, after she stood to greet him with a kiss. "I'll pick it up," he said and then added, looking down at her appreciatively, "You've done enough cooking for a while."

"Sure. I won't be here much longer but I can wait until you're finished to leave. My place tonight?"

"OK, I'll swing back by," he said, kissing her lightly. Then heading down the hallway, he went to the elevator to go up a floor. He went in the direction she'd pointed him to get to Kennedy Reynolds' corner office.

Danbury was already seated in a chair in front of Reynolds when Matthew tapped on the partially open door and Reynolds motioned him in and told him to have a seat. Seated beside Danbury, across from Reynolds, Matthew felt the tension in the room but there was silence. Danbury tapped a pen on the notebook he held, as if waiting for something.

After what seemed like ten minutes to Matthew but was probably far less, Reynolds said, "I don't know what you hope to accomplish by harassing me about my financial information. You know that, without some evidence and a search warrant or a subpoena, I don't have to provide you with anything."

"It wasn't a demand," said Danbury firmly but cautiously. "It was a request."

"Request denied," said Reynolds quickly. "Without sufficient evidence, you will not be granted the subpoena you need to garner that information. You have no evidence because I'm not guilty. It's as simple as that."

"If you're innocent, then prove it," said Danbury. "Tell us about the altercation with Washburn in the stairwell. Or show us the past month of financial transactions. All that originated from accounts at the First Trust Bank of Raleigh."

"Surely, Detective, you know how this works. If you want that information, you'll have to go through the proper channels. And you," he turned to Matthew. "You were in the stairwell immediately after the incident. If Mr. Washburn had said anything to incriminate me, I'd already have been taken downtown. That hasn't happened so he either refrained from comment or exonerated me entirely of any guilt. Either way, I do not have to cooperate with you or provide you with any additional information, banking or otherwise."

Matthew chose to take a different approach. "Mr. Reynolds, if you are innocent as you say and you held no animosity toward Mr. Washburn, then surely you want to know what happened to him and why. If it is related to the altercation in the stairwell in any way, that will eventually come to light."

"It is not," said Reynolds looking down his nose. "There is no relevance whatsoever."

"Depending on the motive then, you or any of the other senior partners here could also be at risk," Matthew added, well knowing that the legal mind operated on cool clean logic unless trying to evoke emotion on behalf of a client in the courtroom. "Have you considered that? Helping to determine who killed Mr. Washburn could prevent future murders. Including your own."

"I am not in any more danger personally than I ever am I can assure you. I have made enemies in my profession."

Changing approach again, Matthew asked, "You want to know what Mr. Washburn said to us in the stairwell after you left, don't you?"

Reynolds merely shrugged and said, "Curiosity on the matter does not overcome me."

Just as Danbury seemed poised to interject, his phone rang and he checked the display. "I need to take this. Excuse me just a minute."

"We're finished here," said Reynolds. "I did tell you that I had nothing more to add when you requested this meeting. You are most certainly excused."

Matthew rose from his seat, but instead of following Danbury out of Kennedy Reynolds' office, he lingered in the doorway and suddenly asked, "You aren't guilty of anything more than losing your temper and momentarily allowing a chink into that carefully crafted armor of yours, are you?"

"I beg your pardon?" said Reynolds, somehow managing to look down his nose while looking up at Matthew, though his patrician face displayed more surprise than disdain.

"You didn't kill Jamison Washburn yourself nor were you involved in his murder," said Matthew, casually, is if he were stating a well-known fact.

"I did not and I was not."

"Are you being framed? Or was the incident in the stairwell just accidental perfect timing from somebody's perspective?"

"I don't know for certain."

"But you have your suspicions that someone might be setting you up?"

"Perhaps."

"Do you know who?"

"No."

"But you know why, don't you? You know why someone might have set you up."

"I do not. I merely know the means by which someone might have ensured an altercation between me and Washburn. The timing of it they could not have predicted."

"Then why won't you tell anyone what the altercation was about in the stairwell? If it was unrelated to the murder or something minor and you can prove that, why not explain and remove the suspicion?"

"Because it's personal. And it's not anyone's business."

"Personal to you? Or to Washburn?"

"Why should I answer you when I've explained to no one else?"

"Because," said Matthew, retaking the seat opposite Reynolds, though uninvited to do so, "I'm probably the only person who now believes that you're innocent of the murder. If whatever the altercation was about wasn't worthy of murder, as you claim, then why not exonerate yourself by explaining it? That also moves the focus of the investigation off of you so that the real murderer can be found and apprehended."

There was a long silence in which Matthew chose to wait him out and maybe even let the silence become uncomfortable without filling it himself. He feared that he'd just be excused as Danbury had been. At long last the man looked over at Matthew and simply asked, "Why do you believe that I'm innocent?"

That was the last thing Matthew had expected him to say and "I had a dream" sounded like an insane answer. After pondering a careful response for a moment, he said, "I think you're a lot of things, and I'll admit that I don't like most of them, but a murderer isn't one of them, is it?"

If he had expected anger from that gut-level honest response, Matthew didn't get it. Instead he got a look of resignation of fate, acceptance on some level, from Kennedy Reynolds. "I understand," he finally responded.

The surprise must have registered very clearly on Matthew's face because Reynolds continued, "We are all, at least on some level, a product of our environment, are we not?"

"I'm not sure I know what you mean," said Matthew. "We all have choices to make, choices about what we do and how we treat people around us, how we relate to them."

"True," said Reynolds slowly, "But the patterns in which we relate to other people, are they not learned behaviors? Instructed perhaps by years of expectations about how we should think of ourselves and how we fit into the space-time continuum on this planet that we occupy."

This conversation went far deeper to a philosophical level much more quickly than Matthew could ever have imagined, dream or no dream. "In the nurture versus nature debate about what forms a human psyche," said Matthew, remembering his psychology classes from his undergraduate years in college, "you're saying that nurture plays a greater role than nature? More so than free will or personal disposition?"

"Generally speaking, yes," said Reynolds. "We are formed to a large degree by those who raised us and shaped the world we were born into. I was born into a world of privilege, for better or worse, and there were many expectations about my behavior and choices. Surely you had expectations thrust upon you as well? You became a doctor, an esteemed and honored profession."

"That was the career I chose," answered Matthew honestly. "My intentions were to help people by choosing that career path. My parents supported my interests and encouraged me as I grew up but they didn't dictate that choice."

"I see," said Reynolds. "Then you were a very fortunate young man."

"You're insinuating that your parents forced you to become a lawyer?"

"Forced is a bit strong. But there were certain parameters within which to choose, you see. Certain schools that were acceptable choices and certain career paths that were as well."

"And there would have been consequences had you not chosen accordingly?" Matthew asked, finding himself being pulled into the discussion. Intrigued with seeing and hoping maybe to understand the depth of the man he'd thought was one of the most arrogant snobs he'd ever met, he leaned in slightly.

"There have been consequences, yes. I was to have gone into law simply to follow my mother's family legacy and become either a renowned judge or politician."

"That's not in your career path now?"

"Hardly. I would never have moved to North Carolina had it been. I enjoy practicing law and I excel at it. I have what they call a poker face, apparently unreadable, which serves me well and leaves the opposing counsel and all of their carefully coached witnesses constantly guessing and scrambling to catch up. I've won some rather impressive cases. Were you in the profession, certainly you'd already know about those. Were you new to it, you'd have studied some of them as part of your pedagogical program."

"I see," said Matthew. Looking beyond the arrogant confidence the man perpetually oozed, he asked instead, "Why did you choose to come to North Carolina?"

"That is an entirely different story but it is integrally connected to the rest. The dispute with Washburn, the reason I went by his office, other than to apologize, which I fully intended to do. The quid pro quo arrangement I was going to propose," said Reynolds, pausing to stare at Matthew, as if he were only just seeing him for the first time.

"Except that he had someone already in his office," continued Reynolds. "I chose to return to my office here, tie up a few loose ends to be gone for a few days, and get away to the mountain cottage for a long weekend. I thought I could apologize and discuss the arrangement I had in mind with him when I returned later. Except that there was no later. He was murdered before I had the chance to follow through with any of it."

Before Matthew could fully process this new information, Kennedy Reynolds leaned forward and suddenly asked, "Would you care to go for a drink?"

"A drink?" asked Matthew, incredulous. "A drink with you?"

"Yes, of course. Do you suppose you could tear yourself away from Ms. Patterson quite long enough for a drink?"

Both dumbfounded and intrigued, Matthew found himself agreeing to drinks and Kennedy Reynolds reached across his desk, drew a business card from the brass holder there, and jotted something on the back of it. Sliding it across the desk to Matthew, he said, "Meet me here."

"Matron Lane? Isn't that in downtown Raleigh? Off of Hillsborough Street?"

"It is."

Matthew knew perfectly well that, unlike Reynolds, he did not have a poker face. An eyebrow raised subconsciously, and he was sure the surprise registered clearly on his face. The arrogant man from the proper families wanted to meet him on Hillsborough Street across from the end of North Carolina State University's campus? As if the shock of that wasn't enough, he was glad to be sitting down when he heard the rest of the story.

"That's across from the bell tower, just at the end of the North Carolina State University campus?" Matthew finally asked dubiously.

"It is."

"Isn't there a sub shop there on the corner and some infamously bawdy fraternity houses down at the end of that dead end street?"

"I see that you know the area well."

"I grew up in Raleigh and several of my family members attended that university."

"There was and there were, yes," confirmed Reynolds. "But I live there now."

"You live there?"

"I do. That whole area is being bought up by a development company and they're building storefronts along the streets with apartments and living quarters above. An attempt at being very cosmopolitan, don't you think?" Before Matthew could answer, Reynolds continued, "The sub shop that was on the corner had been razed and the fraternity houses were going to be. Those properties were being sold. I saw an opportunity for a tidy investment and I outbid the development company. I made a few enemies in the process, I'm sure, but I'm quite used to that. I had a building designed to my specifications two years ago and I moved into the top floor of it just recently. It's not exactly the Waldorf Astoria, but I quite like it."

"You're inviting me to your house for drinks?" asked Matthew, thinking he must be still dreaming because this was completely surreal.

"Don't look so shocked. I like you, Matthew Paine. You're honest, you say what you think, and you see me as I am. You neither bow down deferentially nor bow up defensively."

"OK, drinks," said Matthew, standing. "I'll just let Cici know I'll be back a little later for dinner."

"Wonderful. I'll meet you there. If you should arrive first, just tell the valet that you're visiting me and he'll take good care of your car. I'll call ahead. What sort of vehicle do you drive?"

"I have a black Corvette C7."

"I'll let them know to expect you," said Reynolds, picking up the phone. "I'll see you there," he added, effectively dismissing Matthew from his office.

On his way out, Matthew went back down two floors to Cici's office to tell her where he was going and that he would be late for dinner. He tried to explain the situation as best he could, though it was still a bit muddled in his own mind.

"You're going where?" demanded Cici. "This is December the sixteenth, Matthew, not April first and I'm nobody's fool."

"I'm not joking, Cici. Danbury and I were in Reynolds' office and Danbury left ahead of me to take a call. I hung back and said something to him that apparently caught his interest. He's decided that he likes me."

"He what?!" exclaimed Cici. "Matthew, you've had more than a mild aversion to the man ever since you met him and you haven't done a great job of hiding that fact. Neither have I, unfortunately."

"I know. It's why he says he likes me. Because I'm honest and straightforward."

"Wow. Well, you're a likeable enough guy, I guess," she teased him. "But I would never have imagined you getting to be all buddy-buddy with Kennedy Reynolds. Not in my wildest imagination. Any idea what time you might be over for dinner? Should I order out?"

"It's a little after six now," he said, "Let's aim for seven-thirty and yes, if you don't mind ordering whatever you want, I'll be happy to pick it up on my way in. Just text me where shortly after seven."

"OK, seven-thirty it is. This should be an interesting dinner conversation tonight. Do be careful, Matthew. I'm not thrilled with the possibility that you're having cocktails with a killer who already poisoned one person with a drink."

"That's just it, Cees. I don't think he did."

"Really? Since when? That must have been some discussion you had in his office just now."

"I'll tell you all about it over dinner."

"OK, just please be careful. I love you, Matthew."

"I love you too, Cees," he said, leaning over and kissing her quickly before heading out down the hallway, down to the lobby, and handing in his temporary badge at the front desk. He paused a moment in the elevator as he was on his way down to the parking garage to wonder where Danbury had gone. Pulling his phone from his pocket, he saw the answer to his question.

Danbury had texted him, "*Saw you were talking. Sounded like progress. Going back to the precinct. Call me when done.*"

The elevator was apparently a dead zone for a satellite connection, so Matthew waited until he was in his car in the parking garage before calling Danbury from the car phone. While Matthew was maneuvering out of the parking spot and down through the deck, he heard Danbury's usual, "Hey Doc." And then, "Looked like you were making progress. How'd it go? What'd you learn?"

Pulling the Corvette out of the parking garage and turning right onto Wilmington Street, Matthew responded. "You won't believe me when I tell you, but Reynolds has decided that he likes me and invited me over to his place for a drink."

"He did what?"

"I know. Hard to believe, huh?"

"Very. Did he tell you anything helpful?"

"Not really, at least not yet. We had a deep philosophical discussion about nature versus nurture of the human psyche."

"Come again?"

"Hey, I took psychology classes in undergrad. Sociology too."

Turning left on Edenton Street and following the curve onto Hillsborough, Matthew told Danbury about his conversation with Reynolds until he reached the address that was scribbled on the back of the business card. As he approached, they ended the call and he promised to call Danbury when he left. The sun had already set an hour before and he could see the university's bell tower lit with Christmas colors in the waning evening light.

Matthew made the final turn into the U-shaped drive that circled under the second story on the front of the new building at the corner of Hillsborough Street and Matron Lane. It was an attractive building, though Matthew thought perhaps it would be more in line with Cici's taste than his. It was white with glass and steel, seven stories, including the ground floor that was partially disrupted with the drive. It sported more steel and glass under the drive-through entrance and on the top story, Matthew noticed, than the five in between.

As he pulled in, Matthew hoped that this encounter with Reynolds would be enlightening and not more of the cat and mouse game that the guy had been playing so far.

25 ~ Revelations

Kennedy Reynolds had indeed called ahead and, as soon as Matthew pulled into the entrance, a valet appeared at his door and said, "Good evening, Dr. Paine. Mr. Reynolds is expecting you. I'm sure he'll call down when you're ready to leave and I'll have your car waiting for you right here."

"Thank you," said Matthew, as he got out and pulled a sport jacket from the back seat.

As he stepped into the building that was deeper, down Matron Lane, than it was wide across Hillsborough Street, signage on a kiosk informed him that there was a hair salon and clothing boutique as well as several other stores down to the left. A long counter flanked the right wall of the lobby.

"Dr. Paine?" said a disembodied voice from the direction of the counter before Matthew could wonder which way to go.

"Yes," said Matthew, walking that way. As he approached, he saw a very short man behind the counter whom he hadn't initially noticed but who had apparently noticed him and called out.

"Mr. Reynolds is expecting you. He's just a bit behind you but I've been instructed to send you up and his staff will attend to you upstairs. The elevator is just there to the right," he motioned beyond the desk. "Push the button for the top floor. It's been programmed to take you right up."

"Thank you," said Matthew as he followed those instructions.

As he disembarked on the top floor an older and very distinguished looking man, of medium height, clean shaven, with short salt and pepper hair and deep-set eyes stood waiting. In a clipped British dialect, the man asked, "May I take your jacket, sir?"

"Yes, thank you," replied Matthew, handing it over and thinking he'd found Jeeves here instead of at the Washburn home.

Matthew felt as if he'd stepped onto a movie set as he handed over his jacket and looked around. He was standing in a foyer of sorts with marble floors and more of the glass and chrome. Beyond that to his right were heavy wood-paneled doors with brass trim. On either side of the doors, tall slender evergreens stood in large matching pots and the trees sparkled with tiny fairy lights and small brass and glass Christmas ornaments twinkled in the lighting. Through those doors, the scene was entirely different.

The British gentleman led him into a long hallway off of which more pairs of tall wood-paneled doors were set on both sides. All of them were closed. Matthew thought the arrangement odd in that there were no rooms visible at all from the main hallway. Like the man who had created the space, it was all very closed-off and unwelcoming.

A chandelier that was probably Swarovski Strass crystal from the opulent look of things, thought Matthew, hung from the center of the hallway and lit it with dazzling reflected light. A long wooden library table ran along the wall to his right and a mirror in a matching elaborately carved frame hung above it. A plush Oriental rug ran the length of the center of the hallway with polished hardwood floors peeking out around the edges. The long hallway ended abruptly in two tall wooden double doors at the other end.

"In here, sir," motioned the man that Matthew assumed to be the butler or perhaps the Majordomo of the household as he opened the first pair of double doors to the left and ushered Matthew inside. "Mr. Reynolds will join you here shortly. Please have a seat and make yourself comfortable. Would you like a drink while you wait?"

As Matthew entered a room that looked to be a study with highly polished wood, brass, and leather furnishings, he could smell cigar smoke hanging in the air. There was an undertone of something more heady, woody or balsamic and earthy. As he looked around, he saw no greenery or Christmas decorations of any sort.

"I'm fine thanks. I'll wait for Mr. Reynolds."

"Very well, sir," said the man, bowing slightly, and exiting the room, pulling the doors closed behind him.

Intrigued, Matthew realized that he was alone in Kennedy Reynolds' inner sanctum and he very much wanted to snoop around the room to see what he could learn. Resisting that temptation, he paused a moment to take in the long rectangular room with hardwood floors that were mostly covered, except for the edges along the walls, by a muted oriental rug. He chose a heavy deep green leather chair off to his right that offered a view of the entire room except for some shelving behind him and he looked around as he sunk into the chair.

A large wooden desk that was arranged at an angle occupied the far end of the room to his right and heavy drapes hung across the far wall, floor to high ceiling, behind it. There was an ornate wooden table beside where Matthew sat that held a large oriental lamp on the other side of which was a chair matching the one he'd chosen to sit in.

The rest of the seating area, comprised of a long leather sofa and ornately carved coffee table that matched the end table beside him, was in front of him. Behind that was more shelving, floor to ceiling, that contained books, vases, and other objects d'art which had apparently been collected by Reynolds. All of it had a decidedly Asian feel. Part way along the wall, the open shelves turned to cabinetry with closed doors and then it turned back into shelving farther along the wall as it reached the desk.

Just as Matthew was settling back into the chair after having taken all of this in, the doors opened abruptly and Kennedy Reynolds stepped through them. Matthew studied the man carefully, as he had not done previously. He was still dressed in the same charcoal gray pin-striped suit that wasn't quite black, which he'd had on earlier. His paisley silk tie was still perfectly in place. Underneath was a white starched shirt, unmussed by his day in the office. Gold cufflinks flashed at his wrists as he reached up and closed the doors behind himself, probably eighteen-carat gold if Matthew had to guess.

His pressed perfection was replete with black shoes perfectly shined with no scuffs, his pants cuffs breaking just across the tops of them at exactly the right angle to break in the right spot at his heels. He glided confidently across the floor, as if he were walking onto a Broadway stage, the leading man that everyone has come to see. He looked down his nose and said, in his now familiar haughty tone, "I trust that you've been made comfortable and offered some refreshment?"

Matthew stood as he nodded, "I was offered a drink but I chose to wait for your arrival. Did you say you'd only been in this space a short time?"

"Yes, a little over a month."

How the space could be so recently occupied and yet look like the man had lived in it for years, and probably his family for generations before him, Matthew didn't know. He said as much aloud, "It's very impressive."

Scrutinizing Matthew's face closely, Reynolds seemed to be satisfied that the comment was genuine as he nodded and moved over to the cabinets, opening the doors on one section of the top and bottom. Behind the top cabinet was a collection of bottles in myriad shapes and sizes that covered two full shelves and a collection of matching cut crystal whiskey, wine, and highball glasses on another.

"What would you like?" he asked Matthew. "Just name it."

Not being a heavy drinker, Matthew didn't have a complete sense of what he was looking at in the collection of bottles. He had a few favorites, but he wasn't sure they'd be on Kennedy Reynolds' shelves so he simply asked, "What's your drink of choice?"

"I concoct my own. A bit of bourbon, brandy, and crème de menthe over ice with a splash of club soda and a mint garnish," he replied.

"That sounds good," said Matthew. "I'll have one too."

Reynolds pulled down two tall glasses and set them on the counter top. A gold watch that graced his left wrist flashed under his shirtsleeve. Everybody, noted Matthew, hadn't moved to the watches that synced with their smart phones, case in point Kennedy Reynolds. But then the watch he wore was probably eighteen-carat gold and some very expensive brand, likely one that Matthew had never even heard of.

Matthew watched silently as Reynolds opened a door beneath to reveal a slender ice machine, scooped out the ice, and measured it carefully into each glass. He began measuring and pouring in jiggers of liquid from bottles that he pulled down, one at a time, and then returned to their proper place. Apparently satisfied with that effort, Reynolds opened another door in the bottom cabinetry that exposed a small refrigerator, reached in, pulled out a bottle of club soda and opened it with a hiss. Splashing it into each glass, he replaced the bottle and removed from the mini fridge a small glass of mint sprigs in water. Stirring each glass gently with a stirring stick that he'd removed from the cabinet, he added the mint leaves and handed Matthew one of the glasses while taking the other. He motioned for Matthew to join him as he stepped around the back of the sofa and sat down regally on one end of it.

Returning to the chair opposite the sofa that he had just vacated, Matthew sipped his drink.

"You're a brave man," said Reynolds, breaking the silence.

"Why is that?" asked Matthew.

"You're drinking a concoction prepared for you by a man accused of murdering another by poisoning his drink."

Matthew refrained from mentioning that Cici had said the same thing. He just simply answered, "As I stated earlier, I don't believe you killed Mr. Washburn, either directly or indirectly."

"By what evidence did you arrive at that conclusion?"

Still unwilling to lead with "I had a dream," Matthew instead chose to return to the more philosophical conversation they'd begun in Reynolds' office at the law firm. "In my experience, everyone is hiding something, Mr. Reynolds, absolutely everyone. I don't think anyone can live long on this planet and not have secrets, things they've done or seen or experienced that they don't want anyone else to know about and which they refuse to discuss. You are no different."

"You may call me Kennedy," he said, looking down his nose with a nod of his head. "The primary difference is that most people aren't being accused of murder and still refusing to share secrets that could exonerate them entirely, or at least cast reasonable doubt as to their guilt."

"That's also true," said Matthew.

"But you're wondering if the secret currently being kept outweighs the possible risk of being charged and convicted of a heinous crime. At what point will I decide to reveal the secret if the scale should begin to tip in the other direction."

Matthew just chuckled at this and said, "Something like that. I'll admit I'm curious as to the quid pro quo arrangement that you mentioned wanting to approach Mr. Washburn with before he was murdered."

"Let's just say that he was unaware that he owed me anything until I had enlightened him as to the fact. Having done so, I was trusting that he, being an honorable man, would want to help me with a rather delicate situation that I find myself in."

Matthew raised an eyebrow and found himself leaning forward in his chair with some sort of vague expectation that he was going to be let in on the secret before he left Reynolds' penthouse apartment.

"Are you curious about why I chose this particular property and then paid a ridiculous price to obtain it?" asked Kennedy Reynolds, seeming to change the subject entirely.

"I have no idea why you would do that," said Matthew honestly.

"I'll show you, said Reynolds. He rose, taking his drink with him, walked behind his desk, and pushed a button on the ledge underneath. The heavy drapes behind him opened to reveal a window, floor to ceiling, of thick double-paned glass. Between the layers of heavy glass were louvered blinds. Reynolds slid his hand further along under the edge of his desk and pushed another button after which the louvered blinds somehow rose into the ceiling in the space between the layers of glass.

From the angle that Matthew was seated, which was the same angle at which the desk was placed, the bell tower at the end of the university campus was clearly visible. Matthew watched, both confused and transfixed, as the lighting on the tower changed from green to red and back again, holding longer on the red color. That made sense, thought Matthew, because the school's colors were red and white. But why Kennedy Reynolds should want a view of the tower, he had no idea and lots of curiosity.

"That explains very little, I realize," said Reynolds. "But I treasure that view."

"You never attended the university here, did you?" asked Matthew, feeling like he was grasping at the proverbial straws. When Reynolds sadly shook his head, Matthew began to catch on, "But someone who is important to you did, didn't they?"

"Yes, exactly," said Reynolds, approvingly. Matthew felt like a student having just provided the correct response that the instructor was seeking.

There was a long pause as Reynolds, drink still in hand, circled the desk and stood in front of it, staring out at the bell tower. "In my office," he finally began, breaking the silence but then pausing. Finally, he continued, "In my office at the firm, we discussed how the human psyche is formed, both by nurture and by nature. You asserted that human will, that innate nature, an indomitable spirit, is stronger than the nurture of the human being, did you not?"

"I suppose I did," said Matthew. "Or at least equally as strong."

"I quite agree. As I'm sure you know by now, my family history is a long and highly esteemed one. One of which I am undeniably proud, but I was never allowed not to be!" Reynolds added vehemently. "I've been told the entirety of my life that I'm above almost everyone else because of it. It was drilled into me that I needed to act better, to be better, always a cut above the rest because I'm from this aristocratic family. I have been under tremendous pressure to live up to that."

Surprised by the outburst and uncertain as to why the guy would share this information here, now, and with him, but curious as to where he was going with this discussion, Matthew waited him out.

26 ~ QUID PRO QUO

Reynolds perched on the edge of his desk, staring out the window as if he were mesmerized by the changing lights on the bell tower. His gaze seemed to extend far beyond the tower into a time and space where Matthew couldn't follow. Finally he said, "When I went off to college, I chose Harvard because I wanted to pursue a degree in law. Really it was either that or Yale. It was an ivy league school. A legal degree that could lead to an appointment or election as a judge or politician was an acceptable career path to my parents."

"My parents insisted that the school be ivy league, you see, and any other sort was beyond the realm of possibility. In answer to your question, no I did not attend this university because I would never have been allowed to do so."

Matthew remained quiet until Reynolds continued. As he talked, he relaxed and his face was transformed from the arrogant countenance to glow with a smile that graced his entire face, spreading beyond his mouth to his eyes, "While I was at Harvard in the fall of my junior year, I met the most remarkable woman. A light emanated from her very being. She possessed a resilient and determined spirit like none I had ever encountered, before or since. She was beautiful, deeply intelligent, and had a clever sense of humor, like no woman I'd ever met."

Matthew, assuming that Reynolds was talking about his deceased wife, recalled being told that she had died about three years before. He felt a wave of sorrow for the man, something that he'd never have thought possible for someone as haughty as Kennedy Reynolds, but he said nothing to disrupt the story that was being shared with him.

"I was unabashedly in love with her before the end of that spring semester. Foolishly, I brought her home with me at the end of the school year. I wanted to show her my home, introduce her to my family, and bring her into my world. I wanted our oneness of spirit to transform into a oneness of lives. I suppose I was blinded by my love for her and I lost sight of the reality of our situation."

After he hesitated for several minutes, Matthew wondered if he were going to continue at all. Finally Matthew asked softly, "Which was what exactly?"

Reynolds turned back to face Matthew, as if he'd forgotten he were in the room.

"Our family lives were quite disparate. She, with her brilliant mind, had received a scholarship, a full ride to attend Harvard. She had told me that she was from a small town outside of a city in a state I'd never been to and knew very little about. I'll admit that I'd asked her precious little about her home life and I knew very little of her upbringing or her family background. Until I brought her home after our spring semester and my mother pried every last detail out of her over dinner the evening we arrived."

After taking a deep breath and steadying his hand on the drink it still clutched, he continued, "It was as if we'd been living in a bubble, Celeste and I, and Mother popped it in about fifteen minutes. I was horrified as I heard my mother calmly telling Celeste that she had no family background, she was without a proper upbringing, and she could not possibly function in our world. Carefully unstated but fully obvious was that my family had no wish for her to learn to do so. Mother didn't sugar coat it and my father merely nodded along in agreement."

"My father, you see, was merely the marionette to my mother's puppet master in many ways. Don't misunderstand. He was brilliant in his own right and took entrepreneurship to a grand new level. He inherited money, certainly, but he diversified by creating new and extremely successful businesses. But when it came to anything involving home or family, my mother was the maestro of that symphony, a bit of a dragon lady if you were so bold as to cross her, which I had not in any meaningful way up to that point."

"Initially I was in shock at my mother's words, but I believe that

Celeste was immediately devastated. She rose from the table and ran from the room without a word. I think I just sat there, dumbly, before anger gripped me and I too rose to leave the table. My mother reprimanded me for the faux pas and I committed a far more grievous one when I turned and yelled at her, 'Mother! How could you? She's a guest in our house!' Mother merely spread her hands, dismissively, and said, 'You'll thank me one day.'"

Matthew was watching in rapt attention as Reynolds took a deep drink, as if to regain his courage, before he continued. "I went in search of Celeste and I found her repacking the few things she'd unpacked in her room. I tried to talk to her but she ignored me. I could tell she was deeply hurt, but she was utterly calm as she finally looked up into my eyes and said, "Your maid has already called me a cab. I'm leaving, Ken. Don't try to follow or find me.' I could do nothing but watch as she marched out of the room, down the front steps, and out onto the front veranda. The cab pulled up, she got in, and that was that."

"You never saw or talked to her again?" asked Matthew, unable to contain his burgeoning curiosity. Obviously, he concluded, this woman, Celeste, he'd called her, wasn't Kennedy Reynolds' recently deceased wife.

"I did not. But it was not for lack of effort on my part," he added. "I wrote letters to the only address I could find for her. She wasn't listed anywhere that I could find. Then, before all of the social media of today, it was possible to be reclusive like that. If you weren't listed in the phone book, your records weren't necessarily available. The internet was being developed and the world wide web had been made available, but it was far from complete and searches yielded nothing further that was useful."

"She never answered your letters?"

"She never opened them. They were all returned marked 'Return to Sender.' When the first few I'd written were returned that way, I packed some clothes, took my car, and headed south. I knew the name of the town she had said she was from and that's where I went."

"What town?" asked Matthew.

"Durham," replied Reynolds, holding up a hand as if to ward off

Matthew's objection before he'd made any. "I know, Durham is not now nor was it then a small town. I spent most of the rest of the summer searching for her, asking questions, showing her picture to anyone who would look. I thought I'd found her once. A woman who answered a door in a neighborhood that I'd been told a young woman matching her description had lived in looked very much like her. But the woman told me that no one by that name lived there before promptly closing the door in my face. I watched that house for weeks, driving by and parking at odd hours, but I never saw Celeste. My parents had frozen my bank accounts and I eventually ran out of cash and had to give up and go home."

Matthew was admitting to himself that this was the saddest story he'd heard in quite a while, possibly the saddest love story he'd ever heard, but he remained quiet hoping to hear the rest of it.

"I returned to Harvard that fall, though to my great disappointment Celeste did not. I was lonely without her but determined to complete my degree and move on, away from my mother's control and away from the world where perfection was prerequisite to all else, both physically and in terms of mental acuity. I wanted nothing more than to escape the world in which I was required to have weekly hair trims so that not one hair would ever be out of place and manicures every other week."

Matthew glanced down at Reynolds' hands, elegant with long tapered fingers and perfectly manicured fingernails, all filed evenly short, but not too short. He obviously didn't bite them, Matthew thought, but he was gaining an understanding of how barbaric that would be perceived to be.

"Everyone in my world was perpetually perfectly coiffed and turned out. I had not questioned that until I met Celeste. She was a free spirit who couldn't be bothered with such trivialities. My mother blamed my reformed attitude on her, of course, and redoubled her efforts to ensure that I met a proper young woman and followed the correct career path."

"And did you?" asked Matthew, unable to refrain any longer.

"Mother ensured that I did, which is how I met Gracelyn, the woman I later married. Our parents introduced us at a social gathering the spring of my senior year at Harvard. While the excitement that I had experienced with Celeste was never there, we were very companionable and shared many interests, having long conversations together about them."

Swirling the ice in his glass, Reynolds continued, "As I was finishing my law program, there were certain expectations that I should move forward in that relationship. I suppose it made logical sense and ours was more a marriage of convenience."

"I loved Gracelyn, of course," he quickly added. "Just not in the same way that I had loved Celeste. By that point I had come to expect never to feel that way again. We were engaged and then married after I passed the bar and joined a prestigious law firm. It was all exactly as it had been planned to be at my birth. I was an only child, you see, so all hopes and dreams for all posterity were pinned soundly on me. Gracelyn and I were married for seventeen years but we never had children of our own," he added sadly.

"I never forgot Celeste though. After marrying Gracelyn and then losing her a little over three years ago, I decided to try again to locate Celeste. I hired a private investigator and, of course, internet searches are far more informative now."

"And did you find her?"

Matthew was startled when Reynolds stood suddenly and said, "Come with me."

Out through the double doors and to the left, Reynolds marched more than glided, down the long hallway and threw open the doors at the end of it, as Matthew followed hesitantly in his wake. They entered a large bedroom into which he figured his whole condo might fit nicely. In one corner, was a baby grand piano. Intrigued, never having seen anyone place a piano of that size in their bedroom before, Matthew walked over and touched the ivories under the open lid.

"Do you play?" asked Reynolds.

"I do."

"What genre?" asked Reynolds, interrupting Matthew's thoughts.

"A smattering of lots of things," answered Matthew. "I've been told I have an eclectic taste in music. And you?"

"Mostly ragtime," said Reynolds, to Matthew's surprise. Mozart,

Chopin, or Beethoven he'd have expected, but ragtime? That took a complete command of the keyboard as both hands would be flying across it in opposite directions at once.

"That's impressive," said Matthew.

"Except at night. But then that's why the piano is in here. When I can't sleep, I get up and play until I'm tired. It's soothing."

"I understand," said Matthew, who frequently used his acoustic guitar to unwind at the end of a stressful day. "Except that it's usually on my guitar, not my keyboard, and it's usually just whatever flows from my fingertips. It's not practiced or rehearsed, just free flowing."

Reynolds nodded, seeming to understand the concept, before he said, "Pardon me" and stepped around Matthew. He slid the piano bench all the way out from under the edge of the baby grand piano. As he opened it, Matthew realized that it had been slid underneath the huge piano backward. The inquisitive look on Matthew's face must have been obvious, he thought, as Reynolds said, "It's a great hiding place. Nobody but me ever goes in there or ever has, even when Gracelyn was still alive. And if anyone thought to, they'd not bother with it when they realized that it was backward. You have to pull it all the way out to open it."

Matthew just shook his head in amusement, unsure if he was encountering reticent brilliance or the paranoid schizophrenia of a disturbed mind. Mostly certain that it was the former and not the latter, he watched Reynolds pull what appeared to be an old cash box from the piano bench. If it had ever had a shine to it, that was long gone and rust had started to appear at one of the corners of the gray box. Reynolds laid that on the bed as the piano beckoned to Matthew and he asked, "May I?"

"Certainly."

Appreciative of the enormous finely crafted and perfectly tuned instrument before him, Matthew began to play softly Handel's "Messiah" from the sheet music on the stand. "Wow," he said. "That's such a rich sound." Noticing the sheaves of sheet music on the stand behind Handel's "Messiah," which he thought was appropriate for the season, he saw music from classical composers from various countries and time periods. Pachelbel in Canon D, Chopin's Nocturnes, which he thought was a good choice for relaxation, and several others peeked out at him.

Reluctantly, Matthew pulled himself away from the piano and moved to the center of the bedroom as Reynolds entered a bathroom and dressing area, flipping on light switches as he went. From what Matthew could see of those rooms from where he stood in Reynolds' bedroom, he knew the area to be bigger than his own bedroom in his condominium.

Matthew watched as Reynolds stepped into a long closet at the other end of the bathroom that was filled with suits and shirts and shoes on rotating hangers and reached above them to a shelf, pulling down a large wooden box with brass fittings. Taking it out and placing it gently on his bed with the metal box, he turned to Matthew, and said, "Perhaps not here." He stacked and lifted the boxes, turned on his heel, and glided back down the hallway and into the study where they'd been, closing the doors behind Matthew.

Placing the boxes gingerly on his desk, he turned to Matthew, looking down his nose before opening the old metal one with a key on a ring that he'd retrieved from his desk drawer. Inside Matthew saw a manilla envelope labeled "Celeste" with a stack of papers beneath it. Reynolds pulled the envelope from the box and laid it on the desk. Then he opened the wooden box with a second key on the ring from his desk drawer. In it Matthew could see at least two large manilla envelopes. From it Reynolds retrieved a manilla envelope labeled "Ella," which he set aside on his desk.

Opening the clasp on the first envelope, Reynolds pulled out a single picture and handed it almost reverently to Matthew. A lovely young woman with curly long brown hair and big brown eyes was smiling broadly at him from the photograph. She was standing, in full graduation gown and cap with tassels, sashes and regalia, in front of the bell tower that was across the street from where he now stood in the penthouse of Reynolds' building.

"It's the first picture I'd seen of her in over twenty years," said Reynolds. "It's how I learned that she had graduated from this university the year after I'd finished at Harvard. I wasn't initially sure why it was a year later because we were in the same class, only a few months apart in age. But then the private detective I'd hired found the answer to that too." Without saying anything else, he handed Matthew the other envelope he'd pulled out, that was labeled "Ella," and nodded his permission for Matthew to open it.

Matthew opened the clasp and slid the stack of photographs and papers that the envelope contained onto the desk. As he sifted them apart with his finger by the corners, the life of a young woman, from infancy to high school graduation and beyond, appeared before him. The same woman he'd seen in front of the bell tower, only older, appeared in several of the pictures with her. Underneath the pictures was a copy of a birth certificate.

"Celeste has a daughter," said Matthew, reading the names and dates.

"Celeste has MY daughter," replied Reynolds, fervently. "That's why she graduated a year later. She was already pregnant when I took her home to meet my family and she either didn't yet know it or she chose to withhold that information from me. Celeste has refused me access to Ella. Though Ella is grown now, at twenty-three, she apparently knows nothing of me at all. Celeste never told her who her father was and she is vehemently opposed to me contacting her now. Nor will Celeste agree to talk to me in person about any of this. She said that Ella has had enough trauma in her life and that meeting me would simply cause more. Celeste despises lawyers and she was particularly upset, beyond any reason that I could then begin to imagine, when I told her the name of the firm I work for."

"But I have to see her, you understand," Reynolds said, almost pleadingly. "I have to meet Ella. Even if I never tell her that I'm her father. I moved here to find Celeste, but now she and Ella are all I can think about. An event in Ella's life is the reason for the unfortunate incident you partially witnessed in the stairwell and for Celeste's hatred of the law firm I represent."

"When you punched Washburn?"

Reynolds nodded, and Matthew knew he must look as confused as he felt, one eyebrow raised in response.

"I'm sure you fail to see the connection now, but if you will agree to help me, I'll enlighten you. It does not provide me with an alibi for the murder exactly, but it will provide some insight as to why I went to apologize to Jamison and ask for his help, as sort of a quid pro quo."

Intrigued, Matthew just said, "OK, I'll help if I can."

"Let's have a seat and I'll explain," said Reynolds, sliding the pages back into the envelopes and then leading the way to the seating area. Matthew retrieved his drink from the coaster he'd sat it on as he resumed his seat, and waited for whatever Reynolds was preparing to disclose.

"About five years ago, my daughter was a freshman at the women's college farther down Hillsborough Street." Matthew nodded. Having grown up in Raleigh, he was familiar with it. Reynolds continued, "She had attended a fraternity party at one of the houses down this street behind us here and, from what I read in the court records, something was slipped in her drink."

Matthew thought ironically that there was a lot of that going around, but he said nothing, merely nodding, for Kennedy Reynolds to finish his explanation.

"Apparently, Ella woke up upstairs in one of the bedrooms sometime later, naked, realizing that she'd been violated. The last thing she reported remembering was being with a guy who turned out to be the son of one of the biggest clients of Markham, Denton, and Washburn. The records indicate that she was able to identify him from pictures later."

"Oh!" said Matthew, leaning forward expectantly.

"I knew none of this when I came on board as one of the partners with the firm a little over two years ago. That part was purely coincidental. One of life's little ironic twists, I suppose. I had found Celeste and come to see the bell tower she'd been photographed in front of when I realized that this property was for sale and I went head-to-head in a bidding war with the development company that has been redeveloping most of Hillsborough Street to get it. I had no idea that there were any further ties here when I bought the property, but I had all of the fraternity houses down Matron Lane razed last week after I learned of it. Well ahead of the development schedule for the property."

Reynolds paused, looking sadly down at the drink in his hand, the ice in which was nearly gone, though he swirled it around and took a long swallow before continuing. "I learned of Ella's tragedy just a couple of weeks ago when someone slipped an envelope under my door that contained the results of a search on her name in one of the legal databases."

He rose from his seat and pulled a second large manila envelope from the wooden box that he hadn't closed or locked earlier. "This is the envelope that was under my door. It contains the details of the rape trial and it was then I also learned that Washburn had been the one to defend the client's son and have all charges dropped. Of course, I was livid."

"You found that under your door?"

"I did. Early one morning."

"When was that?"

After considering for a moment, Reynolds responded, "It was on a Tuesday. It would have been December the third, I suppose. Nearly two weeks ago."

"Who else knows about Celeste and Ella?"

"No one that I know of here."

"And the envelope with the information just showed up?"

"Precisely. I came in to work that morning and nearly tripped over it when I opened the door."

"Interesting," said Matthew. "My apologies for interrupting. You were telling me what you'd learned from the information in the folder."

"Right. Open it and have a look," he said, returning to his seat and handing the envelope to Matthew. "It's all there."

Matthew opened the clasp and slid pages that looked to have been printed from a computer into his lap. He flipped through the pages as Reynolds continued.

"The record stated that, like most young women in that predicament, Ella testified that she had felt dirty and she wanted to be clean. She went back to her dorm on her own campus and showered, scrubbing as she said in her statement layers of skin off in the attempt. She shared what had happened with one of her friends, who talked her into going to the local hospital and having a rape kit done. Ella had showered, of course, and removed much of the evidence but that which remained was horrendous."

Swallowing hard, he continued. "She'd been raped by multiple people. Two were still identifiable, but the DNA evidence against the client's son was inconclusive. DNA on the other two and partial DNA data with Ella's ability to pick the son from pages of photographs should have been enough to convict all three. After Jamison was finished with the case though, all three of them walked free. Free to do the same thing to other unsuspecting young women. I wasn't there to protect her from any of it. But I should have been. I certainly should have been! I blame Celeste for that somewhat, but no less so myself."

"I had approached Jamison with this information earlier on Saturday and I found his response quite unsatisfactory. He didn't remember the details of the case. He said he'd review it and get back to me. I ran into him in the stairwell walking up to the gala event and brought it up again but he started making excuses. There was at least one too many of them and I punched him, taking out much of my anger and frustration with this whole situation on him."

"I immediately realized how barbaric that was and I went straight downstairs, washed up in the washroom, composed myself, and then went to find him. Both to apologize and to get his help with righting a few wrongs, which I figured he owed me. Quid pro quo."

"I see," said Matthew. "And now you're asking for my help. With what exactly?"

"I need someone to get through to Celeste. Someone who isn't me, but with a lighter touch. Unbiased. I suppose it isn't too difficult to imagine that I haven't exactly made friends since I've lived here."

Matthew refrained from commenting on that but instead asked, "You want me to talk to Celeste for you? How would that work? She has no idea who I am. Why would she agree to talk to me at all? About anything?"

"Perhaps Ms. Patterson could get through to her more effectively, woman to woman. At least to open the channel of communication. I need the opportunity to apologize most sincerely to her. I want to meet my daughter, with or without her permission, but I have never loved anyone like I loved Celeste, so I'd far prefer to do so with her blessing and her involvement."

"I see," said Matthew again, then checked his watch. Setting his drink back on the coaster, he said, "Speaking of Cici, I'm due at her house in a half hour for dinner. Tell me what part of this I can share with her. You've kept this secret buried for so long. Are you saying you want Cici to know about it now?"

"You may tell Ms. Patterson. But only Ms. Patterson. I do not wish to have any of this aired for public consumption in any way. I will work out a way to bring the two women together if she's willing to help. And one more thing."

"Yes?" said Matthew, as he rose from his chair.

"If you are able to meet with Celeste, she needs to know that Mother has full knowledge of all of this."

"Oh?" said Matthew, surprised. "I assumed that both of your parents were deceased, given the way you'd spoken of them in the past tense."

"My father is deceased, yes, and he never knew that he had a granddaughter. When I decided to move down here, my mother demanded to know my reasoning. I told her. She was livid and threatened to disinherit me. She insisted that I was young and could still remarry, the 'right' sort of woman of course, and produce children. When I refused, she cut off all contact with me. It was important to both of my parents you see, continuing the family lines. We had only barely resumed communication when I found out about Ella's existence. Unsure how Mother would respond, I took the risk and told her. I don't believe I had ever heard Mother speechless before that."

"And how did she take it?"

"Suffice it to say that Ella will be a very wealthy young woman. Mother is prepared to recognize her as the Reynolds heiress. She wants to change her name, of course, but I have no intention of pushing that issue with Celeste. If I can get Celeste to agree to meet with me and begin to include me in their lives, it's enough. At least for me."

"Is there a man in the picture? For Celeste I mean?"

"If there is, it's not apparent," said Reynolds. "In my wildest dreams, I want that man to be me again. Maybe that's asking far too much of her, but I'll never rest without giving that my best effort."

"I will explain all of this to Cici over dinner tonight and solicit her help. Or at least try to. She really doesn't like you, you know?"

"I'd be shocked if you told me that she did but she'll agree if you ask her to. Because she really does like you."

Reynolds saw Matthew out himself after calling down to have the car brought around from who knew where. "No, pressure, no pressure at all," Matthew muttered to himself as he left Kennedy Reynolds' apartment and went down to retrieve his car from the valet. That's what he got for being an honest and approachable guy, he supposed, sucked into the black hole of other people's problems.

27 ~ NEW DIRECTIONS

Matthew called Cici from his car phone first and got the information about the restaurant she'd ordered dinner from. Apparently, Matthew thought, we're having sushi. They both loved sushi so, like their favorite Italian restaurant, it was usually a safe bet when they hadn't discussed what they wanted.

"It's order number twenty-six," she said. "And then when you get here, I want to hear all about what Kennedy Reynolds wanted to talk to you about. I can't imagine him inviting you over for drinks! That man has been a thorn in my side continually, so arrogant and condescending."

"You won't even believe me if I tell you."

"Give me a hint?"

"Are you sure you want to know now?"

"OK, now you definitely have to tell me."

"He wants my help."

"Help? Help him? He wants you to help him? With what?"

"Us actually. He wants us to help him."

The phone line was incredibly quiet and Matthew knew that this information must have truly shocked Cici because she was rarely ever speechless. Finally she said, "He wants my help? Why would he think I would help him? With much of anything? Ever? What on earth could he possibly want my help with?"

"It's a long story. Why don't I call Danbury now, pick up dinner, and explain it all to you while we're eating our sushi?"

"OK, I guess I can wait to find out what you just got us into," she said and Matthew could see her rolling her eyes at him in his mind as she said it.

"Not us. Just me. If you choose not to get involved, that's entirely your prerogative."

"OK, be safe, Matthew, and I'll see you in a few minutes."

They said their goodbyes and Matthew clicked the car system to call Danbury.

"Hey Doc," said Danbury on the second ring. "What did you learn?"

"A plethora of things that I can't tell you about. I can tell you, unequivocally, that the altercation in the stairwell had nothing to do with the murder. Reynolds was planning to apologize for losing his temper and ask Jamison Washburn for his help with the matter that provoked the altercation."

"You're sounding like him now. You've spent too much time with a lawyer," said Danbury.

"I spend lots of time with a lawyer," laughed Matthew.

"You know what I mean. Your lawyer speaks English. At least most of the time. And what do you mean you can't tell me?"

"What Reynolds shared with me is an extremely private matter. He didn't know until recently that Washburn had unwittingly been involved in any of it. I will tell you this. The information that led him to understand Washburn's involvement was slid under his office door in an envelope. He said he nearly tripped over it early one morning a couple of weeks ago."

After a momentary pause, Danbury summarized. "Somebody gave Reynolds information. That made him angry with Washburn. For something Washburn had done. Without knowing that he did it?"

"Sort of. Washburn knew that he did it several years ago, but Reynolds had no knowledge of the incident. Neither of them knew that it had anything to do with Reynolds until somebody shoved that information under Reynolds' door. My point in telling you this is that if someone was trying to create that altercation, it's someone with access to the thirty-second floor. That access is limited and tightly controlled, as you've seen. Reynolds might answer more specific questions about how he received the information, though he won't likely divulge to you what that information was."

"If what you say is true," began Danbury.

"I have no reason to believe that it isn't," said Matthew. "It does involve a highly important and potentially volatile personal situation on Reynolds' part. He has information to support the story he shared with me. I saw the contents of the envelope that he found on his office floor. I have no reason to believe that it isn't true. It doesn't completely exonerate him from the murder, but it does explain the altercation. And that the reason for the altercation is not a likely motive for murder."

"OK, Doc," said Danbury, sighing deeply. "I'll take your word for it. But that does lead us in a new direction. If the envelope was meant to cause problems."

"Exactly," agreed Matthew.

"And how would anybody else know? Information that you say Reynolds didn't know. And Washburn didn't know it affected Reynolds. Who put that together?"

"Somebody who might be framing Reynolds must have done some digging. Murdering one senior partner and framing another for that murder. Maybe it's someone with an axe to grind with the law firm itself?"

"But internal. Information was slid under a locked door. Like you said. After hours. What day was it? Did he say?"

"Well, yeah. Because I asked him. He found it first thing in the morning on Tuesday, December third."

"Had he been in the office the day before?"

"OK, now that I didn't think to ask him," admitted Matthew. "But I can."

"Or I can."

"If you do, explain that you know nothing of what the envelope contained, only that someone fed him information that likely turned him against Washburn and that someone might be the same person who killed Washburn. The timing on it all is just too coincidental otherwise. And you don't believe in coincidence."

"Neither do you."

"Touché. Why did you leave Reynolds' office today? Did that have anything to do with this case? Or was it unrelated?"

"It did. Two things. We have a line on Bartles. And the catering server. Somebody accessed the funds. The ones the catering worker transferred. That led us to Salt Lake City."

"He's in Utah?"

"We believe so. We're working with police there. They have his last known location. It's under surveillance."

"Oh," said Matthew. "This is the guy who didn't exist prior to two years ago?"

"Right. And then quickly developed a RAP sheet. Entirely suspicious. On so many levels."

"And Bartles?"

"Returned earlier today. From a trip out west somewhere. He's agreed to come in. He's being questioned first thing in the morning."

"Huh. If he agreed to come in for questioning, he's either really cocky and thinks he's above the law or he really has nothing to hide involving this case."

"I'd vote for the former. From what Annabelle Washburn told us of him. We'll see what he says in the morning."

"I'm picking up sushi for Cici and me tonight. Do you want me to ask Reynolds about whether he was in the office the day before he found the package? Or do you want to?"

"Do you mind asking?"

"Not at all. I'll need to circle back to him after I talk to Cici anyway."

"You're telling Cici his deep dark secret?"

"At his request I am. He thinks maybe she can help with this scenario too."

"Huh. I wouldn't bet on it. OK, Doc, enjoy the sushi," said Danbury and he was gone.

*****

Over their dinner of salad and sushi, Matthew carefully laid out Reynolds' predicament and his request of Cici.

"Wow, the man might actually be human after all," marveled Cici.

"Does that mean you'll consider talking to Celeste?"

"I suppose so. If you're in, then I guess I'm in for a penny, in for a pound," she said, sounding to Matthew exactly like she'd just come from London. "But why does he think that Celeste would be amenable to talking to me about him?"

"I don't know. I suppose he was just thinking woman to woman might be preferable to being approached by a strange man. Though that's what he was apparently going to ask Jamison Washburn to do. He figured it was a quid pro quo for the damage he'd done by getting Ella's rapists off without any repercussions whatsoever. I guess maybe Washburn apologizing and asking for forgiveness was going to be step one in getting Celeste to talk to Reynolds."

"How long ago was that, exactly?"

"The rape?" he asked as she winced. "I think he said about five years ago. I saw a copy of Ella's birth certificate. He said it was her freshman year in college when this happened. She was born in November and she will have turned twenty-three last month. That all adds up so he must have said five years ago. Why?"

"I was just wondering if I was already at the firm and might have remembered the case, that's all. I wasn't obviously. I was in law school five years ago."

"I remember," said Matthew, brushing her cheek with his fingertips. Just as he was about to lean over and kiss her, his cell phone went off. He wasn't the physician on call this week, but he figured he'd better check it anyway. Leaning back on Cici's leather sofa where they'd opted to eat their sushi, he pulled the phone from his pocket and saw that it was Danbury.

"Hey Doc. We got him."

"Which him?"

"The catering server. Joseph Hayden. You just saw him by the elevator, right? You weren't introduced to him? At some other time that night?"

"If it's the same guy, yeah, I just saw him and I would have had no reason to be introduced. After Jamison Washburn was found, I wasn't back in the room much anyway."

"OK. He's being transported. Back from Utah. After they process him. He'll be back here tomorrow afternoon. Can you pick him out of a lineup? The catering manager, Margaret, she didn't know he was there. You're the only one who saw him. Or at least who remembers seeing him."

"I can try."

"What time can you be downtown?"

"Um…" said Matthew, trying without success to remember his schedule for the next day. "I don't remember when I see my last patient for the day. Can I call you back when I get home?"

"Sure Doc. Just let me know. And I'll set it up."

"OK, I'll give you a call back."

Cici looked over at Matthew with doleful eyes. "You have to go, don't you?" she asked.

"I do. I needed to go through my patient schedule for tomorrow anyway and do some chart updating that I didn't get to before I left today. The latest news is that they've found the guy from the catering company who called in sick the night of the gala event, and Aubrey Bartles has agreed to come in for questioning in the morning. I'm fairly sure the catering worker was the guy I saw standing by the elevator just as we walked in from the stairwell. Danbury wants me to identify him when they bring him back from Utah tomorrow. He'll be questioned in both the Washburn murder and that of Alicia Laws, the other catering server who called in sick but showed up anyway. Both of them must have disappeared sometime around the time of the murder."

"Wow," said Cici. "Maybe that means we're close to finding who killed Mr. Washburn. I surely hope so. Did I tell you that the Medical Examiner is finished with the autopsy and Mrs. Washburn has scheduled the service for Friday afternoon?"

"No, you didn't. Do you know what he found? The ME, I mean?"

"I don't. I'm not sure if they told Annabelle anything about that. If they did, she didn't mention it to me. Abby is helping her with all of the arrangements and she's been there quite a lot since we left. She might know if Annabelle knows. I'm so glad Abby's there with her. What a terrible time to give the personal assistant you didn't even think you needed the month off!"

"Good. I'm happy to hear that you and Abby have been able to help," he said, hesitating. "Well, I guess I really should go. See you tomorrow?"

"Of course," she said sliding into his lap and kissing him so that the last thing on his mind was leaving her just then or ever. Eventually she pulled away and slid off his lap. After he pulled himself together, he helped her clean up their containers and glasses, and then he reluctantly kissed her goodnight before slipping out of her front door and sliding into the Corvette for the drive home.

On the way, he called Kennedy Reynolds at the number jotted on the business card alongside the address. He hadn't given Reynolds his phone number so he wasn't sure the guy would pick up, but he eventually did just as Matthew was certain that he'd get forwarded to voice mail.

"Hi Kennedy," he said, remembering that he'd been told to call him by his first name. "This is Matthew Paine. I just left Cici's and we're in. We'll help you talk to Celeste." The line was quiet and for the second time that night, Matthew thought he might have just made a lawyer speechless.

"I'll admit that I'm flabbergasted. How did you convince her?" he asked. Before Matthew could answer, he added slyly, "Never mind. I probably don't want to know."

Ignoring the innuendo, Matthew asked, "What is it that you want us to do exactly?"

"Make an initial contact with her. Build a rapport and then pull her aside and explain why you're really patrons of her business."

"She owns a business?"

"She owns a landscape architecture company on the outskirts of Raleigh. I'll give you the name and address."

"Can you text it to this number after we get off of the phone? I'm driving."

"Certainly. I'm not much on this texting thing, but I can manage. Let me know if you have any more questions or need more information."

"OK, I will."

"And Dr. Paine?"

"Yes?"

"Thank you."

"Call me Matthew and you're welcome."

They ended the call and Matthew wondered how he'd approach a landscape design company. As he turned into his short driveway and his headlights swept his meager front yard, he had an idea. Whether or not he and Cici decided to sell both houses and consolidate into another one after she returned from London, his yard could use some work. There were three small bushes planted in front of the house beside the porch and that was it. The condominium came that way and Matthew hadn't thought to do anything to improve it. Until now.

Pondering this possibility, Matthew parked the Corvette in his garage, dropped the garage door, and let himself into the house, turning the alarm off as he went. He was immediately met by Max, who was rubbing up against him and winding between his legs.

"Come here, Big Guy," he said, scooping up the big cat and scratching him under the chin and behind his ears. Sliding the satchel containing his computer off his shoulder and onto the sofa, he set the cat down there too so that he could pull off his jacket and add it to the satchel before meandering into the kitchen to care for Max. He refreshed both the food and water bowls and left the big gray tabby there happily munching on his dinner.

Pulling his computer from the satchel, he set it up on the little desk in his living room and pulled up the EMR tool his office used to access his patient records. After looking over his schedule, he texted Danbury, "*I finish up with patients by 4:30 tomorrow. I could be downtown by 5:30.*"

As he was logging the patient data he'd meant to enter earlier, he heard his phone ding and picked it to see that Danbury had sent him a thumbs up. As he was putting it back down, it dinged again and he saw that Kennedy Reynolds had sent him an address. Following Danbury's lead, he clicked to send a thumbs up emoji and went back to his patient records.

Checking his schedule for the next day, Matthew was relieved to see that it was lightening up a bit as they got closer to Christmas. He had a chunk of time, in fact, between two in the afternoon and his last appointment at four. That would likely get filled with walk-ins. Maybe Sadie Peterson had been right about children being little Petri dishes walking around swapping specimens, thought Matthew in amusement. Now that the children were out of school for Christmas break, his schedule looked much lighter this week.

Matthew added water after checking the level in the Christmas tree reservoir and locked up, turning most of the lights off. He set up his coffee maker to brew automatically before he got up the next morning and, as he glanced out of his front window on his way to his bedroom, he noticed tail lights from a car driving slowly away. That was unusual, he thought, because he lived at the very end of his condominium complex with nothing but a dead end, trees, and utility lines on the street beyond his driveway. There was only one way in and no way out from there.

Dismissing it, he went back to his bedroom and laid out his clothes for the morning, slipped into his warm flannel sleep pants and soft T-shirt, and washed up. After crawling in bed, he saw a text from Cici, "*Are you still up?*"

"*Just got in bed,*" he texted back.

"*I miss you. I wish you were here.*"

"*Me too. Dinner tomorrow night? I meet Danbury at the Raleigh Police Station downtown at 5:30 but that shouldn't take long.*"

"*OK, I can get it this time. Your place or mine?*"

"*Either. But mine has the nice tree,*" he teased, knowing that she didn't care one way or the other about his Christmas tree.

"*And Max,*" she answered. "*Deal. Your place it is. I'll bring dinner.*"

They texted their "I love you" messages and Cici sent a plethora of different hearts. Matthew sent a few back and felt content as he rolled over and snuggled under his warm blankets thinking about the woman he loved and potentially helping Kennedy Reynolds to reconnect with the woman he loved. Even the Kennedy Reynolds of the world could be in love, he marveled. It wasn't quite sugar plums dancing in his head, but it gave him warm happy Christmas thoughts as he drifted off to sleep.

28 ~ Dawning

Removing Max from his favorite spot around Matthew's head, Matthew rolled over in bed to silence the annoying noise coming from his phone. He saw a text from Danbury that had just come in which said simply, "*Talked to Bartles. Call for details.*" Matthew knew that Danbury needed and got very little sleep but apparently neither did Bartles if Danbury had already talked to him at six-thirty in the morning.

"I need coffee before I talk to Danbury," muttered Matthew as he headed for the kitchen. He could smell the lovely fragrance of the pot of coffee that was waiting for him. Pouring the requisite heaps of cream and sugar into his favorite mug, a present from Angel which said *World's Best Uncle*, he decided that he needed a long hot shower before talking to Danbury and went to get one.

Having taken care of Max and finished most of his morning routine, he was just cleaning the kitchen up after cooking himself breakfast when he saw the call come in from Danbury. Picking it up, he heard the abrupt, "Hey Doc. Just wanted to check in. I'm driving to Wilmington. To transport Joseph Hayden. He's being flown in there. The team bringing him in can't get him further. I have to go get him myself. If I want him here today."

"Are we still on for the five-thirty meeting?"

"Should be. We'll be back before that. And Bartles looks clean. Thought you'd want to know that too."

"Unrequited love wasn't the motive for the murder after all, huh?"

"Doesn't look like it. Bartles was on his way to Tennessee. The night he got pulled. He has a PI looking for his daughter. The guy thought he'd found her. In Tennessee. Bartles' ex-wife disappeared with the daughter. Several years back. He's been searching for her since."

There was a lot of that going around, noted Matthew. Interesting, he thought, that both of the primary suspects were trying to connect with their estranged daughters in one way or another the night of the murder.

"Oh yeah," responded Matthew aloud. "I think Annabelle Washburn told us about that. He still hasn't found his daughter, the other Annabelle?"

"No. He says Tennessee was a dead end. At least by the time he got there. After being held overnight. He gave us access to the PI he hired. And all of the investigative notes. The guy told him that day. The Saturday of the gala event. That his daughter might be in Tennessee. Bartles left immediately. He provided the email for us. And the PI is being questioned. Sometime later today. Bartles is looking less likely. He's cooperating fully. Or at least he appears to be."

"Maybe. If he can hire a PI, he could hire other people, too. Hopefully questioning Joseph Hayden will give us something then," said Matthew. "If Hayden had a motive or was hired by someone who did, then that would explain his appearance and disappearance around the time of the murder the night of the gala. Otherwise, why was he there at all? One more coincidence that probably isn't coincidental. Maybe you can get something out of him."

"Maybe. If he doesn't lawyer up first. He hasn't so far."

"I know one law firm that'll refuse to represent him."

"Conflict of interest. They couldn't anyway. Can you ask Reynolds about the day before the envelope showed up? If he was in the office that day. And when he left if he was."

"Yeah, I'll ask."

"See what Reynolds has to say. I'm heading for Wilmington. I'll see you at five-thirty." Before Matthew could respond, Danbury had disconnected the call.

On his way out, Matthew had an idea and went to retrieve a folder from the small wooden file cabinet in the spare bedroom that doubled as a home office. Checking the weather forecast and seeing the possibility of some nasty weather, Matthew opted to drive the Element. Pulling the key off the hook by the door, he locked up and turned on the security system on his way out.

On the way to work, Matthew called Cici to ask her about his idea. "Good morning, Matthew," she said in a chipper manner when she answered.

"Hey Cees, I had an idea for this afternoon. What does your schedule look like?"

"It's pretty clear this close to Christmas. I don't have an actual client list here anymore anyway. I've been dedicated to the one client in London. Why?"

"You know how we discussed talking to Celeste for Kennedy?"

"Matthew, honestly, I feel like we're back in middle school passing notes, 'Do you like me? Check yes or no.'"

He had to laugh at her analogy but he persisted, "I think the yards on both of our houses could use improvement, don't you?"

"You mean some sprucing up?"

"Yeah, maybe some flower beds or interesting plants to improve our property values. I admit I've done nothing in my yard at all since I moved in. The little bushes in front of the house beside the porch are all that's there. It has no curb appeal."

"Curb appeal? Are you being serious right now?"

"I am. Whether we agree to sell both properties when you get back from London or not, it couldn't hurt to give them a little pizazz, right?"

"Pizazz? Matthew, what have you been smoking?" she laughed, but sounded pleased with his reasoning about adding curb appeal to sell both houses.

"I don't know where that word came from. I think I just heard it on a radio ad or something, but I am serious about talking to Celeste about our properties."

"OK, what did you have in mind?"

"Let's go meet her this afternoon."

"Don't you have a full schedule?"

"Surprisingly, I don't. I have only one patient after two this afternoon and I think I can hand him off easily enough. It's a guy with a chronically infected ingrown toenail that I've referred to a podiatric surgeon twice now. He hasn't listened to me yet. He just keeps coming back for antibiotics, so I don't feel too bad about not telling him the same thing for the third time. Maybe if one of the other physicians tells him the same thing, he'll finally hear it."

"You want to go see Celeste this afternoon?"

"How does two-thirty work? I can pick you up and we can go together."

"OK, sure. Do you have any ideas about how to broach the subject of Reynolds with her?"

"No idea. I'm hoping meeting her and starting the conversation will spark something that we can use to connect with her."

"We can try I suppose. I'll be at the Washburns this morning and in the office after lunch, so you can pick me up there at two-thirty."

"Great, see you then."

After they'd said their goodbyes, Matthew began to ponder what Cici had said about how they would broach the subject of Kennedy Reynolds with a woman neither of them had ever met before. He was hoping for some inspiration, some dawn of understanding or revelation that would help with the segue.

Lost in his own thoughts as he was, Matthew didn't notice the car that had followed him all the way down Highway 20, which had become Center Street as he entered the historic little town of Peak and crossed the railroad tracks. He paused at the light alongside the old train depot on his left that was used for city purposes, including the Chamber of Commerce. He caught a glimpse of the nondescript gray sedan, just as it turned onto Winston Avenue behind him. It kept going after he turned quickly left onto Chapel Street, the one-way street that looped behind the cultural arts center and in front of Peak Family Practice, his office building.

He did a double take, realizing that he'd seen the car following him before. Why, he wondered, would anyone be following him? He had a very limited role in this murder investigation and all of the drama that had unfolded around it. At least so he thought.

*****

Having swapped a walk-in patient who came in at eleven-thirty for the patient he had scheduled at two with Megan Sims, Matthew had worked through his lunch break as a result. He was belatedly munching on his lunch as he drove to pick up Cici. He hadn't talked to Kennedy Reynolds about his plan and he wondered if Cici had. She'd likely talked to Reynolds as little as possible, he thought, as he pulled in front of the building and she appeared through the front doors, right on time.

Sliding into the car, she leaned over and kissed Matthew before buckling her seat belt. "OK, let's go see what we can do," she said happily.

"You seem excited about this now."

"I've never seen a bigger transformation in anyone as quickly as in Kennedy Reynolds," she admitted slowly and incredulously. "He's thanked me three times already and I was only in the office a couple of hours."

Matthew just laughed. "Love makes you do some weird things sometimes."

"I won't argue that point at all. I can't believe we're going to go do this now. And I wouldn't have but that you talked me into it."

"How is Annabelle Washburn holding up?"

"Reasonably well. She had the plans in place already. She just had to implement them and get the obituary updated with the time and date for the service Friday."

Matthew had put the address in his phone and he was following the directions out of town to the west. He followed Hillsborough Street across the inner beltline and had passed the fairgrounds when he was sure that he spotted the gray sedan a couple of cars behind him again. It was so nondescript that it was difficult for him to know for certain.

"Hey, Cees, don't turn around to look," he said as he stopped for a stoplight. "But have you seen a gray sedan following us or you before? If you check your rear-view mirror, it's about three cars behind us in this lane."

"I haven't seen a gray one," she said. "But I was sure I'd seen a silver one several times as I was coming and going from home. I thought it must be somebody from the neighborhood who was just on the same schedule as I am and headed in the same direction to work downtown. But I didn't go to work this morning and I'm pretty sure I saw it driving to the Washburns too. That doesn't make any sense though. Why would anyone be following either one of us?"

"I have no idea and maybe we are just paranoid. But I'm beginning to think not. Keep your eyes peeled as we turn up here."

"OK, our turn is just down there," said Cici, helping him navigate and pointing to a street on the right. "This is asking belatedly, but do you think we needed an appointment?"

"I have no idea. I guess we'll find out," he said, making the turn.

The cars between them went by including the gray sedan, but the traffic was too close to see the license plate number or anything of value. It kept going as Matthew made his way slowly down the little side street that looked mostly industrial with signs for a few businesses on both sides.

Parking the Element in a gravel parking lot beside an old low brick building that looked like a renovated warehouse, Matthew pulled his coat and the folder he'd retrieved from his office that morning from the back seat. Before he could get around to the other side of the car, Cici had already slid out and donned her coat.

Matthew offered his arm, which Cici took as she navigated the gravel parking lot in her signature spiked heels. They entered double glass doors into an open lobby that had modern and classic furniture blended together in a sitting area off to their left, where a tall green Christmas tree stood glittering in the corner. Soft Christmas music was being piped in from somewhere. They approached a counter that Matthew noticed was either granite or marble or some other shiny slab excavated from the earth. That was appropriate, he thought, for a landscape business.

The woman behind the counter rose and greeted them asking how she could help. Immediately noticeable was a clipped British dialect, which Matthew thought would sound out of place in any landscape businesses he'd have imagined. The atmosphere is this office was far different than he'd expected. Instead of the grit and dirt on concrete floors that he'd pictured, the whole space was shiny, light, and airy. The old warehouse had been renovated into a decidedly upscale business.

"Good afternoon," Cici returned the greeting. "We're interested in having our yards landscaped."

"Yards?" asked the woman. "As in plural?"

"Well, yes," said Cici.

"We want 'yards' to become 'yard,'" added Matthew, putting his arm around Cici, "So we're looking for curb appeal for both properties."

"Did you have an appointment?"

"We didn't," Cici admitted. "Did we need one? For an initial consultation?"

"Not necessarily," said the woman. "This is our slow season. We aren't always in the office this time of year."

"Great, because we hear that Celeste is a rock star with landscaping," gushed Cici, getting fully into the role.

"You know this isn't really the time to plant," said the woman. "That's mostly in the fall. But we can plan now, plant some in the spring, and do some heavy watering through the summer months if you haven't sold the properties by then. Do you have sprinkler systems in place?" she asked.

"Yes," said Cici as Matthew said, "No."

"But I could add one," said Matthew, hopefully. "Do you do that too?"

"We contract that work out, but yes, we can plan the system based on what we lay out for the garden area."

Cici asked, "What part of the UK are you from? I've just come from London and I'll be going back for a month or so after the holidays to finish up some business."

"A tiny place you will never have heard of," she said sweetly. "It's quite a distance from London, a few hours away."

"Oh, try us. We did a bit of touring around the countryside when Mathew was visiting over the summer," said Cici.

"I'm originally from Corfe Castle, though I attended University in London."

'We've been there!" said Matthew. "It's in Dorset, right?"

The receptionist just nodded, smiling. "It is," she said, seemingly surprised.

"It's southwest of London and there's a village there that's below the original castle structure on the hill, for which it's named. Isle of Purbeck peninsula, right?"

"It is!" said the receptionist excitedly.

"It's lovely," said Cici. "Matthew is a huge history buff so I kept that in mind as we were touring around the countryside outside of London. We went to the Isle of Wight on the way back to London."

"You said you wanted to meet with Celeste?" asked the receptionist. "Have a seat for just a moment and I'll see if she has some time to talk to you about your projects."

"Thank you so very much," gushed Cici.

"That went well," Matthew said quietly as they went to have a seat in matching club chairs in the waiting area. "If she has any sway with Celeste at all, we're off to a great start."

After a few minutes, a woman with dark curly hair that hung beneath her shoulders and was streaked with the beginnings of gray, came through a doorway beside the front desk and approached them. She looked to be in her mid-thirties, but by the history Matthew had gathered from Reynolds, he knew she was in her mid-forties instead. Celeste had aged well, he thought.

"Hi, I'm Celeste Mason," she said, shaking their hands in turn as they introduced themselves to her. "How can I help you?"

Again they explained their plan to add curb appeal to their separate abodes and how Matthew would need to add a sprinkler system to his.

"Certainly. We can create a plan for both yards, either to implement all at once or in phases, depending on your goals and the size of the properties."

"My condominium backs up to the corner of a golf course and then woods," explained Matthew, "So, I should really consider doing something to the back yard as well to enhance the view from my patio area. I brought my plot map that shows my unit on the end of the complex and the yard," he said, pulling the folder out that he'd had tucked under his arm.

"Perfect," she said. "That'll be a huge help. Do you know where the utility lines cross it?"

"I think it's on the drawing," he said.

"Come on back to my office and let's see what you have," she said. "I can send someone out to look at both properties and give you some ideas about how to enhance their value with some plantings, simple or complex, depending on what you want to accomplish."

As they followed her through the door by the desk, the receptionist looked up and smiled at them, nodding. "If your goal is to sell both properties, you might want to consider a minimalistic approach with these two properties and then something more complex for the one that you purchase," said Celeste.

"That sounds reasonable," said Matthew, thinking that a good idea and an even better sales technique for continuing business into the future.

She invited them in and they took seats opposite her around a huge metal and white table. She asked for Matthew's drawing, unfolded it, and flipped a switch, illuminating the table as they looked at the layout of his yard. They discussed the sun exposure and soil that was currently in place and what would grow best where with the least amount of care. Matthew liked her ideas and decided this would work out nicely as long as she continued to work with them after they told her why they were really there.

"My house is in Quarry and it's on a tiny lot," said Cici. "So, like Matthew, the challenge will be doing a lot with a little space. I like what you've suggested for his yard. I don't have my plot map with me, but I'll drop one by for you. Seeing you today was sort of a spur of the moment thing. You came highly recommended."

"Oh? Who recommended me?" Celeste asked quickly.

Matthew thought this segue wasn't quite right yet, so he supplied, "You can get recommendations for any business online these days," and then quickly changed the subject, thinking to ease in from another direction and build the sort of rapport that they had with the receptionist. "I see you went to North Carolina State University," he pointed to the matted and framed diploma hanging behind her.

"I did."

"I'm from Raleigh and I grew up as a Wolfpack fan," said Matthew, flashing up the wolf sign with his fingers. "Most of my family graduated from there, though I admit that I didn't."

"It's an excellent university. I have a degree in Environmental Engineering," she answered. "But I went in a bit of a different direction and took design classes too while I was there. I worked for a landscape design company for six years after I graduated and they always seemed to have far more business than they could handle. They focused on industrial clients and larger jobs mainly and turned away lots of smaller ones like yours. I do some of both, but I left there and built this business on the smaller jobs. I really enjoy those. They're so much more personal."

"I have a confession to make," said Cici, determined apparently to broach the subject at that moment. "You were specifically recommended to us by someone I work with who has never used your landscape services but who knows you personally from some years back."

Matthew raised an eyebrow subconsciously, realizing it in his surprise to see Celeste mirror that by raising one of her own. "Who might that be?" she asked, quizzically.

"Kennedy Reynolds," Cici said softly and Matthew watched as understanding was dawning on Celeste's face. He could see a range of emotions there that ranged from anger to disbelief, perhaps fear and then to something softer that played across Celeste's face. A poker face she did not have, he thought as he hoped that she wouldn't throw them out of her office.

"You seem like nice people," she finally said. "And I'm happy to work on your landscaping projects. But I don't want to talk about him."

"He wants to talk about you," said Matthew, deciding to fully cross the line because it was either time to go big or go home now that the subject had been broached. "He says you're the only woman he's ever truly loved."

"He's married to someone else!" objected Celeste, turning a bit red.

"He was married to someone else," said Cici softly. "He's been a widower for several years now and he really wants to see you, to talk to you."

"He does," agreed Matthew. "He said that he came looking for you when you left Harvard, but he realized too late that he hadn't asked you enough questions about where you'd grown up or where your parents lived. He said he spent a summer down here looking for you."

"I know. He found my sister. But I didn't want to talk to him so she just told him that no one by my name lived there, which was true. I didn't live with her. I didn't want him to find me. Did he tell you the story?" When Matthew nodded, she added, "His mother is the most horrid woman I've ever had the displeasure to meet. I didn't see him bucking her, giving up his family heritage or inheritance for me. I still don't, so we really don't have anything further to discuss on that matter."

"But he has," said Matthew. "He's told his mother about Ella and that he moved here to find you."

That seemed to catch Celeste off guard and she stared at him wide-eyed, so Matthew took the opportunity to elaborate.

"I won't lie to you and tell you that he's a wonderful person because neither of us liked him at all until he took me into his confidence about this whole matter. He becomes a different person when he talks about you and your daughter. It's like his hard edge of arrogance disappears. He said his mother told him she would disinherit him if he moved down here, short-circuiting the career she had planned for him as a judge or politician. He told her that he was coming to find you anyway and he moved down here a couple of years ago. As I think you already know, he's working at a law firm that both of you wishes he weren't.

He hired a Private Detective to find you and learned about Ella. But only a couple of weeks ago did he learn about the connection between the law firm he works for and your daughter."

At this, Celeste looked away and her eyes teared up.

"I'm sorry," said Cici, glaring at Matthew. "I know this is none of our business and we shouldn't be discussing some of this with you. But Mr. Reynolds punched the attorney who gave the boys a pass," she said delicately. "That attorney, just for the record, was a really caring person who didn't have the whole story on that case. If he had, he'd have refused to represent the boys."

"Was?" asked Celeste, her expressive eyes widening. "Ken didn't…did he?"

Taking a deep breath, Matthew said, "The attorney is recently deceased and Mr. Reynolds has been accused of the murder."

"He was murdered?" asked Celeste, the horror of that revelation showing plainly on her face and in her voice.

"He was and Mr. Reynolds has no alibi," said Cici. "Matthew now believes that he's innocent and wants to help him exonerate himself.

"Kennedy is consumed by reconnecting with you and meeting his daughter," began Matthew. Seeing the panic on Celeste's face, he added, "And he's prepared to do that without revealing that he's her father if you prefer it that way. Anyway, he's so focused on connecting with the two of you that he isn't at all concerned about the possibility of being charged with a murder that he didn't commit."

Celeste had sunk into her chair and her face was ashen white. Nobody spoke for what seemed to Matthew like an eternity and she finally said quietly, "Ken was a great guy in college. But his mother would never have accepted me. And you do marry the family. If she'd known I was pregnant back then, she'd have probably put a hit out on me," she said, trying to make a joke that fell flat. "More likely, she'd have tried to buy me off to get me to do exactly what I did and disappear. I didn't need her help to do that, though, did I?"

"She's prepared to accept you and Ella now," said Matthew. "Kennedy admits that some of that is due to the lack of heir for the family name and inheritance. But they have reconnected and she is determined to extend that family title to Ella."

"What?" said Celeste. "Doesn't he have legitimate children from his marriage?"

"He doesn't. Nor does he want any others now. Your daughter could be a quite wealthy young woman," said Matthew.

"I never wanted that for her when she was growing up," said Celeste. "I wanted her to have a normal home life. Not like the one that Ken apparently grew up in."

"And now?" asked Cici quietly.

"She's a grown woman now," conceded Celeste.

"You're saying that maybe it's time for her to decide for herself?" prompted Matthew.

"I guess I am," she agreed. "I will agree to talk to him but on my terms. He will come here. In my space, not his. I don't want to talk to him alone though. I need an out if it doesn't go well. Would you maybe be willing to…" and she left the sentence hanging.

Matthew and Cici smiled at each other surreptitiously as Cici answered, "That's fair and we'd be happy to. He's desperate to talk to you," she added.

"What does tomorrow afternoon look like, around three maybe?" asked Celeste. "I know that's rushing it, but I don't want this hanging over me through the holidays. My schedule is fairly light this time of year. I've long ago finished the Christmas displays for my contract clients and I was just working on some layouts for home and garden shows in the late winter. I'm sure Ken probably can't schedule that quickly though."

"From what he said, I think Kennedy Reynolds would drop anything and everything to see you," said Matthew honestly. "If your criterion is that one or both of us come with him, let me check my schedule. It's lightened up now that the children are out of school for the holidays." When Celeste looked at him quizzically, he added, "I'm a physician in a family practice in Peak."

"Oh!" she said. Then, she added, "Yes, I'd like to have you run interference. I haven't seen him in over twenty-three years and I had no intention of seeing him now or ever. But if all you say is true, then I will at least talk to him. I suppose I owe that much to my daughter."

"It is," said Cici. "And I can bring my plot map in for you to work from on my property too."

After they'd said their good-byes, they left and Matthew called his office from the car to check his schedule and ask to shift some patients around. Remembering Dr. Rob's offer, he asked if Maddie, the office manager, would check with him first. He'd already swapped with Megan to be off this afternoon, though she seemed happy enough to make the swap.

"There's a new app out that will enable me to see my patient schedule remotely from my phone. I really need to download that," he told Cici. "Maddie is working on moving or swapping two patients I had scheduled for tomorrow afternoon. I only had the two after lunch."

Next he called Kennedy Reynolds, who was more elated than either Matthew or Cici could have imagined. As Matthew had predicted, he said he'd move whatever he needed to move in order to see Celeste.

"I need to go downtown to identify the catering worker Danbury is bringing in," Matthew told Cici after he got off the call with Reynolds. "Do you want to come with me or go back to your office now?"

Cici checked her watch before answering. "It's only four now, so I guess I'll go back to my office for an hour or so anyway."

"OK," said Matthew as he backed carefully out of the spot and turned right onto the side street. Hillsborough Street was crowded and it took him a few minutes to make the left turn without a light at the small T intersection. Just as he pulled out, he saw the gray sedan come roaring up behind him, "Hang on, Cees!" he exclaimed before they felt the impact of the car running into them from behind.

29 ~ NOTHING RATIONAL

Matthew held onto the wheel and managed to brake enough not to ram the car in front of him. Before he could react, he saw from his rear-view mirror that the gray sedan slammed on brakes and spun in a 180-degree U-turn behind them. It then sped off in the other direction as fast as the congested road would allow before slipping onto the shoulder of the road to get around the traffic and it was quickly out of sight.

"Cees, are you OK?" asked Matthew, as he pushed down the deployed airbag and pulled to the side of the road. With the curtained airbag on the side, he hadn't immediately noticed that the car behind him, which had been behind the gray sedan, followed him onto the shoulder.

"I think so," she said, pushing down the airbag on her side as well. looking herself over, still stunned. "What was that about?" she demanded, suddenly angry.

"I have no idea, but it was nothing rational," said Matthew as he clicked to call Danbury and slid out of the car during the next break in traffic.

"Are you OK?" asked the driver of the car who had pulled over with him and rushed up to check on them. "That maniac came out from a side road, around me, and rammed you. I think I got it on my dash cam."

"Oh good!" said Matthew, realizing that the guy was standing there. "I think we're OK. Thank you. I'm calling it in now."

"OK, I'll go see what I got on the dash cam," said the guy as he made his way carefully back down the shoulder of the busy road to his own car.

When Danbury answered, Matthew explained what had happened and that he would be later getting downtown than he'd planned. He also explained that he was reasonably sure that the car which had hit them had been tailing him for a couple of days. Matthew wasn't totally oblivious to being followed and figured he'd learned a few things since the previous April when he'd first met Danbury and gotten more involved than he'd have liked in several murder investigations. So much for being early getting downtown to the police station and having a quiet night at home tonight, thought Matthew. Danbury said he'd send officers to the scene and Matthew began to circle the Element to check the damage.

At first, his heart sank when he saw the rear quarter panel of the driver's side. The back had buckled so that the gas flap was sunken beneath the section behind it, now raised. His Element was an EX, so the tailgate matched the rest of the silver paint not the bumper, but both were severely damaged. The bumper and the bottom of the tailgate were scrunched in, he saw as he walked behind it. The driver's side of the bumper was pushed into the tire and the other side was hanging on the ground. He fervently hoped that the frame wasn't damaged as he circled the driver's side again but he couldn't be certain of that. And then he got angry.

Matthew could feel the anger rising up in him. If it had been an accident, he'd have felt completely different. But this wasn't an accident. Somebody had purposefully targeted him and he was fuming. He tamped down the anger, taking deep breaths as he turned to Cici who had climbed out of the other side of the Element and was circling behind it to join him.

"Are you sure you're OK?" Matthew asked in genuine concern, pushing his anger aside to focus on what was immediately important.

Cici just nodded and said, "I'm fine."

The guy in the blue Toyota Camry who had pulled up behind them rejoined them triumphantly. "I got him!" he announced. "My dash cam isn't top of the line, but it isn't half bad either. I have a license plate number," he said, handing Matthew a slip of paper that seemed to be a gas receipt with a tag number scribbled on it. "And I can send you the video of the accident if you'd like?"

"Thank you so much," said Cici, stepping forward and introducing herself.

"Yes, thank you," Matthew added, introducing himself as well. "I really appreciate that. And so will my insurance company if we can catch this guy. If he has insurance."

Before they could say more, two Raleigh police cruisers pulled in, one in front and one behind them, both with lights flashing. After handing over his license and registration, Matthew explained that the blue Camry behind him was not involved in the accident but the driver had seen it and recorded it on his dash camera.

While the officers got all of the relevant information from the Camry driver, including a copy of the video so that the guy could be on his way, Matthew called his insurance company. It was a company that his family had dealt with for years, so he was relieved to hear them offer to send him a tow truck and set him up with a rental car until it could all get sorted out.

"Can you send a flatbed?" asked Matthew. "I'm not sure if the frame is bent, but the bumper is mangled, half dragging, and half pushed into the rear wheel. I don't want to cause any more damage by trying to drag it. I fully intend to repair this vehicle."

"I'll see what I can do," said the very helpful voice, before explaining the ratio of cost to repair and the value of the vehicle, should he need to use his own comprehensive coverage for the repairs.

"I understand," said Matthew. "I'm hoping to have the driver apprehended and hold him fiscally accountable. We have a license plate number."

"Good luck, Dr. Paine. I'll get this called in now. Shall I also send someone from the rental company to pick you up?"

"Yes, please," said Matthew, very impressed with the agency that eagerly offered such assistance. He wasn't certain if it was the agency itself or if it was because his father had grown up with the owner of the agency. Either way, score two for his father's friends this Christmas season, he thought.

"I'm glad you weren't driving your Corvette," said Cici.

Matthew grimaced. "I know you're trying to make me feel better but you know this car isn't made anymore, not since 2011. This little car has held its value exceptionally well and it has a dedicated fan following. I could have sold it quickly and easily many times if I had wanted to. I didn't want to lose it then and I don't want to lose it now. It's a great car. Or truck. I think it's actually classified as a truck."

"Then you'll get it fixed," soothed Cici. "Just like new."

"I hope so. It didn't have a scratch on it. I took very good care of it over the years. And those were a lot of years. My parents bought it for me in high school and I drove it all the way through college and my medical program."

*****

After all of the paperwork was filled out and signed for the police report, the Element had been towed. Though it had been loaded on the flatbed that he'd requested, Matthew hated to see it so mangled as it was being hauled away. He and Cici had been picked up by a rental car company and taken to the rental agency where Matthew requested to rent a Toyota Camry in honor of the helpful driver from the roadside. After signing yet more paperwork, Matthew was finally able to get the rental car from the parking lot. Glancing at his phone as he waited for the traffic to clear before pulling out of the rental lot, he realized that it was almost six-thirty.

Though the day had been exceptionally warm again for December, the temperatures were dropping quickly after the sun set and it was already dark and cold. As they drove away from the car rental agency, Christmas lights shone brightly all around them but Matthew felt his Christmas spirit waning.

"I don't know about you, but I'm hungry," said Matthew, realizing that was at least half of his problem. "Want to grab some dinner before we go to the police station? Or are you coming with me? Would you rather have me drop you back by your office?"

"I could use a bite. And I'm fine to go with you. I'll get to the things that I intended to do this afternoon in the morning."

With that, they made a quick stop by a deli and picked up

sandwiches to go. The crinkling of paper food wrappers and occasional slurping of drinks was all the sound there was as they drove into downtown Raleigh. After parking in the now familiar deck behind the police precinct, he and Cici got out and pulled their coats from the back seat where they'd stashed them. Hand in hand, they made their way wordlessly down the sidewalk, across the entrance drive, around the building, up the steps, and inside.

Stopping at the front desk, both provided their identification and they were issued temporary clip-on plastic badges and instructions to find Danbury. He was in the observation room, the fourth door on the left. They tapped and the door opened. Danbury retook his seat in front of the double-paned window. "Come on in," he said. "Meet Joseph Hayden. Get a good look. See if he's the guy you saw."

That name sounded familiar to Matthew on some level that he couldn't identify and it niggled at the corners of his mind as he stepped forward. A scraggly looking guy seated despondently behind the metal table in the interrogation room stared down at the floor, so it was difficult to get a good look at him. "Maybe," Matthew said. "Can you get him to stand up facing the door and slumping just a little?"

"That shouldn't be a problem," said Danbury. "I haven't seen him stand up straight yet. I'll be right back."

The door opened into the interrogation room. The sound was turned off so that Danbury's voice was muffled as he said, "Joseph Hayden. Stand up. Take two steps toward me."

The guy jumped, then stood and walked toward Danbury in the doorway. As he'd said, the guy seemed to perpetually slouch, but it wasn't his demeanor that was bothering Matthew. It was his name. Why it was so familiar, Matthew couldn't determine but he squinted at the guy, then closed his eyes and tried to recreate the scene from the Christmas Gala in his mind. Opening his eyes again, he took in the guy standing in the next room. After a moment, Danbury said something else and the guy sullenly schlepped back behind the table and plopped into the chair, face in hands and elbows propped on the table.

When Danbury returned to the room, he asked, "So?"

"It looks like the same guy, but I can't be completely certain of that because I didn't get a great look at him the night of the party. But it has to be, right? What are the odds that someone who so closely matches that description and was in the caterer's clothing the night of the event was someone other than the guy who worked for the caterer? His name is what's bugging me though. It's familiar from some other context recently but I can't place where or why."

"That's not his real name. It can't be. He didn't exist before two years ago. Not under that name. We've taken his prints. They're being run through databases now. Hopefully they'll tell us who he really is.

"Has he told you anything yet?"

"Not much. He's been processed in. But he lawyered up when he got here."

"Hmm..." said Cici. "May I?"

Danbury looked momentarily confused. "What are you thinking?"

"I am a lawyer," said Cici. "I could just introduce myself as such and talk to him. Of course, there is the little matter of false pretenses and getting anything he says to be admissible in court. I won't say that I'm his lawyer, of course. In fact, if I make it clear that I'm not his lawyer but I'm just checking on him, then it should be admissible if he says anything helpful."

"That's sneaky," said Matthew. "Will it work?"

"His lawyer could show up any minute," replied Danbury. "But I've been thinking that for the past three hours. It's worth a try."

"OK," said Cici, "do you have a legal pad handy? I left my bag in the car."

"Let me go find you one," said Danbury as he left the observation booth and Cici followed him.

Matthew remained behind, lost in contemplation with his knee jumping in concentration and foot bouncing as it was propped on the bottom rung of the high stool where he was perched. Why had someone rammed them from behind and then driven off? Was it some sort of warning? If it was, a warning of what? Was this the same someone who had been following him in recent days? What did he or Cici, either of them, have to do with the murder investigation? Or was it something else entirely? And where had he heard the name Joseph Hayden recently?

As he pondered those thoughts, suddenly it all became clear. He stood up from the stool, happy to be the only one in the room, as the realization hit him and he was horrified by the implications. Joseph Haydn was a classical Austrian composer in the eighteenth and very early nineteenth centuries. Matthew had just seen some of his music on the stand of Kennedy Reynolds' baby grand piano.

Sinking back onto the stool, he wondered if his dream could have been wrong this time. His insistence that Reynolds was innocent had been based not on any concrete evidence, just the dream. Was he helping a cold-blooded murderer? Matthew had dreams twice before when he was working on investigations and they'd been right so he had blindly trusted this one, but this one was different. The other dreams had been about peripheral people, one a victim of murder and the other a neighbor. Both dreams had led him to better understand people in his realm but neither had exonerated anyone from guilt.

Hearing the voices of Danbury and Cici who were coming back down the hallway, Matthew stepped out to tell them what he'd figured out.

"Cici, if you decide to bring up any names to see if he recognizes them, ask him about Kennedy Reynolds."

"Kennedy Reynolds? I thought you'd decided that he was innocent."

"I thought I had too, but I just remembered where I'd heard the name Joseph Hayden before. I didn't hear it, I saw it. On the stand of Reynolds' piano. Hayden was an Austrian classical composer. We know that's not this guy's real name and it's too much of a coincidence, don't you think? The guy with this name showed up about two years ago. About the same time as Kennedy Reynolds. Reynolds plays classical music and has Hayden's sheet music right there in front of him on his baby grand. If he were helping someone get a new identity, it's a great name. Unlike Mozart or Bach, Hayden was a lesser-known composer."

"Oh," said Cici.

"Circumstantial," offered Danbury. "But definitely worth following up."

"I agree," said Cici. "OK, I'll see what I can get out of him."

Matthew realized that he was fidgeting as he watched Cici enter the room and introduce herself. "I'm a lawyer but not your lawyer," she clarified. "Your lawyer still isn't here yet, so I just wanted to check in on you."

The guy looked up at her lasciviously and then looked her up and down, not bothering to hide the fact at all. "Could you be my lawyer?" he asked in a dialect that wasn't southern but what it was wasn't readily apparent, at least not to Matthew.

"No," said Cici, ignoring the fact that the guy was nearly drooling on himself as he checked her out. "Your lawyer has been contacted, but I just happened to be in the building. Do you need anything?"

Still looking lustfully at her, he paused and then seemed to choose his response more carefully, "I'd like a smoke," he finally said.

"We can always ask, but they will likely refuse that request until after you're questioned. Did they Mirandize you?"

"Who?" he asked, as if trying to be funny while looking like a cat about to eat a canary.

"Read you your rights, explain that anything you say can be used against you, that sort of thing?"

"Oh yeah. Twice. Once yesterday in Utah and the big dude did it again when he picked me up at the coast."

"OK, then I guess you just have to wait. Have they asked you anything yet? About known associates or places and times you might have been at any given locations?"

"Yeah, the big dude was asking if I was at some Christmas party working for a catering company. I told him I might have been," he said slyly. "And he asked me if I knew a chick who worked there. I told him I might have met her."

"What was her name?"

"Alicia Laws," he said with a knowing smirk. His right hand rested on the table and three of his fingers moved rapidly. They weren't drumming exactly. It was an odd twitching motion as if they had a life of their own.

"Did he ask you anything else?"

"He asked me about records they can't find on me. I told him I kept a low profile."

"What about in Utah? Did they ask you any questions?"

"Oh yeah, a shit ton of them. They asked about my address. I guess that's on my driver's license so I told 'em that."

"Did they ask you about any other people?"

"Yeah, some lawyer who got himself whacked," he said with the smirk. As he spoke, the fingers moving on the table quickened. There was something familiar about the motion, that particular sequencing gesture, but Matthew couldn't place it.

Matthew admired Cici's calm when she heard that response because he knew that she had great respect for Jamison Washburn and truly adored both him and his wife. But, he realized, it did make her circle for the kill faster.

"Jamison Washburn?" she asked, as both Matthew and Danbury leaned forward to watch the guy's face.

"Yeah, I think that was him."

"What about Aubrey Bartles?"

"Who's she?" he asked, looking less amused with this process, as if he were getting bored with it.

"Kennedy Reynolds?"

"Like the tobacco company? I could really use that smoke now," he said noncommittally.

"I've got to get back to my office. You have had dinner, right?" she asked, as if genuinely concerned for him but Matthew knew her too well to be fooled by the act.

"Yeah, they fed me. Wasn't half bad," he said. "Hey, I need to take a leak."

"OK," said Cici, rising and walking to the door. "I'll have one of the male officers come to escort you."

"Can't you take me?" he asked, leering openly at her.

Without another word, she turned on her heel and left the room.

Matthew could hear her closing the door firmly, but without slamming it, behind her as Danbury opened the door to the observation room for her.

"He's pretty slippery," said Cici as she stepped in and closed the door quietly behind her. "He's obviously done this before. I didn't need this," she added, handing the pen and legal pad back to Danbury. "Did you get any impression at all?"

"Marginally," said Danbury. "In between him ogling you. He smirked and looked away. When you mentioned murder victims. Both times. He gave no reaction to the other names."

"You're saying that he's a psychopath who gets his jollies from murdering people and if we're talking about someone he's killed, we get a reaction?" summarized Cici.

"Either that or people he knows," said Matthew. "He didn't give any reaction to either of the other two names. I couldn't tell if he was serious about thinking you'd said Audrey instead of Aubrey, though. That wasn't clear."

"Not to me either," admitted Danbury. "He's hard to read."

Just then Danbury's cell phone chirped and he clicked to answer it. "Danbury here." Matthew and Cici waited patiently and quietly, perching on stools, through a series of Danbury's "Uh huh, uh huh," responses until they heard him ask, "And it was where? Got it. OK, thanks."

Looking expectantly at Danbury, Matthew finally asked, "What?"

30 ~ Concerning

Danbury rubbed his chin with his thumb and index finger, as if trying to determine where to begin. "They found the car. The one that hit you. Abandoned. And burned."

"Oh," said Matthew and Cici in unison.

"They got the VIN number. It was stolen. So were the plates. The plates belonged to a pickup truck. The only connection is the location. Both were from Durham. And the car was left there. Burning in an empty lot. Behind a defunct grocery store. No prints have been found yet."

Matthew felt his hopes of having his Element easily restored quickly sinking. He was thankful that he had his own comprehensive coverage on both of his vehicles, but he figured that this would make it more difficult. "I'll let my insurance company know in the morning, but they'll want the police report, I'm sure."

"Yeah, I can help with that. I'm sorry, Doc," Danbury was saying as his cell phone went off again.

"Danbury here," he repeated into it. Again Matthew and Cici waited through a series of, "Uh huh, uh huh," responses. "OK, got it. Thanks."

Turning to Matthew and Cici, he said, "Maybe we're getting somewhere. The fingerprint report came back. From our John Doe. AKA Joseph Hayden. We got a hit. He's twenty-eight years old. With a RAP sheet longer than my arm. He disappeared three years ago. Fled murder charges. In Utah."

"Oh," said Cici. "They'll seek extradition back there then, won't they? Will you be able to question him first?"

"If his attorney ever gets here," answered Danbury. "And if we keep it quiet. His true identity. From the guys in Utah. Just until I can question him."

"Didn't they check his prints to know who he is?" asked Cici.

"They should have. They'd have kept him there. If they had. It's odd."

"That's what I was thinking, it is odd. Well, I guess we're done here for the evening?" asked Cici, standing from the stool.

"Yeah, I guess so. As for repairing your car," Danbury said to Matthew, "I'll get the report. I'm sure they wore gloves. In the burned vehicle. Or at least wiped it down. We won't likely find them."

"Gloves!" exclaimed Matthew, turning back to look at the guy behind the glass. "This is our guy! He was there the night of the murder! He was wearing gloves as he stood by the elevator, but his fingers were doing that odd twitching motion on his thigh that I saw him do just now when Cici asked about the two murdered people. He has another 'tell,' it's not just the smirk. Watch his hands when you're able to question him again."

"Wow!" said Cici, looking admiringly up at Matthew. "You do notice details, don't you?"

"Sometimes," said Matthew. "And others I'm just a run-of-the-mill clueless male," he added jokingly.

Danbury promised to keep them posted if he learned anything new and Matthew and Cici walked out. "I'm going to call Kennedy," said Matthew as he was leaving the parking garage of the police station heading back to parking garage of Cici's office building.

"Really?" asked Cici.

"If it still matters, I need to ask him how late he was in his office the night before he found the information about his daughter's rape on his office floor. And I guess I'll set up a time to meet with him tomorrow for us to go talk to Celeste. I want to talk to him about composers in person and see if I get any reaction to Joseph Hayden's name at all."

"We need to be extremely careful," said Cici. "Somebody has been following us and they tried to run us off the road. Maybe we're getting too close and they're worried."

"Yeah, maybe so," answered Matthew, as he checked his rear-view mirror for what seemed to him like the hundredth time and then poked his phone to call Kennedy Reynolds while he was stopped at a stoplight. After multiple rings, the light turned and Matthew handed the phone, on speaker, to Cici because he lacked the dash holder for it in the rental car that he had in both of his cars.

"Hello?" a voice finally answered as Matthew was preparing to leave a message. "Matthew?"

"Hi Kennedy. Yes, it's Matthew. I'm in the car with Cici and you're on speaker. I have a question for you and then an update."

"OK, what do you want to know?"

"The envelope that showed up under your door with the disturbing news about your daughter. You said it was there first thing in the morning on Tuesday, December the third, correct? Two weeks ago today?"

"Yes."

"Do you know what time that was when you arrived and found it?"

"It was early, probably seven or seven-thirty. I had a court hearing that morning and I needed to do some final preparation for it."

"And the night before? Monday, December the second, do you know what time you left your office?"

"It was late, for the same reason. It was probably nearly eight that evening before I left the office."

"OK, thanks," said Matthew and hesitated, trying to sound casual, but concerned that he was connecting a murderer with a very nice innocent woman. "We talked to Celeste this afternoon, Cici and I, and she's agreed to talk to you. What does your schedule tomorrow afternoon look like?"

Matthew heard a deep intake of breath on the other end of the line and then a choked voice replied, "She'll see me? I can't believe it! Thank you, Matthew. And Cici, I owe you both my undying gratitude!"

Cringing at Kennedy's choice of words, Matthew responded, "You're welcome. How does three tomorrow afternoon work for you? She wants us there too as a buffer I think. I'm working on clearing my afternoon schedule and Cici has agreed to the arrangement." Matthew realized that he hadn't called the office back to confirm that his afternoon was cleared, but he had great faith in the people he worked with, unlike the guy he now spoke with.

"I'd move heaven and earth to get to see her again," he said and Matthew thought he heard the guy's voice choke again on the words. That didn't sound like the voice of a killer. But neither did it sound like the voice of the man they'd known him to be up until that point. It was the softer side of a hardened man, but hardened by what, Matthew wondered. Grief? Loss? Or past sins?

"OK, I'll meet you at your office at two-thirty, how's that?"

"That's the best news I've had in twenty-three years!" Kennedy Reynolds exclaimed.

"OK, I'll see you then."

"Thank you, Matthew. I can't begin to thank you enough!"

They said their good-nights and Matthew had a thought after they'd disconnected the call, "Cici, there aren't any cameras on the floors where your offices are, right? Due to client confidentiality concerns?"

"That's right. There was a big hoo-hah about it right after I was hired. Some of the attorneys felt like it provided extra security, not a breach of client confidentiality. But the named senior partners wanted nothing that could ever be subpoenaed as evidence against any of their clients."

"When you say named partners, you mean Markham, Denton, and Washburn, right?"

"That's right, why?"

"How did Reynolds weigh in on it? Do you know?"

Cici thought about it for a minute and said, "I don't think he had much to say about it that I remember. There were a few who were very vocal, one way or the other."

"Any who stand out as not wanting the extra security?"

"I remember Mitch was vehemently opposed to it. He said his clients would be very upset if they knew their coming and going was being recorded."

"Huh," said Matthew. "Coming and going. There aren't any cameras in that one elevator that goes all the way to the top, or in the stairwells for those top three floors, right?"

"Right."

"What about the stairwells on the floors below?"

"I don't honestly know. Thankfully, I've never had to climb up or down thirty floors in that building."

"And the lobby?"

"Yes, there are cameras there, I'm pretty sure. We don't own the whole building, so we have no control over that area."

"And the parking garage?"

"There are cameras there, yes."

"Can you call Danbury?"

"Sure," said Cici, poking her phone.

"Hey Doc. What's up?" he heard Danbury's voice say, grateful that he chose that word order and didn't imitate a certain cartoon bunny.

"I just got off the phone with Kennedy Reynolds. He said he left his office late, like something before eight on Monday December the second, the night before the envelope was supposedly slid under his door. And he arrived early on Tuesday, December the third, between seven and seven-thirty. We know there are no cameras on those top three floors, but maybe we can check to see who left later than Reynolds that night or arrived earlier the next morning from the lobby or parking garage security footage."

"Great idea. Thanks for that intel. I'll get my team on it. I'm going in to question Hayden now. His lawyer finally arrived. He didn't give much away before. But I have a bomb to drop on him now. His real name. I'll let you know how it goes. Later, Doc."

Before Matthew could respond at all, the line went dead. Typical

Danbury, he thought. The guy had lots of work to do to be considered anything other than abrupt. As he pulled into the parking garage of Cici's building, Matthew looked for the cameras and spotted two near the elevator. He got out to inspect her rental car carefully. Nobody hiding in it, nothing in the trunk, and nothing obvious stuck underneath, he noted. He kissed her longingly and they said their good-nights.

"Be sure to watch your mirrors and call Danbury if you suspect that anyone is following you," he cautioned. "You can always come to my place for the night. Do you want me to follow you to yours to pack a few things?"

"No," she said, with determination in her voice. "Coming to stay with you will be deeply unsatisfying right now. And I'm a grown woman. With a security system and cameras all around my house," she added. "I'll be fine. Sleep well, Matthew."

He kissed her one last time and got into his car, waiting while she started up her rental car and backed out carefully. He followed her out of the parking deck, looking behind them and up and down the streets as they pulled out.

After watching his rear-view mirror all the way home, Matthew pulled into his garage, happy that he'd remembered to remove the remote garage door opener from the Element, and dropped the door behind him. He entered the house, resetting the alarm system behind himself, and went about his evening routine, caring for Max, laying out and setting up everything for the next day before dropping into bed exhausted.

It wasn't even that late, he realized, but it had been a long and stressful day. He picked up a book he'd been reading and tried to get into it as Max jumped up onto the bed and began bathing himself. Still worried about Cici for some nebulous reason that he couldn't put his finger on, he texted her to be sure that she had gotten home without any incident. Getting an affirmative response, it was only then that he was able to fully settle in for the night hoping to have a deep and dreamless sleep as the silent stars went by.

31 ~ DÉJÀ VU

Matthew was thankful for an uneventful morning on Wednesday. He'd been able to clear his afternoon schedule after two that afternoon and he'd just gotten through his morning round of patients when he felt his cell phone vibrate in his pocket. He'd missed two earlier calls, he knew, because his phone had been muted but he had felt it vibrate while he was in with patients. As he stepped from the hallway into an alcove, he clicked to connect and heard his father greeting him for the usual mid-week check in.

"Hey Dad, how're things on your side of the capital city?" he quipped, trying to be evasively clever as he decided how much, if anything, of what had transpired the day before to share with Joc. After a moment of small talk, Matthew decided to share and explained the events of the previous day to his father.

"You have no idea who was behind the wheel?" asked his father about the guy who had tried to run him off of the road, sounding concerned.

"No, like I told the police officers, the guy was wearing what looked like a ball cap and sunglasses. I couldn't see his face to know what he looked like. And the license plate information obviously didn't help at all. I was just about to call the insurance company back to give them the updated status. I called before they were in the office this morning. I guess people are taking off time right before Christmas. I don't blame them. They were more than helpful yesterday, so I'm thankful for all of your friends and connections from over the years, jewelers and insurance agency owners."

"You're crediting me for special treatment, huh?" his father chuckled.

"Likely so," he said.

"I'll let you get back to the grind, son. I just wanted to check in and I'm glad that I did. Let us know if there's anything we can do to help while your car is getting fixed."

"Thanks Dad, will do. Talk to you later."

"OK, bye Matthew."

Checking his phone, he could see that both Cici and Danbury had called him earlier. He started with Danbury, figuring he'd save the best for last.

"Hey Doc," said Danbury. "We've requested the security footage. From Cici's building. The evening through the morning in question. It can't be sent digitally apparently. Some security concern or other. An officer is on the way over there now. With a device to load the footage on. I'll let you know what that turns up. We had to ship Hayden back to Utah this morning. We didn't get anything concrete. The 'tell' you noticed is consistent. That thing he does with his fingers. It's almost as good as a lie detector. But not admissible as evidence unfortunately. We like him for both murders. But he's a hired gun. We can't find any connection. Not between him and Washburn. Or Bartles. Or Reynolds, unfortunately."

"There's nothing else you can do to nail him?" asked Matthew, clearly concerned, when Danbury took a breath.

"Not yet. But we're still working on it. What we really want is to know who hired him. We might have been able to offer a deal. But for his past record. We tried to bluff on that. His lawyer called us on it. Our forensic data techs are finally having some luck though. With the money transfer. Backward to the First Trust Bank of Raleigh account. The bank is helping as it can. Without breaking any laws."

"Wow, you've been busy since last night," said Matthew. "I just went home and went to bed."

"It's why I get paid the big bucks," Danbury joked. Matthew chuckled with him before Danbury added, "You're meeting with Reynolds today?"

"Yeah, we're going with him to see Celeste this afternoon at three."

"Be safe out there. And let me know if anything else pops. With Reynolds. Or anything else."

"Will do," said Matthew and Danbury disconnected the call.

"Abrupt much?" asked Matthew to air as he poked the phone to call Cici back.

She was in her office that morning, he learned, and she was calling to beg off of the afternoon plans. Initially he wasn't sure whether he was more annoyed or relieved that Cici wouldn't be joining him and Reynolds to visit Celeste that afternoon. At first he was relieved, thinking that she'd be safer if she weren't involved in any of that transaction. He thought so right up until she told him why she couldn't join him.

"Mitch has asked to meet with me this afternoon so that I can start getting him up to speed on the London clients. It's a huge amount of work and knowledge to transfer," she said, "so I can certainly understand him wanting to begin to chip away at that mountain."

As Matthew was quiet, trying to figure out how to word his objection and not sound like an insanely jealous ex-boyfriend who hoped to lose the "ex" part of that status in a little over a month, Cici said, "I'm sure you're not thrilled with this, Matthew. But if he's willing to take this on and allow me to come back three months early, I need to be available to do the knowledge transfer on his schedule as much as possible. I can hardly argue with his timing because he's doing me this huge favor."

"Is he really though? Isn't this a high-profile client? And wasn't he interested in taking them on initially too?"

"He was, but I think he was their second choice because I had more international banking experience already. It's where I started with internships in law school." She paused for a moment before adding, "Please, Matthew, do be careful with Reynolds this afternoon. I'm just getting you back and I don't want to lose you again."

"I'll do my best. You be careful too, for all of the same reasons," he admonished. "Do you want to get dinner this evening when I get back to your office with Kennedy?"

"Let's play that one by ear," said Cici. Then, she quickly added, "Of course, I'd love to, but we'll have to see how long Mitch wants to work this afternoon. I think my eyes would glaze over after a couple of hours but his might not. It's a lot, but I think I have it well organized."

"OK," said Matthew. "I can be flexible. I'm not a fan of Moorestrom obviously. I think he's shifty and way too smooth, plastic, in a sense. But I do appreciate his willingness to take on this client and allow you to come home sooner. Let me know when you're finished for the day?"

"Deal," she said, "I love you, Matthew. And don't you ever forget that."

"I love you too, Cees, and I haven't. Don't you forget it either," he added. She laughed as they disconnected the call and Matthew headed for the front desk to pick up the lunch order that he'd placed that morning with the daily lunch train.

*****

After updating his patient charts for the day and checking his schedule for the next day, Matthew called his insurance company to give them the report. They were helpful and promised to provide a check as soon as they heard from the repair body shop with an estimate. If, they told him, the other driver could be located and brought to justice, they would pursue reimbursement from that driver. Otherwise, they'd cover Matthew's repairs as long as they didn't exceed three quarters of the value of the vehicle.

A bit discouraged by this news, though he didn't think he had any reason to be because his Element would surely be repaired, Matthew took the rented Camry and headed toward downtown Raleigh. He called Kennedy Reynolds on the way.

"Hi Matthew," said Kennedy, sounding anxious. "Are you on your way?"

"I am. It's what I was calling to tell you."

"OK, I'll meet you in the parking garage. We can take my car."

"But," began Matthew.

"I'm sure you're perfectly willing to drive, but I just prefer my own car. It's roomy and more comfortable than anything else I've ever driven or ridden in. You should consider getting one yourself, as tall as you are," he added.

"OK," said Matthew, not feeling up for an argument with an attorney about driving. "I'll see you in about twenty minutes."

"I'll be downstairs in the parking deck waiting," Kennedy responded and they said their good-byes and disconnected the call.

If Matthew didn't know better, he'd think the guy was nervous. But did he really know better, he wondered. If Kennedy Reynolds was as genuinely in love with Celeste as he claimed, and had been for over twenty-three years, then maybe he really was nervous. Christmas miracles, thought Matthew. If the arrogant attorney who could stare down anyone and win was nervous, then pretty much anything could happen. But was he also guilty of murder, Matthew wondered, remembering the Austrian composer's work he'd seen on the baby grand piano.

As he made his way north and east up Highway 64 into Raleigh, Matthew found himself checking his mirrors constantly and wondered when he'd stop watching for a tail. Then he wondered when he'd be able to stop watching. Would he know when it was safe to live his life without worrying anymore? The thought disturbed him as he pondered what that would mean for how he lived his life.

Pulling into the parking deck, Matthew saw Reynolds standing by the elevator looking uncomfortable as he shifted from foot to foot. Matthew pulled alongside and Reynolds motioned, "Right over there. Park beside the Bentley or as close as you can get," he said, looking down his nose. That must be a practiced and long ingrained mannerism, thought Matthew, and one that he hoped the guy would try to avoid as they met with his lost love.

Matthew parked and retrieved his sport jacket from the seat beside him. The warmth of the day before had dissipated overnight and the temperatures were more in the normal range for Raleigh in December, above freezing but still chilly and breezy. As he approached the Bentley, Matthew heard Reynolds release the lock on the passenger side and he slid in. As promised, the car was roomy and comfortable. It felt like a boxy tank to Matthew and he had a sudden wave of nostalgia for his Element.

"I'm sure you know exactly where you're going and the best route to get there," said Matthew.

"Of course," replied Reynolds. "I've been by it more times than I care to admit. I didn't risk stopping to go in and see her in person because I got such a cold reception earlier. I was afraid she'd swear out a restraining order against me without ever hearing me out. Thank you again for giving me that opportunity. What did you already tell her to get her to agree? Anything?"

"The truth. According to my observations and what you told me."

"Which was?"

Matthew felt like the proverbial bug pinned to an entomologist's board, still squiggling to be free but realizing that the attempt would prove to be futile because he was talking to a renowned attorney, so he answered truthfully. "I told her that I'd love to be able to tell her that you were wonderful and dearly loved but that we didn't like you at all at first. Not until you decided to share your story with me. And that changed everything once I understood your feelings for Celeste and your desperation, and yes I think Cici used that word, to find her and connect with your daughter."

"That you were there, given all of that, probably spoke volumes. And that did it?" asked Reynolds dubiously.

"Not yet, but the truth at least got her to listen to us. She thought you were still married so we straightened her out on that score. And then she brought up the little matter of your mother and I think she finally softened when we told her that you'd faced your mother down and won. That you'd risked disinheritance to move down here and look for her. I don't think she thought you'd ever do that."

"Perhaps in years past I wouldn't have, but now that hardly seems important. If Mother had chosen to leave the entire family fortune to her favorite charity and disinherit me completely, so be it," he said. "All the money in the world isn't worth a sad and lonely existence when there's someone you love out there."

"I fully agree. We did tell her that your mother had come around and was now supporting you finding Ella as her heir. I left out the bit about the last name change demand. I figured you two can work that one out."

"Thank you, Matthew. I'm actually jittery. Maybe you should have driven after all," he said.

Barely had he gotten the words out when Matthew heard a yell and realized that it had come from his own mouth as a huge pickup truck bore down on them and slammed into right front quarter panel in front of the driver's side. Everything began to move in slow motion, but with crystal clarity in Matthew's mind. To its credit, thought Matthew as the Bentley spun and bounced backwards, it didn't flip over. He wasn't sure that the Toyota Camry would have held up nearly as well and he'd have been in the driver's seat of that vehicle.

When the Bentley came to rest, the back end was on the railroad tracks that paralleled Hillsborough Street on the other side of the road from the fair grounds and it was facing east, the opposite direction from which they had been heading. Matthew's mind raced with things he knew he needed to do as he pushed down the deployed airbags. Trying to piece together an order of operations of what he should do first, time seemed to speed back up again. Was he OK? He'd have some nasty bruising where the seat belt had grabbed him, he thought, but he shook his limbs and moved his head around. He thought he was OK but when he turned to check on Kennedy Reynolds next, the guy was anything but.

"Kennedy, can you hear me?" he asked, pushing airbags gently out of the way. Reynolds was slumped over the steering wheel as far as the seat belt, which hadn't released, would allow. Matthew clicked to release his own seat belt and leaned over to examine him. He could see blood gushing down the other side of the man's face and he wasn't moving. Matthew quickly checked his pulse and was relieved to find one. Head wounds always bled a lot more than those in other locations, he reassured himself, as he checked to see if Reynolds was breathing. He was, so Matthew unlocked the car, slid out of his side, and was trying to run on wobbly legs around to Kennedy's side to better assess him.

"Call an ambulance!" he heard himself shout as he saw, in a blur, the occupants of other vehicles near him emerging and running toward the smashed Bentley.

He couldn't get Reynolds' door open. The front portion of it near the hinge was smashed too badly, but the window was no longer there so he was able to reach in and recheck the pulse and begin to assess the injuries. Reynolds' left arm hung at an odd angle and Matthew figured the shoulder was dislocated and the arm probably broken, but it was the head wound he was most concerned about. A huge hematoma was already forming on the side of his face, taking up most of it. He's still breathing and he still has a pulse, Matthew reassured himself, hoping against internal hemorrhaging but he didn't dare move Reynolds, not without a backboard and the equipment to do so without causing further injury.

Managing to find a shirt in the back seat, which he'd gone back around the car to pull from a gym bag and retrieve, Matthew used it to put pressure on the head wound, holding it carefully without shifting Reynolds' head. After what seemed like an eternity but was probably only a few minutes, he heard distant sirens. An ambulance and fire truck pulled up behind him and two paramedics and an EMT, as the guy identified himself, had jumped out and come running.

"Matthew Paine, medical doctor," he identified himself back to them. "He has a pulse and he's breathing, but the door is smashed closed. I can't get it open and of course I haven't moved him."

"We've got it, Dr. Paine," said one of the paramedics. "Your head is bleeding too. Go sit down at the ambulance while we work on him."

He was bleeding? Matthew hadn't realized that he was until he reached up and touched his forehead. What had he hit his head on, he wondered. The airbags had kept him from connecting with the windshield, hadn't they? At least he'd thought so. Stunned by this realization, he followed their orders and went with the EMT to sit on the open back of the ambulance, watching while the guy worked him over. Examining the wound and then putting pressure on his head with a cloth and telling Matthew to hold it there, the guy went over the rest of him. The EMT shone a light in each eye and all of the other things that Matthew would have done to someone else, had he not been the patient. The paramedics had crawled in the Bentley with Reynolds from the other side, one in the seat Matthew had vacated and the other in the back seat behind the smashed driver's seat.

It felt surreal, like Matthew was watching a movie, as he watched the firemen maneuver the jaws of life into place. One of them yelled back over his shoulder to two police officers who were arriving on the scene, "Call it in, there's a train due by here in less than ten minutes!" One of the officers turned on his heel and jogged back to one of the police cars. When Matthew looked in the direction he was heading, all he could see were blue and red lights flashing through the waning winter afternoon light and cars pulled onto the shoulder of the road. He shivered involuntarily and the EMT wrapped him in a silver emergency rescue blanket.

"You're gonna need a couple of stitches, Doctor Paine," the guy said. "I don't think you have a concussion, but they're probably going to want to keep an eye on you. You know, observation. There's a second bus coming. We'll transport you when it gets here."

"Thank you," was all that Matthew could think to say. He was confused, he realized, and he couldn't quite put the pieces together to figure out what had happened. Vaguely he remembered a massive pick-up truck hurtling in their direction. It was a huge black Ford, he remembered because he'd seen the blackened badge on the front of the black grill clearly. Looking around, he didn't see it anywhere. "Do you know what happened to the truck that hit us?"

"It was a truck? We didn't know what hit you," replied the guy. "You're the only injured here. You bounced off a couple of other cars before you came to a complete stop, but none of the others were injured."

"What?" asked Matthew, looking around. His mind began to clear and he switched the hand holding the cloth with pressure on his head and reached into his pocket, relieved that his phone was still there. He pulled it out and poked it to call Danbury.

"Hey, Doc. Tell me you're not out on the railroad tracks right now."

"I am," Matthew confirmed. "How'd you know?"

"I was up front. I heard the call come in. I knew you'd be out that way. Details weren't provided. Are you OK?"

"I'm in far better shape than Kennedy Reynolds is right now," Matthew said. "He insisted on driving and he has a Bentley, which is basically a tank. Otherwise, I wouldn't be." He shuddered as he realized the truth of that admission.

"And Cici? Is she OK?"

"She wasn't with us. She ended up meeting with Mitch Moorestrom this afternoon. He's volunteered to go back to London with her to take over that client so that she can come home. He's proposing that they overlap by a month. I'm not thrilled with that, but I can't really tell you why I don't like that guy. He's just, I don't know how to describe him. Fake, I guess," Matthew realized that he was babbling and made himself stop.

"I'll be right back," said the EMT as he jogged over to the Bentley.

"What happened? The accident," said Danbury, refocusing Matthew's wandering mind.

"We were hit on Reynolds' side of the car by a huge black Ford truck that I've been told isn't on the scene anymore. It came out of nowhere. I didn't see it tailing us and I didn't see it coming. It's hard to tell what's here or isn't. There are people and cars and emergency vehicles everywhere. But it's weird. We were headed west, the truck hit us on the driver's side, yet we ended up across the other side of Hillsborough Street on the edge of railroad tracks. We spun and slid, I know. But I can't figure it out."

"Déjà vu," muttered Danbury. "Can you stay put?" asked Danbury.

"No," said Matthew. "They don't think I'm concussed, but I have a cut on my head that's apparently deep enough to need stitches. They're going to transport me to the hospital to get stitched up and probably poked and prodded some more as soon as a second ambulance arrives. There's a fire rescue truck here too, but I guess they don't want to use that one for whatever reason." He realized that he was beginning to babble again, just telling Danbury about what he saw around him, and clamped his mouth shut.

"OK, I'll meet you there. Rex?"

"It's closest, but let me ask."

The EMT returned and he confirmed the hospital just as the second ambulance arrived. Matthew updated Danbury and, in a complete role reversal, Matthew ended the call abruptly. "How's Reynolds?" he asked the EMT.

"The driver?" asked the EMT. "Stable, but still not conscious and he's lost a lot of blood. They nearly have him out. Is there anyone we can call for him?"

"Celeste," muttered Matthew to himself. Aloud, he said, "There isn't really. I'll call to tell the person we were meeting with that he won't be making it today."

"Is this your jacket?" he asked, holding out Matthew's sport jacket to him. Matthew hadn't noticed that he was holding it when he returned.

"It is. Thanks," said Matthew, taking it from him and putting it on.

"Anything else you can tell me about him or his health that might help?"

In a moment of clarity, Matthew was thankful for Cici, Danbury, his friends, and mostly for his family. Had he driven the Camry and the roles been reversed, there were lots of people who would need to be called, and any of them could have provided this information on his behalf. "I wish I could tell you," Matthew answered. "I don't know him that well. His name is Kennedy Reynolds and he's an attorney with Markham, Denton and Washburn in downtown Raleigh. He has no family except a mother up in Massachusetts, I think. He's about forty-five, and he seems to be in reasonably good health."

"Thanks. That helps. They should have him out shortly. Maybe his phone can help us if he has the ICE setting on. Is it in his pocket? They haven't found it in the car," said the EMT as he walked Matthew over to the other ambulance that had just arrived and helped him climb aboard, getting him settled on the gurney, which was raised at the head.

"I'm not sure. I didn't see his phone out anywhere in the car. He knew where he was going, so he wasn't using it to navigate."

The EMT aboard the ambulance checked Matthew's head wound and did all of the same things that the guy by the side of the road had done. When she was happy that he wasn't in any sort of imminent danger, she settled back into the seat and Matthew pulled his phone out. He was tempted to call Cici, but he figured she was working with Moorestrom and he wanted now more than ever to avoid having her think that he was jealously checking up on her.

Instead he pulled up the number for Celeste's landscaping company.

When the receptionist with the British dialect answered, Matthew got straight to the point, "Matthew Paine to speak to Celeste Mason, please. It's important."

"Yes, sir," she said and he heard Christmas music while he was put on hold for the transfer.

After a moment, Celeste answered uncertainly, "Hello?"

"Hi Ms. Mason, It's Matthew Paine. I was calling to tell you that we won't make it this afternoon. There's been an accident."

"What sort of accident?" she asked cautiously.

"We were involved in a hit and run on the way to see you," he replied. "I'm being transported to the hospital now, but only to get stitched up.

"You're what?!" she exclaimed. "Where is Ken? Is he OK?"

"The truck that hit us hit his side of the car," said Matthew. "He was stable when I left but still unconscious," he said, deciding to ignore HIPAA verification of her status as Reynolds' emergency contact because she was the closest that Reynolds had in the way of next of kin that he knew how to reach. He was acting in friend not physician mode and he knew that Reynolds would want her to know why he hadn't shown up when he was supposed to. If Matthew was being totally honest with himself in his rationalizations, he'd have also admitted that he had no desire to speak with Reynolds' mother after everything he'd learned of her, even if he did know how to contact her.

"He's not being taken to the hospital now too?" she asked, sounding genuinely concerned.

"He will be, but they were having to use the jaws of life to get him out of the vehicle. When I left him, his heart rate was strong and he was breathing on his own. He had two paramedics in the car around him working on him when I left and they almost had him out. He should be transported right behind me. I'm being taken to Rex. I'm assuming he will be too. But I just wanted you to know that he was nervous but excited to be coming to see you. He wouldn't have missed it for the world, if he could have helped it."

"I thought," she said, stifling a sniffle. "I thought he'd changed his mind and decided not to come. I was angrily berating him already.

Wow. Just wow," she said.

"I'm sorry to be the bearer of bad news, but I thought you'd want to know, and I knew without a doubt that he'd want you to know."

"Thank you, Matthew. He's going to Rex, you said?"

"I think so, just a second," then putting his hand over the phone, he looked over at the EMT and asked her, "Do you know if the other injured man from that accident will be transported to Rex as well?"

"Probably so," she said, "but let me check. Is that his wife you're talking to?"

"His ex," said Matthew, without clarifying ex what.

After a quick conversation with someone on the radio, the EMT said, "Yes, they've just gotten him out and on a backboard. They're loading him onto the other ambulance and they'll be running with lights and sirens to Rex."

Matthew had noticed that the ambulance he occupied had employed neither lights nor sirens and he was thankful for that detail because it meant that nobody thought he was critical. It could have gone so differently had he insisted on driving, he thought again. Closing his eyes, he just took a moment to be thankful and to pray for the well-being of Kennedy Reynolds. In that moment, he was reassured that Reynolds, despite the sheet music, had not killed anyone. He knew the guy was probably guilty of a lot of other things, and he wasn't sure how he knew it, but he knew that murder wasn't one of them.

Who then was guilty he thought as his eyes popped back open.

32 ~ MISCREANTS FOR HIRE

After being stitched up in the ED, Matthew was still under observation before being released when Danbury showed up, flipping back the flimsy curtain that separated Matthew from the rest of the hustle and bustle of the area.

"Hey Doc. How're you feeling?"

"I have a headache," Matthew admitted. "But otherwise, I think I'm OK. I can leave in about another half hour, I think. Are you sticking around? I don't have any transportation here."

"Yeah, I'm going to check on Reynolds next. Not that they'll tell me much, but I'm going to try. Tell me what you remember," said Danbury. "And then I'll give you the updates."

Matthew recounted the phone conversation with Reynolds in which the guy had insisted on driving. Then he explained how he'd gotten in the car and they were talking as they drove to see Celeste when suddenly they were struck by the oncoming truck. "That thing came out of nowhere," said Matthew. "One minute we were driving down the street, and I don't even know how the truck crossed over and slammed into us like that. The next minute we were spinning, sliding, and we crossed over the other lane of oncoming traffic. We landed facing east, the direction we had come from, with the back half of the car on the railroad tracks. I pushed the airbag away and checked myself over."

Taking a breath, Matthew continued, "Then I unbuckled my seat belt I think and tried to check Reynolds. He wasn't responsive but his pulse and breathing were both strong. I got out and circled the car but his door was smashed in and it wouldn't open. I think I yelled for someone to call 9-1-1. They must have. After I'd checked Reynolds over, I was holding his head in place while putting pressure on the gash and monitoring him as best I could one minute and then the sirens and lights came tearing in the next. The paramedics took over and sent me to the ambulance. I didn't even realize that I was bleeding," he said, sheepishly looking down at his blood-stained shirt.

"Did you see anyone behind the wheel? You said it was black, A Ford pick-up, right?"

"Yes, a huge one. And no, I didn't get a look at the driver. At the time it seemed to move in slow motion, but really it all happened so fast, and the impact was on the other side of the car. I didn't see who was behind the wheel, just the grill of the truck, which is how I knew it was a Ford. Both the grill and the badge were blackened but both were above the hood level on the Bentley. That truck was huge."

"Yeah, we found it. Abandoned. Less than a mile away."

"Stolen and with stolen plates again?" asked Matthew.

"Yes and no. They went for easy this time. The plates matched the vehicle. They stole the whole thing. That makes sense. If they were planning to use it then ditch it. The other car. It was following you around, right?"

"I'm pretty sure it was, yeah."

"For how long? When did you first notice it?"

"I'm not sure. I don't remember when I first noticed it. It's all kind of a blur right now," said Matthew.

"They were more careful with that one. Selecting something nondescript. Switching plates. It would take longer to trace it. If it were spotted."

"Did they burn this one?"

"No. It'll be towed. To our facility. Forensics is on it. But they're backed up. I doubt they get to it. At least not before Christmas. This was sudden. As you observed. Witnesses and dash cams confirm it. That truck struck you from the other direction."

"How could anybody have known that I'd switched vehicles and was riding with Reynolds unless they had me under serious surveillance? I was watching my mirrors the whole way over to the office to meet him and I saw nothing consistent."

After thinking it over for a moment more, Matthew added, "I am the common denominator, aren't I? Cici wasn't with me today. If they were after Reynolds, they wouldn't have hit us yesterday. If they were after Cici, they wouldn't have hit us today. But why me?" Matthew said, more miserably than angrily, though the anger was rising again. "I have very little to do with the Washburn murder investigation. Why target me?"

"That's the right question to ask," said Danbury. "I agree with you. They knew that Cici wasn't with you. If they saw you get in the car with Reynolds. And they must have. But it gets worse."

"Worse?" asked Matthew, sitting up straight on the hospital bed. "Worse how?"

"There were multiple vehicles involved. At least two. Probably more. You had to have had a tail. Likely more than one. Switching off behind you. So that you didn't notice them. But that truck was waiting. They knew where you were going."

"Oh man! You're right," agreed Matthew. "They must have known where we were going and when. But they who? Who would be after any of us? Why? And how could they know the destination or the timing?"

"I don't know yet," admitted Danbury. "But there are plenty of miscreants for hire. If you know where to look. Likely whoever is behind it was nowhere nearby. Either time. Who did you tell? About your plans this afternoon."

Matthew searched his memory trying to remember. "Cici knew obviously. And you and Kennedy Reynolds. And Celeste. I didn't explain any of this to anyone at my office. I can't think of anybody else I mentioned it to. Maybe Cici said something to someone."

"Would she have?"

"Cici!" said Matthew, reaching into his pocket to retrieve his phone. "She should be safely ensconced at her office pouring over files and information with Mitchell Moorestrom. I didn't want to bother or worry her, but I need to check in because she needs to be on her guard. What if it isn't just me they're after? What if Cici just happened not to be in the car today?"

"Good point. I'll leave you to that. I'm going to check on Reynolds. Be right back."

Matthew poked his phone to call her, but Cici's phone rang and then went to voice mail. He disconnected the call but then reconsidered and called her back, leaving a voice message telling her that he'd been hit again and run off the road. Warning only that she needed to be extra careful, he left out the details about how badly Reynolds was injured and that both of them were currently at the hospital.

Thinking that maybe she had her phone silenced for the meeting, he also sent her a text message asking her to call as soon as she got the chance. He was beyond worrying about seeming jealous and needy now. That was clearly not the case and she needed to be on high alert. When Danbury got back, he'd get him to go straight to her office. He wanted to find her himself, he thought.

The attending physician returned with a resident in tow and Danbury was right behind them. The little bay got quickly crowded, though Danbury was hovering just outside it.

"Can I go now?" asked Matthew, now anxious to get out of the hospital to go warn Cici.

"Let's see," said the doctor, checking the chart and then checking Matthew's pupils for what seemed like the hundredth time. Matthew understood the necessity of ensuring that he did not have a concussion before he could be released, both for his own protection and that of the hospital and physicians. He was worried about Cici though and he needed to find her.

"Rest this evening and by tomorrow you should be feeling more normal. Do you need a ride?" asked the doctor. "You probably shouldn't be driving this evening."

"Right here," said Danbury, behind them.

After they were all satisfied that Matthew wasn't in any imminent danger of developing any unforetold adverse reactions to the accident and that he wouldn't be driving, he was released from their care.

Matthew asked about Reynolds, hoping to see him in the ED before they left.

"He isn't back here," said Danbury. "He wasn't brought to the ED. I was told that he wasn't able to be questioned. And maybe I could check back later. Probably tomorrow. To see if he was in a room."

"That's cryptic," said Matthew. "If he bypassed the ED, my bet is that they took him straight into surgery. I wonder if he ever regained consciousness."

"I can find that out," said Danbury. As they made their way out to the front lobby, he poked his phone and asked whoever answered it for an update on the accident, specifically on the Reynolds victim. As they came into the open lobby area, Matthew heard a familiar voice raised a bit frantically at the front desk and he turned to go that way.

"What is it?" asked Danbury, following. "I'm on hold," he added, pointing to the phone.

"Celeste," said Matthew, as he stepped up to the desk.

"Oh Matthew! Are you OK?" she asked as she looked down at his shirt that looked like an ink blot of dried blood. When he nodded affirmatively, she asked frantically, "Where's Ken? They won't tell me anything because I'm not an immediate relative."

Stepping up to the counter, Matthew said, "Hi, I'm Dr. Matthew Paine. I'm a family practice physician in Peak and I was involved in the accident with Kennedy Reynolds."

"Ah, hi Dr. Paine, how can I help you?"

"I know that he was brought in right behind me and that he was taken into surgery upon arrival. I was there on the scene to begin to assess and treat him. This is Celeste Mason." Then conspiratorially, he added. "She's his ex but they are working on reconciling." That she wasn't his ex-wife was a clarification he thought he'd risk not sharing because he needed to get to Cici and somebody should be there with Reynolds.

He glanced back at Celeste, who didn't flinch in any way at this statement. She apparently had a poker face when she most needed to have one, Matthew thought. Either that or, in her own mind, she wasn't disputing what he said.

"I see," said the receptionist. "If you're his physician, I can share his status and location with you. I'll need his permission to share that with his ex-wife," she said. "Unless she's still listed as his emergency contact in any of the *Manage My Health* portal information."

"That I don't know," said Matthew, choosing to ignore the implied question about whether or not he was Reynolds' physician. Who knew, after all of this he might well become so. "I don't have access to his chart right now," he tried for levity, shrugging his empty hands. "I would need to get back to my car and my computer to access any patient records. But I'd like to know Kennedy's location and status before I go if you can share that information with me. So that I can check in on him later when I get cleaned up."

"Huh," said the woman behind the desk, looking down at the computer monitor as she clicked away at the keys. "It doesn't look like Mr. Reynolds has added much information to his portal information. I see neither a primary health care provider nor an emergency contact listed."

"That sounds like him," said Matthew, as if he knew the guy well. He didn't, he realized, but it still sounded like Kennedy Reynolds not to have bothered with any of that.

"What's his full name?" she asked hesitantly.

Stepping forward, Celeste said, "Kennedy Edward Reynolds."

"Date of birth?" she asked.

Celeste provided that without hesitation.

"Birthplace?"

Celeste spieled off the name of a town in Massachusetts that Matthew had never heard of.

"Next of kin?"

"Our daughter and his mother. His elderly mother is still in Massachusetts. So we're it," she said.

Clearly, Celeste must have loved him as fiercely as he claimed to love her if she still remembered all of those details about him, thought Matthew.

"OK," said the woman and gave them the location of the waiting room.

Torn, Matthew knew that Celeste might well need his assistance upstairs but he was still worried about Cici. He couldn't reach her and she had neither called nor texted him back. In the end that won out.

"Celeste, I really do need to go get cleaned up," said Matthew as they walked away from the counter heading for the elevators that the receptionist had pointed them to. "If they ask for his wife or family in the waiting room upstairs, just tell them that you're his ex."

"OK, I can do that," she said as Danbury approached.

"I don't know much," he said. "Reynolds hadn't regained consciousness. When they left the scene. To bring him here."

"That doesn't surprise me," said Matthew. "Because they skipped triage down here and took him straight up to surgery." Turning back to Celeste, he said, "You have my number. Can you text me when you know something?"

"I will. Thank you, Matthew. For everything." He just nodded, and he and Danbury went back through the lobby and out the doors. They didn't have far to go. Danbury had parked close by.

"One of the perks," he said, obviously noting Matthew's surprise. "To Cici's office?"

"Please," said Matthew, climbing in.

"Doc, you're kind of," began Danbury, gesturing to Matthew's bloodied shirt over which he'd put his sport coat that was also probably bloodied but it was a dark color and not as obvious.

"I think I have a spare," said Danbury, getting back out and going to the back of his big black SUV.

"Here," he said, climbing back in and handing a golf shirt across to Matthew.

"Thanks Danbury," said Matthew, appreciatively. "Do you always carry clothing around with you?" he asked as he pulled off the jacket and then carefully pulled his collared three button shirt over his head. Noting a couple of sore ribs in addition to the bruising on his shoulder, he pulled Danbury's shirt gingerly back over his head. It was a little bit big but not horribly so, if he put his jacket back over it, he thought.

And he'd definitely do that to ward off the chill of the dusk. It was nearly six and the sun had already set, though there was still a soft glow on the horizon as they pulled out.

Looking over at Danbury, who hadn't replied, he thought the big detective looked sheepish.

"Ah, that's not your go-bag for your job, is it? Unless we're talking about going over to Penn's," he teased and knew for certain that Danbury had flushed just a bit with that good-natured ribbing.

Danbury still didn't respond except to grunt, so Matthew settled back into his seat to relax but then he realized that he hadn't inspected his own injury. Leaning forward slightly, he flipped down the sun visor and slid open the vanity mirror. The edge of his hair had been shaved back slightly on the right side of his forehead and he sported a bandage over what he thought had been five stitches. I might not be raising the eyebrow on that side for a while, he thought, but it could have been far worse.

Settling back in, he rode in silence without arguing over the music this time because Danbury had the radio set to a station that was playing Christmas music continually. Though their taste in music was usually diametrically opposed, that they could both agree on, thought Matthew. Danbury pulled in front of the tall building in downtown Raleigh and Matthew checked to be sure that he still had the key for the rental car in the front pocket of his gray slacks and his wallet in his back pocket.

"You sure you want to drive back? Cici can drive. You can get your car tomorrow. Leave the shirt in here," said Danbury. "You can get that later too."

"OK," said Matthew. "Thanks Danbury for everything."

"OK, Doc. Let me know if," and he let the sentence hang for a few seconds. "If you learn anything else."

"Will do," Matthew waved as Danbury drove off and he turned to enter the building. Glancing over at the huge tree in the lobby as he entered, Matthew felt like it had been ages since he'd swapped the ornaments around on it. Months at least. Not days.

Approaching the front desk, he saw that it was empty but he didn't hesitate to click the button to call someone out from wherever they were holed up. The door behind the desk swooshed open and a tall woman he hadn't seen before emerged.

"How can I help you, Sir?" she asked, staring curiously up at the bandage on his head.

Deciding it wasn't the time for humility, he played the card, "Dr. Matthew Paine here to see Cecelia Patterson."

"I can call up for you. Are you a client with an appointment?" she asked, dubiously checking her watch.

"No, I'm her boyfriend," he said without hesitation. It sounded right in his head as the thought formulated and just as much so as he heard himself say it aloud.

"Oh, OK. Identification please?"

Pulling out his wallet, Matthew handed over his driver's license. After studying it, the woman clicked some keys on the computer keyboard in front of her and then handed his ID back with a temporary plastic badge. "Clip this to your shirt and display it at all times," she said. "Right through there, take that far elevator on the right. Use the badge to access the top floors."

"Thanks, I know the drill," he said, already walking away before she'd finished talking. He leaned over to hover the chip in the temporary badge over the card reader without pulling it off and punched the button on the elevator to take him to the thirtieth floor. Usually, he thought the elevator was exceptionally fast as it zoomed quickly skyward, but today it felt like an eternity. After he'd found and talked to Cici, he could relax, he thought. He would hang around until she finished with Moorestrom and they'd leave together, and he didn't care what objections the guy might make about it.

Stepping off the elevator on her floor, he saw nobody else about as he made his way down and around to her office. The door was closed, so he tapped gently on it. There was no response from within. He jiggled the door handle and found the door locked. Maybe they were working in Moorestrom's office or a nearby conference room that was bigger, he thought. Meandering through the hallways, he finally saw an administrative assistant through a glass panel in one of the doors. He had met her, he knew, but he had no idea who she worked for or what her name might be.

Opening the door and slipping into the office, he said quickly, "Hi, I'm Matthew Paine and I'm looking for Cecelia Patterson."

"Oh, hi Dr. Paine," she said. Apparently, she knew him or at least of him, even if he couldn't remember much about her. "I haven't seen her in a while. I don't think she's here."

He hadn't thought to check the parking garage for her car because she'd have seen his text messages or heard his voice message if she'd left, surely, so this was odd.

"She was meeting with Mitchell Moorestrom this afternoon. Over three hours ago," he said, checking his watch. "Do you know if he's here?"

"I haven't seen him all afternoon. I can ring his office, if you'd like?"

"Yes, please," he said and waited while she flipped through a little card deck on the side of her phone and then picked up the receiver and poked in the extension number. He waited while she waited.

"It went to his voicemail," she reported. "Apparently, he's not in his office either," she added, stating the obvious.

"Are there conference rooms around that they might be working in?"

"A couple," she said, flipping the card deck again and poking more numbers. After a succession of three, Matthew was growing alarmed.

"Any place nearby that Moorestrom likes to go for work sessions? A coffee shop or deli? Brewery?"

"Not that I'm aware of. They'd not be likely to go to a public place like that if they're meeting about clients, confidentiality and all. I can call his cell, if you'd like?"

Something in Matthew was alarmed at that suggestion, and he simply said, "That's OK. I'll keep trying her cell. Thank you," he waved as he left the office. Checking to see if her car was in the parking deck was a next logical step, but he wanted to be certain that she really wasn't here first, so he walked the rest of Cici's floor before he got back in the elevator and rode up one. The thirty-first floor was also a ghost town until he got near the end of the hallway where he'd found Jamison Washburn slumped over his desk in his office.

Lights were burning brightly down at that end of the hallway and he could hear a noise that he realized was crying. He stopped in his tracks, pausing momentarily. He didn't want to intrude, but he resumed his path when he thought about Cici and not knowing where she was and if she was OK. Peeking through the outer office door, he saw a woman sitting at the messy desk and she was indeed crying.

Tapping lightly, he pushed the door open. A pretty blonde woman looked up at him from behind the messy desk to the right of the inner office. "I'm sorry to bother you," he began. "But I'm looking for Cecelia Patterson. She was supposed to be here working this afternoon with Mitchell Moorestrom. She's not in her office and she's not answering my calls."

"Oh," said the woman, snatching a tissue from a box on the desk and blowing her nose loudly. "I haven't seen either of them today. I was just in cleaning out my things. I worked for Jamison Washburn, but he's," she said, choking on her words and not able to finish the sentence.

"I know, I was here that night," said Matthew. Noting the alarm in her face, he stepped forward, "I'm Dr. Matthew Paine," again using the title, which he rarely did, to put her at ease as he introduced himself.

"Rhonda Cauthren," she said, standing and beginning to offer her hand, but then pulling it back, embarrassed, because it was holding a tissue into which she'd been blowing her nose.

"I'm very sorry about Mr. Washburn. He was beyond resuscitation when we arrived, though I and another physician did try. I really need to find Cici," he said. "Can you think of any place they might go to work this afternoon if they chose not to be here? Any nearby coffee shop or deli that has a room? I know they wouldn't be out in the open anywhere to discuss private client information," he added, having just heard that himself. They would, as the other assistant had pointed out, be somewhere private. Normally, he'd have realized that himself, but he knew he wasn't thinking entirely straight just then.

She paused a moment. "Not that I can think of, no. Did you check the conference rooms? There are only two on this floor. There's the big one on the floor above us but there are a couple of smaller ones up there too."

"Would you mind showing me?" he asked.

"OK," she said, tossing the tissue on the messy desk that he couldn't see she'd managed to "clean" at all yet. Passing him through the doorway, she headed briskly down the hall. "There's this one," she said, pulling a key ring from the pocket of her sweater and opening the door to an empty room. She flipped the light switch on and then back off again.

He followed her down the hallway and around the corner. "And then there's this one," she said, repeating the process with the same result. "These are the only two on this floor. I guess because the senior partners have big offices with tables in them for talking to clients."

Senior partners, thought Matthew, realizing that he hadn't yet told anyone there about Kennedy Reynolds. He turned to her abruptly and asked, "Is Kennedy Reynolds' assistant still here?"

"I don't think so. I think she said she was leaving early today because he was."

"He did. And then he was in a car accident. Can you reach her? Somebody here should know about it."

"Mr. Reynolds? Is he OK?"

"He was in surgery when I left. Can you get the word to her and the other senior partners? He's at Rex."

"OK," she nodded, the alarm showing clearly in her face. "I'll let them know."

"Thanks. I'm going up to check the top floor. Cici isn't answering her phone and nobody has seen her this afternoon. I'm starting to get worried." Pausing, he added, "Can you check with Reynolds' assistant and the partners? And if I leave you my number, contact me if any of them know where she could be?"

"Sure," she said, reopening the conference room door she'd just closed, flipping on the light switch, and pulling one of the notepads with the firm's name and logo splashed across the top of it from the middle of the table. She found a pen in the stack of supplies in the middle of the table and handed them over to him.

He jotted down the number, thanked her again, and all but ran for the elevators.

After searching the top floor without finding Cici or anyone else, he descended to the lobby floor, turned in his badge, and got into another elevator to descend to the parking deck. As the doors opened and he stepped out, he looked down through the parking deck and saw Cici's rental car in the well-lit but nearly deserted deck, part way down. He felt the back of his neck prickle in alarm. She wasn't where she was supposed to be, she wasn't answering her phone, and he had no idea where she was or if she was safe.

33 ~ Nonstop

Matthew thought that this particular Wednesday in December, though one of the shortest days of the year, was one of the longest of his life. He jogged down to Cici's rental car in the lot, feeling his headache intensify with the effort, and looked around it. There was nothing there to give him any clues. The inside was empty of anything personal, the doors were locked, and there was nothing on the outside to give him any indication of anything amiss.

Feeling like he must be a little paranoid, he went to the trunk and tapped on it. "Cici?" he said aloud. Getting no response, he pulled out both his car key and his phone. His rental car was still in the lot, just to the other side of the elevator so he jogged back that way and, ignoring the pain in his head, slipped into the car and started it up. He called Danbury and told him what was happening.

"I don't know what to do," said Matthew. "Or where to look. I thought about going by her house but how would she be there if her car is still here?" While he was talking, he reached for his satchel and pulled out a bottle of Ibuprofen and a protein bar. He had no water, but there was a travel mug with cold coffee from that morning that he grabbed and grimaced as he chased down the Ibuprofen with the stale cold coffee.

"I'm at the precinct," said Danbury. "Why don't you come over here. Maybe if we can access her phone," he began, sounding like he was thinking out loud.

Just then, Matthew saw a text come in. "Wait, I have a text from Cici," said Matthew, relieved. "I'm putting you on speaker, hold on."

Pulling up the text to read the message, he realized that the momentary relief he'd felt was fleeting.

"I need you. Something's off with Mitch. I'm at his house. Dropping a pin. I'm going to call in a minute. Mute yourself and just listen. But get here."

Reading it aloud to Danbury, he quickly texted back, "*Coming.*" Poking the pin that she'd dropped to start the route to her, he put the phone on the console beside him and tore out of the parking deck. "I'm coming to you," he said to Danbury. "I'll be there in just a minute."

Danbury said, "I'll be parked out front. Pull in behind. Leave the car running. Get in mine. It's faster."

It was the one time that driving like a maniac seemed completely sane to Matthew and he paused long enough to gather his nerve and then drove through the metal arm beside the exit booth without stopping to deal with his parking stub. Hearing it buckle and then scrape the rental car as he drove through, he heard the metal arm clatter loudly onto the pavement behind him but he didn't slow down.

"Cici's calling now," he told Danbury. "I'm clicking over and muting myself."

Matthew reached down and poked the buttons to mute himself and accept her incoming call. He strained to listen as he paused for stoplights and then tore through them. Christmas lights, stoplights, street lights, they were all a blur as he heard Cici say, "Thank you for your concern, Mitch. I didn't remember telling you that I'd been run off the road yesterday."

"You mentioned it," said a noncommittal voice that was farther away.

"I really don't think that I did," he heard Cici say.

"Slow down, Cees," Matthew said aloud to her, coaching her as if she could hear him. "We're on the way, but slow down."

"You must have, Baby. How else would I have known?" Moorestrom's voice cooed, as if talking to an actual child. Matthew cringed on Cici's behalf because he knew she'd hate being called "baby" as much as she'd hate the tone of voice the guy was using with her. But then, who wouldn't?

"I suppose I must have," she said to Matthew's relief. He heard a rustling noise before she added, "Were you planning to order out for dinner? Or are we going out somewhere?"

"We can have it delivered," Matthew heard the voice say. "What are you in the mood for? Besides me, of course."

"Really? You're still up for that?"

"Because of your female problems?" Matthew could hear the derision in the voice and feel his own ire rise as Moorestrom added, "That'll hardly slow us down."

"Maybe Chinese takeout with fried rice?" he heard Cici ask. Matthew could hear the strain in her voice though she was trying to sound casual. He knew that she'd said that for his benefit because Cici wasn't fond of Chinese takeout and she particularly detested fried rice. She was letting him know that she was playing along but nothing more.

Matthew turned the corner and pulled up in front of the police station, slamming on brakes to keep from rear-ending Danbury's SUV. He grabbed his jacket, the protein bar, and his phone. Flinging the door open, he jumped out and ran for Danbury's SUV. Climbing in, he clicked to the map that was pointing him to Cici and held it up for Danbury's inspection. Danbury used two fingers to expand the view, studied it for just a moment, and then handed the phone back.

"Chinese it is then," he heard Moorestrom's voice say on his phone. "What are you doing?" Moorestrom's voice sounded accusatory, but it was fainter this time and they had to strain to hear him. Matthew reached over and pushed the volume button multiple times on his phone, trying to turn it up but it was already maxed out.

"This is a lovely piano," Cici's voice said smoothly and clearly. "You play, I assume?"

"Of course. I'm a maestro. I can serenade you later if you'd like," Moorestrom's voice answered her.

Taking off from the curb, Danbury reached down and flipped or poked something to activate the blue lights in the grill on the front of the big SUV. From the rear-view mirror, Matthew could see that behind them an officer ran out of the building, down the steps, and got in Matthew's rental car, looking at it oddly in the process. Matthew saw two more cars, one marked and one not, pull out from the small street behind the station to follow Danbury. The Raleigh police building became a blur in the rear-view mirror as Danbury turned left onto South McDowell Street, slowing at the intersections, but making his way through each one without stopping.

From the seat beside him, Danbury said, "Yeah, up US 1 and north. Off of Wake Forest Road. Then Falls of the Neuse. Looks like a secluded area. A wooded section on the outskirts of the city." When Matthew looked over, inquiringly, Danbury just tapped his ear and Matthew could see some sort of communication device there that he hadn't noticed before. Danbury followed the curve in the road as it became Capital Boulevard and hit the gas.

"You have a great selection of music here," Matthew heard Cici's voice say. "I've heard of most of these. But who's Joseph Hayden? That one isn't familiar." Again, Matthew knew that Cici was talking to him and telling him that she suspected Mitchell Moorestrom of being behind the murders. Glancing over at Danbury, Matthew saw him nod in acknowledgment that he too had heard what she'd said.

"He's an Austrian composer from a couple of centuries ago. Brilliant really but highly unacclaimed. We can understand that, can't we, Baby? Let me order dinner and I'll play some for you."

"That would be lovely," said Cici and Matthew knew that she must be struggling and giving the performance of her life, not on a piano and not on a stage but performing none the less. There was a momentary quiet lull on the phone, though Matthew could still hear background noise so he knew the connection held.

"Chicken Manchurian is my favorite so I'll order two," he finally heard Moorestrom's voice say. "Did you know it's actually Indo-Chinese not purely so? I'm not a huge fan of Chinese cuisine, but I love Indian, particularly curry. Yes, let's do Indian. I like that far better than Chinese."

Having talked himself in circles, the guy had conveniently but effectively dismissed Cici's request and substituted his own choice. Matthew knew that Cici wouldn't care since she wasn't actually a Chinese takeout fan herself and she wouldn't be likely to eat anything he was ordering anyway if Matthew could help it. She was just biding her time and giving him clues until he could get there. What was on the menu for dinner was completely superfluous.

"That's fine," she said, obviously going for complicity at this point and trying not to rock the boat.

After a few more moments of silence, Matthew looked over to see that Danbury was doing seventy up Capital Boulevard through the city and cars were getting out of his way. The two cars following were both running with lights and sirens. Nobody else on the road was arguing with them. Slowing slightly, they followed the exit ramp off to the right, then curving to the left, they crossed back over Capital Boulevard to take Wake Forest Road north.

Moorestrom's voice announced, "OK, done. It'll be here in about twenty minutes."

"So will we," Danbury said softly as Matthew heard Cici say, "Great."

Then louder, Danbury said, "Hey, Hanks, they've ordered Indian take out. That might be our way in. Is North Raleigh backup en route?" After a pause, he said, "OK, thanks."

"Whatever will we do until dinner arrives?" Moorestrom's voice said in what must be his seductive bedroom voice.

"You could play for me" said Cici quickly.

"Or play with you."

Matthew heard an odd chirping noise and then Moorestrom angrily asked, "What the hell was that?"

"I have the hiccups," said Cici's voice sweetly and submissively. "I guess I'm just nervous."

"With me? Baby, you never have to be nervous with me. I'll take good care of you."

Anxiously, Matthew looked over to see that Danbury was still well above the speed limit on Wake Forest Road as they approached Whitaker Mill Road.

"Maybe you could play for me now," suggested Cici. "I love piano music. It's calming." Cici must have turned doe eyes or puppy dog eyes on him, Matthew thought, as he heard the chirping noise again.

"I had other ideas, but if it gets rid of the hiccups, I can do that," said Moorestrom. "I'm a patient man. I've waited years for you already and we have all night. I want it to be perfect for me."

That, thought Matthew, was the crux of it. They blew through the intersection of Whitaker Mill Road as Matthew thought that he had been entirely right in his assessment of the guy as plastic and fake. What he'd missed, he now admitted to himself, was that the guy was also a sociopath, probably a psychopathic sociopath. Ben Teddy apparently had nothing on this guy. He cringed at the comparison in his mind. Teddy had been a serial killer who was handsome and charming. He'd lured unsuspecting women in and killed them violently. Enjoying it, he'd admitted later after finally being apprehended, thus ending his killing spree permanently.

Moorestrom had lured Cici in, getting her to trust him as he helped her to get promoted early. She'd struggle with all of this later, Matthew knew. If he could just get there in time to prevent her from being raped or worse, she'd struggle less. This was the guy who had poisoned Jamison Washburn he was now certain. By proxy of the guy calling himself Joseph Hayden, granted, but he was convinced now that Moorestrom was the mastermind behind it all. Why, Matthew wondered. What was his motive?

As if reading his mind and providing the answer, Moorestrom said, "We have the perfect future together, you understand. The ultimate power couple, which I know is what you've always wanted. Brilliant, gorgeous, unstoppable. We'll both move up now that there's a bit more room at the top of the firm. There will be more room soon. And we're going to thoroughly enjoy London together." The voice got farther away before it added, "And maybe Paris too, the romantic city, before we return and take our rightful places as senior partners at Moorestrom, Denton, and Patterson."

"But, we're only junior partners. And I have far less experience than you do," Matthew heard Cici object as piano music filled the background.

"You just leave that to me, Baby," he heard Moorestrom say above the soft music. "I have it all under control."

Looking around him, Matthew could see that they had crossed I-440, the inner beltline, still on Wake Forest Road and still at high speed until they crossed Old Wake Forest Road. They remained on the same road but, as Raleigh was famous for doing, the road name changed to Falls of the Neuse Road.

"That's lovely, Maestro," he heard Cici say and he thought she had choked on the words but Moorestrom continued playing and seemed not to notice.

After what seemed an eternity listening to the piano music, they had crossed several smaller intersections, slowing only slightly before blasting through them, and then crossed East Millbrook Road in a blur. After blowing through more smaller intersections, Matthew heard Danbury say, "Yeah, we'll cross Spring Forest too." And then they did, in as much of a blur as East Millbrook had been.

Picking up Matthew's phone and glancing down at the map briefly, Danbury said, "We'll turn left on Hollyhawk. Just ahead. Then go under 540."

Suddenly the piano music stopped and Matthew heard Cici say, "Don't stop. That was beautiful."

"We have more important things to do," said Moorestrom.

"Keep him talking, Cici," said Matthew as if she could hear him. "We're almost there."

"Tell me something," Cici said. "I'm entirely curious. What did you mean when you said that there would be more room at the top of the firm and then we'd be title members with our names on the partnership?"

"I'm not sure I'm ready to divulge that information just yet." Moorestrom replied, though his voice was getting closer.

"Why not?" asked Cici.

"It's all a matter of trust, Baby. I'm not convinced that you fully have mine yet. Suffice it to say that I'm paving the way to move up and I'm taking you with me."

Danbury turned left onto Hollyhawk, picked up Matthew's phone to see the path ahead, and then said, "Just over two miles. We'll cross Durant just ahead." After a pause, he said, "Yeah, it's close. Not that far from the lake."

"You don't trust me?" he heard Cici ask. "Why on earth not?"

"There's that little matter of your ex-boyfriend who keeps showing up and pulling you away from me."

"He is my EX-boyfriend for a reason," said Cici, stressing the ex as she said it.

"Yes, and he's entirely boring, right?"

"Incredibly," she responded. "How much longer until the food gets here? My stomach is growling. I'm getting hungry."

"Me too," Matthew heard Moorestrom's voice, much closer, and it was followed by some guttural noise.

"Was that his attempt at a growl?" Matthew said aloud, indignant that Cici had called him boring, though he knew that was totally illogical because she'd say anything she had to in order to keep Moorestrom at bay until he could get there.

They had slowed slightly to cross Durant and Danbury picked up the phone again and said, "One more small intersection. Elderberry. Kill the sirens now. Kill the lights after we cross it. We don't want to spook him. Then veer off to the right."

The night got quiet and Matthew could see houses and streets in this rural area lit in Christmas finery as he saw Danbury reach down and turn off the blue lights that had been flashing in the grill as they blew through the Elderberry Road intersection.

"Down on the right," said Danbury. "Entrance on Fox Trot. I'm going to make a pass. Keep straight. On Rabbit Run. Don't make the right on Fox Trot. Space out. Keep your eyes open."

"There, isn't that better?" Matthew heard Moorestrom ask and his voice became more muted.

"Not really," said Cici. "It's chilly in here. I'd like my jacket back."

"You don't need that. I'll keep you warm," he said. "Trust me, there will be plenty of heat."

"Mitch, could you start a fire? It'll be warmer and provide atmosphere."

"That would be romantic certainly," said Moorestrom as Danbury slowed, veering off to the right onto Rabbit Run and then right again onto an even smaller road, Fox Trot Trail. Were all of the streets out here in the boondocks named for animals, Matthew wondered. Slowly they passed a gated entrance to what appeared to be a driveway on their left and kept going.

"That's it," said Danbury, after consulting Matthew's phone again. "Cameras at the gate. Let's regroup. We plan for a hostage situation. We've heard only him. But it could be well guarded."

Fox Trot Trail was apparently a long loop road, Matthew realized, as they kept veering left before turning right back onto Rabbit Run. "OK, I see you," said Danbury, turning right again into a church parking lot. The two police cars were already there.

"There, is that better?" asked Moorestrom.

"Ah, gas logs. Very nice," Cici responded.

"Yeah, they'll heat up quickly and it'll get cozy in here before you know it."

"I like the tall stone fireplace," said Cici. "And the way you've used so much of the stone on your house inside and out. It's lovely." She was telling them, Matthew knew, what the house looked like. "It's not what I'd expected though. It's very earthy and isolated. I thought you'd live somewhere flashier, more modern."

"This was my parents' house, you know. It's been in my family for years. I've made lots of updates and improvements to it myself," he said proudly. "I keep an apartment in town, of course. But this is where I come for serious contemplation and endeavors."

What she couldn't know, because he couldn't communicate back to her, was that they were already there. He wished that he could tell her he was there somehow to reassure her. Maybe he could, he thought. "She knows sign language," he blurted out. "She's fluent in ASL, American Sign Language."

"That's good," said Danbury meaningfully as he got out of the car and circled to the front, pulling out his own cell phone and poking it. Matthew got out and followed, grabbing his phone on the way. Two officers, one in uniform and one not, approached from the Raleigh police car and two others, also not in uniform, ran up from the unmarked car.

The uniformed police officer had an iPad and he pulled up what Matthew saw was a map of the area, slightly larger than the phones could provide. They all huddled with Danbury over the hood of his SUV, looking it over, pointing and discussing points of entry.

"Hey, Mitch," said Cici. "Can you check the app and see how much longer dinner will be? I love that app. It even tells you who's bringing your order and what kind of car they drive."

"Yeah," said Moorestrom.

"So, is it Muhammad tonight or Carlos?" Cici asked casually in a joking tone. "And are they driving a Camry or a Corvette?"

"Neither," he said brusquely. "It's still five minutes out and Michael is running late."

"Ah, Michael," said Cici. "Let me guess. He's driving a 1983 brown Ford Mustang. Michael sounds like a pony boy name to me."

Matthew marveled at her cleverness to reference an old movie they'd seen together several years prior, a 1983 film adaptation of the *Outsiders* book. After watching it together, they'd started calling Mustang drivers pony boys, their private joke referencing the main character, Michael Curtis, whose nickname was Pony Boy. Even under extreme duress, Cici kept her nerve and her wit. Was she trying to tell him something with that comment? Or merely making a reference that only he would understand?

As Matthew pondered this, he heard Moorestrom ask in annoyance, "A what? No, it's a green Hyundai. Hand me my computer from the table there so that I can pull up my security cameras and let him in."

"Danbury, did you," began Matthew but Danbury was already barking out orders.

"Harrison, road block. Half mile up. Where Loggerhead connects. Fox Trot is a loop road. The others are dead end streets. That and Hollyhawk. The only ways in."

"On it," said the uniformed police officer, jumping into the marked car and turning right out of the church parking lot. Obviously, thought Matthew, that's Harrison. There had been no time for introductions.

"Delano, you're up. You know ASL, right?"

The guy nodded, "How's this?" he asked as he spread his hands apart, palms up. "It's 'here' in ASL."

"Good," said Danbury, his sentences getting choppier than usual as he barked out orders. "Intercept at Hollyhawk. That's most likely. Coming from the south. More businesses that way. Swap with the driver. Make the delivery. Tell her we're here."

The younger of the plain clothes police officers that Danbury had called Delano ran for the unmarked car and sped out of the parking lot turning left.

"What sort of security system do you have?" Matthew heard Cici ask Moorestrom. "It looks complex."

"It's very comprehensive. I don't like company, at least not the uninvited sort," he specified and Matthew could hear the leer in his voice. "I am well protected with the security system. The dogs run the fence lines at night and the cameras are always recording."

"Dogs?" asked Cici.

"Dobermans," clarified Moorestrom. "I have two. Apollyon and Abaddon."

"They sound fearless," she said. Matthew could hear the genuine fear that she'd allowed in her voice as she said it.

"Most definitely. They'd tear you to shreds in a second. But don't fret, Baby, only on command. I'd never let them hurt you. I haven't put them out on patrol yet tonight and I won't until after our food arrives. I want it delivered intact."

"Report on intercept," said Danbury. "Dogs in the compound. Have mace and tasers ready."

"I'm going," Matthew said to Danbury as he heard Moorestrom cooing at Cici to comfort her fear.

"We've got this," said Danbury.

"This is Cici," said Matthew. "I'll go in the trunk if I have to, but I'm going."

Ignoring Matthew, Danbury said to the remaining officer, "You're out here. Coordinating. Until Harrison comes back. North Raleigh team circles rear. We go in when Delano comes out," said Danbury as he rubbed his chin in apparent concentration. Matthew had seen him do it many times before. "Matthew, how's your shot?"

"About eighty-five percent accurate most of the time, why?"

"Not good enough. We take out the cameras. Silenced shots. When Delano comes out. Hanks and Connors. That's you. Then we go in. Hostage situation. All protocols in place," he said and Matthew knew he was talking to the two officers and into the com device because he had no idea what that meant. "Stand by," Danbury added, nodding to Matthew but apparently talking to all.

"Good, Delano. Make the swap," said Danbury. Matthew assumed that meant that the young officer who'd headed south had intercepted the incoming delivery driver.

"Harrison, back here. Point on comms. Hanks, Connors, gear up. Night gear," said Danbury as all three rounded the back of the SUV and pulled night vision goggles and black coats from the rear storage area.

"Here," said Danbury, tossing a set to Matthew as he climbed in the SUV. "Let's roll."

34 ~ Rescue who?

Realizing that he'd missed conversation between Cici and Moorestrom, Matthew had only half heard the guy brag about being an expert dog trainer and handler and that his dogs had been trained by the best in the field. If Cici had given him any further information, he'd missed it. He didn't think she had because Moorestrom had been talking most of the time that Danbury and the team were planning their approach. Matthew felt an adrenaline rush as he climbed back in the big SUV, gratefully pulling on the black jacket against the dipping temperatures while carefully holding his phone and the night googles.

All four doors had barely slammed when Danbury spun the vehicle around and pulled out to the left, almost immediately turning left again to traverse the loop road they'd been on previously in reverse.

"Hanks, you're with me. We cross over. Approach from the left. Connors, you're with Matthew. I'll drop you short. Approach from the right. We hold until Delano comes out. Then we take the cameras out. And move in. Before the gate closes."

"Roger that," said Connors aloud and Matthew remembered his bad joke to the elevator operator the night of the gala event. It seemed like an eternity ago, Matthew thought. If he could just go back then knowing what he knew now things could have been so different. For Cici. For Reynolds. For all of them.

Cici continued asking questions, sounding as if she were intrigued and impressed about the dog training. "That's good, Cees, keep him talking, nearly there now," Matthew muttered softly to her, willing her to hear him as Danbury pulled to the edge of the narrow road and

Matthew and Connors donned their night vision goggles and slipped out and into the edge of the woods.

Moorestrom had apparently tired of the subject. "Let me fix you a drink," he said instead.

Don't drink that, Cees, Matthew was thinking as if by willing it, he could procure her safety. Don't even put it to your lips, he thought, wishing that he could knock it out of Moorestrom's hand.

"What's your favorite?" he heard Moorestrom ask. Then the narcissist quickly answered for her, "Never mind. I'll fix two of my favorites. You'll love it."

"You're going to need to mute that," said Connors to Matthew. "When we approach."

"Right." said Matthew, listening intently to be sure that Cici was not drinking anything that Moorestrom had concocted. They could see the back brake lights flash briefly from the big SUV about a half mile down the road and then all was dark and quiet briefly until a green car pulled into the pool of light at the gate.

Matthew could hear the squawk of voices, both over the phone in his hand and from the security intercom system at the gate. Delano identified himself as Michael the delivery guy and Moorestrom questioned him thoroughly about what he was bringing in and from where. Matthew was impressed that Delano had the wherewithal to have gotten that information from the real driver and he provided the requested information readily.

Though he couldn't see them around the tree line, Matthew heard the protest of metal gates opening that sounded like they needed to be oiled. The next sounds he heard came from the phone in his hand as a chime sounded and Moorestrom said, "Dinner's here."

Cici answered, "Thank goodness, I'm famished."

Matthew could hear voices as Delano handed over the food and then all was momentarily quiet.

"What do you want? A tip?" asked Moorestrom.

"No, Sir. That's included from the app if you choose to add one."

"Then why were your hands out?"

"I was just waiting for you to check your order. Most people do that before they let me leave."

"Oh, I'm sure it's fine," said Moorestrom and Matthew heard the sound of the door slam shut. From that point, everything happened so fast that it was impossible for Matthew to know what was going on. He heard a thwap and then a scream from the phone, definitely male he consoled himself. Connors beside him said, "Go!"

Silencing the volume on the phone, Matthew thrust it in his pocket and jogged along behind Connors. Pausing, Connors dropped the night vision goggles to look up into the light and took a single shot that could be heard but not loudly. Matthew heard a second shot, almost consecutive with the first one, and Connors and Matthew met up with Danbury and Hanks as all four looked down from the lights and jogged into the compound. Delano positioned the green car in the gate, preventing it from closing and jumped out, following them in on foot.

As they approached the house, Matthew wasn't sure if communication was still happening over the com system or if they were all as quiet as they sounded. He saw Danbury motion with his hand and Delano and Hanks veered left while Matthew followed Danbury and Connors to the right, ducking down in the bushes in front of the house. Connors, he realized, had disappeared down the side of the house.

They crouched only briefly because they heard yelling from within. Danbury, motioning Matthew to follow, stepped up on the front porch and with two well-placed shots, removed the door locks. They pulled off the night goggles and entered the well-lit house. As Matthew rushed in behind Danbury, who still had his gun raised, he saw Hanks approach through the house from the back and veer off down a corridor. Connors followed him in and ran up the open staircase.

What Matthew saw in front of him took his breath momentarily.

Standing above Moorestrom, who was jerking around in the fetal position on the floor, was Cici. With a flashlight in one hand and one of her spiked heeled shoes in the other, she was beating him over the head, pummeling him alternately with both. All the while, she was yelling at him, "And this is for Matthew's Element! And this is for that woman Alicia Laws! And this is for calling me Baby!" On she went, releasing all of her anger and adrenaline on the guy until Danbury motioned for Matthew to intercede.

Matthew wrapped his arms around Cici and lifted her gently. She was still flailing away at Moorestrom, but in midair. Pulling her backward as Danbury knelt and cuffed Moorestrom, who was bleeding profusely but still writhing on the floor, Matthew said, "Cici. Hey Cees, it's me."

She whirled on him when he relaxed his hold and she looked up at him. "Did you hear what he called me? And how he was talking to me?" she exclaimed, still wielding the shoe and the flashlight angrily.

"Cees," said Matthew, taking the shoe out of her hand and dropping it to the floor.

"Oh," was all she said as, lowering her hands and hiccupping softly, she dropped the flashlight beside the shoe. He leaned over as she reached up and flung her arms around his neck and held on tightly.

Lifting her off her feet as he stood up straight, Matthew pulled her back with him into a large plaid-upholstered chair in the corner of the room. It was an informal room, he noted briefly, done in jewel tones and plaids and stripes, with a baby grand piano in the other corner. It sported wide board floors, high-beamed ceilings, and as Cici had said, a feature wall with the fireplace of stone. It was a very outdoorsy masculine space, but it was not a personal space. There were no pictures or knickknacks at all and it was notably devoid of Christmas lights or decorations, either outside or in. In Matthew's opinion that spoke volumes about the occupant, indicating a lack of emotional attachments.

Hearing the thud of multiple sets of heavy footsteps, Matthew looked up over Cici's head as both Hanks and Connors yelled, "Clear!" re-entering the room from the directions they'd left it in.

"The basement is clear too," said Delano, who approached from the back of the house. "But you're going to want to see this, Danbury."

"OK. Hanks, you can process him. When he's cognizant," said Danbury, sounding amused as he stepped back from Moorestrom.

As the police officers went through the house and Hanks stood guard over Moorestrom, Matthew heard sirens from outside. The officers from the north Raleigh station had arrived belatedly to the party. Matthew held Cici to him, as she was happily curled in his lap, as if he'd never let her go. Looking up, he noticed the two tumbler glasses on a coffee table. It was a wide and low table that looked like the massive base of a huge oak with a glass top.

"Cici," said Matthew in alarm, pulling her back to look into her face. "He didn't force you to drink anything, did he? You didn't even touch that glass to your lips, did you?"

"Of course not," she said, indignantly. "I switched the glasses. He was drinking whatever he'd poured for me."

At this Moorestrom regained some sense of understanding as he swiveled himself over trying to sit up and said pejoratively, "I wasn't going to poison her, you idiot. It's just a mild sedative. I want to marry her not kill her."

Looking over at him, Matthew felt his left eyebrow on the side of his face that was not obstructed with the bandage lift in amusement. He didn't bother with a reply. Looking up, Cici seemed to have just noticed the bandage and said, "Matthew, what happened to your face?"

"I'm sure Moorestrom over there could explain it. And why Reynolds was in surgery when I left Rex hospital a little while ago." He realized the truth of that statement, even though it felt like several days since the accident that afternoon. "He had his miscreants slam into us."

"I didn't even know about that," she said, angrily and menacingly at Moorestrom.

"Are you OK?" she asked Matthew. Reaching up, she touched his face beneath the bandage, the concern showing clearly in her own.

"Mostly. I have a few stitches up in my hairline. It'll heal. I'm in better shape than Reynolds, but thankfully he insisted on driving his Bentley. It's a tank. Celeste was there waiting for him to come out of surgery when I left," Matthew indicated Moorestrom. "Cees, what did you do?"

"Oh that," she shrugged. "That flashlight," she pointed to the one she'd dropped on the floor across the room. "It's a taser in disguise. It was here the whole time. I just didn't know where he'd put my satchel and I had to find it. It's behind this chair. I saw it when I followed him to the door to get the food delivery. Then when your guy signed that you were here, I used the diversion while Moorestrom's attention was on the delivery guy to grab it. When he walked in with the food, I zapped him with it."

"Wow,'" said Matthew. "You didn't really need rescuing, did you?"

"No, I just needed to find my satchel and I needed a diversion. Did you hear him talking to me?" she demanded.

"I heard the whole thing," said Matthew. "Or at least most of it. Until we were moving in."

"Then you heard everything that mattered," she said. "He all but confessed to killing Jamison Washburn. That and helping that horrible guy change his identity and become Joseph Hayden. I'm sure if Danbury digs long enough, he'll find evidence of both. His plan was to kill Mr. Washburn and frame Kennedy Reynolds to clear two senior partner spots at once so that he could move up into one of them."

"I did no such thing!" Moorestrom growled from the floor, but he looked ridiculous and not at all menacing, feet splayed in front of him, arms cuffed behind him, and bloodied all over. He was no longer a threat to anyone. Cici had seen to that.

"We'll get him for abduction and several other things, even if we don't yet have the evidence to charge him with murder," said Hanks.

As he said it, Danbury entered the room and went to the front door to meet the officers who'd arrived from north Raleigh. Over his shoulder, Danbury said, "We'll get him for a lot more. Just from his basement."

"It's pretty sick," said Delano, looking a bit pale as he appeared behind Danbury. "We've called a forensic team and they should be out here ASAP."

"Mirandize him," said Danbury to Hanks. "Delano, go swap the cars back. Let the delivery guy go. With our apologies. For ruining his night."

"Sure, boss," said Delano as he slipped past four uniformed officers on the porch and headed down the driveway to the green car still parked in the gateway.

"We could use the help," said Danbury. "We'll be here awhile. I need to get this guy downtown. Hey, Harrison," he said, and then paused. "Yeah, come on in. Take him downtown. And process him."

A few minutes later Harrison, the officer who had hung back because he was in uniform, arrived and hauled Moorestrom to his feet. He and Connors escorted Moorestrom out and into the marked police cruiser. The forensic team that Danbury had called arrived shortly thereafter and there was a lot of coming and going from the basement. When Cici asked what they'd found down there, Danbury just grimaced and said, "Nothing good. You don't want to look."

After giving instructions to everyone about processing the scene, Danbury turned to Matthew and Cici and said, "Let's go. I'll take you wherever you want to go. Ms. Patterson," he said formally. "We'll need a statement. The rest can wait until tomorrow. Moorestrom can cool his heels overnight. We've got more than enough to hold him."

Cici just nodded in agreement as Matthew answered, "Our rental cars are both downtown, but I have a spare at home."

"Yours isn't in great shape," said Danbury. "What did you do to it?"

"I didn't bother with the ticketing system when I left the parking deck. Cees, your management company for the building might not be too happy with me. Neither will the rental agency."

"What? You drove through it?" When he nodded, she just laughed as she got up to reclaim her shoes, coat, and satchel. "I can't begin to tell you how many times I've wanted to do that. Oh Matthew," she said, pulling her phone out of her jacket pocket, "We're still on a phone conversation! At least I didn't disconnect it. Did you?"

Retrieving his phone from his pocket, he just shook his head as they both clicked to disconnect the call.

When they were organized, Danbury pulled his SUV into the driveway. "Where to?" he asked as they climbed in.

"I really am hungry," said Cici and both men laughed at her. After all she'd been through, Matthew wasn't at all sure how she could be hungry.

"My protein bar," said Matthew, picking it up. "I completely forgot about that. And I'm hungry too now that you mention it, Cees. I'll share it with you." Then to Danbury, he added, "Just take us back to her office building to get her statement and that rental car. If mine is OK at the precinct until tomorrow, I'll deal with it then."

"There's no place safer for it," said Danbury as he pulled out and began to make his way back through town.

*****

After taking care of Max, Matthew settled with Cici on his leather sofa to eat the belated dinner they'd picked up on the way. It was after eleven, he realized. They'd been looking in all the wrong places and chasing down the wrong shunned person, he thought as he glanced over at Cici. He knew that he didn't want to lose her again. Not now, not ever.

"Cees," he said, "I've gained some perspective on all of this." He didn't get a chance to finish his statement because his cell phone vibrated in his pocket. The phone hadn't been charged after their prolonged one-way conversation and he was surprised that it still had any battery life left. Knowing that he wasn't on call, he pulled it out to check the display anyway.

"It's Celeste," he said to Cici.

He poked his phone to connect the call, "Hello?"

"Matthew, he's out of surgery and in recovery," said Celeste excitedly in his ear. "I'd love your interpretation of what they just told me because I'm not sure what that was. The upshot I think was that they expect him to recover. It'll be a long road and he'll need lots of help. I need you to promise me something, swear to me really."

"What's that?" he asked, feeling more than weary after the day he and Cici had both just survived.

"I need you to swear to me that everything you told me yesterday is true. All of it. Every last bit."

"It is, Celeste. It's all true. He told me that he's always loved you and that he doesn't want to live any longer without you in his life," he glanced over at Cici, thinking that this was the gist of the speech he had been about to give her.

"Thank you. That's what I needed to know. They won't release him alone without somewhere for him to go with someone to care for him. The doctor said they'd go over everything with us tomorrow. If all goes well, he could be released in a couple of days. I was thinking about bringing him home with me to take care of him. But I needed to know, I needed to be certain," she hesitated. "I don't want to go through that again, losing him and trying to start over with my life."

"I know exactly how you feel," he said, glancing at Cici again.

"I'm sorry to call you so late. But I thought you'd want to know that he's out of surgery and it went well."

"I did, Celeste, thank you for letting me know."

"You're welcome."

"You can call me tomorrow if you'd like, and I can interpret whatever they tell you and help you to prepare for bringing him home with you. The hospital should supply an Occupational Therapist who will help with that transition too."

They said their goodbyes and he turned back to Cici. He was preparing to try again to explain how worried he'd been that he'd never have the chance to tell her all of the things that he felt for her, all of the future he wanted to plan with her.

Just as he was about to try to convey that information, Cici looked up and said, "Matthew, you know this means that I have four more months in London, right? With Moorestrom out of the picture, I have to finish up with my clients."

"Cici," said Matthew, leaning over and scooping her up. "Honestly, I don't care. I'll be right here waiting for you when you get back."

She wrapped her arms around his neck as he kissed her with all the longing and pent-up passion that he had been holding back.

35 ~ Mourning After

The Saturday morning after Jamison Washburn's funeral service Matthew was pondering how quickly the month had flown by and how close Christmas was. How, he wondered, as he sat beside Cici on his sofa enjoying the Christmas tree and chatting about their future plans, could it be just four days away?

Cici reached up and pushed Matthew's soft short brown hair back on the right side of his face to examine the bandage covering the stitches. Then she leaned up and kissed it. "I don't have to go back to London, you know. I could just refuse to return and stay here. I want more than anything to be here with you."

"I'm afraid you'd regret it. If not immediately, eventually. I know you, Cici, and you'd hate not finishing something you started and finishing it well."

"I suppose. I gained some perspective with all of this Mitchell Moorestrom business. It has shaken me, I'll admit. I've been afraid that I've lost any ability I've ever had to accurately assess character. I've been looking at everyone around me differently and wondering if they're really who I thought they were."

"Including me?"

"For about five seconds," she shrugged. "But I've known you a long time and you've always been there for me. I know who you are and where you come from. Your family is wonderful too. You've always supported me, encouraged me, and never asked me to be anybody other than who I am. There's not much in my life that I wouldn't give up for you, for us, to make us work. My job, my house, any of it. It's just not that important anymore."

"I'd never ask you to give up any of that."

"I know and that's exactly it! You're genuine and focused on what matters. You're supportive of me being me and you never tried to change me into someone I'm not. Thank you for that. I wish you could say the same thing about me," she said, staring down at her hands.

"What do you mean?"

"I mean, I fell for the polished successful appearance that Mitch represented. I didn't fall for him, just the lifestyle that he portrayed. I tried to change you into that shiny façade too. I'm sorry for that. Does that make sense?"

"I suppose so."

"But none of it was ever real. It wasn't even who he was. It's just a shell, an illusion. Do you know when that finally became clear to me? When the understanding fully dawned?"

"When?"

"It was when I was with Mitch at his house. I started to suspect that something wasn't right when he was cagey about letting me leave. I felt trapped."

"Is that what happened to make you text me? I haven't asked you much about it because I didn't want to upset you. I wanted to enjoy Christmas together and the time we have before you fly back out for London."

"It was fine at first. I was showing him the files I'd created. But then he started acting really weird. I'm pretty sure I caught him sniffing my hair. I got up to take a glass to the kitchen and when I got back to his living room my satchel was gone from beside the coffee table. I asked him where it was and he gave me some noncommittal answer like, 'Oh, it's around somewhere.'"

"Then, he apologized for the 'goon,' that was his word, running us off of the road in the Element. He said I wasn't supposed to have been in the car which was a direct admission to his knowledge, if not his direct involvement, in trying to run you off the road and cause you serious injury. He was trying to get you out of the picture."

Before Matthew could interject, she added, "And he was stalking me! It was him outside of the Washburns' house both times, and it was him trying to get in. He wanted to know that I wasn't shacked up with you."

"He told you that?"

"As much as. He said he wanted to be sure you weren't taking advantage of me. As if! He said he wanted to be sure I was OK. It wasn't Aubrey Bartles after Annabelle at all."

Matthew just nodded, without commenting.

"That was when I slipped off to the bathroom to text you. He was odd about that too, like he didn't want me out of his sight. I told him I needed to take care of a female problem, picked up my purse, and asked for the bathroom. He escorted me to it and I think he was listening outside the door, at least at first. When I came back, I went over to the piano ostensibly to admire it, but I was really looking for my satchel. Then I saw the sheet music on the stand there and it all clicked into place in my mind."

"When he first started acting weird, I tried to laugh it off and make a joke about it. He asked me, 'What are you doing?' and I told him I was just being silly. He said, 'Don't, it's unbecoming.'"

"I love it when you're silly," said Matthew softly.

"Me too. In that moment, I realized two things. The first was that I hadn't enjoyed been silly enough lately until I came back here with you. I love being silly with you. Our inside jokes and all of the things we shared when we were dating before. I didn't realize how important that is or that I'd missed it so much. And the second was that I wanted that chance to be silly with you again. Endlessly. I knew I needed to get out of there."

After a pause she added sadly, "I guess you're right that I have to go finish what I started in London. I'm going to miss you, Matthew."

"Me too, Cees, me too," he agreed, pulling her close.

He shared her sentiment entirely but he didn't want to think about her being gone until they'd said their final goodbye at the security gate of the airport. He'd deal with it then. For now, he just wanted to enjoy every second he had with her.

Looking at her watch, she said, "What time are we meeting Penn and Danbury for brunch?"

"In about twenty minutes. We can be there in ten," he added, turning her to him and kissing her while he still could.

*****

As they were having brunch at Peak Eats, Danbury asked about the funeral service the day before and how the Washburns were faring.

"As well as can be expected, I think," said Cici. "Elizabeth is going to live there with Annabelle and commute to Duke, at least for her spring semester and through next fall. Annabelle was talking about selling the house and moving into something smaller and more manageable but she said she'd been told not to make any drastic changes in her life for at least the next year."

"That sounds like wise advice," said Penn. "Stability after tragedy is best I think."

"It was good to see Eugene Miller there and looking well. He was the other doctor who responded to the call for help when Mr. Washburn was found and he was inadvertently exposed to the poison too," Cici explained to Penn.

"It was good to see him there," Matthew agreed. "They caught his secondary exposure to the poison in time to treat him. Who was that with him at the service?"

"His son and daughter-in-law, I think," said Cici. "They're trying to talk him into moving closer to them. Rumor has it that they're expecting and he's excited about being a grandfather, so my bet is that he moves quickly in the new year."

"That was a really nice speech that Mr. Markham gave about Mr. Washburn," observed Matthew.

"It was," agreed Cici. "And he's right that the foundation of the law firm has been fundamentally shaken with Washburn deceased. With Kennedy Reynolds recovering and Mitch Moorestrom charged with murder and myriad other things, it is a setback. He was smart not to mention any of that."

"Speaking of Moorestrom," Matthew said, turning to Danbury. "What's the latest?"

"Some good news for Reynolds. We got fingerprints. From the Ford truck that hit the Bentley. On the back of the rear-view mirror. One good thumbprint. That was a rush job. They didn't clean up well. The driver is in custody. And pointing the finger at Moorestrom. Not by name. But by bank account routing information. He clammed up about hitting your Element. We'll likely tie him to that too. At least as a tail. If not as the driver that hit you. We're close. Your insurance company will be happy."

"We can prove that Moorestrom helped Hayden," continued Danbury. "With the new identity. And he funded Mr. Washburn's murder. Probable cause got us the warrants. The warrants got us the fund transfer data. Transfers left Moorestrom's account to both caterers. And to the miscreants. The ones he hired to track you. And then run you off the road."

"Wow," said Cici. "What about framing Kennedy Reynolds for Mr. Washburn's murder? Have you been able to pin that on him too?"

"Not yet. It's just a matter of time. But probably irrelevant."

"How so?" asked Cici.

"Because there are so many others. Charges that we can prove."

"Tell me something," she said. "Those other charges have to do with what was in that basement, don't they? In Mitch's basement."

"They do," said Danbury, scratching the stubble on his chin.

"Don't you think I earned the right to know about that? After what I went through?"

"It isn't pretty, Cees," interjected Matthew. "Are you sure you want to know?"

"You know?"

"Yeah," he nodded. "But I'm not sure that you want to."

"I do. Sometimes I feel a wee bit guilty," said Cici, holding her thumb and forefinger apart just a bit, "for whaling on him like that."

"I think Danbury can help you with that," chuckled Matthew.

"Let's start with the easy part," said Danbury.

"OK, shoot," said Cici.

"How old did he say he is?"

"Thirty-four, I think. Something like that, why?"

"Add ten," said Danbury.

"Mitchell Moorestrom is forty-four?" she asked in surprise. When Danbury and Matthew both nodded, she said, "Well, I totally missed that one. I thought I was a much better judge of people than that."

"You are," said Matthew. "He's a very practiced liar. And you had no reason not to believe him. He had helped to get you promoted quickly so you trusted him. Why wouldn't you?"

"Thank you, Matthew. That's very gracious of you. Now the basement," she stared expectantly at the two men.

"He hasn't always been a lawyer," said Danbury.

"He was a botanist and he had a whole apothecary in one section of his basement where he'd mixed literally God only knows what," added Matthew. "Including poison hemlock that was found down there too."

"Wow!" said Cici, looking confused. "A botanist? I never saw him as the outdoorsy type. Except maybe when I got to his house. It was spotless but it had a woodsy feel to it."

"And he lured you there? Under what pretense?" asked Danbury.

"No pretense really. He was pretty casual about it. He said we could relax at his place for the afternoon while we went over the information for the London clients that he was going to take over from me. We were going to discuss all of the legal ramifications of everything that I had put in place so far and everything that I was planning to do to finish up in the new year."

Leaning back, she added, "I was resistant at first and I should have gotten a clue from his face when I told him that I wanted to get back in time to have a late dinner with Matthew. It clouded over somehow but I thought he was jealous."

"Jealous is an understatement, Cees," said Matthew.

After a momentary pause, Cici took a breath before asking earnestly, "What do you mean about his jealousy being an understatement?"

"His idea of 'relationships' with women is sicker and more warped than you can imagine," Matthew answered. "He has to own them, control them. They have to do exactly what he says exactly the way he expects."

"And you know this how?"

"The basement," said Danbury. "It had been, ah, occupied. By several women. We don't yet know how many. DNA evidence points to at least three. That count is likely to rise."

"Occupied how?" she asked sounding truly alarmed.

"They were imprisoned down there, Cees," explained Matthew. "Until they did something he didn't like or until he got tired of being 'married' to them," he said with his fingers in air quotes. "Then he moved on to the next one. The three the police know about so far were reported as missing but never found."

"Oh!" said Cici, sinking down in her seat.

"Feel better now about whaling on him?" asked Matthew as he put his arm around her.

"Not entirely," she said after a minute. Then she sat up straight and vehemently added, "I wish I'd done worse to him than tase him and beat him!"

"I'm glad I never had the displeasure of meeting this creep," said Penn. "And remind me never to get on your bad side," she added to Cici with a grin.

Matthew chuckled and kissed Cici on top of the head. He'd always loved her passion and fire. He was thrilled that she'd somehow morphed back into the woman he'd met in college when he was in his medical program and she was finishing up her undergraduate degree. That woman was passionate about helping people, champion of the underdog. Since she'd been home this past month, he'd seen much more of that Cici than he had in the last couple of years they'd been dating before they had broken up.

As their omelets, oatmeal, grits, toast, and all of the trimmings arrived at the table, the conversation turned to passing condiments and if anybody needed refills on coffee or juice. Mallory, the flirtatious waitress, was serving them, but minus the toothy grin and dimples. She seemed resigned to the fact that both of the previously most eligible bachelors in town had women with them.

"Just one more question," said Cici as she put her napkin in her lap. "Did Mitch really have Dobermans there?"

"He did," said Danbury.

"What happened to them?"

"We impounded them," said Danbury with a grin.

"You took them to the pound?" asked Penn.

"Not exactly."

"What then?" asked Cici.

"He was telling the truth. About how well trained they are. They'll make excellent additions. To our K-9 unit."

"Oh!" said Cici, and she chuckled at Danbury's play on words. "I'm happy to hear that something good came out of all of that."

EPILOGUE ~ TWO AND A HALF WEEKS LATER

The looks from Matthew's family that he had taken to be critical, usually aimed over Cici's head, had finally faded and disappeared. Cici was back in his life to stay. Whether just resigned to the inevitability or fully accepting of the fact – and Matthew wasn't entirely sure which – his family had welcomed her with open arms. To his delight she had finally chosen to bask in their welcome and joined wholeheartedly in all of the Christmas celebrations with them. The tennis bracelet he gave her had been a huge hit and she was impressed that he'd remembered the one she'd seen in London but refrained from buying for herself.

Spending their last day together, the Saturday after New Year's, before she had to fly out to return to London for the next four months was bittersweet. They'd decided to do something lighthearted and go car shopping for her. They'd test driven a BMW Z4, a Mercedes SLC and, just for grins, a Mercedes SL-Class Roadster. Then they migrated to the new Porsche 911 and stopped by to check out Corvettes. Matthew was elated that the dealership had one of the new C8 mid-engine Stingrays and they test drove that too.

After a full day they returned to Cici's house where Matthew was helping her to pack. As he stood by her bed watching her pile things on it, he said, "You know we can ship over anything that you don't want to have to carry."

"I know. I left most of my things in my flat there. The more difficult part will be shipping it all back in four months. One other thing," she said, jumping up and leaving her bedroom. Matthew waited perched on her bed until she returned with a manilla folder. "Here," she said.

"You'll need my property plot map to work with Celeste on planning the landscaping here."

His surprise must have shown in his face as she added, "I trust you. You have excellent taste. In pretty much everything," she added, as she ran her fingers over the diamond tennis bracelet that sparkled as it dangled from her wrist.

"We can't plant until spring anyway," said Matthew. "You'll be back around that time."

"But you can go ahead and plan it out. If you want my input or have questions, just email me whatever you're working with Celeste on. But honestly, Matthew, whatever you lay out with her will be lovely. I like what you planned for your yard a lot."

"She is really helpful and insightful, isn't she?"

"Extremely. It's so sweet to see her and Kennedy together. He's become a whole different person. And Ella. She was in pure ecstatic wonder to meet him and to finally know who her father is. It sounded like she thought she had a hole in her life until she met him, one that she hadn't ever shared with Celeste."

"It is rewarding to help unite a family, isn't it? I've told Celeste that I'll have plenty of free time on my hands over the next four months if she needs any more help with Kennedy."

"They hired a wonderful nurse," said Cici. "How'd you work that one out anyway?"

"Who, Malcolm? He was Allan Lingle's caregiver in Peak. Everybody was thoroughly impressed with him long before he'd ever finished his nursing degree."

"Oh, yeah. I do remember hearing Penn mention him when we had dinner with them last month. With Kennedy as a reference, he could do private care easily enough from now on," said Cici. "If he decides not to go back to a hospital. Those are some long and arduous hours, which you know far better than I do. I watched you do your rotations in medical school."

"I think he went to that specific hospital to move closer to his sister. She lives in an old shack up near the lake on the state line. She's a character."

"You've met some interesting people while I've been gone, haven't you?"

"I guess I have," Matthew agreed.

"I wonder what other interesting people you'll meet while I'm gone these next four months," she mused. "Just none that turn your head, I hope."

Matthew sighed. Looking deeply into her eyes, he said, "That you don't ever have to worry about. Four months sounds like an eternity right now."

"It does to me too," she agreed. "But we can talk every day on FaceTime and text and share pictures. I'll be back before we know it."

"I hope you're right," he said, taking her in his arms and then scooping her up onto her bed.

*****

As Matthew drove away from the airport the next day, his heart was heavy and his mind was consumed with thoughts of the time they'd had together over the holidays. As he drove home in the far-right lane of I-40 heading back to Peak, he was driving like an old man below the speed limit.

So lost in thought was he that he barely noticed his cell phone vibrating in his pocket. He hadn't been playing music and he knew where he was going by rote, so he hadn't had it out. Reluctantly he clicked to answer it on his car system.

"Hey Doc," he heard Danbury say. "Where are you?"

"I just dropped Cici at the airport and I'm headed home."

"Are you still a medical consultant? Or was this a one-last-time gig? Because you were involved?"

Matthew hadn't really thought about this but he sighed deeply before answering, "I guess I'm still consulting. I'll need something to do over the next four months to keep my mind off Cici."

"Happy to hear it. I need you up here. We've got a body. Frozen in a covered pool. I'll drop you a pin."

Before Matthew could agree, object, or even think about it,

Danbury had disconnected and was gone. "Déjà vu," said Matthew aloud, as he saw the text come in and clicked to get the routing information. Checking the rear-view mirror, he hit the gas and slid over into the left lane.

"Frozen?" he muttered to himself. "How could a body be frozen in a pool now? Temperatures haven't gotten down to freezing for at least the past week, even overnight."

About the Author

Lee Clark is a North Carolina native, originally from Raleigh, with family roots in Virginia. Clark attended Campbell University, obtained a degree in Journalism from East Carolina University, and then a Master's in Technical Communication from North Carolina State University. After working in the software technology industry for over 20 years, creating and building highly technical user information for software developers, Clark decided it was time to pursue a true passion – fiction writing.

The Matthew Paine character is a fictional character, though inspired by two very important men in the author's life, brother Sean and son Will. Both will see characteristics of themselves in the character and identify with some of Matthew's struggles.

Lee Clark, an admitted coffeeholic, still resides in North Carolina with spouse, two mostly grown children who are in and out, and a small petting zoo of dogs and cats.